W9-CKI-474

# A Heart Revealed

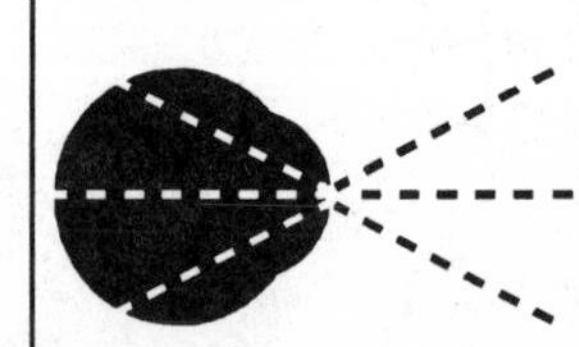

This Large Print Book carries the Seal of Approval of N.A.V.H.

A PROPER ROMANCE

# A Heart Revealed

Josi S. Kilpack

**THORNDIKE PRESS**
A part of Gale, a Cengage Company

Farmington Hills, Mich • San Francisco • New York • Waterville, Maine
Meriden, Conn • Mason, Ohio • Chicago

A Proper Romance.™
Thorndike Press, a part of Gale, a Cengage Company.


Thorndike Press® Large Print Gentle Romance.
The text of this Large Print edition is unabridged.
Other aspects of the book may vary from the original edition.
Set in 16 pt. Plantin.

**LIBRARY OF CONGRESS CIP DATA ON FILE.
CATALOGUING IN PUBLICATION FOR THIS BOOK
IS AVAILABLE FROM THE LIBRARY OF CONGRESS**

ISBN-13: 978-1-4328-5933-6 (hardcover)

Published in 2018 by arrangement with Deseret Book Company/Shadow Mountain

Printed in the United States of America
1 2 3 4 5 6 7 22 21 20 19 18

*To Thomas Richards and Amelia Hey,*
*my personal link to England.*
*Thank you for the legacies.*

■ ■ ■ ■

# Book One

■ ■ ■ ■

*London*

# Chapter 1

*April*

Thomas knew the moment Amber Sterlington entered Almack's ballroom. Not because he was watching the door, or because someone spoke her name. No. The reason Thomas Richards knew when Miss Sterlington entered the room was because every gentleman straightened his bearing and turned his head in her direction. Simultaneously, the women in the room either narrowed their eyes or raised their chin a fraction of an inch in the feminine version of the same response. Amber Sterlington was the Rage of the Season, after all, and in the space of a glance and a breath, the room was changed by her arrival.

Thomas cared little for the attention *society* gave to her, but like everyone else, he reacted to her arrival by standing a bit taller in case she looked his way. The truth was that Amber Sterlington was quite simply the most attractive woman he had ever seen, and he was as struck by her arrival as every other man.

In the month he'd been in London, this being his third Wednesday night ball at Almack's, he'd seen Miss Sterlington nearly a dozen times at a variety of events, and his reaction to her had been equally profound each time. When his notice passed, he berated himself for it, wanting to believe himself a man apart from such fancy. She would marry for title or fortune or both — everyone knew it — and as a younger son of a modest Baron, Thomas offered neither, which made his attraction toward her that much more vexing.

Her sultry laugh washed over him, serving as yet another defining quality that set her apart from the trilling young women of the *ton*. Everything about that woman was equal parts distracting and irritating to Thomas, who in every other case felt himself to be a logical, determined, and well-balanced sort of man.

"As you were saying, Mr. Richards?"

Thomas returned his attention to the young woman standing before him, holding a glass of lemonade in her delicate hands and looking at him with the wide-eyed expression of interest he expected had been taught to her by her mama, a woman who had made no secret of how eager she was to marry off her youngest daughter.

He was not entirely opposed to Miss Carolyn Morton. She possessed the manners of genteel birth and did not seem the type who would drag her future husband to London because she loved the social atmosphere Thomas found so tedious. It was her level of intellect that worried him. Despite the dire warnings against having a bluestocking for a wife, Thomas wished to find a bride with whom he could converse on occasion. He had not realized it would be so difficult a prospect. While a great many of the season's debutantes had been taught of literature and art — two areas of study he also enjoyed — none could give much critical opinion on either topic nor did they know the slightest bit regarding matters of economics or politics.

But Miss Morton *was* an agreeable girl, and Thomas had been so distracted by Miss Sterlington's entrance that he had broken off his reply regarding his thoughts on the current parliamentary session.

"Yes," Thomas said, remembering the conversation he'd let slip away. "As I was saying, I am hopeful that parliament will address the agriculture reforms Northern

England is in such desperate need of. As mining gains greater investment, I fear for the future of the herds and fields that England is dependent upon. Should the mining industry continue to take such liberties with the land and subsequent water rights they are buying out at an alarming rate, I shouldn't doubt that we'll be importing beef from the continent. A repulsive solution, to my mind, when we have the resources to be self-sustaining if parliament will but protect the interests that are most certainly theirs as well as those of all England."

Miss Morton nodded, but he'd seen the blankness enter her expression and knew he had gone too far afield with information of no interest to his companion. In an attempt to repair the situation, Thomas bowed slightly and smiled at the girl most chivalrously. "Would you care to dance the next quadrille, Miss Morton?"

The light he'd cast out of her face with his talk of cows and corn immediately refreshed itself, and she nodded so quickly that the curls on either side of her face jiggled as though they too were excited to take the floor. Miss Morton smiled, revealing broad front teeth he would not mind so much if the girl were a bit more engaging to talk with. "I would most definitely like to dance a quadrille with you, Mr. Richards."

"Capital," he said with a slight incline of his head. "I shall return for you when this set has finished."

She bobbled those curls again as Thomas made his way through the crowd toward one of the assembly rooms not so tightly occupied. He could only abide crowds for so long, and he needed a moment to himself before leading Miss Morton across the dance floor. Thomas caught sight of Miss Sterlington holding court with half a dozen suitors and felt his jaw tighten in another seemingly uncontrollable reaction.

He had come to London because it was reasonable to expect that a man in search of a wife would find one amid the young women who came for the entertainment season that coincided with the parliamentary session. Yet after a month in London, Thomas had yet to meet any young woman who could hold his interest for the length of an evening. He thought of Miss Sterlington and shook his head at the irony that the only debutante who drew his attention was one he could never have.

Thomas found a nearly empty corner where someone had, blessedly, opened one of the diamond-paned windows. He took the liberty of pushing it open a bit more to get some cooler air on his face; he would never go so far as to call London's air *fresh,* but the outdoors was far better than the stuffiness of the ballroom. He looked toward a garden some distance away and felt a wave of melancholy as he took in the trees and walking path.

He missed Yorkshire, where he'd lived all his life and where his father and oldest brother were buried. He missed the moors and the cattle and the sheep of North Riding. He missed fishing in the River Wiske that ran through his families' estate lands, walking through mud in his wearing boots, and eating apples right off the tree when they were in season. He missed his mother and his brother and his niece, Lizabeth, who was adjusting to the birth of her baby brother, the next Lord Fielding. And so help him, Thomas missed the simple country dances where attendees did not feel the singular pressure of having to find a marriage amid the crowd.

"Just one season," his mother had begged two months ago, revealing a plan that had been some time in the making on her part. "I feel certain that once you commit yourself to your lands you shall never leave Yorkshire again." He could not adequately relieve her fear on that count and therefore agreed to her wishes.

"Tell me it is not The Honourable Thomas Richards." Recognition of the nasally voice behind him was instantaneous, and Thomas was smiling before he turned around to see a dandy of a fellow looking at him through a quizzing glass tied to his waistcoat with a black ribbon. "Pray, I don't believe it!" the fop said with a pretty stomp of his green, square-toed shoe. He put one hand on his hip, lowered his glass, and looked at Thomas with growing astonishment. "Thomas Richards at *Almack's*? In *London*?" He shook his head and closed his eyes while taking a dramatic breath that flared his nostrils. "No, no, you must be an imposter. The Thomas Richards I knew, bless him, would never make such an appearance. No, it would go against all he stood for, I am sure."

Thomas laughed and put his hand out for his old schoolmate. Though they were different sorts of men, Thomas had counted Fenton as a great friend for many years. "I for one would be far more surprised if Viscount Fenton *weren't* at Almack's. In *London,*" Thomas countered in mimicked cadence. "The true question of the hour is why I have been in this city for nearly a month and I am just now seeing him."

The two men shook hands, and Thomas was reminded through the power of his grip that, should Fenton choose to, he could lay Thomas flat in a trice. He'd done exactly that more times than Thomas cared to remember when they were suitemates at Oxford and trying to prove who was the stronger man, as young men often did in any number of competitive games.

"How are you, my friend?" Thomas asked, disposing of the jesting tone.

"I am very well," Fenton said, his voice low and even now that he was not putting on a show. "Have you truly been in London a month?"

"Nearly so," Thomas confirmed. "Darwood said you were in Brighton."

Fenton nodded. "That I was, but the company bored me and so I gave it up. And what luck that I did. It is splendid to see you again. How are you enjoying the city?"

Thomas opened his mouth to reply only to have Fenton cut him off before he'd said a single word.

"Ah, let me guess," Fenton said, returning to his foppish allocution and putting a hand to his chest. "You are repulsed by the dinginess of it, bored with the frivolous entertainment, and only here because you desire what every man both wants and fears — a wife."

Thomas laughed again. "My answer was far less patronizing."

"And far less honest, no doubt."

Thomas did not argue. "If you must know, my mother sent me. She would like me to find a suitable wife and feels I shan't find her in Yorkshire."

"Well, how many women are there in Yorkshire?" Fenton asked, raising his eyebrows to emphasize the question. "Other than your mother, of course, and your brother's wife, which you need not consider, there can't be more than two or three women in the entire county, let alone any of marriageable age. I can't help but think your mother had the right of it."

Thomas did not attempt to hide his smile. "I suppose this is the point in our conversation where I try to convince you that Yorkshire is not the uninhabited wilds you perceive it to be."

"Perhaps, but then I shall refuse to believe it — as always — and you will end up with your nose in a joint over defending your homeland and I'll feel wretched for taking things too far." He waved his hand through the air. "Better not even to start."

Thomas laughed again and clapped his

friend on the back, taking note of the striped satin coat of green and gold, which matched Fenton's extravagant shoes, far different from Thomas's conservative evening dress consisting of a black coat, gray waistcoat, and buff-colored knee breeches.

"Oh, I am glad to see you, Fenton," Thomas said sincerely. "London has improved by spades just by you being here. Darwood is somewhere in the crowd."

"Darwood is a singularly obnoxious fellow. I should prefer to avoid him as long as possible." Fenton sighed and fluffed his lace cuffs with exaggerated attention.

"I can only guess that your father continues to harangue you regarding your modishness?" Thomas asked, indicating Fenton's extreme clothing.

Fenton gave Thomas a conspiratorial grin and stepped closer so as to be heard while lowering his voice. "He despises it," Fenton said with a gleam in his eye. "Almost as much as the women adore my sense of style." He lifted his chin as though posing for a portrait.

Thomas shook his head in mock disappointment and tsked loudly. "If I'd had any idea the high collars you sported at university would lead to this, I'd have burned them while you slept."

Fenton laughed, then did away with his foppish façade once again. "Now," he said, crossing his arms over his chest, "tell me about your plans while you are in town — other than wife hunting. Do you need an introduction to any of the gaming hells? Have you joined any clubs? I'm a fan of Brooks myself. Great tables."

"I'm not such a gambler," Thomas said, shaking his head. As the heir to a wealthy earldom, Fenton had a far different situation than Thomas did.

Fenton raised an eyebrow. "London makes a gambler of many a man."

"Perhaps if they have a deeper purse than I do." Thomas had no reason to be vague regarding his situation. "I am to be self-made, and the only thing standing in my way of it, is a proper wife."

Fenton turned his head slightly, regarding Thomas with a questioning look. "One with a fortune?"

Thomas colored at the suggestion that he expected his wife to make his living. "Certainly not," he said. When Fenton pulled back, Thomas knew he'd spoken too sharply. He repaired his tone as he continued, "I have made an arrangement with my older brother: most of my annual inheritance for the fields near Romanby. In the long term I shall be far better for the investment and am still left with a modest inheritance."

Fenton's eyebrows rose throughout Thomas's recounting and his arms dropped to his sides. "You gave up your inheritance? I've never heard such a thing."

Thomas shrugged as though his decision was a common one when in fact he had come up with the idea himself. Most men would not give up the security of guaranteed income to make their own way. "I believe in time that the land will more than make up for the forgone income," he said simply. After Charles — the eldest of the three brothers and their father's heir — had died, Thomas had more fully realized how dependent they all were on lineage and inheritance. He also better understood that as generations — specifically his own posterity — became more distant from the security the title offered, he wanted something of substance to pass on. It was a unique perspective amid the noble class to be sure, but one that settled so comfortably in Thomas's mind that he did not doubt the wisdom of it.

The sound of a familiar and distracting voice prevented Fenton from making a reply, and they both looked toward the interruption. For the second time that evening, Thomas straightened in response to Amber Sterlington, who was walking arm in arm with her younger sister whom Thomas recognized from other events. For the second time that evening, he was taken off guard at the effect Miss Sterlington had on him. And for the second time that evening, he noted that he was not the only man so affected by her presence. Fenton struck a posture of distinction and bowed toward the women, looping his hand as he lowered it nearly to the ground.

"Miss Sterlington," Fenton said as he rose. He glanced at her companion and inclined his head. "Miss Darra. What a lovely happenstance to receive your company this evening."

Amber Sterlington fixed Fenton with a playful look that sparked instant jealousy in Thomas.

"What a lovely happenstance for us that you are receiving, Lord Fenton," she said in that haunting voice, acknowledging that she and Fenton knew one another. She put out her hand, which was covered in a white satin glove. It matched the white satin gown that opened in the front, revealing the light green underdress that set off Miss Sterlington's similarly green eyes to distraction.

Fenton took her hand and bowed over it

with an easy manner Thomas wished he himself possessed. "You look absolutely breathtaking tonight, Miss Sterlington," he said. "Like a goddess brought to life."

"Oh pish," Amber said, shaking her head as she returned her hand to her sister's arm; Miss Darra was a beauty in her own right though Thomas doubted many people noticed. "It's bad enough that Almack's is such a sad crush week after week, but the requirement that debutantes may only wear pasty colors is not to be countenanced." She waved toward him. "Is it not offensive to your sensibilities that you can appear in all manner of pattern and color, and all of us females are relegated to look like infantile dowds?" She pouted — such a pretty pout — and let out an equally pretty breath. "I tell you, it's not fair, Lord Fenton. Not fair at all."

"Ah, but you look like an angel in white, my dear, and, for you particularly, white is quite the canvas for your hair and your eyes. I can't fathom why you would be cross toward such regulations when they show *you* off to your very best light."

Amber smiled, her mood repaired by the compliment that, while true, was over the top of anything Thomas could say. Did it not embarrass Miss Sterlington to hear such outrageous flattery?

As though to answer his unspoken question, Miss Sterlington reached up and fingered one of the long auburn ringlets draped over her shoulder while giving Fenton a coy look. The rest of her hair was piled on top of her head, a mass of curls into which small white flowers with diamond centers had been woven. The only other jewelry she wore was an oval pendant — amber, as her namesake — that hung just below her collarbone, drawing the eye, which then naturally looked over the rest of her.

Where so many of the debutantes looked as though they were barely women at all, Amber Sterlington had a figure worthy of admiration. Her inquisitive green eyes — with gold flecks, Thomas noticed — smooth skin, and vibrant hair left him no doubt that the other young women could not hold a candle to her. So mesmerized was Thomas that he did not realize Fenton had introduced him until Thomas heard his name said out loud.

Thomas felt his mouth go dry when Miss Sterlington's gaze settled upon him. "I'm very p-pleased to meet you, Miss Starringt — I mean, Miss Sterlington." He gave a quick bow nowhere near as elegant or graceful as Fenton's had been.

"Likewise," she said, but she looked back to Fenton before she'd even finished her polite reply. "Now, I escaped the crush of the ballroom in order to have a private word with my dear sister. Would you two gentlemen excuse us for a moment? I fear that once my absence is noted, I shan't get another moment's peace. I must insist on a bit of privacy, and this is perhaps the only vestibule available. Do you mind?" She offered another pout, and this time Thomas and Fenton equally fumbled for words as they assured her they were not the least bit put out by her need of a private corner.

"Good grief, is she not a diamond of the first water?" Fenton said, somewhat breathless from their quick retreat back to the crowd of the ballroom. Thomas was surprised that Fenton was so undone by the woman; he had dealt with her quite calmly up until the end of their exchange. Thomas felt even lower as he acknowledged that only a man of Fenton's station had a chance of gaining Amber Sterlington's attentions.

Thomas pulled at his collar. The awkward exchange had left his heart racing and he was beginning to sweat. "She must think I'm an absolute nitwit," he said under his breath as he and Fenton moved toward the refreshment table. The more distance he put between himself and the girl who rendered him such an idiot, the more his irritation increased. "Why could I not react like a grown man?"

"Don't be so severe upon yourself," Fenton said, patting Thomas's arm as he picked up a cup of ratafia with his other hand. He took a drink and made a face — ratafia was a mild drink and obviously not what Fenton was hoping to encounter. "There's not a man in London who can keep his head around such a woman as Amber Sterlington. The breeding of a wife and the appeal of a mistress."

It did not make Thomas feel better to be reminded he was as besotted as every other man. Nor did it improve his mood when he realized he had missed the beginning of the quadrille promised to Miss Morton. With a groan, he excused himself of Fenton and soon found Miss Morton blinking back tears near the balustrade. Miss Morton did not deserve such treatment, and he felt badly for causing her distress.

It was too late to join the dance so Thomas spent the duration of it coaxing Miss Morton from her mood through compliments of her appearance — she did look lovely in her light blue gown — and a humorous account of a gentleman being chased by a dog through Hyde Park the day before yesterday. By the time the next dance was announced, Miss Morton was giggling behind her hand. He asked her to stand up for this set and she gratefully accepted his invitation, giving him a chance to redeem himself, for which he was glad.

It was after thanking Miss Morton for the dance some time later, and avoiding her mother's approving eye as he departed her company, that Thomas saw Miss Sterlington again. She had likewise finished the set with a young man in full regimentals, and he was bowing over her hand in a simpering manner that left Thomas embarrassed for him.

A moment later, however, a mad thought seized Thomas's mind and before he knew it, he was standing in front of her at the exact moment she was quit of her former partner and had not yet accepted another.

"Might I have this dance, Miss Sterlington?" Thomas heard himself say as though it were not him at all. He could feel the flush in his cheeks and the sweat beneath his collar as those beautiful green eyes looked him over, a bit more than he thought was warranted.

"Sir," she said, her eyebrows coming

together. "We have not had a proper introduction, therefore I certainly could *not* dance with you." Her tone was not as rich and playful as it had been when she'd bantered with Fenton.

"Lord Fenton introduced me to you not half an hour ago, within one of the assembly rooms." No sooner had he said it than he realized how pathetic he sounded, begging for her remembrance of something she hadn't given enough attention to remember for herself.

"I'm sure he did not," she said sharply, lifting her chin and taking a step back. "Besides, Lord Norwin has asked that I reserve the waltz for him. . . . Ah, there he is." She stepped to her right in time to lift her hand to a man wearing a blue superfine tailcoat and satin knee breeches.

In a moment Miss Sterlington was gone, the sound of her laughter trickling back to him as she took her place with Lord Norwin on the dance floor. Thomas came to himself in time to see numerous attendees look away; the quickness of their diverted glances evidence that they had seen the set down he'd just received. From the looks on their faces, they were not sharing in his embarrassment; rather they were taking his measure just as Miss Sterlington had.

Overwhelmed with embarrassment, Thomas turned to the staircase and quit Almack's without a word to anyone, not even Fenton. It was unfashionable to leave the dance before supper but Thomas could not stay another minute.

As he made his way back to his rented rooms in a less fashionable district of town, he brooded over all the things he had hated about London prior to this evening and how much more he despised them now.

As the third son of a Baron — and a modest, Northern Baron who had little connection in London — without enough fortune to raise him above what he lacked, Thomas Richards knew his place among the aristocracy. He was acknowledged but not afforded, accepted but not sought after. That he was decent, generous, hardworking, and intelligent had always seemed to him a reckoning of sorts — a way of balancing what he did not have with those virtues he possessed. Until tonight, he had believed that he was, for the most part, equal to other men of higher rank in the ways that mattered most.

Now, however, he felt sure he would never forget the look on Amber Sterlington's face that had said, clear as church bells, that while he might consider himself an equal, she did not. Perhaps that would be enough to rescue him from the reaction he had each time he saw her. Regardless, he vowed never to put himself within reach of her opinion again.

# Chapter 2

Amber Sterlington turned the page of the most recent edition of *The Ladies' Monthly Museum* and spoke without looking up. "Make Darra attend, Mama," she said, reviewing the renderings of the new fashion plates and finding them near enough the designs from the last periodical that they were barely worth her notice. "You know I don't like to attend events alone."

"You won't be attending alone," her mother, Elsinore Sterlington, Viscountess of Marchent, said from the seat in front of her mirror as her lady's maid, Nelson, put the finishing touches on the perfectly afforded chignon that set Lady Marchent's auburn hair — a faded version of Amber's own — to perfection. "I'll be in attendance," her mother said. "And you are never lacking for company."

"It would not countenance for me to have my mother hanging about me, and you shall want to visit with the other matrons." Amber kept to herself that other than her younger sister, Darra, she did not have female acquaintances to shore up her confidence like so many young women found in each other. It was to be expected that the debutante who drew most of the attention would be at odds with her competitors, and having her sister at her side kept Amber from noticing how the other girls talked and laughed together so easily. "Darra gives me companionship, Mama, make her attend."

"As I've said, she is not feeling well. You would have me force her to go?"

"Yes, I would," Amber said without hesitation, though she did not meet her mother's eyes in the mirror and felt a sting of conscience at the insistence. She turned another page and reviewed an array of half boots that looked like every other half boot she'd seen since coming to London nearly six weeks ago. "She is not *ill,* Mama. She is pouting over the obvious preference the gentlemen have of my company."

Lady Marchent didn't comment, but turned her head side to side, inspecting herself in the mirror. "You may go, Nelson," she said to her maid. "Mind you prepare my lavender morning dress as I will be receiving tomorrow."

"Yes, your ladyship." Nelson bobbed a quick curtsey then gathered up the linens left over from having helped Lady Marchent dress for the evening before she left the room as silently as she'd come.

Lady Marchent's expression was critical as she observed her reflection and patted the underside of her chin that was becoming fleshy as she approached her fortieth year. "Age is an odious taskmaster," she said, frowning as she stood. The skirts of her gown rustled as she shook them out and then fixed Amber with a pointed look. "You would do well to remember that and procure yourself a husband before you tempt the fates by waiting any longer than you already have."

Amber put the periodical down on the empty portion of the cushioned bench and returned her mother's look with a precocious one of her own. "I am barely nineteen, Mama. Hardly in need of such dire warnings."

Men of title and fortune — or both — had taken considerable note of her these past weeks, and once she clarified her choice of whichever gentleman she decided upon, she had no doubt an arrangement would be made. Once she married, the level of affection she enjoyed from numerous suitors would come to an end, and she would be left with only the regard of her husband, which would surely be far less exciting.

She was not a romantic in pursuit of a love match — such an arrangement always seemed to involve one party settling below his or her station. Instead, she focused her ambitions on choosing a husband who would secure her a similar position in society that she'd always known and give her the foundation she needed to make a name for herself alongside him as her mother had done in her own marriage. To factor love, beyond a future potential of their match, into her consideration could obscure her goals.

"I shall never understand why you chose to wait until now to have your season," Lady Marchent continued, looking through the contents of her reticule she would take with her this evening. "I should not have allowed it."

"You truly do not know my motivation?" Amber asked, unwilling to believe her mother's claims to ignorance. "It is your very example I have been following."

Her mother looked at her with an irritated expression, and Amber continued.

"You were married at seventeen to a *Viscount*, Mama," Amber reminded her.

Though the Viscount of Marchent was her father, he rarely interacted with his daughters, reserving his attention for her younger brothers, his numerous estates, and his interest in parliament. He did not hold a seat himself but followed closely the enactments of the government and shared his opinions with his friends who had representation. "And, pray remember, Father was already in his title at the time of your arrangement. You know as well as I do that there are very few prospects already in possession of their title attending this season, and there were even fewer last season, which is why I chose to wait."

"There are a handful of apparents who have made their affections for you known."

"Yes, but Daniel Greenley's father is in his prime, and I shan't be surprised if he doesn't keep his seat for another score," Amber said, singling out her most ardent suitor. He'd proposed to her half a dozen times at least and would post the banns by morning should she accept him. "David Harrington won't inherit until his uncle passes and should his uncle marry and procure an heir of his own — I have seen the ridiculous man at any number of events around town eyeing the widows — Mr. Harrington has no recommendation at all. Mr.

Morrison is nearly your own age, Mama, and I would be settling for only three thousand pounds — never mind that his estate is in *Leeds.* Lord Fenton is a shameless flirt whose intentions are unreliable at best, Bertram Welshire is in need of a fortune to repair the damage his younger brothers have made on the family coffers, and Lord Norwin is simply a bore — though he might be my best prospect as his father did not return to parliament this year due to an illness that has not yet been disclosed through the gossip lines. It's rumored he has nearly ten thousand a year settled upon him, however, and his family *is* well connected."

While Amber did not have female friends, there were plenty of girls who would associate with her for connection, and Amber made use of them by procuring whatever *on-dit* they possessed. Amber never shared what she learned with anyone else but simply filed it away for her own purposes.

Seeing the surprise on Lady Marchent's face turn to admiration of her eldest daughter's shrewdness, Amber finished her commentary. "I have heard, however, that the Earl of Sunther may be returning to London within a fortnight. With the title so new upon his shoulders, he's most certainly mindful of the need to secure himself a wife and an heir." Amber looked at her mother with a smile. "Do not think me a simpleton in my pursuits only because I have not shared with you the workings of my mind. I am the eldest daughter, Mama. I plan to make you and Father proud and ensure that my children are raised with the same level of distinction I have known."

"I regret to have doubted you," her mother said with a complimentary smile. "I fear that with so many events demanding my attention I had forgotten to consider what a wise girl you are." She crossed the space between them and took Amber's hands in a rare display of affection. "I shan't let my concerns interfere with my confidence in you." She leaned in and pressed her cheek ever so quickly against her daughter's.

Amber inhaled the scent of her mother's perfume and closed her eyes. Her mind turned to the times of her childhood when she'd so often pined for her mother's return to Hampton Grove, the estate where Amber and her siblings — her younger sister, Darra, and her three brothers, two of whom were now at school — had spent their childhood. It seemed as though Mama was always away, and Amber had not yet lost the ache of wanting her mother's attentions.

Amber clearly remembered the day Mama had come home from a stay in Bath and looked upon her eldest daughter in surprise. "Why, you are becoming a woman," she'd said to Amber, who was barely fifteen. "And a lovely one at that. We must attend to your education in the graces that will secure you the future a beauty such as you deserves. A woman gets one chance to secure herself any power in this life, you know, and we shall make certain you do your family credit."

For the first time Amber had a place in her mother's life and had from then on kept a sharp eye toward the world in general in hopes of becoming everything her mother wished her to be. Tonight, Amber felt the validation of her efforts. She ignored the stirring within her that wished it had not taken so much accomplishment to earn Mama's attention.

Lady Marchent pulled back from the near-embrace and smiled. "I shall talk to Darra about tonight's attendance," she said. "I don't want you to be out of sorts for the night's assemblies. I shall also be sure to ask after Lord Norwin's father at the dinner party. Mrs. Heyworth is sure to know the circumstance."

Amber nodded her approval. She'd known

Mama would comply with her, and she enjoyed the internal victory she felt at having been correct in that expectation.

Lady Marchent released Amber's hands which were left cold from her withdrawal. "We leave in just over an hour, and I am sure your new abigail awaits you quite anxiously."

"Then perhaps she will be eager about my presentation," Amber said, frowning at the memory of the difficulties she'd had with her prior maid, Helen, these last weeks.

Amber quit her mother's rooms and returned to her own bedchamber where the new maid was waiting with Mrs. Nitsweller, the housekeeper. Just as Lady Marchent had supposed, both women seemed anxious about the time left to prepare Amber for the dinner party.

"Miss Sterlington," Mrs. Nitsweller said. "Might I introduce to you Suzanne Miller, your new maid."

Amber kept her gaze unaffected as she looked at the woman who bobbed a curtsy before her. "It is an honor to have been requested to assist you, and I thank you for the position," the woman said.

The new maid had surprisingly high tones, not the Cockney accent Helen had retained. Suzanne was also older than any other maid Amber had had, likely in her thirties. Amber hoped that her age communicated experience.

"I am to call you Miller, then?" Amber asked. She'd never had an actual lady's maid, who would traditionally be addressed by their surname. Amber turned her attention to Mrs. Nitsweller when the answer was not immediate.

"She is more of an abigail than a lady's maid as she has served multiple women in a household before now," Mrs. Nitsweller said, causing Amber to purse her lips in disapproval. "But she is very skilled and well recommended. She even reads some. In a few years' time, I'm sure she will arise to that station."

"So I shall call you Suzanne," Amber said coldly so that both women would know of her irritation that she'd been told this woman was a lady's maid when she was not one.

Suzanne nodded and kept her eyes on the floor.

"Might I leave you to your toilet?" Mrs. Nitsweller asked, her introduction complete.

Amber nodded and waited for the housekeeper to leave before she explained her expectations to the new maid. She always dressed before the rest of her toilet, with a cape to shield her clothes. She preferred at least a portion of her hair to be worn about her shoulders in order to show off the color and curl. She did not fancy tightly curled fringe at the sides of her forehead though she would tolerate long ringlets so far as they reached her chin at least.

Beads, flowers, ribbon, and feathers were appropriate so long as they did not distract from her natural beauty. She was partial to gold, white, and green accessories as they brought out the color of her eyes and hair.

She had a diamond tiara she wore on occasion but not often as it was such a memorable piece. It was kept in her father's safe and only Lord or Lady Marchent could retrieve it. Her other jewelry was stored in her mother's room; Suzanne would need to coordinate with Nelson to procure whatever items best fit the event's dress. The only piece she kept in her own room was the amber pendant she wore whenever an occasion warranted the unique and personal item.

"Very well, Miss," Suzanne said when Amber finished. "I shall do my best to meet your expectations."

"Be aware that if you do not, you shall not last a fortnight in this household," Amber warned. There was no reason to be less than honest with the underling. "I was far too indulging of my former maid's inadequacies, and I will not be so generous again."

"Yes, Miss," Suzanne said again, bowing slightly in response.

Convinced she'd made her point, Amber turned her back to the woman so Suzanne could help her out of her day dress and into the silver crepe evening gown she'd chosen for the night's events. They would be attending two assemblies tonight: an evening party and a coming-out ball, though Amber felt it ridiculous that the girl's parents were holding it so late in the season. She'd seen the girl at two different events and found it very bad *ton* to have a ball touted as a debut when the girl had already made appearances. Still, there promised to be a good turnout, several of Amber's admirers would be in attendance, and Amber's parents were well acquainted with the family.

There was always a goal to be achieved regardless of the event, and she was prepared to make the most of it.

# Chapter 3

At ten minutes past the hour at which they were supposed to leave, Amber hurried into the closed carriage that had been waiting for far too long.

"You have made all of us late," her mother reprimanded as the footman closed the door.

Amber put a hand to her chest. The high stays, pulled tight to accentuate her small waist and large bosom, made it particularly difficult for her to regain her breath. "It is not my fault," she said between tight breaths. "The new abigail is hardly worthy of the recommendation she received." The carriage lurched forward, and Amber reached out to brace herself against the side until the carriage had gained a rhythm on the cobblestones. Once she could draw a full breath, she continued her complaint. "It took her three attempts to arrange my hair in a style I am still only half pleased with."

She sat back against the cushions and crossed her arms, keeping to herself that in order to create the full topknot, Suzanne had rolled a pair of Amber's stockings into her hair. The very idea was humiliating. Amber had never needed padding or props to give herself the appearance of a thick coiffure. She reflected on the complaints she'd had these last weeks about Helen's styling. Now Amber had a new maid but was still unhappy with the results. What could be the cause?

Feeling the anxiety of such thoughts far stronger than was comfortable, Amber cast her eyes upon her sister — younger by barely a year — pouting in the corner of the carriage as she looked out the window. At least her mother had convinced Darra of the importance of her attendance tonight. At least that.

"I'll have no patience for a case of the doldrums tonight, Darra," Amber warned.

Darra turned her eyes on Amber, matching her glare. "I do not feel well tonight. I should be abed."

"You should be at my side, exactly where you belong," Amber countered. "You are simply put out that Mama did not order you a new gown."

"You have had three new gowns just this

month," Darra spat back, leaning forward in her seat a bit which further convinced Amber that her younger sister was not ill at all. "I have had nothing new since just after we arrived in London."

"*You* are not expected to make a match this season," Amber replied. "Next season you'll have all the attention, and I need not remind you that it is because of my —"

"Your *generosity,*" Darra cut in, looking back to the window and pulling her velvet cape tighter around her shoulders. "When the idea was presented for us to have our first seasons together, I thought it would account for more than simply serving as your companion." She said it with such lack of feeling that Amber felt a prickle of regret in her chest. It had not been her desire for Darra to be miserable, and she had noted her waning interests as the weeks had passed. But Amber needed Darra's attention at these events and was unwilling to drop the argument.

"Have you not danced 'til the early morning hours with men of consequence and fashion? You have not had your own maid instead of sharing with mine? You have not mingled with the upper crust of society?"

"That is enough," her mother said, though her tone was not intent enough to render

Amber silent.

Amber kept her eyes fixed on Darra, who was not looking at her. "You shall return next season with all the polish and manner of a woman rather than a wide-eyed debutante who knows nothing of the polite world. Forgive me for not feeling sympathy toward your discomfort when you are most certainly the larger beneficiary of this experience."

Amber awaited Darra's rebuttal, but her sister simply leaned her head against the back of the cushion and made no answer.

"Leave your sister at peace," Lady Marchent said. "You wanted her attendance and she is here." She turned to Darra and patted her shoulder. "We shall have a new gown made for you, my dear. It is not my intention that you should be left out."

Amber turned away, irritated that her mother had risen to Darra's defense. She had always suspected a preference on Lady Marchent's part to Darra's quiet and inquisitive nature and moments like this seemed to confirm it. Since coming to London, a competitive spirit had sprung up between the sisters. Amber suspected it was due in part to them both vying for their mother's attention, which she had expected would be more heavily turned in her direction.

In the rush of her new abigail's failings, Amber had not retrieved her wrap and shivered a bit in the cooling temperature of the evening. Or perhaps the shiver was in response to the mood of the carriage.

Amber watched the town houses passing outside the carriage and could only hope that the pending society of the evening would push away the dark thoughts and feelings that currently plagued her. By way of distraction, she reviewed her expectations of the evening, the compliments she would receive and the requests for carriage rides and morning visits that would result from the company she kept. Her mood would certainly be restored through the attentions of her suitors. Surely Darra's mood would improve as well, but even if it did not, Amber would not allow her sister's pouting to set the tone of the evening.

# Chapter 4

It was after one o'clock in the morning when Amber next approached her bedchamber. She was unhappy to have left the ball early, but Darra had worsened by the hour and finally begged Amber to go home as her throat was inflamed and her head pounded.

Amber had acted quite put out by the early departure, but in truth she felt badly for having forced Darra's company when she truly *was* ill. She told her sister during the drive home that if she'd known she felt *so* poorly she'd have never insisted on her company, but Amber was quite sure Darra believed her words as much as Amber did, which was not at all. Even given the fact that Darra's complaints had been honest ones, Amber was glad to have had the evening.

She'd been seated next to Lord Norwin at dinner and found his manner more relaxed and personable than it had been during prior events. Perhaps because it was the first time they had been given opportunity for such lengthy conversation. He seemed impressed in particular with her talk of horses. She had little enjoyment of the animals but knew a great deal about them due to her mother's insistence that she be able to converse about what was most gentlemen's favorite topic. That Amber knew the perfect places to laugh as he regaled her with stories not as humorous as he believed helped a great deal as well, and he became more and more comfortable as the evening progressed.

On the ride home, Lady Marchent told Amber that according to Mrs. Heyworth, Lord Norwin's father, the Earl of Lanketer, *was* rather poorly. Enough so that Lord Norwin might soon be allowed to occupy his father's seat in the House of Lords, perhaps permanently. Not only did that stand to forecast that Lord Norwin could become the Earl at any given time, it also meant that his parliamentary seat would require he return to London every season. The expectation of living in London for at least a portion of the year was a significant recommendation for Lord Norwin's suit, which Amber was considering to encourage.

Amber's head was full of such thoughts as she pushed open the door of her bedchamber.

"How was your evening, Miss?"

The unfamiliar voice gave Amber a start. She'd had to ring for Helen after ten o'clock, but it seemed Suzanne had waited for Amber.

"The evening went very well." Amber had all but decided to let the maid go in the morning, but now thought perhaps she should sleep on it to make sure she didn't react rashly. It hadn't been a simple task to replace Helen and could be some time before her mother would be able to procure a maid of higher recommendation than Suzanne.

Amber held out her arms so Suzanne could undo the straps and clasps of the evening gown, turning when needed and stepping out of the gown when Suzanne had pooled it at her feet. Suzanne removed Amber's petticoat next, then the stays, and then the shift, laying them neatly over the dressing bar as she did so. Amber took note of the woman's attention and admitted to herself that despite Amber's displeasure with her hair tonight, she'd received numerous compliments. Only Amber knew she owed the presentation to a pair of stockings.

Suzanne helped her into her nightdress and dressing gown before Amber sat down at her mirror, feeling the heaviness of sleep reach her eyes as Suzanne began removing the pins from her hair. It seemed as though it had taken a hundred of them to hold everything in place tonight.

"Miss?" Suzanne asked, causing Amber to open her eyes and meet the woman's reflection in the mirror. "Might I speak plainly?"

*Speak plainly?* Suzanne had been under Amber's employ for less than a day. What a presumptuous woman! The request was so out of place that it piqued her curiosity, however, and kept Amber from responding with the irritation she felt. "You may."

Suzanne kept her eyes on Amber's hair as she continued removing the pins. She tucked each pin in the pocket of her apron, obviously nervous, which meant the servant had not asked for such a liberty without understanding the risk she took in doing so.

"I am quite distressed at displeasing you on my very first night. In hopes of improving my service for tomorrow, I thought to become more familiar with your wardrobe and tastes. I explored your bedchamber, and

I found the box in the back of your wardrobe. Do you know it?"

"Why would a box in the back of my wardrobe concern you?" Amber snapped. "I have any number of boxes for hats and trinkets."

Suzanne looked up and met Amber's eyes in the mirror. "Yes, Miss, but this box was different. It was filled with . . . hair."

"Hair?" Amber asked, confused. "A wig?"

"No, Miss, *your* hair." She took a breath and did not meet Amber's reflection as she spoke more quickly. "If you know of it I will not mention it again."

Amber's irritation was profound. "Are you completely addled? I have no idea what you are talking about."

Suzanne pursed her lips as she threaded the stockings out of Amber's hair. The bulk of her hair fell down Amber's back once it was released, causing her scalp to tingle with relief. Suzanne went to the wardrobe, opened it, and returned with a wooden box similar in size to the cigar boxes Amber had seen in her father's study, though not as fine. Suzanne set the box on the dressing table and opened the lid.

Amber gasped as she looked upon the contents, which were just as Suzanne had said — tangles of hair in Amber's exact shade. "What is this? I have never laid eyes upon this in my life."

"I took the liberty of talking of it to your mother's maid, Nelson, and she confided that your former maid had said you were losing hair at an alarming rate. She'd gone about collecting it."

"Collecting my . . . hair?" Amber was too shocked to feel anything but confusion as she stared at the box.

"She was afraid it might be blamed on her if you took notice of it."

"Of course it shall be blamed on her! She was below her appointment and obviously rough amid her duties."

"I can understand why you would assume as much," Suzanne said, her words hesitant as she continued. "But when I was working on your arrangement tonight, I noted much hair falling to the ground. More than I have ever seen. Even now, upon removing your pins I am shocked at how much hair has come out with them." She stepped around Amber and opened the wide pocket on the side of her apron where she'd been depositing the pins as she removed them.

Amber was taken aback at how much hair was gathered there. She could barely see the dark-colored pins amid the auburn strands. She thought back to the concern she'd felt earlier that evening regarding the difficulty with her hair and felt a coldness in her chest. She turned in her chair and looked at the section of rug beneath Suzanne's feet. The dark strands of hair — seemingly dozens of them — stood out on the blue and gray rug.

Amber lifted a hand to her head. She'd barely given her hair any of her own attention since arriving in London as Helen had taken on the responsibility. Prior to leaving Hampton Grove, however, she had at times attended to her own styling when the maid she shared with Darra was attending her sister. She had memory of her thumb and middle finger not touching, so thick was the girth of her gathered hair. She pulled her hair together now and noted that her thumb overlapped her finger to the first knuckle. Her breath caught in her throat, and she turned sincerely frightened eyes upon her maid.

"What does it mean? You must know of this based upon your experience with other ladies."

Suzanne shook her head, looking truly distressed. "I have worked with hair that has thinned with age, of course, and I have attended to wigs and hairpieces for different matrons — that's how I knew a set of stockings could give you the proper appearance this evening — but I have never known of anyone losing hair like this, Miss. And certainly not among young women like yourself. Not ever." She stepped behind Amber again and gingerly took the hair from Amber's hand and parted it in the back. "If you'll but use your hand mirror and turn your back to the dressing table glass, you will see what concerns me the most."

Feeling light-headed, Amber did as Suzanne suggested, holding the hand mirror in front of her face and turning around on her stool to see the larger reflection in the looking glass. It took a few movements of the mirror before Amber saw what Suzanne wanted her to see, and she gasped, lifting her hand to what she could only explain as an empty spot. It was an inch or two in width, and she hit Suzanne's hand away in order to run her own fingers over the smooth patch of skin. Stunned by this discovery, Amber dropped her hair and turned back to the mirror, replacing the hand mirror on her dressing table.

While watching herself in the mirror, she ran her hand through the length of her hair, then stared at the strands left woven around her fingers. Too much. She shook the hair off her hand and watched it float to the floor. "Leave me," she finally said, quick and sharp.

"Miss, I am —"

"Leave me," Amber repeated with a hiss this time, fixing the woman with a glare. "And do not gossip about this to the other servants as you did with Nelson. I will not stand for it."

Suzanne cast her eyes to the ground and bowed out of the room without a word, collecting Amber's garments as she did so.

Once the door was shut, Amber first looked at the hair on the floor then at the hair in the box still open on her dressing table. It looked like a tangled pillow, and she thought that perhaps it looked like more than it was, but upon closer inspection, she could tell the mass was densely organized. She imagined Helen gathering the strands from the floor after attending to Amber in the mornings and evening and hiding them in the box for fear of making it known.

Amber looked at her reflection and tried to quell her concerns with the fact that her hair *looked* the same as always from this perspective. The dark auburn locks, so coveted by every girl with drab blonde or mousy brown hair, hung in large, loose waves halfway down her back. It was full at the crown and shone beneath the candlelight of her room like polished copper. But when Amber gathered it together again she could not deny the difference compared to when she'd last gathered it in her hand at Hampton Grove.

Her gaze caught sight of the boar's hair brush that, usually, her maid would use to brush out her hair before plaiting it for the night. With apprehension Amber picked up the brush, pressed the bristles against the crown of her head and pulled it through her tresses. There was far more hair left behind on the brush than should be there. She moved the brush to the other side and pulled it through again. More strands were woven through the stiff bristles to the point where she could hardly make out the bristles at all.

*Stop,* she told herself, fearing that with each stroke she was causing further loss. She threw the brush on the vanity as though it were hot to the touch, then reached for it again in order to pull the hair quickly from it. She gathered the strands from the floor as well, resulting in a messy handful she then shoved into the box of hair. She quickly closed the lid, ran to the wardrobe, and hid the box in a back corner before slamming the door shut.

*No one can know of this,* she said to herself as she stared at the closed door.

Suzanne could help Amber keep her appearance while Amber sought out a solution to this tragic turn. But Suzanne claimed to have never encountered something like this. There had to be a reason that her hair was dropping off. Was she ill and unaware of it? Perhaps she was not getting enough rest due to the late hours she kept and the number of engagements she accepted — life in London was very different from the pace of life in Somerset. Maybe she was drinking too much wine at dinner parties — something her parents had never allowed prior to her season. Or perhaps she was not drinking enough — some people swore that wine would improve one's health. Perhaps her diet was compromised or, maybe, the pressure she felt at being such an unparallel was taking more of her energy than she'd expected. It was not easy to withstand so much scorn from her rivals night after night, no matter how pretty their manners were when she was in their company.

Amber returned to her place before the mirror and carefully plaited her hair over one shoulder, watching her movements and being mindful not to pull too much against her scalp. She tied the end of the plait with a bit of string Suzanne had left on the dressing table. Looking at her reflection, she could not deny that the thickness was fairly half of the plait she recalled seeing in the mirror at Hampton Grove — *that* plait had been nearly as thick as her wrist.

Feeling dizzy, Amber blew out the candle before making her way to her bed, where she burrowed under the covers and stared at the darkened walls for quite some time before sleep overtook her.

The last conscious thought she remembered before falling asleep, and the first thought she had when she awakened the next morning, was the one she'd already admitted — no one could know. She would behave as she always did, flirting and complimenting and drawing the eyes of the men of the *ton.* There would be no change in her behavior, therefore no one would suspect anything amiss. One's reputation was determined by perfect execution of behavior, appearance, and manners. Amber could not let anyone know she was anything less than exactly what she ought to be.

# Chapter 5

Thomas checked the watch pinned to his waistcoat as the hansom cab he'd hired for the ride across town slowed to a stop in front of the Earl of Chariton's London house. It was not quite eleven o'clock, and he hoped the lateness of his arrival for the card party would not offend his hosts, Lord and Lady Chariton — Lord Fenton's parents.

Thomas had meant to arrive earlier but had gone to a ball, which had not been well attended. He'd stayed later than he'd planned so as to dance with as many women as possible and attempt to preserve the evening for the hosts, the Thorntons. He was acquainted with them from Lancashire and therefore knew that their son had recently died following an accident in Scotland. The mourning period had prevented the Thorntons from coming to London until now, leaving them in the unenviable position of trying to find their footing amid people who had been making the rounds for weeks.

As this was their first daughter to be presented, they did not come with many connections to recommend them. The social climate of London during the season could be temperamental at best and prejudicial more often than not, as Thomas had been reminded by Amber Sterlington nearly a fortnight ago. Even with so much distance from the event at Almack's, his neck flushed hot at the reminder of the set down.

He had skipped the Almack's Wednesday night ball last week and decided not to appeal to the patronesses for a May voucher. The embarrassing situation had encouraged him to accept invitations to events with smaller crowds which better suited his personality. He had not missed Almack's for a moment and, in accepting such invitations, had managed to avoid Miss Sterlington almost completely.

Once he stepped down from the carriage, Thomas paid the driver and then straightened his black-and-violet striped silk waistcoat. Fenton's encouragement to purchase a few nicer pieces of clothing had the happy effect of helping Thomas feel more on the level.

"Does no good to look the part of a rustic amid roses, Richards," Fenton had said one afternoon after the two had enjoyed lunch at Brooks. "You don't have to be a dandy to give *some* attention to fashion." Thomas would have to find a way to thank Fenton for the encouragement without inviting his friend to tease him for it. It could be a tricky business affecting that balance with someone who was as watchful for a joke as Fenton.

Thomas had been to the Earl of Chariton's London house on holiday forays when he and Fenton were attending Oxford, and it appeared much the same: a fenced-in flower garden out front, a wide porch, and two stories above ground. Thomas let himself through the gate and heard the sound of laughter and voices as he made his way up the steps. A footman opened the door to his knock and took Thomas's greatcoat — with only two capes, much to Fenton's dismay — before directing Thomas into the yellow and blue drawing room located at the front of the house and set with four card tables for the evening. Thomas could hear additional voices from down the hall, indicating that Lord Chariton's study must have been opened for the night's entertainment as well.

"Richards!" Fenton said, crossing to him from the fireplace where he stood in conference with Sir Barney Crosby, a man with whom Thomas was newly acquainted. " 'Pon my soul I thought you'd snubbed us."

Thomas took Fenton's outstretched hand and gave it a hearty shake. "You have my most sincere apologies, Fenton. I'm afraid I landed at an event slender on gentlemen."

"Ah, had to dance with a bunch of country cousins, eh?"

"Lovely young ladies," Thomas corrected him, then paused as he thought back to some of the women he'd stood up with. "Well, mostly lovely young ladies."

Fenton laughed loudly and took a sip of brandy from the glass he held. "Let me introduce you to the room," he said, putting a hand on Thomas's back and starting the introductions at the table nearest the door. Many of the guests were familiar and extended him warm welcomes, furthering Thomas's confidence that he would feel at ease amid this group. At the last table was a girl Thomas had seen before but had not been introduced to.

"And this is Miss Laurel Ranbury," Fenton said after introducing the other guests at the table, including the woman's mother,

Lady Ranbury. "Sir Ranbury and his family are from Sheffield — isn't that near the jungle you hail from, Thomas?" He raised his eyebrows mockingly, and Thomas shook his head as he turned his attention to the girl at the table who lifted her hand, allowing him to bow over it.

"Lord Fenton is certain that anything north of Nottingham could not possibly be civilized," Thomas explained as he released her hand. "I'm afraid my jungles are even further north than yours. I hail from Northallerton."

"My father's cousin lives in Northallerton," the girl said with amiable confidence. "Mr. Clarence Gordy — do you know him?"

"I do know Mr. Gordy," Thomas said, smiling a bit wider. "He was an associate of my father's, though I'm afraid I haven't seen Mr. Gordy since my father's passing three summers ago."

"I'm sorry to hear of your father," Miss Ranbury said with a frown. "I'm afraid it's been some time since I've seen my uncle as well. Next time I do, I shall ask after your family . . ."

Thomas picked up the unspoken question once she trailed off. "My father was Walter Richards," he supplied. "Former Lord Fielding, a title now held by my eldest brother, Albert."

He was glad to see that her expression didn't falter at his admittance of not having a title of his own. He would ask Fenton about Miss Ranbury's family at another time to see if their positions matched. Not because he feared her to be below him, but to make certain that she was not of such a high esteem that his interest would be unwelcome. He was particularly sensitive to such a thing after his attempt to dance with Amber Sterlington.

"It is nice to meet a northern gentleman," Miss Ranbury said with a smile.

"Laurel," Lady Ranbury said from across the table, "either take your turn or find someone to play your hand rather than keep us waiting while you flirt the night away."

"Mama!" Miss Ranbury said, color rising to her cheeks as she looked wide-eyed at her mother. "You are beyond the pale this evening. Lord Fenton, do not give my mother any more to drink. The wine has quite gone to her head and dreadfully affected her manners."

"I shall willingly refuse her pleas for refreshment and drink anything she requests myself to make doubly sure she is denied it," Fenton said, with a sharp bend at the waist. "Pray, excuse us as I continue introductions in the next room. But do come find us when you finish your round, Miss Ranbury. I haven't seen Mr. Richards so engaged in conversation in some time."

The table laughed. Thomas smiled but once they'd exited into the hall on their way to the study, he punched Fenton lightly on the shoulder. "Must you embarrass me in front of everyone?" Thomas said quietly. "It was hard enough to keep my confidence amid new introductions without being thrown to the wolves."

"Oh, don't think of it," Fenton said, waving the glass in his hand and nearly spilling his drink in the process. "I can only get away with such shameless behavior if I embarrass everyone equally, and I only invite people of the best humor to my parties. You should have heard what I said about Miss Sterlington's hair upon her arrival. I daresay I may have taken that one too far." He laughed at the recollection even as Thomas came to a stop and took hold of Fenton's arm. He pulled Fenton past the yellow and blue drawing room to the small parlor at the front of the house which was lit but unoccupied.

"Amber Sterlington is here?" Thomas asked, glad the alarm didn't show in his voice, though he feared his actions communicated the intensity of his feelings without him having to display it in the tone of his words.

"Most certainly," Fenton said with a wide grin. "I find her vastly enjoyable to look upon, and if you can ignore the headdress she chose for reasons only the angels of heaven can know, she is quite fetching tonight. Green will always be her color, but pink does wonders for her complexion."

Thomas kept his expression stolid, at least he hoped he did, as he took a breath. "Fenton, I have no desire to be acquainted with her. Will you mind ever so much if I leave?"

Fenton's eyebrows leaped up his forehead. "The devil you say! I thought Miss Sterlington was vastly enjoyable for you to look upon as well?"

Thomas had not told Fenton what happened at Almack's but expected his friend to know about it all the same. It had been such an embarrassment that he had assumed it was interesting enough *on-dit* that those in view of the situation had spread the tale far and wide. But perhaps the younger son of a Baron being set down by the Darling of the Season was not impressive enough to be whispered about. Thomas hated that he was a bit disappointed by the realization, but then relayed what had happened. Fenton's face showed sincere regret as Thomas concluded his report.

"I surely would not have invited both of you if I had known," Fenton said in the sincere voice Thomas preferred to the dandy tones. "I have no desire to put you in an awkward position, but I'm sure you see that I have managed to put myself in the suds due to my ignorance. I had hoped you would like Miss Ranbury who, though I know she is no great beauty, is a very personable young woman and someone I felt might be just the match for you. Her family does not have airs and are well accepted here in town. For you to leave just after having made her acquaintance would be very bad *ton* for the both of us."

*What a muck-pen,* Thomas thought to himself. He considered the truth of Fenton's statement and searched his mind for a remedy. "Perhaps you could spare me the introduction to the second room then, and I shall simply give Miss Sterlington distance on my own as best I can."

Fenton frowned. "I'm afraid my home will not provide the kind of distance you would prefer. I am sincerely sorry. Perhaps another introduction could repair it. There are so many people at Almack's and —"

"I want no further introduction," Thomas said with an adamant shake of his head. "And I am quite happy to take responsibility to avoid her if I can but have your blessing to forgo the convention of your introduction to the other guests in the study."

"Of course," Fenton said. He raised one eyebrow while shaking his head, marking for Thomas the transformation back into the façade he employed amid society. Fenton downed the last of the drink in his hand and smacked his lips, eyeing the now empty glass. "I believe I am in need of Lady Ranbury's allotted drink. My nerves are raw with all this complication." He waved his hand through the air and made his way to the study where the food and drinks must be laid out while Thomas returned to the drawing room.

When the set at one of the tables finished, Thomas joined the next round. The company could not be more pleasant, and he enjoyed himself almost enough to forget about a certain lady in the other room until he noticed Mr. Pembroke and Sir Crosby straighten in their chairs at the same moment Miss Ranbury lifted her chin. He did not need to turn toward the door to see the cause of the change as the honeyed voice of Amber Sterlington soon washed over him.

Much to his dismay, his heart rate increased and the temperature in the room went up by degrees as he pulled his shoulders back and adjusted his position in the chair so he would not appear to be slouching. Blast that abominable woman!

Thomas studied the cards he held. "Sir Crosby, I should like to trade for the miss," he said, even though his hand was adequate.

Miss Sterlington took a seat at the table behind him — far too close for him to attempt to be unaware of her.

"Certainly," Sir Crosby said as all eyes returned to the game. Thomas's table continued through the round though he performed very poorly and then he excused himself from the next set, claiming to be in need of refreshment. He did not look at Miss Sterlington as he left the room to fortify himself with a glass of brandy and conversation with guests in the study.

"Where are your parents this evening?" Thomas asked Fenton some time later, realizing that neither Lord nor Lady Chariton were in the study as he had expected. Fenton did not live in the London house, of course, instead staying in a very nice set of rooms far enough away to give him privacy. It was odd that he had been put in the position to host a party at his parents' home when they were not even in attendance.

Fenton rolled his eyes. "My father stayed for an hour before excusing himself for another engagement. Mother was not feeling well but stayed on until just before you came. I think London does not go well with her." He frowned, reflecting the close affection he shared with his mother and his obvious concern for her health.

Thomas shared his best wishes for her recovery while not commenting on Lord Chariton's absence. It was ill-mannered for him to have left, but though Thomas found the man personable enough, Fenton made no attempt to show his father any tolerance, and therefore Thomas knew better than to make Lord Chariton the focus of the conversation. Instead, he changed the subject, asking after a visit to Tattersalls that Fenton had mentioned the previous week.

Once enough time had passed for Thomas to regain his composure, the need to see Miss Sterlington took him back to the drawing room where he stood in the doorway, sipping his brandy while attempting a casual survey of the room. His eyes could not help but land on Miss Sterlington each time she spoke or laughed. Her voice drew him in like a net, further irritating him each time it did so.

She had shown her character so poorly when she'd dismissed him that he had hoped his reaction to her would have adjusted accordingly. Obviously it was not enough to know she was highbrow, rude, and unpleasant. He stood behind her, out of her sight unless she looked to the doorway, but in full view of the back of her head and the graceful curve of her neck and shoulders. He was close enough to hear her voice and, perhaps, smell her perfume, though he couldn't be sure it was hers.

Her gown *was* quite lovely, just as Fenton had said. It was a muted shade of pink fitted high with fine lace along the collar and puffed sleeves. Pearls defined the bodice, which accentuated her womanly figure that drew far too much interest from the men in the room. She wore more daring necklines than most debutantes, and yet received no judgment for it, which was both interesting and irritating. Certainly the males of the species would not be so attentive to her if she dressed with a bit more modesty. Yet even as he attempted to place the blame on her, he knew he was the one in keeping of his own thoughts and ought not to blame her manner of dress for his own weakness.

He moved his attention to the headdress Fenton had found so worthy of teasing. It was an arrangement of ribbons, beads, and flowers, which almost looked like a hat, though it was not. While overdone compared to the relatively conservative nature of her dress, it didn't seem particularly disagreeable. Her hair still shone like dark embers beneath the recently installed gas lights, and her eyes glittered most beautifully when she turned her head enough for Thomas to see her face in profile.

Thomas forced himself to look away and was glad he had when he saw Miss Ranbury glance toward him and give him a small smile. He smiled back and hoped she hadn't noted his inspection of Miss Sterlington. Comparing the beauty of the two women was unfair by half, and he had no desire to make Miss Ranbury feel small. Miss Ranbury returned to her game, and Thomas watched her a bit longer, but his eyes were drawn back to Miss Sterlington the next time she spoke. Luckily, he was in better control of his reaction and thoughts. In fact, rather than ponder on his own mind, he found himself wondering at hers.

She was seated next to Lord Norwin; the very man she had refused Thomas for at Almack's. The two of them sat very close together, and Thomas realized that Lord Norwin was attempting to teach Miss Sterlington the finer points of loo. Odd, since loo was thought of as a woman's game, making it appropriate for mixed company and penny bets.

A quick glance across the room revealed the other Miss Sterlington — Miss Darra — seated at a different table and seeming to handle her game quite sufficiently. She glanced at him but looked away before he had the chance to acknowledge her notice. He wondered if *she* remembered him from Almack's and hoped that she did not.

"So, I want to play the highest spade, my lord?" Miss Sterlington asked her teacher in consternation, her voice an octave higher than usual, more girlish. From Thomas's position he could not see her face, but he *could* see her cards over her shoulder. She held the jack of spades, a very good card for a simple pool round when spades were the leading suit.

"Right you are," Lord Norwin said. "If you haven't a spade, you must discard something else."

"Oh pooh," she said with a pout and removed the queen of hearts from her hand — a card she ought to hold on to in case hearts were played in another round. "I'm sure I'll never learn to play this game," she said, casually keeping her cards away from

Lord Norwin's gaze even as he leaned toward her in such a way as to invite her to let him see.

Thomas watched the game progress as again and again Miss Sterlington intentionally set herself at a disadvantage. He could have accused her of cheating except that she was losing. Each time she lost a hand or withdrew — most times without need — she pouted and then revived amid the compliments of the other players on the table — all of whom, Thomas noted, were men quite enraptured by her grievances.

When one of the men won the round, she laid the compliments on rather thick, remarking on their fine skill and astute play. Considering the moves she'd chosen, it was not difficult to ascertain that Miss Sterlington understood the game; she had to know the rules well in order to play so poorly.

*What a fascinating act she is playing out for them,* Thomas thought as he noted how the men's opinions of themselves seemed to rise with her compliments. With the realization of her manipulation came a sense of relief to know that she was making a different kind of fool of these men than she had with him. What would they say if they knew?

"Will you join us, Mr. Richards?"

Thomas looked away from Miss Sterlington's table to see Lady Ranbury's eyebrows lifted in invitation. She was an older version of her daughter with a genuine air about her.

"I would be pleased to join if you've an open seat," Thomas said, moving toward the table.

An older gentleman rose and made a joke about trading his seat for Thomas's glass of brandy.

"You're welcome to it," Thomas said, holding out his glass.

The man laughed. "I was teasing you, my man."

"Were you?" Thomas replied as though surprised. "You do not want brandy that's been adequately warmed by my hand?"

The man laughed again, as did the rest of the table. "I'll get myself a double in the next room and return ready to best the lot of you." He made an exaggerated motion of glaring at the table, and they all laughed at his joke.

Thomas took the abandoned seat and enjoyed two rounds before the strain of being attentive to his game while listening to Miss Sterlington at the next table began to give him a headache. The gentleman whose seat he'd taken returned to the drawing room, giving Thomas the opportunity to make his good-byes, stealthily avoiding Miss Sterlington's table. She did not look up at him despite the occupants of the room taking a turn in their farewells, and once Thomas quit the room he let out a breath he hadn't realized he'd been holding. Her laugh followed him out, as did Fenton.

"You behaved admirably," Fenton said when they were quite a distance from anyone who might overhear the exchange. "I hope you were able to enjoy yourself despite the discomfort."

"I'm grateful for the invitation and even more grateful to have stayed. Thank you for being a man of honor about the situation."

"You had a good time, then?"

It was rare for Thomas to see Fenton in need of reassurance, which proved to him what a good friend Fenton truly was to be so concerned for Thomas's comfort. "I did, my friend," he said. "Perhaps we could luncheon tomorrow and you could help me know how best to go about furthering my acquaintance with Miss Ranbury."

Fenton's face broke into a full smile. "I knew you would like her. Shall we say one o'clock at my club?"

"That would be ideal," Thomas said with a nod as the footman helped him into his coat and hat. "Until then."

Thomas had to walk a few blocks before he could signal a hansom cab, but as he did so he reviewed the evening and allowed himself some modest pride at having endured what could have been a most uncomfortable experience. That he'd gained a different perspective on Miss Sterlington was not the least of his accomplishments, and it set his mind at ease a great deal to know that he could never have been happy with a woman so false. Beauty could never be as important to him as character.

# CHAPTER 6

*May*

It had been two weeks since Suzanne had first used the stockings in Amber's hair, and as Amber watched her maid's face in the mirror she had to fight back tears.

"It is worse, isn't it?" she asked in a soft voice, worn-out with the worry and concern that had plagued her day and night since first discovering the blight that had come upon her. She'd been mindful of all the things she'd promised to reverence: sleep, healthy foods, and avoiding late nights. She'd read of a recommendation that an increase of meat in one's diet could result in thick and shiny hair, and she had more than once made herself sick in her attention to the ham and beef and poultry she'd asked her mother to add to the cook's menus.

Given her specific attention to her health, she had come to realize that she *felt* vital and strong; she was not fatigued or achy, nor was she feeling dull witted. Her body felt as well as ever, but her hair continued to shed every night, including tonight, when she feared she would not be able to leave the house at all.

Suzanne had used increasing amounts of ribbon, flowers, and all manner of accessories, often spending hours to complete a style that was merely passable. Amber no longer accepted afternoon engagements so that Suzanne could have the extra time for her styling before she dressed for the evening. It did not escape Amber's notice that the compliments to her hair, once so frequently made, had decreased now that the use of the hidden stockings had become a daily occurrence. The only time she was without them was when she could expect to wear a bonnet for the duration of an event.

Tonight, Amber was to attend the opera in the Earl of Sunther's box. He had returned to London three nights ago and sought Amber out at once. Their parents were connected and a match between them would be acceptable by all parties. His attention gave her confidence that she had not lost her appeal, and she was relieved that the flamboyant expectations of opera dress could countenance even more elaborate accessories to disguise the increased thinness of her hair. However, it had been nearly two hours since the maid had begun attempting a suitable coiffure only to undo it and start again several times.

"It is worse," Amber said again, anxious for her maid to give her assurance that she was mistaken.

"I cannot hide the stocking completely." She met Amber's eyes. "What about a turban, Miss? I'm told they are all the rage."

Earlier in the season, Amber would never have considered such a matronly affectation. "Can you conform to a style that will allow some of my hair to show through?"

"I could create two or three ringlets down the back," Suzanne suggested as she began removing the pins she had placed and taking out the ribbon. "It would look as though it were a portion of your hair."

When her hair was down again, Amber looked at her reflection and blinked back tears. The area on the back of her head that Suzanne had first made her aware of was now larger, and another had formed above her left ear, allowing Amber to see her scalp through the hair that fell over it. The color of her hair looked brighter than it had when there was more of it — but more orange than auburn and not nearly as rich. In a word, she looked wretched, like a decrepit old woman on the edge of death.

*Am I dying?* she asked herself as Suzanne brushed the newly-shed hair from her fingers and apron. As had become her habit, she picked the hair from the floor and disposed of it in a linen pillowcase she'd procured for this very purpose — there was too much hair to fit in the box any longer. Suzanne excused herself from the room to retrieve a length of silk that would work for the turban, and by the time the maid returned, Amber was wiping at the tears she'd been unable to hold back.

"There, there," Suzanne said, awkwardly patting Amber's shoulder. "I promise it will look lovely. You'll be the envy of every girl there, but I cannot remedy a splotchy face and swollen eyes."

"I shall not be the envy of anyone." Amber wiped at her eyes with a handkerchief she had found in the top drawer.

Perhaps it was time to ask for her mother's help, but the idea frightened her. Admitting a fault to Lady Marchent filled her with dread. What would her mother say? Would she blame Amber? Was it blame that Amber deserved?

She thought back to the counsel her mother had given her about tempting fate by drawing out the attentions of eligible men. If only Amber had not delayed her season. Had she come out last year, she would be established already. Had she not been so determined to enjoy herself in London *this* year, she could have secured a match by now. Already it was May; the season was half over.

"See there, Miss, it's lovely. Look at how it draws out the color of your eyes."

Amber looked at her reflection, the tears nearly dried though her eyes were still pink around the edges. The silk Suzanne had found was a soft gold, with shimmers of silver throughout. The maid did not build the turban high, but kept it close to Amber's head. She finished by pushing a white and a green feather into the folds.

"Where did you find this?" Amber asked as she took note of exactly what Suzanne had said; the color *did* emphasize her eyes. Perhaps it *could* work.

"I feared we might need something of this sort and was able to find this at a shop. I thought it would look right nice with your silver gown."

Amber straightened in her chair and felt heat rush up her chest as she more fully understood the implications of this change. "That is a ball gown. I had set aside the blue *robe a la Russe* for tonight." It was a beautiful gown of velvet, with cutaway sleeves, beading at the neck, and a ruffled collar in the back. It had come from the dressmaker just last week.

Suzanne frowned. "The blue won't match the silk, and the collar would not look right."

"Then why did you not procure a silk to match my gown?" Amber said, horrified by the turn of events. "I can't wear a ball gown to the opera! Certainly not one I've been seen in before."

"Has the Earl seen the silver gown?" Suzanne asked rather boldly. "Did he not return to town since you last wore it? Perhaps you could borrow Miss Darra's gold mantle and wear your gold chains to disguise the look of it for those who might remember it."

Amber pursed her lips, unhappy with the suggestion even as she realized the hour was too late for her to come up with a better solution. Suzanne had not stopped her work as they'd talked and was now using her fingers with a bit of pomade to shape into ringlets the hair left about Amber's shoulders. There was no time to use papers to set the curl the way it ought to be, and Amber felt her spirits fall again as she accepted that this result would not look quite right either.

Her anxiety increasing, she snapped at Suzanne throughout the rest of the preparation and did not acknowledge her when she left the bedchamber some time later.

Amber went straight to Darra's room where they argued over the golden mantle until Amber agreed that Darra could have use of the *robe a la Russe.* They were close enough in size that Darra's slighter frame would allow the velvet to drape, elongating her figure even as it emphasized Amber's curves.

"I don't know why you are so insistent on wearing that wrap upon your head," Darra said once she had committed to the trade. "It looks positively old-fashioned." She narrowed her eyes, blue like their mother's. "Perhaps you think that if *you* wear such a stuffy accessory all the other girls will do so as well, then you'll laugh at the lot of them for following your lead."

"Am I so horrible?" Amber said, more hurt than she expected to be by her sister's accusation. "Do you think all I do is design ways to make myself superior?"

"Since our arrival in London, it is all I've seen from you," Darra said, her tone as cutting as her words. They held one another's eyes, and when Darra's expression fell for a moment, Amber wondered if perhaps her sister sensed Amber's unspoken hardship.

How she longed to pour out her troubles to a compassionate ear and be assured that things were not so frightening as they seemed.

Instead, Darra lifted her chin, and her expression was at once hard and arrogant. "I shall look far better in your gown than you shall ever look in my mantle." With that, she quit the room.

"I expect you are exactly right," Amber said to the silence as she crossed to Darra's wardrobe and removed the mantle, not allowing a second wave of tears to release themselves. She had to be at her very best tonight. With her condition growing worse by the day, she lived in fear that after having dismissed so much attention earlier in the season she might end up without a match at all.

# Chapter 7

It took all of Amber's energy to keep up the appearance of confidence and security throughout the opera. The Earl was complimentary of her dress and hair — sincerely, she felt — and attentive, which made it easier for her to laugh when she should laugh, pout when she should pout, and flatter him shamelessly. He responded as she hoped he would and asked her to ride out with him through Hyde Park the following afternoon in his barouche. It was the first time he had invited her on an outing.

"A ride through Hyde Park tomorrow sounds lovely, though I must be returned home by three o'clock," Amber said to Lord Sunther with a coy grin and a pat of her fan against his arm. "I need sufficient time to ready myself for the evening party at the Whiteacres. Will you be attending, do you think? It promises to be a delightful event with the very highest of company." She had already procured the morning gossip that confirmed he'd been included on the guest list. Amber had to resist touching the turban or trying to make it more comfortable. It felt odd to have such a confining piece on her head, and it itched terribly.

"If I know you shall be there, I will make certain to accept the invitation that arrived just tonight," he said, smiling at her. He was not particularly handsome with too thin a face and ears that could not be disguised even with his longish hair combed into a Brutus style. But he was attentive and kind. Was he kind enough to accept her situation if she hid it from him until they married? Would he be the type of man to make the best of it?

Such thoughts threatened to ruin her resolve to act her part and so Amber set them aside and complimented him on the superior view of the stage afforded them by the rented box. He seemed to take great delight in her compliments, and she determined to consider what other aspects of his person and interests she could expound upon during their carriage ride tomorrow. She could wear a bonnet, which would be a relief to her nerves.

When the Sterlington party returned to the town house on Park Street near midnight, Amber felt as though she could think freely for the first time all evening. The night had been a success, but the effort to maintain her role of carefree and confident debutante was exhausting. She knew that if the society she worked so hard to impress knew the truth, they would want nothing of her at all. Though she wanted to believe that Lord Sunther would not dismiss her should they marry and then he learn of her secret, he would have to come to terms with her deception as well as her condition eventually. It would be easier if she had no qualms regarding her behavior — such as had been the case when she saw herself as whole and desirable. Now she knew she was offering less than she was leading Lord Sunther to believe, and the realization of how poorly she was using him did not sit well with her.

Suzanne was waiting in Amber's bedchamber as she always was, and assisted Amber with the removal of Darra's mantle, which she draped over the bench at the end of Amber's bed while asking about the evening.

"It was bearable but only just," Amber said tersely, not hesitating to take her mood out on her maid. She settled herself on the stool before her vanity and looked at Suzanne in the mirror. "This *silk,* as you call it, is as coarse as burlap. It itched the whole evening through."

Suzanne made no comment as she began unwrapping the turban from Amber's head. Amber closed her eyes, enjoying the release of pressure and wished it could take other tensions with it. If the Earl had been in town for some weeks, she could countenance pushing for a proposal on their ride tomorrow. As he had only been in town for three days, however, and this would be their first ride together, it was far too forward and might work against her by creating a wariness in him. She needed more time for him to fall in love with her and offer her a sincere proposal.

"Oh, Miss," she heard Suzanne said, her voice heavy. Amber blinked her eyes open and looked first at Suzanne's wide-eyed expression reflected in the mirror before looking at herself. Her gasp was audible as she gingerly lifted a hand to the front left portion of her head which had no hair at all. The patch above her ear that she had noted earlier in the evening had expanded, like wine spilled on a rug. The pale skin was smooth beneath her touch: warm, and completely . . . bald.

*It can't be,* she said in her mind. She placed her hand over the offending portion as though to hide it and turned in her seat to see full clumps of hair at Suzanne's feet. She looked at the portion of silk still in Suzanne's hands and could see several stands of her hair woven into it as well.

"I was simply trying to brush out the tangles," Suzanne said. "I do not know what —"

"You put the silk on too tight," she accused her maid as her ears filled with a rushing sound. This *had* to be Suzanne's fault, never mind that Helen had been collecting Amber's fallen hair prior to Suzanne's arrival. The maid *had* to bear responsibility. "You hate me, you have always hated me, and you are determined to ruin me!"

"Miss," Suzanne said, sounding shocked as she took a step back, "I have naught but helped you all this time. I have —"

"You have rendered me an atrocity!" Amber yelled back, her rage overflowing her ability to reason. "Until you came, all was as it should be. Your attention to me has changed everything. Were you sent from the household of a rival? Have you conspired with a suitor whose attentions I have thwarted?"

Amber paused for breath as Suzanne cowered near the bed, her head hung so that

Amber could not see her face. Amber did not hear the creak of a door hinge until it was too late. She snapped her head to the side in time to see Darra and her mother standing in the doorway, horror on their faces.

They stared at Amber for what should have been a breath, though Amber could not draw air as she took in the wide eyes of the interlopers. Their expressions finally brought her to herself, and she let out a strangled cry. Raising her hands to her head, she desperately searched for a hiding place and saw the open door of the wardrobe.

She ran to the space created between the open door and the wall and sank to the ground. The realization that her secret was no longer a secret pounded her mind like a hammer against stone.

"Leave us," she heard her mother snap a moment before the door to the bedchamber closed. There was silence, and Amber curled over herself, covering her ragged head with her arms, unable to catch her breath due to her corset and gown. She heard the wardrobe door close, revealing her to the room, and she pulled even tighter to the corner, wishing she could disappear completely.

"Show yourself to me," her mother commanded.

Amber shook her head. She could not do it. She could not bear to have them see her.

"Darra," she heard her mother say a moment before Lady Marchent grabbed one of Amber's arms, pulling it away from Amber's head. A moment later, the softer touch of Darra's hand on Amber's other arm pulled it away as well. She tried to fight them, aching for her corner even as she was drawn to her feet and forced into the center of the room. Knowing she could not prevent their inspection, she covered her face with her hands and sobbed.

For some time her mother and Darra were silent, until Amber controlled her emotion enough to drop her hands and lift her swollen eyes to meet those of her mother's, which looked at her with both shock and disgust.

"You stupid girl," her mother said, each word falling like hot coals at Amber's feet. "What have you done to yourself?"

# Chapter 8

Amber sent her regrets by messenger to Lord Sunther first thing the next morning, claiming she was ill and could not ride out with him. She spent the rest of the day in her bedchamber with one of her mother's ugly mobcaps on her head. Her mother did not appear until the afternoon when she followed a maid who carried in a tea tray. Lady Marchent did not stay long and instead simply relayed that Dr. Hankins would attend her in the morning, until then the household had been told Amber was ill and Suzanne had been sworn to secrecy. Amber was hungry for some encouragement, some hope, but it was misplaced. Her mother left her to her own company after only a few minutes. Amber pressed her face into the pillow and cried alone.

Dr. Hankins came to Amber's bedchamber at ten o'clock Monday morning. He wasn't an old man, perhaps not quite her mother's age, even, and she could not take her eyes off the powdered wig he wore, a reminder of the style of her mother's time as a debutante in King George's court.

The extreme fashion that included wigs and hairpieces was outmoded when the French Revolution drew sharp attention to the extravagance of the aristocracy. France was not so far away from England for English noblemen and noblewomen to avoid taking note.

Amber had heard tell and seen portraits of face paints and full stays, hoop skirts, and heavy brocade fabrics of vibrant color — the court dress required of each debutante when she was presented, but avoided in every other venue. Amber had often felt grateful to live in an age of greater discretion that, she felt, allowed a woman's more natural charms to show through the pretense of earlier fashions.

Now, however, with her natural charms threatened she wished for a powdered wig to hide her truth and perhaps face paint that could further hide her fear.

"I shall need you to remove the cap," Dr. Hankins said, sitting down on the foot bench after Amber sat on her dressing table stool.

At the doctor's request, Amber raised a

hand, carefully expanded the cap, and lifted it off her head, mindful of pulling on the hair she had left. Several strands of hair fluttered into her lap.

The doctor made no reaction, for which she was grateful, and stood to cross over to her. She closed her eyes in hopes it would lessen her humiliation as he touched her hair, lifted the remaining tresses and making noises such as "Hmm," and "Ah." He began pulling on certain sections, and Amber bit her lip, not in pain but in fear he would loosen the strands still connected. She'd been so gentle of them herself, though it hadn't seemed to make a difference. Lady Marchent stood just inside the door, standing silent sentry of the exchange.

"And you lose more hair daily?" Dr. Hankins asked, still inspecting.

"Hourly, it seems." She swallowed the rising emotion and finally looked up when he stepped away. "What is to become of me? I fear I have contracted something severe."

"What of the other hair about your person?" he asked, returning to his seat.

"Pardon?" she asked.

"I see that your eyebrows are mostly intact — what of the other hair? It is typical for all of a person's skin to be covered in fine hair, you see. Surely you are aware of this."

Amber nodded but was terribly embarrassed by his question. "I can't say I've been particularly attentive." Had he said her eyebrows were *mostly* intact?

"I should encourage you to be attentive, then." Finally his eyes moved to her face and met her gaze. His expression was sympathetic, and she felt tears rise in her eyes at his genuine concern.

"Other than this symptom, are you experiencing any other discomfort?"

"No," Amber said, shaking her head and wishing he would let her replace the cap. "I feel quite well, other than the nervousness this has created."

Dr. Hankins nodded while looking at her head, his thick eyebrows pulled together beneath his wig. "I am afraid I have never encountered a situation such as this before," he said. "Hair loss is usually accompanied by other physical symptoms that indicate a severe illness. Without other discomforts — as you've told me — I'm afraid I am unaware of what could be the cause of this."

He must have seen Amber's expression fall as he smiled and leaned toward her slightly. "You should take comfort to know that you are likely not experiencing anything that will endanger your life. There are all manner of complexities about the human body, and while I am not experienced with this particular situation, I shall consult some journals and confer with colleagues before I return to —"

"No," Lady Marchent said, stepping into the room and drawing Dr. Hankins's attention. "You are to talk to no one of this. I explained that upon your agreement to come."

"I shall exert the utmost discretion, Madam, but it would be a benefit for me to hear of other practitioners' experience."

"I explained that this was for your knowledge only," Lady Marchent said, fixing him with a reproving look. "I shall hold you to your word on that."

Dr. Hankins held her eyes a moment then nodded. "I shall return on Thursday morning, then, and hope that I can find information within my own resources before then."

"We shall hope for that as well," Lady Marchent said.

The doctor and her mother took their leave while Amber replaced the cap on her head and tucked her hair into it without inspecting her reflection. It was too gruesome to look at. Once the cap was in place, she scrutinized the dark brows in the mirror, remembering Dr. Hankins's comment regarding them, and realized that the left one was not as thick as the right. She leaned in further and blinked her eyes, noting her long dark eyelashes — another enviable feature — but was unable to tell if they were affected.

When the hinge of the door signaled an entrance, she tugged her cap a bit lower in hopes the shadow of the brim would hide her brows. Lady Marchent closed the door behind her and approached Amber still seated at her dressing table.

Lady Marchent pulled a small, dark-colored jar from somewhere amid the folds of her morning gown. "I procured this from a cart-man yesterday afternoon, but I hoped the doctor would have a better course. It is a blend of herbs and medicines from the Orient. You are to apply it morning and night to stimulate your scalp. It should help contain the hair loss. I feel it best for us to pursue this course as we await Dr. Hankins's return. We've no time to waste."

Amber eyed the jar with trepidation. "Perhaps we could wait until after the doctor returns and —"

Lady Marchent fixed her with a look that communicated her lack of patience.

"I'm sorry," Amber said, hanging her head.

"I am doing all I can to help you."

"I know that," Amber said, swallowing tears she knew would not be well received; her mother did not know how to react to emotion any more than Amber did. They had been raised to be strong and in possession of their feelings, not to give into them. "I shall do whatever you ask of me."

When her mother left the room sometime later, Amber rang for Suzanne to whom she gave a brief accounting, acting the part of the cool and confident mistress, much like her mother's treatment of herself had been.

*Perhaps that is what everyone does,* she thought. *We pass our discomfort to someone else so as not to carry so much of it ourselves.*

Suzanne picked up the jar and removed the lid. Her face crinkled, and she lifted a hand to her nose, opening her mouth as though to protest.

Amber fixed her with a hard look in the mirror, and Suzanne seemed to think better of whatever argument she was designing. Amber removed her cap without looking at her reflection. Instead, she watched with increasing anxiety as Suzanne dipped her fingers into the jar to extract a portion of the thick, yellow substance. Only when she was prepared to apply it did Amber fully look at the entirety of her reflection.

Her heart seemed to freeze in her chest at

the sight. The portion of her head from the crown to her left ear was smooth as an egg now. She couldn't see the back portion that had first been a concern but she could see daylight through the remaining strands of her long hair.

"I put this on the affected areas?" Suzanne asked, her eyebrows pulled together in concern.

"Is that not what I already instructed you?" Amber snapped, concealing her nervousness with irritation. She could not expect Suzanne to have confidence if Amber did not show an increased amount herself.

Suzanne stepped closer and extended her paste-covered fingers toward Amber's head.

Amber startled as the slightly cool substance first touched her scalp, then wrinkled her nose as a stink of camphor and rotting leaves assaulted her. It was strong enough to clear Amber's lungs and nasal passages, and it turned her stomach. She attempted to breathe through her mouth as Suzanne covered the baldness with a liberal amount of putrid ointment.

Suzanne put the jar on the dressing table — the smell further assaulting Amber's nose due to its nearness — and pulled back the hair covering the space on the back of Amber's head. She dug out another handful of the vile mixture and applied it accordingly. The cooling sensation alerted Amber to how much hair was missing in the back, and to her surprise, Suzanne parted her hair again on the right and applied more of the mixture to two smaller areas of baldness Amber did not know existed.

When Suzanne finished, she replaced the cap on the jar and asked permission to leave the room in order to clean the ointment from her hand.

Amber excused her and then attempted to plait the remainder of her hair in such a way as to disguise the bald patches. There was no concealment of her appearance any longer. The mixture was greasy and yet sticky too, and she wondered if it would be absorbed into her skin or if there was an amount of time she should leave it before wiping it off? She would surely have to wash her hair to facilitate the removal and feared that a washing would cause even more hair to fall out.

The coolness of the salve's application was beginning to change into a heat, and Amber shifted uncomfortably on her stool, avoiding her reflection. She wanted to cover her head with the cap, but worried about soiling it with the ointment.

In need of distraction, she recovered the

most recent copy of *The Ladies' Monthly Museum,* which she had already read through four times, and flipped through the pages as she waited for Suzanne to return. The heat of the ointment became more pronounced, and Amber's discomfort increased. She tried harder to distract herself with an article about increased fashion for lace and ermine trim.

The uncomfortable heat turned to burning and then sharp pains began to shoot through her scalp. She paced back and forth across the room and took deep breaths, waiting for the discomfort to pass. Surely it would pass!

It did not.

Finally, she ran for the bellpull. She did not reach it before there was a quick knock and the door to her bedchamber opened. The itching and burning felt fit to boil her skin.

"Miss?" Suzanne said from the doorway.

"Where have you been!" Amber yelled a moment before she noticed that Suzanne was holding up the hand she had used to apply the monstrous mixture. The fingers and palm were red as though scalded, raw and blistering. Amber met Suzanne's frightened eyes. "What is this?" she asked, her voice edged with sincere concern even as the pain of her head seemed to intensify.

"Mrs. Yarrow is preparing a salve she feels certain will soothe us — she uses it for kitchen burns," Suzanne said. "She fears there is something amiss with that ointment." Her eyes moved to look at Amber's head and went wide. "We must get all we can from your head as quickly as possible, Miss." She hurried to the bellpull. "But I'm afraid I shan't be able to do it alone."

A chambermaid and Nelson were soon attending Amber, and although it upset her to have other servants involved, she was without any other recourse. It took all of Amber's genteel breeding not to show the increasing level of her pain and fear as Nelson ordered a tub of warm water and, in turn, soap for Amber's head and hair.

Suzanne could do naught but run back and forth from the room in search of the items Nelson ordered. Amber felt as though Nelson were peeling the very skin from her skull as the maid attempted to remove the ointment, and bit her lip to keep from crying out in pain.

"Now, dip your 'ead in 'ere, Miss," Nelson said after having washed Amber's hair three times and then procuring a bin of cooled water. The washings had left Amber as wet as if her entire person had been put in the bath; the goal had been speed not comfort. "The cold will do good for the blisterin', methinks. I need to see about the salve Mrs. Yarrow was preparin', then I'll return to attend to ya."

*Blistering,* Amber repeated in her mind as Nelson helped her lean over the tub and dip her head in the cold water. Even though Amber was finally alone and able to release the emotion she had withheld thus far, she couldn't cry with her head inverted like it was. She focused on taking long draws of air and attempting to take comfort in the fact that her head did feel better, despite her shivering and the continued throbbing of her scalp.

When Nelson returned, she helped Amber stand; her legs were shaky from having knelt over the basin for so long, and she had to be assisted to the dressing room stool. Nelson carefully used a soft towel to pat Amber's head and remaining hair.

"Has my mother been told of what's happened?" Amber asked once Nelson wrapped the towel around her head.

The maid did not meet Amber's eyes as she turned back to the basin and used another towel to mop up the floor around it. "I informed Lady Marchent afore she left, Miss. She said she would look in on ya when she returned."

Amber pinched her lips together and looked into her lap, noticing the dark strands of hair that stood out from the pink and white of her dress, the entire front of which was soaked through. She worked to control her emotion before standing and stepping around Nelson to look into the tub. Even more auburn strands stood out against the porcelain bottom. How much could be left with this much gone?

"I should like to cut my hair, Nelson," she said, hating the tremor in her voice. She continued to stare into the basin as though it would somehow give her strength.

Nelson looked up at Amber in surprise, her gray eyebrows high on her forehead. "Miss? But a girl's 'air is 'er crowning glory."

The term made Amber's chest tighten. How many times had she heard that very idea shared when people admired her hair? How many times had Amber taken such compliments as further proof that she was above those people who were not as graced as she?

"I can't bear to see it coming out a bit at a time, and there's too much gone for new hair to ever become equal to what remains. I should think that arranging what's left in a shorter crop will make it easier for me to cope."

"Shall you wait and speak to yer mother first?" Nelson asked.

Amber lifted her chin. "If that is what I wanted, I would have asked for that from the start. Fetch some shears from the kitchen. I want it cut before you apply the remedy."

Half an hour passed before Suzanne laid a thin plait of still-wet hair, tied off at both ends, on the dressing table. Though her hand was bandaged and surely as painful as Amber's head, Suzanne had offered to do the job herself, which Amber appreciated though she hadn't said so out loud.

Amber stared at the braid for several seconds, stunned to see the proof of what had been done. Without a word, Suzanne went about trimming up the remaining hair on Amber's head.

Amber dared not admit, even to herself, the depth of feeling she experienced with each snip of the shears. It still felt as though she were trapped in a nightmare.

"Is there anything else I can do for you, Miss?" Suzanne asked when she finished, stepping back and putting the shears in the pocket of her apron.

"No, Suzanne," Amber said, too spent to remember the superior tone. She glanced at the white bandage wrapped around the maid's hand. "You may go."

"Thank you, Miss." Suzanne had placed a cloth beneath Amber's stool to catch the cuttings and folded it before leaving. "I'll tell Nelson that you're ready to be attended to with Mrs. Yarrow's salve. My hand is feeling much better since I treated it. Perhaps a hot bath would help you warm yourself?"

Amber nodded, but her eyes went back to the bound hair on the dressing table once the door shut. She reached up and ran her fingers over the woven strands. Her hair was beautiful and looked so strong and vibrant, woven together like that.

"It will grow back," she told herself in a soft voice another type of mother might have used to console her daughter in a situation such as this. "It will be as beautiful as ever," she continued in the nurturing tone she had only ever known in her imagination. "Until then, I shall love you no different than ever I did." The last words were broken by a suppressed sob, and Amber finally lifted her eyes to the reflection she had been avoiding.

Suzanne had cut the remaining hair so it followed the contours of Amber's head. It looked soft and smooth and very much like a man's hairstyle — or it might if hair had covered all of her head. The portion afflicted with the ointment was no longer smooth, but ragged and red with blisters.

*Gruesome,* Amber thought. *Horrid. Ugly. Vile. Cursed.* For every word of compliment she had ever received, there was now a word of derision and condemnation. *Abominable. Wretched. Disgusting. Repulsive.*

When she could think of no other words, despair overcame her.

*What will become of me?*

"Perhaps someone will want you for your money and connections," she answered herself out loud, feeling the brittleness of the realization that those were the only things she had left to entice a husband. How ironic that until now those things were all she had wanted from him.

# Chapter 9

Amber stood at her bedroom window, looking upon London just beginning to wake. The clear morning promised another sunny day, and Amber could scarcely contain her yearning to be part of it. It was Sunday, just over a week since Lady Marchent and Darra had learned of her circumstance, and she had not left her bedchamber since. Suzanne attended to her throughout the day and her mother looked in, but it had become increasingly clear that the Sterlingtons were going about their lives without her. Dr. Hankins had been told to communicate with the family only in writing. Amber felt it was to prevent her mother from taking blame for the ointment. He had found no solutions but would keep researching. Judging from the reduced amount of notes and flowers she had received these last few days, all of London was going about their lives without her.

She heard the door open and tugged at her cap as she did every time someone entered. Since cutting off the length of her hair there was no need to have anyone see her without the cap. She had even draped a blanket over her looking glass so as not to be caught unawares by her reflection.

"Good morning, Miss."

Amber turned in time to see Suzanne set the breakfast tray on the small table that had been moved from the corner of the drawing room to Amber's bedchamber. Amber hadn't asked for it, and her mother hadn't explained its appearance; it was simply brought in five days ago by a footman an hour before supper. As though Amber would forever eat her meals in this room.

She looked at the tray Suzanne had set down — toast, tea, eggs, and sausage — then turned to look out the window again while the maid poured the tea. Two women walked arm in arm down the sidewalk and though the time of day was not fashionable for a stroll, she felt a deep longing to be outdoors stir within her.

"I would like to dress today," Amber said when she turned back to the room, making a decision in an instant; the view from her window still fresh in her mind. It wasn't fair that everyone else should go about their lives and she could not, but so long as she supported the notion that she could be hidden away it would certainly continue. "I would like to wear the blue morning gown."

"Yes, Miss," Suzanne said, unable to hide her surprise. "Ring when you finish your breakfast —"

"I won't be eating breakfast in my bedchamber today," Amber said. "Are my mother and sister in the morning room?"

"Yes, Miss," Suzanne said, even more surprised.

"I would like to be ready in time to join them before they leave for church services."

Without her hair to arrange, Amber was ready in a short time. She removed the blanket from her mirror and took comfort in the fact that her eyebrows looked balanced and her eyes were bright. She pinched her cheeks and bit her lips to bring out the color while attempting to convince herself that having no hair showing from beneath the cap did not look so unnatural. She turned the ruffled fabric of the cap so that the blue bow was over her right ear. Then she took a breath and exited the room, feeling strangely foreign in the house she had made visits to all her life.

The upper hallway was empty, and she

held her head high as she moved to the stairway, down to the main floor, and toward the back of the house where the morning room was located. She lifted her hand to push open the partially closed door, but the sound of voices made her hesitate.

". . . get some new slippers and feathers, Mama? The ball at Carlton House is Saturday, and I should love to wear something new."

"I suppose a few more accessories are in order," Lady Marchent said amid a chink of silverware against china. "But there's no time to go to Bond Street tomorrow, not with the visit to the Fergusons and Mrs. Carmichael's garden party in the afternoon. We'll have to go shopping on Tuesday."

"Do we have to go to the Fergusons?" Darra pouted. "Their son looks at me as though I might pull a sword point on him and call him out."

Lady Marchent laughed, and the sound ran through Amber as though it were the very sword Darra had mentioned. That her mother and sister could talk and laugh as though there was nothing ill in the world was stunning even though Amber had already realized this morning that the lives of the people around her were continuing — only hers had been put aside. Somehow she had assumed that her mother and sister might not be so lightly affected by her absence, and it made her heart ache with a dismissal she felt foolish for not having expected.

The baize door opened at the far end of the hall and rather than explain to a servant why she was standing in the hallway, Amber took a breath and pushed through the doorway of the morning room.

Darra was facing the door and describing the style of hat she would like to arrange when Amber stepped into the room. Darra's words dropped off, and Lady Marchent turned to see what had drawn Darra's attention. They were both dressed in their Sunday finest, as though they would be attending church as a family.

In that instant Amber chose her strategy for this meeting: if they were to be unaffected, she would be as well. She pulled her shoulders back, lifted her chin, and arranged a casual smile on her face as though today were any other day and she had not been stashed away in her bedchamber for the past week.

"Amber," her mother said in a tone that did not hide her surprise. "I thought your maid was bringing a breakfast tray to your room."

"She brought a tray," Amber said lightly, moving smoothly to the sideboard where she picked up a plate and began to fill it from the selection of breakfast items laid out. "I see the cook made lemon buns." She looked over her shoulder and smiled playfully. "I had feared that perhaps I was being denied a full selection, and it appears I was exactly right." She put a lemon bun on her plate, took an extra-large slab of ham, and moved to take the seat opposite Darra at the table. She smiled sweetly at her sister. "How are you, Darra?"

Darra regarded her for a moment, obviously distrustful of Amber's mood. Finally, she looked away and set about spreading jam on a piece of toast. "I am well," she said simply.

"I am *so* glad to hear as much," Amber said, exaggerating her smile to match her tone. Acting this part was familiar and yet uncomfortable too. Perhaps because she had not played the role for so many days. Or perhaps confronting what could not be acted away left her less impressed with the falseness she could master so easily. "Did I hear you talking of a ball? I'm afraid I did not hear the date."

"Saturday," Darra said, glancing up briefly before looking to their mother seated at

Amber's left. The look exchanged between them filled Amber with remarkable jealousy. All the time that Amber had spent in her bedchamber, sick, frightened, lonely, and morose, had allowed her mother and sister to grow closer with one another. She chewed a bite of ham slowly, and then carefully cut another as she processed through this understanding without allowing it to show upon her features.

"Perhaps I shall be able to attend then," Amber said once she swallowed her bite and speared the next on her fork. "I have some ideas on how I can reenter society. I long to renew the acquaintances I worked so hard to procure."

"You cannot attend," Darra said quickly. "Nothing can hide what has been done. Everyone will know."

Amber shrugged and pinched off a bit of the lemon bun. "Everyone will *not* know, and you shall see that my absence has simply whet the appetite of my admirers so that when they see me they shan't notice anyone else." Darra's face darkened. Amber continued though it was not with enjoyable intent so much as growing fear at her sister's defensiveness. "And their concern for my having been ill for such a time will have them *pouring* out their sympathies, I am sure. I am the Rage of the Season after all."

"They have forgotten you," Darra said, dropping her toast onto her plate. "You are most certainly *not* the Rage of the Season anymore."

The words sliced through Amber's façade, and she narrowed her eyes. "And I suppose you flatter yourself into thinking that *you* are the rage now? That you can somehow replace me in the eye of every bachelor in London? Do not get so high in your opinion of yourself as to ignore why you are here at all, Darra. Do not —"

"That is enough," Lady Marchent said, silencing Amber. "I'll not have you rail against your sister when she has done naught to deserve it."

"Naught to deserve it?" Amber said, turning toward her mother. "Do you not see that she is using my ailment for her benefit? That she is primping about as though —"

"I said that is enough." Her mother fixed her with an icy stare. "If you are going to sit with the family, then you will engage in polite conversation and keep your razor tongue in check. You should thank her for upholding the story of your illness."

Stunned at her mother's reprimand, Amber looked down at her plate, adequately chastised. There was no doubt as the breakfast continued that Darra and her mother would have preferred she have remained in her room. The thought left her terribly sad and wishing she'd never come down despite knowing she could not stay in her room forever.

After some time had passed, Lady Marchent touched Amber's arm, causing her to look up at her mother. Lady Marchent smiled softly. "I am sorry to be so cross," she said, then flicked her eyes to Darra as though including her in the apology. "We are all trying to make the best decisions we can to move forward. We must be patient."

Did she mean that Amber should be patient about not attending events? "Mama," she said when she had adequately organized her thoughts in a way she hoped would make her intentions clear. She placed her knife and fork on either side of her plate and put her hands in her lap. "I would like to attend the season again."

Lady Marchent removed her hand and took a thoughtful sip of her tea. "I don't know how that is possible, Amber. You cannot expect that the affections you entreated before won't have been changed by your absence and situation."

Amber turned in her chair to face her mother more fully. "My hair is not all I have to recommend me."

"Certainly not, but its absence is . . . unseemly at best. Were you to attend the events as you did before, it would be an embarrassment to your family as well as the hosts. You cannot ask such a sacrifice of those around you any more than you can expect your situation to be overlooked. I have thought more about you returning to Hampton Grove and feel —"

"I need to secure a match," Amber interrupted, unable to comprehend being sent away from London. "I cannot give up every expectation I have wished for, and I am unwilling to walk away from my ambitions."

"You cannot expect a man to look past such a . . . defect," Lady Marchent said. She glanced quickly at Darra, increasing Amber's worry that the two of them had spoken of this topic without her present. Lady Marchent took a breath and continued in a sympathetic tone, "It might be best for you to return to Hampton Grove for the remainder of the season, allow yourself sufficient rest. Should your condition repair itself, you can return next season prepared to exist in society again."

"I am not leaving London," Amber said, unwilling to consider the suggestion even when it was so kindly delivered. "Not after all the effort I put into making the connections I have made. By next season my dresses will be out of fashion and my prospects irrevocably changed."

"Fashion and prospects do not balance out your circumstance," Lady Marchent said, beginning to sound frustrated with Amber's stubbornness. But Lady Marchent had not said that a decision had been made, only that it had been discussed. That left hope for Amber to convince her otherwise.

"I feel certain I can secure a marriage even without my hair."

"Only if you expect to fool a potential husband," Lady Marchent said, looking at her and raising her eyebrows.

"Not forever," Amber said. "But I can delay his discovery of the fact until after we are wed. There is no reason to believe this change will be permanent."

Lady Marchent looked into her teacup while Darra joined the conversation. "You would fool a man into posting the banns despite your condition?"

"Yes," Amber said without apology, looking at her sister. "I would secure my future any way that I am able, and as the eldest daughter I owe it to my family to make an admirable connection." She turned to her mother. "You said not long ago that you wanted to see me cared for. Let me continue toward that goal for your sake as well as mine — and Darra's too."

"No one will look twice at you," Darra said. "They will know something is amiss."

"I was not soliciting an opinion from *you,*" Amber snapped, sending a sharp look at her sister. She looked back to her mother and softened her tone. "My maid has worked with women who needed wigs and hairpieces to remedy thinning hair as they aged. I feel sure she could help me find a solution that will allow me to reenter society without causing embarrassment to anyone. No one need know of my situation, and once I am married, my husband shall adapt. I shall make sure to meet every other expectation he might have of me. I want to make you proud, Mama. I want to remove your worry for my future, and I feel sure this is the best option." Not long ago she would have demanded her mother allow her to reenter society. Now she was begging.

Lady Marchent held Amber's eyes for a moment. She took another sip of her tea while Amber sat rigid in her chair.

Amber pleaded in her mind for her mother to see the wisdom of her idea. If she refused, Amber would have no reason to remain in London. The idea of returning to her childhood home without securing a marriage was too overwhelming to be considered. No, there was only one solution — one course of action she could commit herself too. "Please, Mama. Please do not deny me this chance to find a match." She thought back to the day in her mother's bedchamber when Lady Marchent had said she was proud of Amber's shrewdness. Certainly she could see the wisdom of this suggestion as well.

"I shall have to see what your maid can do before I give my consent to this," her mother said, not relieved of her concern but sounding hopeful at least.

"Mama!" Darra said in shock. Clearly Darra had enjoyed the additional attention she received when Amber was secluded, which only angered Amber all the more. *She* was the Rage of the Season; *she* was the one more admired.

Lady Marchent looked across the table to Darra and Amber was certain she saw regret in *that* expression. "I shall not consent lightly," she explained. "But we have put a great deal into preparing for the season, and if there is a possibility for Amber to make a connection I cannot deny her that, just as I would not deny you."

Lady Marchent pushed away from the

table and stood, looking down on Amber with a calculating expression. "I shall have to see what your maid can do," she said again. "When you are ready for me to approve your presentation, I shall decide upon our course of action." She turned her attention to Darra. "We shall be leaving for church shortly. Do not dawdle over your breakfast."

Amber watched her mother leave the room. Left alone with Darra, Amber turned to her sister and smiled triumphantly. "I am still the eldest daughter," she said with confidence. "*And* the Rage of the Season. If I am sent away, you can expect I shall insist you be returned with me."

For a moment, Darra's expression was unreadable and then her eyes narrowed and she leaned forward. "Did you not notice that the only reason Mama agreed to your plan was because marrying you off to some fool would free her of you?" She stood and glared at her older sister as she threw her napkin on the plate. "Because I certainly did."

# CHAPTER 10

It was five days before Amber had an adequate remedy for her missing hair. Suzanne had searched every wigmaker in London and finally found a quality hairpiece that was near Amber's true color. It was not exact, which was worrisome, but when compared with the alternative of not appearing in society again, Amber was willing to concede. The idea to sew her own hair into a bonnet was abandoned so as not to have two competing hair colors.

In addition to the wig, Amber fashioned a headpiece — essentially a scarf fastened with beads and flowers — that she hoped would be complementary to the new color even as it drew attention away from it. The wig included curls to frame her face and hide the portion where the edge of the hairpiece met against her skin. The wig ended in a length of ringlets that could be tied to the side so as to hang over her shoulder, as Amber had often worn her own hair. Amber was optimistic and yet anxious about the result as Suzanne helped her dress for an afternoon tea. If her mother did not accept her attempts to appear the part, she would likely not be able to attend the ball tomorrow night.

When she was convinced of her mother's favor, Amber sent for Lady Marchent and then assumed a pose of confidence when her mother entered the room.

"The color is not exact," Lady Marchent said immediately.

"I have come up with an explanation for it," Amber said, eager to share her cleverness and ignoring the increasing itch beneath the wrapping on her head necessary for the wig to be attached. She would withstand any matter of discomfort if it meant she could return to society and secure a match. "I have heard talk of colored rinses meant to enhance one's hair color. I shall explain that while recovering from my ailment, I was morose about my pale complexion and made the erroneous decision to attempt one of these rinses." She lifted her eyebrows and chin to emphasize the rest of her story. "It went awry and rather than adding to my countenance it detracted from it. In the process, however, I was reminded again of the ills of vanity. I shall share the experience with abject humility and take it as a chance to laugh at myself, which will then soften people's impression. I think I can use it to my benefit quite well."

Lady Marchent did not seem convinced, but Amber remained hopeful as her mother walked around her, taking in Amber's appearance from every direction. When she faced Amber again, she nodded. "It is my confidence in your ability to manage yourself that earns my agreement rather than the condition of the . . ." She waved her hand toward the wig as though searching for the correct word. "Affectation," she finally said. "It shall be a small group at the Middleton's tea this afternoon where we can judge the strength of your story based on the reception it receives."

"And if it goes well, may I attend the ball at Carlton House tomorrow?" She did not want to appear too eager but being shut up for so long had her trembling with the excitement of returning to society and recapturing her position. "Many of my suitors will be there, Mama. I'm most anxious to return to their favor."

Lady Marchent nodded but still looked reluctant. "If the tea goes well, I shall consider it."

"Not consider it," Amber insisted, a bit restored to her usual strength of character. "You promise I can attend Carlton House if the Middleton tea is a success. I'll let you approve my presentation as I have today, of course."

"Very well," her mother said. She looked over Amber again, and when she met her eye, Amber saw sympathy there. Lady Marchent took one of her hands in both of hers. "I hope I have not given the impression that I have not considered your position within these circumstances. I am not so unfeeling as to realize how difficult this has been for you."

Amber blinked rapidly, taken off guard by the emotion spurred by her mother's compassion.

Lady Marchent continued, "My consideration in keeping you out of society was as much for your good as anyone else's. I should hate for things to not go well and your prospects for another season be diminished if the extent of your circumstance were to be known. The *ton* will not tolerate such imperfection, Amber, and no parent would credit a match of their son to someone with such a blemish. I am uncomfortable to think of this duplicity even as I realize that it is the best option for *my* child."

Amber lowered her eyes, emotional for a different reason than she was before. *Imperfection. Blemish.* The feel of her mother's hand on her face as she lifted Amber's chin left her unsure whether to view her mother as a compatriot in this or someone expecting Amber to fail. "I want the best for all of my children, Amber. Do you believe that?"

"Of course I believe that, Mama," Amber said, eager to forgive her mother's neglect if only they could return the level of comfort they had enjoyed before this horrid turn of fate. More than ever she wanted her mother's good opinion.

Her mother dropped her hand and nodded. "We shall be walking to the Middletons and are to be received at three o'clock. I shall lend you my parasol so you need not trouble yourself with a bonnet that could upset your arrangement upon its removal."

"Thank you, Mama," Amber said with a smile. "I will make you proud, I promise."

"It went so well," Amber said once they were on the street following the Middleton's tea, which had gone famously. Amber's story of the rinse was well received and even sympathetic, making for a most comfortable and companionable afternoon. She now walked side by side with her mother while Darra trailed behind them. Of everyone in attendance, Darra had by far been the least responsive to Amber's charms.

"It did go very well," Lady Marchent said with a nod and a relieved smile. "I was quite pleased with your behavior and how the tale regarding the rinse was received. You were very engaging to the other women and handled yourself very well indeed."

Amber smiled at the compliment and felt the comfortable reassurance that this wig would return her to her place in society. Never mind that her head itched atrociously. "So I may attend the ball at Carlton House tomorrow night, then?"

Lady Marchent hesitated, and Amber felt her grip on her mother's arm tighten the smallest degree.

"You said that I could, Mama," Amber reminded her. "You said if the tea went well I could go to Carlton House."

"It is so soon," Lady Marchent explained. "Perhaps it would be better to wait for a less formal event to make your reentry." She glanced over her shoulder at Darra and Amber followed the look.

"Darra does not want me to attend, does she?" Amber said.

"It is not that," Lady Marchent said. "Only she has enjoyed a different kind of attention since your absence. If she had more time for her to accept that things have changed once again she will be more supportive."

Amber bit back a sharp retort about her mother considering her feelings as much as Darra's. "All my suitors will be there," Amber said instead. "And I am of a mind to make a decision as quickly as possible. It would do no good to refuse such an enviable invitation from the Prince Regent himself and miss an opportunity to secure my prospects."

Lady Marchent remained thoughtful as they passed a gentleman who nodded and bowed to them. They greeted him and then resumed their conversation. "You haven't had time to plan your dress," Lady Marchent said.

"I have the emerald dress I did not wear to the Covington's. My maid can have everything in readiness." She tightened the grip on her mother's arm. "Please, Mama. Let me go. Don't let Darra's discomfort in sharing the attention prevent me from making progress toward my own potential."

Lady Marchent let out a heavy breath. "Let me convince your sister of the wisdom of it," she said, slowing her step and letting go of Amber's arm. "Go on ahead. We'll only be a short distance behind."

"Thank you, Mama," Amber said, smiling so as not to show her disappointment in her mother's reluctance. She leaned in and gave her mother a quick kiss on the cheek before quickening her pace, allowing Lady Marchent to fall even with Darra.

Amber reached the house before her mother and sister, but rather than go directly to her bedchamber, she stepped into the drawing room and closed the door enough to be hidden but still able to overhear the conversation as her mother and sister entered the house. They were only a short distance behind her so she did not have to wait long.

"It is not fair," Darra whined. "I am always pulled about according to Amber's will, and I can hardly stand it."

"I am sorry," Lady Marchent said sincerely, rippling that pool of jealousy not yet dried up within Amber's chest. "But she is quite ardent in her desire to make a quick match and to let an opportunity pass for her to pursue such a thing would work against that. Surely you can see the wisdom of this course. It is in your best interest as well as hers."

Darra let out a breath and lowered her voice, causing Amber to lean closer to the gap in the doorway. "He prefers me, Mama, I know he does."

*He?* Amber thought. *He who?*

"Then you have nothing to worry about, my dear," her mother said. "Your sister has any number of suitors to choose from. Once she's made her match, you will be free to pursue whomever you please."

They continued up the stairs to their rooms, and only after they were gone did Amber come out of her hiding place and continue to her own bedchamber. She rang for Suzanne and then explained the plans for tomorrow as she sat before her dressing table so that Suzanne could remove the pins holding the wig to the binding.

"I must look my very best tomorrow night," Amber said, watching in the mirror as Suzanne lifted the wig off Amber's head and moved it to the pedestal set on a table beside Amber's vanity. She thought of Darra's long dark hair — her real hair. Who was the "he" she had mentioned?

Suzanne untucked the wrapping, and Amber sighed with relief as it was unwound from her head, leaving an oddly satisfying ache behind it. Though she was glad for the success of the Middleton tea, she was equally grateful that her mother had not obligated her for any events this evening.

She felt in need of the time to prepare for tomorrow and felt rather fatigued.

Her reflection took her by surprise and she blinked quickly. Hair stuck out in several directions and the bald portions were still red and scabbed from where the blisters had been. It was truly gruesome, but with the wig it no longer mattered so much. She had successfully attended the Middleton's tea. She would attend tomorrow's party at Carlton House — the epicenter of society.

*It will work,* she told herself, looking away from the horrible reminder of her condition reflected in the mirror as she reached for one of the lace caps Suzanne had purchased for her a few days earlier She put the cap in place and looked back at her reflection. *It has to work.*

# Chapter 11

Fenton introduced Thomas to Waiters on a night when the entertainment was thin and Thomas's patience with wife-hunting was even thinner. The famous club, known for its gaming, was reserved for only the highest of the *ton.* Thomas had enjoyed himself more than he'd expected. That he left thirty pounds richer than he'd been upon arrival improved his opinion that much more. After that first evening, Thomas and Fenton had attended a few other times and after an assembly last night, returned again.

Too many glasses of brandy combined with other distractions sent Thomas home with a pounding head and pockets on the verge of empty. It wasn't until morning, however, that he realized the extent of his carelessness. He had gambled away nearly a hundred pounds in one evening and awoke sick to his stomach for more reasons than one.

He left his rooms in search of sun and wind to clear his head and found himself seated at the back of St. Paul's Cathedral. He was not the only person to seek refuge in the church on a Saturday morning, but he sat long enough to see everyone who had been there upon his arrival be replaced with another set and still did not feel absolved of his regret.

He reviewed his memories of the evening before, more ill at ease with himself each time he ran through his actions.

Why had he accepted that third glass of brandy? It was not like him to be so free with his drink.

Why had he allowed himself to become so distracted by the conversations going on around him that he was inattentive to the cards in his hand? He was usually such a shrewd player.

Why had he kept playing when he'd lost the twenty pounds he'd promised himself as his limit? He was not a man with a sizable allowance that gave him margins for frivolous spending; he knew better.

He did the equations in his head of how much of this year's corn harvest would equate to those hundred pounds. How much would he spend on his workers who planted, raised, and harvested it? How many families in Northallerton lived off a hundred pounds for an entire year? How many other families could only dream of that much?

With elbows braced upon his knees, he let his thoughts wander down equally dark roads that had little to do with money and far more to do with the pattern his day-to-day life had taken on. He hated that he spent the majority of his time pursuing pleasure that often was not that pleasurable. He hated the growing covetousness he felt toward friends with seemingly endless funds at their disposal. He hated the late mornings and too-long afternoons that became late evenings, which resulted in a foggy head, only to repeat the unproductive efforts of the day before, and the day before that, and the day before that. He hated weighing out the merits of every woman he met and wondering if his attentions would be welcomed. He hated that he had not felt drawn to a single one of them — except the one he knew would not welcome him.

The thoughts cycled through his mind and surged through his heart, building like a thunderstorm in his head and chest until he found himself pleading in silent prayer for God to help him find direction. He wanted to be working his land. He wanted to find a comfortable wife. He wanted to please his mother. He wanted to be mindful of his finances. He wanted to ride his horse through the countryside again without caring how his cravat was tied. He wanted to secure his future. He wanted . . . he wanted . . . he *needed* to feel at peace with himself. That peace was proving to be fleeting the longer he stayed in this blasted city. The realization brought his thoughts back to the idea that had plagued him increasingly these last weeks: did he belong here?

Which of the women he'd become acquainted with would be satisfied with a husband who sat in the saddle? Would any of them be able to find comfort on his annual income with the rest of his income being dependent on his harvest and management? Would they be comfortable in a country house not yet built rather than an estate with history and distinction?

As the years went by, the smell of the shop, or in his case, the farm, would cling stronger and stronger to Thomas and affect his standing in social circles. His sons would need to pursue careers of their own despite the land they would one day inherit. He did not expect to have adequate fortune to lay about them as they entered maturity. His daughters would have small inheritances but need to marry well to ensure their comfort, likely to a man of trade, which would move them below the society Thomas himself belonged to, if only just. Had Thomas met *any* woman who could find happiness in such a life? Never mind that each woman he met was compared to Amber Sterlington — her beauty, her figure, the effect her voice had on him each time he heard it. One more aggravation to heap upon the others.

As his mind turned to matters of more immediate attention, he became even more morose. Due to his extravagance, he had spent the majority of the finances he'd brought with him to London. Next week he would need to pay another month's rent of his rooms, which would leave his pockets near empty. He could appeal to his solicitor for an advance on next quarter's allowance, but Mr. Jefferies would inform Albert, and the idea of his brother knowing what he'd done burned in Thomas's chest like a blacksmith's fire. He would have to withstand his brother's censure for the irresponsible management of his funds.

Or, perhaps Albert would clap him on the back and express his relief to see Thomas become as irresponsible as every other man in London. Albert had been the second son when he'd come to London and unburdened by the responsibility of one day becoming the Baron himself. He had therefore been quite the rake — even more so after Charles had died and Albert faced the expectations of an inheritance he was not eager to fulfill. Albert had often said that Thomas was too straitlaced and should embrace the pleasures afforded the younger sons of the nobility. Thomas had never wished for such dissipation, it was not in his nature, and had endured his brother's ribbing with tolerance and amusement. Yet now he had started on that same path — a path that had left Albert at odds with their father after Lord Fielding had ordered Albert back to Northallerton and railed him on the level of propriety he expected. The breach never entirely healed before the old Baron passed. Thomas had no desire to create such chaos within the family, which would not be a concern if his behavior was above reproach.

Thomas sat on the back pew for another half an hour, then bowed his head in another supplication to the heavens. He did not have the means or the interest to stay in London much longer, but he hated the feeling of returning home with his tail between his legs.

*As much as you deserve,* he scolded himself. He quickly attempted to think beyond his self-judgment. *How do I fix this?*

No answer came, and he returned to his rooms, thinking of the upcoming evening's entertainment — a ball at Carlton House. It was an honor to be attending as Fenton's guest, but he would have to pretend his way through it to not be a pall on the frivolity. The very idea was wearying. Following the ball, Fenton would likely encourage him to return to the gaming hells and try to win some of his purse back, but the thought was beyond consideration. Thomas would never step inside those halls again, which meant Fenton would likely no longer be Thomas's escort around town. He could not expect Fenton to avoid such pleasure simply on account of Thomas's regret. Would Thomas present himself at entertainments alone? Would he be turned away from the higher-level events if he showed without Fenton's recommendation? Thomas hated how small he felt, how out of place.

Unable to find any other remedy, Thomas penned a letter to his solicitor requesting additional funds. His neck was still hot with embarrassment as he mailed the letter to Yorkshire. That Albert would find it all very diverting did not give Thomas any peace of mind. He did not like the changes this town was making upon him, and as he readied himself for the evening, he questioned again why he was there at all and why he had come to London for a wife he hoped would never want to return to the city.

# CHAPTER 12

Suzanne helped Amber to dress in a crepe evening gown a rather daring shade of green for a debutante. That Amber had not yet worn it increased her excitement regarding the notice she would surely attract. Suzanne added a diamond and pearl necklace that was to become Amber's upon marriage and four pearl bracelets that added a feeling of refinement to the ensemble.

It was a relief to have Suzanne start on the binding for her head, hiding the gruesome sight from Amber's view in the looking glass. The wrapping had to be pulled as tightly as possible so as not to be easily displaced over the course of the evening, but Amber asked for a bit more ease tonight. She would be wearing it for hours and did not want a headache as frightful as the one she had after yesterday's tea. Once the binding was in place, the wig was pinned to it, creating the bond to her head that allowed her to move freely rather than carefully looking this way and that for fear of upsetting the piece.

Suzanne was proficient in how to style and arrange the wig to its best representation, freeing Amber's thoughts to consider the evening before her. All of Amber's suitors would be at the ball, and she was committed to make a decision tonight. Lord Sunther was her first choice; he would therefore be the focus of her attention.

Though position itself was no longer her chief objective, she did not want to give up on the possibility of an arrangement with the most eligible bachelor of the season. More, she felt Lord Sunther was the kind of man who could come to love her despite all the complications he would unknowingly be presented with in having her for a wife.

"How is it, Miss?" Suzanne said.

Amber looked up as she turned her head to inspect the arrangement. As tonight's event was at the Prince Regent's opulent residence, it was among the most formal events of the season, and Amber had told Suzanne to be additionally attentive.

Suzanne had left one long curl of the dark hair to hang over Amber's shoulder. The rest of the hair had been braided with ribbon the same color as the gown and then wrapped and pinned to give the appearance of a crown of sorts, into which Suzanne had threaded the white flowers with diamond centers. The only concern Amber had with the style was if showing so much hair might draw attention to the change in color. But surely she could repeat the story of a rinse to those who had not yet heard it.

"It will do," Amber said, though she continued to inspect the intricacies of the style. *Did it look like a wig?* she wondered. Her concern served to further convince her of the importance of tonight's ball. She would increase her attention to Lord Sunther and have an official proposal by the end of the week, if not the end of the night. Any one of her other suitors would be overjoyed at such a prospect; surely he would be as well once she convinced him of her interest.

As Suzanne replaced the dressing cape from Amber's shoulders with a white cashmere shawl draped at her elbows, Amber filled her stores of confidence for the evening ahead. It was imperative that she have absolute assurance — tonight would be a night she would never forget.

By the time Amber, Darra, and their parents arrived at Carlton House, it was already crowded. Lord and Lady Marchent made the appropriate rounds of greetings and gave a few introductions to people Darra and Amber did not know. Amber kept a close eye out for her suitors, casting them a smile when they met her eye, but she was eager to see Lord Sunther most of all, and he was the one she did not find amid the crowds.

It was some time before Lady Marchent and her daughters found themselves at the edge of the dance floor, showing that the girls were ready to dance. Lord Marchent had already disappeared into a card room with a group of gentlemen. Amber did not expect to see him again until it was time to leave, assuming he didn't leave in a hired carriage for other entertainments.

Mr. Harrington approached Amber before she'd even had a chance to assess the couples already on the floor. He greeted Darra and their mother before turning his eager attention to Amber. "You are pretty as a picture tonight, Miss Sterlington," he said as he bowed over her hand. "I am glad that you are recovered from your illness. Society was quite dimmed by your absence."

"Why, thank you, Mr. Harrington," she said with a wide smile. "I so worried this color might be too daring." She swished her skirts while looking at him from beneath her lashes. The neckline was the most daring aspect of the gown, and she felt sure he noted it while appearing to inspect the color of the dress.

"Forever not!" he said as though offended by the prospect. "It enhances your beauty to the height of all things charming and . . . and beautiful."

Amber smiled and ducked as though modestly embarrassed by his stumbling flattery. "My mind is very much put at ease by your compliments, Mr. Harrington. Thank you for being ever so kind."

"Of course," he said, dipping his head slightly. "Would you join me in the next set?" His eyes were bright with anticipation.

"Most certainly," Amber said, wishing she had checked the order of dances for the night. She hoped to waltz with Lord Sunther and did not want to waste the opportunity on Mr. Harrington though she had yet to see the former.

"Wonderful! Shall I fetch you a drink in the meantime? Prinny has put out his very best champagne this evening, truly delightful."

"I would love a glass of champagne before the next set, thank you, Mr. Harrington."

"Very good," he said with another quick

bow. With a click of his heels, he was off to the refreshment table in another room. Amber watched him go. Could he be the husband she needed him to be if Lord Sunther did not rise to the occasion? He often proclaimed of her beauty, and she worried at his reaction when he realized that all was not as it appeared to be. She bit her lip as she watched his retreating back.

"Miss Sterlington," a voice said, drawing her eye up to see Lord Sunther's. By the time Amber recovered herself from the surprise of seeing him so suddenly, he had already turned to look at Darra. "Miss Darra."

The sisters offered the proper curtsy at precisely the same moment. When Amber raised her head, Lord Sunther's eyes were still on her sister. Darra looked back at him, a soft smile on her face and a new light in her eyes. In the space of a moment Amber understood the conversation she'd overheard between Darra and their mother the day before. "He prefers me," Darra had said. "He" was Lord Sunther — there could be no mistake of it, and the knowledge filled her chest with fire. How dare her younger sister pursue a man who only knew of Darra's existence because of Amber's reputation.

"You look dashing tonight," Amber said before Darra could speak, determined to undo whatever charm Darra had cast upon him. "I do love that waistcoat."

He looked at his simple gold waistcoat and his ears colored slightly beneath her compliment.

"Amber will be dancing with Mr. Harrington for the next set," Darra interrupted in a shocking display of forwardness. "Were you of a mind to ask for a dance, my lord?"

Amber could scarcely believe her sister's words and was battling between apologizing on her behalf or laughing it off as an ill-timed joke when she looked at Lord Sunther. He was all smiles and soft looks as he stared back at Darra.

"I should most like to partner you, Miss Darra. If you are not otherwise spoken for."

"Not at all, my lord," she said, smiling with the same degree of eagerness Lord Sunther had in his expression.

"Your champagne?"

The far less well-appointed Mr. Harrington held out the fluted glass to Amber with his pudgy hand. Amber smiled as she accepted the refreshment, then thanked him most ardently in hopes of giving a fine display of her graciousness to both men. Beneath her façade of confidence, her heart was racing with both fury and fear.

Lord Sunther moved to Darra's other side, and though Amber attempted to remain engaged with Mr. Harrington in conversation as they awaited the dance, she was aware of the muted exchange between Darra and Lord Sunther and how each was quite comfortable with the other. He did not know that Darra was using him as a weapon against the sister of whom she was obviously jealous and that was unfair to him in the extreme. Amber would not stand for it.

The current dance ended, and Amber set her glass down on a small table so Mr. Harrington could lead her to the floor. She lined up with the other women, Darra to her right. Before the music began, she turned to look at her sister who returned the glance with one equally assured and knowing. The sisters held one another's eyes for a moment before facing forward once again.

They said nothing as they perfectly executed the first steps of the dance, but Amber had no doubt that Darra knew a glove had been thrown all the same.

# Chapter 13

Lord Norwin arrived late, but asked Amber for the next waltz, which she accepted minutes before Lord Sunther asked Darra for the same dance. It was the couple's third dance, and though they had both had a variety of partners in between, Lord Sunther had only asked Amber to dance once, and that after she had flirted so shamelessly she feared the invitation had come only so she would focus more on the dance than on him.

As Lord Norwin led Amber across the floor, she attempted to attend to his conversation despite keeping a sharp eye on Darra and Lord Sunther, who seemed quite amiably engaged with one another. Too amiably.

"So it would seem Lord Sunther is to be the gentleman of your attentions, then?"

Amber turned her eyes to those of Lord Norwin's, which were decidedly out of humor. "Pardon?" she asked, unsure what she'd missed in his conversation.

"You can hardly bear to take your eyes off him," Lord Norwin said. He did not smile nor apologize for his forward commentary. "I would like to make it clear that I will not stand in your way."

"Oh, Lord Norwin," Amber said, embarrassed to have been so rightly caught. "You misunderstand my notice. It is just that —"

"There is no need to explain yourself to me," Lord Norwin said. Amber was as equally struck by his words as his tone, which, though cool, was surprisingly gentle. "My attention has been quite captured by another young woman myself, and I had wanted to be sure of my own mind by paying my attentions to you before I chose to further my situation with her. Do not feel badly for finding yourself in the same position." He smiled, but it did not relieve her discomfort. She could not afford to lose his attentions — *anyone's* attentions. "I wish you quite happy. Lord Sunther is lucky to have your distinction. It will credit him well as he rises to his title so unexpectedly settled upon him these last months."

Amber was spared from having to reply when the last chords of the dance ended and Lord Norwin led her to the edge of the ballroom. He bowed over her hand. "Shall I assume you wish me every happiness in my own choice?" he asked, lifting his eyebrows in expectation.

Amber's first thought was to tell him, "No." She had not made *her* final decision, and the thought of him removing himself from her list of suitors left her anxious. But she was embarrassed enough at having spent their waltz looking upon another man that she took Lord Norwin's hand and wished him, as sincerely as she could, the very happiness he requested of her.

He smiled widely, thanked her for the dance, and removed himself from her company. A few moments later he was bowing over the hand of a golden-haired woman who could scarcely contain her pleasure at his attention. From the look on Lord Norwin's face as he led the girl to the floor, Amber had no doubt that she was the very woman of his favor.

"So it seems you have lost one."

Amber stiffened at the sound of her mother's voice behind her. Her mother could not have overheard the conversation she and Lord Norwin had shared during their waltz, which meant their expressions had said quite enough. Before Amber spoke, she made certain her tone and bearing was quite even. “He has grown an affection for someone else. I shan’t try to interfere with such an attachment.”

Her mother came to stand beside her, but looked upon the crowd rather than her daughter directly. She wore a gray gown that set off her features and blue eyes well without looking as though she were in mourning. Lady Marchent had always been fashionable and admired, so much the kind of woman Amber had expected to be. “You are down to two ardent suitors, then,” Lady Marchent said.

“Three.”

“Lord Sunther prefers Darra,” she said with pointed sympathy. “Surely you can see that.”

Amber could not keep the bite from her words as she turned her head sharply. “Darra well knows my feelings toward him. That she should undermine me in such a way is beyond belief.”

“You were out of society for more than a week,” Lady Marchent said.

“And she made good use of the absence of my shadow, did she not?”

“You cannot fault her,” Lady Marchent said, her voice calm but intolerant. “Nor him. Your sister is quite fine in her manners and a beauty in her own right. I wonder that anyone noticed so long as she was at your side night after night, but once you were not there, her charms were quite obvious and very highly favored."

Amber looked at her mother, sorrow and jealousy and confusion milling about in her head. "Did she not come to London as *my* companion? Is she not to have another season next year without me?"

Lady Marchent met Amber's eyes for the first time in their conversation. "We had many plans for this season that have changed, my dear." The softness in her words made Amber nervous, as though they were a prelude to something decidedly unpleasant. "And we have all faced changes of circumstance. I shall not expect Darra to be your attendant any more than I shall expect you to procure the type of man you initially sought for. It would be in everyone's best interest if you made quick work of procuring a satisfying arrangement and let Darra stay her course."

Amber considered the words, the truth and the coldness of them. "You feel I should *allow* her to pursue Lord Sunther?"

"They have an affection for one another," Lady Marchent said. "Many couples would wish for as good a start. Did you not just tell me that you would not stand in the way of Lord Norwin's attachment? You can give the same consideration to your sister."

"Lord Sunther is the most eligible man in all of London, Mama. For Darra to secure his interests would mean that I would end in a position below her. I am still the eldest sister. Do you not feel bound by the expectation that I marry first and of the higher level?"

"You are in need of a match, and in such cases as this it is not to be expected that you supersede the future station of your sister." Her words were beginning to snap upon the edges, showing the fullness of her feelings. "I will accept whatever censure the *ton* may direct in exchange for the relief of you making an arrangement and retiring from London so as to recover from your condition outside the glare of society."

An acquaintance approached, and Lady Marchent's expression changed to one of welcome as she began to converse with her friend. After a moment, the two matrons removed from the edge of the dance floor, leaving Amber to stew over her mother's words alone.

No one had asked her to dance this set and the awkwardness she felt added to her enflamed nerves. That her mother expected Amber's condition to change her entire future was upsetting. And unfair. Amber had been groomed for this, taught and positioned to set the level. But it seemed that Amber was the only person who thought herself still capable of such a match. Which meant she was the only person to change the mind of everyone who doubted her abilities.

It took nearly an hour before Lord Sunther asked Amber to dance a second time. He had danced a fourth with Darra by then, and even Lady Marchent had shared her disapproval at the impropriety of such behavior; there would be no more dances between them tonight.

Lord Sunther and Amber were set opposite for a quadrille and each time they met up, Amber asked him a question about his family or what he liked best about London, desperately seeking some common topic of discussion she could use to get his attention. She was well studied in literature, history, and music and felt eager to make him mindful of her education as he was an intellect himself. He was polite in his short replies, and Amber knew she needed to make more of an impression.

When the dance finished and Lord Sunther was leading Amber back to the edge of the room, she pulled on his arm and pointed toward an elaborate stairway leading off the ballroom. "I believe the statue room is located up those stairs. Would you escort me to see Prinny's collection?" She turned her face toward him expectantly.

"Certainly," he said, with enough hesitation for Amber to notice, which only confirmed her course.

She pressed against his arm and thanked him profusely. His ears colored at her forwardness but she pretended not to notice. They took the stairs and wandered through the statue room, which was quite impressive although Amber had seen it before. Lord Sunther was quite informed on the history of several of the pieces, and Amber took confidence in his growing comfort the more she asked him about the statuary.

As Lord Sunther moved around a large piece, Amber moved quickly around the other side so it appeared an accident when they met face to face at the front. Amber giggled as though surprised, while Lord Sunther's ears colored and he took a step back. Amber took a step toward him, and he looked down at the neckline of her gown for a moment before looking back into her face. She made sure she did not show any embarrassment of his notice. She reached out to run her finger along the lapel of his coat and watched his Adam's apple bob as he swallowed nervously. His ears were flaming red, but she kept her eyes locked on his own though her chest burned in embarrassment for the lengths she was taking for his attention. How had she come to this? And yet, what other course did she have?

"My lord," Amber said in a throaty voice she hoped sounded seductive and not hoarse. She'd been told her lower tones were already quite exciting to gentlemen, and she hoped taking them a degree lower would only add to the appeal. She moved closer, enough that she knew he could smell her cologne — and hardly ignore the neckline of her dress as he was trying to do since his first notice of it. "I must tell you that —"

"Lord Sunther?"

Amber whipped her head around and narrowed her eyes when she saw Darra standing a short distance away with another debutante. "What is happening here?"

"Miss Darra," Lord Sunther said, taking two large steps away from Amber, his ears nearing to burst into flames they were so bright. "I . . . Miss Sterlington wanted to see the statuary. I studied art history at Cambridge and was telling her of the different pieces. Would you like to join us on a tour?"

Darra looked between the two of them, keeping her expression neutral. She let her gaze finally settle on Lord Sunther and smiled sweetly. "My mother has requested Amber attend to her. My apologies for the interference in your tour."

"Not at all," Lord Sunther said, shaking his head. "We were nearly finished, were we not, Miss Sterlington?"

Amber hardly knew how to react, especially as she looked between Darra and Lord Sunther and saw what her mother had warned her was there — mutual affection. She had already lost Lord Norwin's interest this night, but now she realized she'd lost Lord Sunther even before that. In the process she had betrayed herself with such a low display of her own character.

Embarrassed by her behavior and frightened at her dwindling prospects, Amber walked past her sister and the girl she did not know without speaking, intent on the stairs that led back to the ballroom and away from this place of humiliation. Darra must have followed them up the stairs. Had she known what Amber was planning? The thought embarrassed her even more.

She reached the stairs and lifted her skirts

as she began her descent, her thoughts tangling, her concerns growing, and questions regarding her own character overwhelming any good thought in regards to herself. She heard another footfall on the stairs and turned to see Darra's companion a few steps behind her. Amber did not recognize her and wondered if she was new to London during Amber's absence.

At the top of the stairs was Lord Sunther with Darra on his arm — his ears nearly returned to their normal shade. They looked so comfortable together, so . . . happy. Amber felt tears in her eyes at the full realization. They *had* found a connection between themselves that Amber had not found with any man. Would she ever find it?

What she'd said to her mother about requiring the first choice of men and her desire to outrank her younger sister suddenly sounded so infantile, so beyond the point. Why could Amber not be happy for her sister? Why could she not find someone with such affinity herself?

She was nearly to the base of the stairs when she felt someone brush against her skirt from behind. Startled, she turned to see Darra's friend only one step above her. At the same moment, there was a tug at the back of her head as the girl took hold of the crowning braid of the wig and pulled. Amber grabbed for the girl's hand, but then felt the girl's fingers slide beneath the binding. This girl was not simply pulling Amber's hair without understanding it was not real, she was attempting to remove the wig entirely!

"No, please." Amber could not keep a grip as the girl moved backward up the stairs, holding tightly to Amber's wig as she went. Amber stumbled upward and back, tripping on her skirts. She let go of the girl's arm and grabbed hold of the wig with both hands, pulling it against her head while attempting to hurry down the stairs, away from this fiend and her dark intentions.

The girl did not let go but moved down the stairs with her, a firm grip on the edge of the wig just behind Amber's right ear. Two steps from the bottom, Amber tripped on her dress and fell against the railing. The girl fell with her, knocking her down and causing them both to tumble down the remaining stairs. Amber hit her knee, then her hip, and ended in a heap at the bottom of the flamboyant marble stairs, tangled in the layered fabric of her dress and dazed from the fall.

She was vaguely aware of the girl scrambling away amid the sound of gasps and screams from the crowd concentrated in the ballroom. The orchestra staggered to a stop as Amber attempted to right herself, using her hands to push herself into a sitting position. After regaining her equilibrium, she blinked up at the crowd, took in their horrified expressions that felt too severe, and then gingerly reached up to touch her head as her chest went cold. Instead of feeling the comforting bulk of the wig, she felt nothing but the remnants of her own cropped hair and the remaining damage to her scalp.

No wig. No binding.

She could not breathe as reality descended upon her in the form of pointing fingers, open mouths, and shocked expressions of the *ton* Amber knew in an instant she no longer belonged to.

# CHAPTER 14

The ripple of horrified gasps moved through the crowd like a wave, drawing Thomas's attention away from the gentlemen with whom he was conversing and toward the other side of the room. People were moving that direction, their reactions rising in volume. Thomas was merely curious until he saw Darra Sterlington standing beside Lord Sunther in the middle of the stairway, above the rest of the crowd. Darra's face was pale as she stared at something below her. Lord Sunther was equally shocked, his mouth open and his eyes the size of saucers.

"What's that all about?" Fenton asked, waving idly toward the tightening crowd.

"Perhaps Mrs. Miston's stays finally gave out," Sir Crosby said with a grin. "If so, you owe me forty pounds, Fenton."

Thomas grunted in a semblance of laughter until he heard a cry that struck recognition within him. The sound of sobbing reached his ears a moment later. He pivoted in an instant but was jostled to the side as Lady Marchent made her way quickly toward the source of the distress. Thomas looked at Darra Sterlington for only a moment before falling in step behind Lady Marchent.

The Sterlington family had arrived together shortly after he and Fenton had been introduced, and he had noted Miss Sterlington as he did every time she entered a room. She had not presented as the shining diamond she'd been earlier in the season, her recent illness had dimmed her somewhat, but his reaction to her was as strong and unwelcome as ever. He'd set about avoiding her for this evening, as he always did when they attended the same events. Where was she now? From the urgency of Lady Marchent's movements and the look upon Darra Sterlington's face he feared he was about to find out.

Lady Marchent attempted to push her way through the crowd and Thomas stepped in front of her to help part the guests until they reached the edge of the circle of people assessing the scene. Huddled at the base of the stairs was the very subject of his pondering, curled around herself with her arms over her head as she sobbed and rocked back and forth. Her emerald-colored skirts were askew, and a silver slipper lay discarded some feet away. Had she fallen down the steps? Was she injured?

He moved aside so Lady Marchent could reach her daughter and therefore was close enough to hear Lady Marchent grumble under her breath, "Stupid girl," before she came to a stop several feet away from her daughter.

Miss Sterlington looked up at her mother and in the process revealed herself. A fresh reaction rose through the crowd, and Thomas fell back a step in shock. That hair — so beautiful and admired — existed now only in short tufts interspersed between red welts and scabs. If not for the large green eyes — desperate and frightened — he would doubt it was Miss Sterlington at all. But it *was* her. What had happened?

"Diseased," he heard a woman say behind him.

"Repulsive," a man repeated.

The sound that bubbled up from Miss Sterlington's throat sounded like that of a child. "Mama," she cried.

Her mother did not go to her, however, and though Thomas could not see her face, he imagined Lady Marchent's reaction was not much different than everyone else in the crowd. Was no one to help her? The look on Miss Sterlington's face was of such pain and distress that he quickly shrugged off his coat and stepped forward, in front of Lady Marchent who had not approached any closer than anyone else in the room.

Miss Sterlington looked at him, first with fear and then gratitude as she seemed to realize his intent. She lifted a hand toward his coat, and he helped throw it over her head. She pulled the lapels tight beneath her chin, hiding her horrifying head, and turned her splotchy face to her mother. "Mama," she said in that same pathetic voice. "Help me."

The words seemed to hang in the air, as if her mother were still considering whether assisting her daughter was the best course, but then a servant to Carlton House stepped forward.

The footman helped Miss Sterlington to her feet — she seemed to have injured her ankle — and then turned to Lady Marchent. "Which is your carriage, Madam?"

Thomas looked at the embarrassed expression of Lady Marchent as the woman finally moved to her daughter. She ushered the footman and Miss Sterlington toward a doorway. Thomas stood with the crowd as they made their exit, Thomas's coat disappearing with them. Darra Sterlington followed a few steps behind her mother and sister, her head hung low, avoiding eye contact with anyone. The whispers and twittering continued until the orchestra started up again. *When had it stopped?* Thomas wondered.

The guests slowly began to move away from the scene of Miss Sterlington's humiliation, but Thomas remained rooted in place, reviewing what he'd seen and what it meant. Her head was revolting, just as someone had said, and yet the look on her face, the fear and humility was . . . striking. He could not make sense of it and fought the urge to go after her. If he could think of a purpose in his pursuit perhaps he would do it.

"Good grief," Fenton said as he came up beside Thomas and looked in the direction Miss Sterlington had disappeared. "If that is not the most fearsome spectacle I have ever seen in my life, I don't know what is. And at Prinny's ball, no less." He tsked before taking a long drink of his champagne. "And you're left in your shirtsleeves, almost as shocking."

Thomas looked at his grinning friend, dazed by the events of the last few minutes. "What has happened to her?"

"I've only ever seen a condition like that

on the most disease-riddled rakes," Fenton said, still smiling. "Every man in this room is thanking the heavens for fair warning, or perhaps some men are even now shaking in their boots for what may yet come upon them."

"That is beyond the pale," Thomas said sharply, causing Fenton to raise his eyebrows in surprise as his smile fell. Most times, Thomas appreciated his friend's lightness but not in this. "Miss Sterlington has given no reason for anyone to suspect her virtue. She is not some cur who's made his rounds with lightskirts for a decade or more."

"Begging your pardon, Richards," Fenton said, looking surprised at Thomas's reprimand. "I simply know of no other explanation for such a condition. We have both remarked at her excessive flirting, have we not?"

"If flirting is a reflection of virtue, than you are in serious peril of your own reputation, Fenton."

Fenton did not make a joke of Thomas's rebuttal as Thomas had known he would not. Fenton's morality was higher than that of most men, though he did not draw attention to what most of society saw as a flaw rather than a virtue. Thomas would have expected Fenton's morality to give him more decorum in such a matter. "Touché," Fenton said with adequate humility before finishing his glass. "I think I shall get another drink."

Once alone, Thomas looked about himself to see a few quickly averted glances. Surely the other guests were commenting on the impropriety of him being without his coat at such a high-*ton* event. He shook his head, disgusted with the whole of London and society in general. A young woman had faced public humiliation of the worst kind and yet they still had enough judgment left for his lack of a coat.

Thomas had no doubt that everyone in the room was drawing the same conclusion Fenton had: that whatever had caused the hideous state of Miss Sterlington's hair and head was a result of some immoral action on her part. Miss Sterlington, and perhaps her entire family, could face ruin simply from the rumor of the possibility. Doors would be shut, gossip would infect morning visits, and the attention Miss Sterlington had received until now would turn on her completely.

Another servant approached him and leaned forward to speak softly. "Sir, may I assist you in locating a coat so that you will be properly attired?"

"Thank you, no," Thomas said, keeping his back straight and his chin up. "I have had all the entertainment I can stand for one night. Good evening."

# Chapter 15

Three days after the ball at Carlton House, Amber was summoned to Lord Marchent's study. She wore a mobcap and her dressing gown as she entered the room, head down and hands clasped behind her back.

"Do sit down, Amber," Lord Marchent said, waving her to a leather chair. Amber sat on the edge of the cushion, her body rigid with expectation. Lady Marchent was seated in another chair, her hands folded demurely in her lap.

"I have made arrangements," Lord Marchent said, looking over his spectacles at his eldest daughter. He was a handsome man, with a full head of hair just beginning to gray at the temples and piercing green eyes that Amber had inherited. Unlike many men his age, he had not grown portly and soft, but was as broad as any young buck, but with the presence and severity of a man of title.

More than ever before, Amber marked him as much a stranger to her as any other young woman's father. He was Lord Marchent, and not much else; she wondered if he felt the same detachment to her as she felt to him.

"Your mother has spoken to you about returning to Hampton Grove for the duration of the season," he continued. "She says you do not wish to return there."

Amber shook her head but could not speak, the fear and sorrow was too thick in her throat. She had told her mother she did not want to return to Somerset — too many people would have heard what happened. Too many people would come for gossip disguised as sympathy, and Amber felt such frailty within herself that she knew it would not take much for her to break into a thousand pieces. The faces at Carlton House haunted her.

"I have considered all other possibilities," Lord Marchent continued, "and decided upon an estate in the North Country, away from society and connections that might seek you out. I think it will meet the need most comfortably."

"In Nottingham?" Amber asked. Lord Marchent traveled to his Nottingham estate a few times a year; it was his largest holding of land and therefore quite profitable. He had often remarked that the family would live there if not for its distance from London. Amber had not been to Nottingham for several years and knew no one in that county. It could be a good escape; the estate was not nearly as large as Hampton Grove but would be comfortable for a single occupant not of a mind to entertain visitors.

"Not Nottingham," Lord Marchent said, shaking his head. "This estate is near Romanby — just south of that village, in fact. I travel there but once a year to meet with the caretaker and solicitor. I have thought to sell it in the past, but it brings in profit enough to support itself so I have maintained it."

Amber furrowed her brow. "Romanby?"

"Just south of Northallerton," her father said. He removed his spectacles and massaged the bridge of his nose as though her questions were taxing his patience. "Yorkshire. You'll be safe there and very comfortable as you convalesce. I have sent word to have the house readied for you in time for your arrival."

Amber blinked in surprise and looked at her mother. "It's all decided, then? I have no say?"

"You refused to return to Hampton

Grove," Lady Marchent reminded her. "Your father and I have discussed the options, and this is the best one available. You will be comfortable there, and no one will know of what happened here in London."

"Am I to go alone?" Amber asked. She knew her father would not leave London until parliament finished their session, but surely her mother would not send her so far away alone. Yorkshire was at least a two-day journey.

"I shall come as soon as I can," her mother said, looking into her lap and straightening a fold in the skirt of her morning gown. "I'm afraid that Darra and I cannot be in readiness to go with you now."

"Darra is not to come," Amber spat, filled with the fire she felt each time she thought of her sister's betrayal. "She did this, Mama. She and her friend."

Lady Marchent gave her a look of irritation. "Darra claims no part of it. Furthermore it was Darra's idea to explain that the rinse you had already talked of had gone further awry than we dared to say, resulting in your horrific state. People have been accepting of such an explanation, and you have Darra to thank for the rescue. We need to remain in London so as to show our confidence in your eventual return once you are properly recovered. Should we all leave, it will seem a far greater scandal."

"Your mother will come as soon as she is able," Lord Marchent said, drawing the full attention of both women. "Your maid has agreed to attend you for the duration of time you spend away."

A maid for her companion was hardly compensation for everything Amber would be leaving behind. "Yorkshire is so far away," she said. "Could I not go to Nottingham instead? Then I shall only be a day's journey from all of you, and I am not well enough known there that —"

Lord Marchent fixed her with a look that caused her to drop her gaze to the floor once more. "I have already sent word to have Step Cottage prepared for you. I shall not consider other arrangements."

"Yes, my lord," Amber murmured, still staring at the rug beneath her feet.

"Your maid is packing your trunks even now," Lady Marchent said. "And your father has ordered the traveling carriage readied for your journey. Two groomsmen will attend you for a few days' time upon arrival, procuring you a carriage and seeing to any other tasks of your comfort before they return with the coach. They shall be meeting with your father's steward who, along with your father's man of business in Northallerton, will see that your needs are met."

Amber dared look up at her mother. "I am to leave *today*?"

"We need to regain a sense of normalcy and decorum about this house," her father said. "There is no reason for delay now that I have finished all the correspondence that must attend you. This has not been a simple arrangement to make, and I should think you would express adequate gratitude for the difficulties we have gone to for your care."

Amber nodded her acceptance of his investment but could not speak. Her throat was dry with fear for what awaited her. She had never lived apart from her family, her siblings at least, and to do so at such a distance in a cottage she'd never seen before was shocking to accept. She could not help but feel as though she were being discarded as any other belonging no longer of use to its owner.

Lord Marchent continued, "Despite the intervention of your sister's story to explain it, the horrific scene you created has most certainly come under the attention of London gossips. As long as you remain here, none of us can recover from the burden you have placed upon us."

"You sound as though I did this with purpose," she said, feeling a wave of strength, though she kept her hands tightly clenched in her lap and her eyes fixed on the rug. "As though I would bring this upon us of my own will."

For the space of several breaths the room was silent, then Lord Marchent stood from his chair. "There is no space for blame in this." She could hear the fatigue in his voice; oh, but her parents were a pair for one another with their disregard. The thought did not bring the emotion it once might. Perhaps she had spent her emotion and was left empty of any feeling at all.

Lord Marchent continued, "There are circumstances in life that happen regardless of our will. All we can do is react as best we can so as to have as little impact on the comfort of others as possible. That you have to endure such a thing is unfortunate indeed, but I should think you would not want your family to suffer along with you. I should think that as a woman of feeling and sound mind you should want to protect us from such derision, not ask that we share it with you."

"The country will be a good place for you to be restored," her mother offered. "And we shall all hope for your return to London next season."

Amber shrank away from the thought. Could she expect that anyone would have forgotten her humiliation by next year? She could not imagine it so she focused on the restoration her mother had mentioned. That would be her reason in agreeing to this. She could do anything so long as it would help her find her true self once again. Besides, her father was right. She should trust that her parents wanted what was best for her and not create further difficulty by arguing selfish concerns.

"As your mother said, your maid is attending to your trunks and preparing to ready you for the journey."

There seemed nothing else to say. "Yes, my lord." She stood, curtsied stiffly, and left the room feeling apart from what was happening around her. All of this because she was no longer the perfect debutante, the perfect daughter? She had never before imagined that one aspect of a person could have such power as to change every detail of their existence.

When Amber returned to her bedchamber she found Suzanne doing exactly what Lord and Lady Marchent had said she would be doing — preparing Amber's trunks for the journey north. Upon a closer inspection, she noted the maid's red face and swollen eyes. "What is wrong?" she snapped. Suzanne wasn't ill, was she? That would make the journey even more difficult.

Suzanne shook her head and continued folding Amber's nightdress into the smaller trunk, the one that would attend her at the inns they would stay in along the way. Amber did not know if they would stop over for one night or two, but the thought of staying in an inn at all made her shiver in repulsion. She had heard tales that made her wish they could drive straight through the night, though she had never done that either. She had never had the need to cover such a distance.

"I thought you might want your yellow traveling dress today," Suzanne said. "Which dresses should I set aside for the rest of the journey?" Her voice broke and she sniffled with the last part.

Amber realized that it was not illness causing her maid's disposition. Rather, the woman was . . . sad?

"Did you not agree to attend me?" Amber asked, annoyed and strangely hurt by the idea, which made no sense at all. Suzanne was just a maid and Amber cared not for her opinion.

Suzanne continued pulling items from the wardrobe and laying them on the bed. Amber noted that none of her ball gowns or fancier pieces were being packed, but then she'd have no need for them in Yorkshire. Should she return next season — still a difficult prospect to consider — she would need a new wardrobe to fit the current fashions.

"I asked if you did not agree to attend me?" Amber said when Suzanne still did not answer, not disguising her irritation at having to repeat herself. "I've no mind to deal with a sullen maid amid already difficult circumstances."

Suzanne looked up and her eyes flashed as her hands gripped the gown in her hands. "What choice do I have?" she said, her voice controlled but passionate. "I have been told that should I not attend you to Yorkshire I shall never find employ in this city again. I have lived in London all of my life; my family is here. Forgive me my *sullenness,* Miss, but 'tis not only your future being changed."

Amber backed up a step. She'd never had a servant address her with so much feeling and did not know how to respond. As she thought on the words again, however, she felt a different manner of discomfort. "Who said you wouldn't find employment if you did not attend me?"

Suzanne went back to her work, her cheeks pink but her mouth tightly shut.

"I asked you a question," Amber said harshly.

Suzanne whipped her head up, once again full of passion Amber did not expect. "What does it matter? My fate is bound to yours, Miss, but I shall get none of the sympathy."

"You think anyone is regarding me with sympathy?" Amber said in angry surprise. "I am a pariah. I have lost everything."

"As have I," Suzanne said boldly. "What am I to do in Yorkshire? There shan't be fine clothes to attend to, fashions to style. You haven't even any hair for me to care for, nor anywhere to go. I have already been set about as a chambermaid these last weeks, which is far below my training, and now I shall attend a woman without hair and without kindness in the wilds of the north country and leave behind me every person I've ever loved as well as any prospect of a greater position. I have lost as much as you."

The concept of Suzanne having lost anything at all was overwhelming, and Amber sat on a chair at the small table brought up for her meals as she looked upon her maid . . . no, as she looked upon this *woman.*

With Amber's fall from grace, Suzanne had become an unintended casualty.

Suzanne had likely invested all the years of Amber's life in rising to this point of attending the ladies of the *ton.* She surely expected to attend Amber long enough to transition into the full position of a lady's maid. And now she was to be exiled. Amber thought of Suzanne's words: *"Leave behind me every person I've ever loved."* Amber had never thought of servants having a life outside of the house they worked for. But of course they would.

"Who do you leave behind, Suzanne?" Amber asked, her voice surprisingly soft even to her own ears.

Suzanne had gone back to packing, though she wiped her eyes a time or two. Amber waited for an answer. Finally, after several seconds, Suzanne took a breath. "I have two sisters in London, both with families of their own. My mother is in ill health and living with my youngest sister. We all assist her when we can. Eliza is expecting her fourth child in a few months' time and has had quite a time of it."

Another remark Suzanne had made came back to Amber's mind. *"I shall attend a woman without hair and without kindness."* Why Amber should be affected by a servant's opinion of her she did not know, but realizing how Suzanne regarded her made her feel heavy inside.

Suzanne turned to the wardrobe and removed Amber's stockings and underthings from the bottom drawer. Amber watched her smooth out each piece, fold it carefully, and tuck it into the trunk. Even with her anger and devastation at being forced to leave London she was attentive to her tasks, attentive to Amber.

"I am sorry, Suzanne," Amber said, seized by an emotion she was unable to define. Her best attempt labeled it as regret for Suzanne's circumstance and guilt for being the cause of it. Surely she had come about these feelings naturally at some time in her life, as there was a familiarity to them, but not recently to be sure, as they were foreign too. Suzanne looked at her with hesitation, and Amber took a breath. "It is not right that you should be affected by this after you have served me so well these last weeks. I shall talk to my mother and ask that she find you a position worthy of your station. She has many connections, and I will insist she ensure you a solid post."

"Who would then attend you?" Suzanne asked, hesitant but eager too. "You can't travel to Yorkshire alone."

No, she couldn't travel to Yorkshire alone. Amber looked at the rug beneath her feet as she sought a solution in her mind, then met her maid's eyes. "The groomsmen attending me will be returning to London after I am settled. You could come with me to this estate and return with them to London. You will be gone but a week."

"And leave you there alone?"

"I'm sure I can find a maid in Yorkshire," Amber said, ignoring the fear springing up in her chest of having to show herself to someone new. "Or perhaps I am not in need of an abigail." The idea of not having anyone to care for her person was frightening, but she attempted to keep from showing the emotion. The other servants could be kept at such a distance so as to not even know of her condition. "If you only pack the simpler dresses rather than those with the more elaborate fastenings about them, I could dress myself without assistance. As you said, I have nothing to ready myself for and no hair to be attended."

"I spoke out of turn, Miss," Suzanne said, humbled now that her fervor had passed. Or perhaps because she'd been pardoned from the fate Amber could not escape from herself.

"No, you did not," Amber said. She looked

up to see sincere sympathy on the face of her maid. It nearly undid her, and she blinked back the emotion. "Will you attend me to Yorkshire if I convince my mother to help you find a new position upon your return to London? I shall see that you are financially compensated for the sacrifice as well. Perhaps you could send the payment to your sister so that she might procure additional help for your mother during your absence."

Suzanne held Amber's gaze for some time, looking equal parts relieved and regretful. Amber sensed that she wanted to speak but did not know how to address her mistress now that they had both stepped over the unseen lines of station and address. "I will attend you, Miss," she finally said, her expression softened. "Which dresses would you like me to pack in the small trunk?"

Amber went to her wardrobe to look over her dresses and in the process saw the black coat that had hung there since Carlton House. She pulled it from the closet and looked it over with only a vague memory of the man who had given it to her.

One man amid the hundreds gathered there had given her aid. A man Amber did not believe she was acquainted with, and yet he had been kind to her. She wished she knew how to return his coat to him and thank him for that kindness, but to try to find him would mean reigniting people's memories of what his kindness had intended to hide.

She was to disappear today, slip away from London and people's thoughts, taking with her the shame and embarrassment she had brought upon her family and perhaps this man too — he'd have been left at a ball without a coat. Perhaps he would not want it back anyway after it had been about her head.

She let out a breath and pushed the coat into the back of the closet before fingering through her day dresses and morning gowns. He was without a coat. She was to be without far more than that.

Two hours later, Amber closed the curtain inside the traveling coach, not wanting to see London and all it symbolized fall away from her; not wanting anyone of her acquaintance to see her leaving in shame. She feared she would never come back, and yet she was relieved to be parted from the place of so much heartache. She rested her cap-and-bonnet-covered head against the cushions of the seat and spent the first five miles attempting not to cry. There would be plenty of time for that when she was settled in the country house — Step Cottage, her father had called it — in Romanby, North Riding, Yorkshire.

Alone.

Unattended.

She could only hope she would not call this cottage "home" for long.

# Chapter 16

They stopped overnight at the Crimson Shield Inn, arriving late and leaving early. Suzanne and Amber took their meals together in the room they shared rather than join the other guests in the coaching house. The proprietor said it was the finest room the inn had to offer, but it smelled sour and the sheets were rough.

Once back in the carriage for the second day of travel, Amber could stand the silence no longer and asked Suzanne about her family. The maid was hesitant to talk at first, but Amber continued to prod her with questions until eventually Suzanne disposed of the one-word answers.

Both of her parents had worked in service, but Suzanne's younger sisters had married into the merchant class and were not employed outside of running their household and caring for their children, though her one sister did mending for a few gentry families. Suzanne's father had retired five years ago after an illness left him unable to keep up his duties as a gardener of a grand estate outside of London. He died in his sleep the following summer, leaving their mother to work in the kitchens of a London house until being let go two years ago this August.

"I fear she may not live another winter. The cold is increasingly hard on her." She paused, then looked at Amber and forced a smile. "Which is why I must thank you for talking with your mother of my return to London. I could not bear being away from her or my sisters at such a time. The additional funds you procured will be of great help to them both, for which I thank you too."

"Your affection for them is a credit to all of you," Amber said, not liking the reflection her own family cast through the prism of Suzanne's. "I certainly hope all is well until your return and that perhaps the summer will result in an increase of health for your mother."

"As do I, Miss," Suzanne said.

Amber wondered if she would be missed by her family. When she had parted the London house, her mother had given her a quick embrace and said she would come to

Yorkshire when the season was over. Seeing as it was May, it would be several weeks until the gentry who gathered in London returned to their country estates. Perhaps by then her mother would have missed her and they could start afresh.

A fear nagged her that Lady Marchent wouldn't come, but surely her mother would not abandon her completely. There was such a difference in age between herself and her brothers that she knew they would not notice her absence; they had always been kept to a different schedule as they were sons instead of daughters. It was Amber and Darra who had always been the most closely aligned, both in age and in their equal desire for the attention of their parents. Amber did not want to think of Darra right now. It stung to do so.

"How many nieces and nephews do you have?" Amber asked, eager to keep Suzanne talking as it took her out of her own thoughts.

Suzanne told of her endearment toward her sisters' children, which brought another lump to Amber's throat. Amber had grown up privileged and, in her mind, envied by the lesser classes she interacted with but rarely. The more Suzanne spoke of her family connections created through the affection they shared, the more envious Amber felt. Did anyone within her own society love their children the way Suzanne's family did?

Amber had never seen or experienced such bonds and began to wonder if Suzanne were making fun of her. She eventually stopped asking questions, not wanting to be made a fool of by believing such stories of parents playing with their children, or teaching them the skills of daily life without the help of servants. She struggled to make sense of the jealousy she felt toward Suzanne's situation; she was loved and she knew it. Was Amber loved by her parents? Did she love *them*?

As daylight began to slip away, they stopped in the village of Topcliffe. Amber assumed it was to change horses, and it was, but then she saw the groom talking with a man who he then brought toward the carriage. Amber shrank back against the cushion, alerting Suzanne, who leaned forward to see the men approaching.

"Who is that man with Jeffery?" Suzanne asked. "Do you know him?"

"Of course not," Amber snapped. "I know no one this far north. Why is Jeffery bringing him over?" She pulled at the lace edging of her cap as she watched the men getting closer. She looked to her bonnet lying beside her on the seat — she'd removed it while it was only her and Suzanne's company she needed to accommodate. She quickly put on the bonnet, her fingers fumbling to tie the ribbon.

"Act your part," Suzanne said, drawing Amber's eyes to her. The maid mimicked sitting straight, folding her hands in her lap, and lifting her chin. "You're your own mistress, now. Act the part of a Lady and everyone will treat you as such."

Amber straightened as Suzanne had indicated, prepared to encounter this man, then snapped her gaze back to Suzanne. "Is he to address me directly, then? Should he not be speaking with you until I invite his attention?"

It was Suzanne's turn to look startled, but she nodded quickly and straightened her own posture moments before Jeffery knocked on the side of the carriage. Suzanne unlatched the door, which Jeffery then pulled wide. The man with him was older than Amber's father and dressed in the simple attire of a workingman. He took off his hat to reveal thinning gray hair. He bowed, then looked up with a sincere smile that seemed incongruent with his country clothing and mottled teeth.

He glanced at Amber but then turned his

attention to Suzanne. "I am but right pleased to meetcha, Miss. My name be Paulie Dariloo. I take care of tha cottage where his lordship dun says you be staying this next while. Asked me to meet yer carriage in Topcliffe, he did, and I done been waitin' jus 'alf an 'our's all. Made right good time, yer driver did."

"Yes, he did," Suzanne said nervously.

Amber kept a polite smile on her face but found herself very much on edge. She was as unprepared to take charge of this situation as Suzanne was, but she was no longer a daughter or a debutante with someone speaking for her. She would have to take the position she had left to others all her life or she should have no order and respect here in the North.

"You are too kind to have met us, Mr. Dariloo," Suzanne said after an awkward delay, glancing at Amber who nodded to confirm that she should continue. Suzanne returned her attention to Mr. Dariloo. "You're to give direction to the coachman in finding the cottage, I presume?"

"I'm to lead you in, Miss," he said, waving over his shoulder toward the road that ran in front of the inn. "These country roads can get a might bit ragged an' the road to the cottage ain't an easy one to navigate in the dark. Mr. Jeffery here" — he nodded toward the driver — "says you be wantin' to get there tonight despite it being a late 'our that you'll arrive. That set right with ya?"

"My mistress *would* like to arrive at the cottage tonight, Mr. Dariloo." Neither of the women had any desire to stay in another inn like the one from last night. Amber had barely slept at all for the strange sounds and odd smells of the place, and Suzanne had had to sleep on a straw pallet near the door.

"And ya shall, ya shall," he said, nodding. "The horses are 'bout changed an' then we'll make us a procession, if ya will, to the cottage." He glanced at Amber, who glanced at Suzanne, who lifted her shoulders in confusion. She did not understand this situation any better than Amber did. Amber fumbled for what to do and then accepted that her time to be mistress had come.

"You may address me directly, Mr. Dariloo."

His smile broadened, confirming that she'd read his unspoken request for her attention correctly. "Yer father's man a'business found me just yesterday, he did," Mr. Dariloo said. "To give me the 'structions. But my missus and I got the cottage set to rights fer ya in time. Everythin's in place, it is."

"You're very good, sir," Amber said.

His bushy eyebrows went up. "You don't need to be calling me sir, Miss. I ain't so fine as that, just a caretaker, that's all I is. Glad to be of help to ya for your holiday."

*Holiday?* Is that how her father had explained it? Amber pulled at the strings on her bonnet. "Shall we go on, then?" she asked, nervous and wishing she could have the confident demeanor expected of her. Why should an underling such as Mr. Dariloo put her out of sorts?

"Right ya are," Mr. Dariloo said, backing away, his hat still in hand. "We be ready to go in five minute."

Jeffery shut the carriage door, and Amber leaned back against the cushion, her heart thumping. "How odd that I should be so anxious over an exchange of that sort," she said out loud, then looked to Suzanne after pondering a few moments longer. "Neither of us are who we were in London, are we?"

Suzanne's smile was shaky too. "It does not seem so. You handled yourself very well, Miss. You didn't appear nervous but for the pulling on your ribbon." Amber was surprised at how grateful she was for the compliment. Suzanne continued, sounding calmer. "All that breeding will serve its purpose, I'll wager. It's not been lost just because you find yourself in Yorkshire."

Amber pondered that comment for the rest of their journey. As night fell, Mr. Dariloo hung a lantern from his saddle, giving the coach ample mark to follow. They still seemed well within the country when they turned from the relatively smooth ground to a more narrow and pitted road that wound through clusters of trees and fields.

Eager to see the cottage, Amber and Suzanne were looking through the windows when Suzanne touched Amber's arm. "I think that must be it," she said.

Amber could see the light from two windows set on a hillside a short distance in front of them. Mr. Dariloo turned onto a drive that took them off the road, and by the time the carriage came to a stop, Amber and Suzanne had their necks craned upward in an attempt to get a better view of the cottage. Amber hadn't thought about why the place was called Step Cottage, but understood when she removed from the carriage and looked up an impossibly long series of wide stone steps — at least twenty — that led to an equally impossibly small gray house complete with a slate roof. If not for the white sections of stone that reflected the light of the half moon, it would have blended perfectly with the landscape around it.

"Right pretty place, ain't it?" Mr. Dariloo said as he joined them. He gazed up at the cottage as though it were a castle. "My missus has some mutton stew at the ready. We knew that you would be hungry." He headed up the rough stone stairs. Amber lifted her skirts and followed, afraid to look anywhere but the next step as they were not equally spaced and Mr. Dariloo's lantern did not give a great deal of light. She shivered in the night temperature and tried not to think of the haunted forests and forbidden woods of the fairy tales and fables her governess had read to her as a child. Her traveling boots looked impossibly dainty amid the rough surroundings and anxiety crept up her throat with every step.

At the top, more stones were set together in a small terrace, and there were empty flowerpots near the small inset of the front door. Mr. Dariloo turned the knob, and Amber entered behind him. Once inside she came to a stop and then blinked desperately so her eyes would adjust to the dim interior, lit only by a few candles set into sconces on the wall.

Surely the furniture and upholstery looked

so dark and heavy because of the lighting. Certainly it was not a braided rug at her feet, or burlap hung as curtains over the windows in the room on her left meant to be a parlor; it was no bigger than a closet.

In front of them was a narrow stairway heading to the second level, while to the right was a corridor that led straight back into what looked like a kitchen — there was no door to hide the functional part of the house from that of the common space. The area directly left of the front door was complete with a foot bench, umbrella stand, and shelves she imagined were meant for hats and things. There was one other doorway framed by heavy dark wood further down the hall past the parlor.

"It is so small," she said under her breath. It could hardly be called an estate, and she wondered for a brief moment if this were a joke. Perhaps this was Mr. Dariloo's cottage and the finer house was some ways off.

"Is *this* Step Cottage?" she asked in a frightened voice. "It is not a cottage at all."

"Aye, 'tis a clever title to be callin' it a cottage." He laughed as though there were any humor in this situation. "But it's a fine 'ouse and tight as a drum. Not many 'ouses have timber supports on the inside like this'un. You be findin' the library an' parlor

’ere on the first level an’ the kitchen to the back.”

*No dining room?* Amber had never been to a house without a well-appointed dining room, let alone lived in such a place.

Mr. Dariloo continued, “The sleepin’ rooms be upstairs. Jus’ the two though the one ain’t properly set up.”

Two bedrooms!

Mr. Dariloo rocked back on his heels and grinned widely. “An’ that smell you be savorin’ is Mrs. Dariloo’s mutton stew — good hearty tuck for ya at the end of yer journey. ’Ead on down to the kitchen, an’ I’ll see about ’aving yer trunks brought up before them grooms put up the horses in the stable. It’s a bit down the road — not so ’igh on the ’ill o’course.” He waved them toward the kitchen.

Suzanne gave Amber a look that prompted Amber to follow her despite wanting to run back to the carriage and insist there was another destination in mind.

When they entered the primitive kitchen, Amber felt her mouth fall open. A short, round woman stood over a cooking pot that swung out from the fireplace on a hook. She smiled at Amber and Suzanne, showing teeth the same shade of brown and gray as her husband’s. She began to jabber to Suzanne, but Amber was too overwhelmed to hear much of it and sat on one of the benches set at a small, rough-hewn table in the corner. The servants' quarters of Hampton Grove were better turned out than this *cottage,* and Amber felt a fire in her stomach at the thought of living here.

*This is where my parents sent me?*

A bowl of stew was set before her, and she stared at the brown gravy mixed with chunks of meat and vegetables and thought of the four-course meals that had been standard at Hampton Grove and of the even finer meals the chef prepared for them at the London town house. Pheasant, creamed potatoes, asparagus with hollandaise sauce.

She had never sat in the kitchen for a meal in her life, and she had never eaten such rustic food as mutton stew, which was decidedly peasants' fare. She looked up from the bowl to see Mrs. Dariloo open a door off the kitchen that she showed to Suzanne. A single room for servant quarters? Where would the housekeeper stay? What about the chambermaid?

Amber's heart began to race as she realized how the life she'd known had slipped away during the miles they'd traveled. The plaster on the walls wasn't smooth and colored, but a thick rough white, with bits of straw forever stuck within it. She closed her eyes. This could not be right. There must be a mistake. But when she opened her eyes again, she still saw the atrocious stew in a lopsided wooden bowl.

"Yer mistress cun take off th' bonnet," Mrs. Dariloo said to Suzanne though she looked at Amber. She clasped her hands together below her ample bosom, which was covered in an apron no servant at Hampton Grove would see fit to wear for the stained dinginess of it. "No need t' go oot tonight."

The horrid accent grated upon Amber's sensibilities even further, and she came to her feet quick enough that the bench scraped against the floor. "Show me to my room," she said, her voice quivering as she attempted to contain the level of emotion rising within her.

"But, yer stew, Miss."

"Show me to my room!" she yelled, then clamped her mouth shut. Suzanne looked at her with a tight expression, and Amber narrowed her eyes defiantly. Suzanne was used to such poverty and could not possibly understand the feelings rushing through Amber's head. She felt as though she had toppled from the top of a mountain peak and landed in a heap of broken bones. Perhaps that was exactly what had happened when she'd fallen down the stairs at Carlton House.

Suzanne whispered something to Mrs. Dariloo, who nodded and led them out of the kitchen corridor and up the narrow stairs Amber had seen when she first entered the cottage. She removed a candle from one of the foyer sconces before heading up the stairway, moving far too slowly for Amber's tastes and casting dark shadows on the narrow walls as they ascended. Amber dug her nails into the palm of her hand to keep from pushing the woman to move faster.

At the top of the stairs, they entered a small alcove with a door straight back and two doors facing one another across the hallway. Mrs. Dariloo moved to the right-hand door, turned the knob, and pushed open the heavy door. Amber followed her inside and let her eyes scan the room. It was long and narrow and very close in style to the horrid room at the inn she had barely survived the night before.

The ceiling pitched in line with the roof, leaving only space enough for a dresser, a bed, and a chair. There was a single window at the far end. A washbasin was set on the dresser, and Amber could see the edge of a chamber pot beneath the bed. The fireplace set against the interior wall was shared with the next room. A row of hooks on the wall served in place of a wardrobe.

It was unlike anything Amber had ever seen before, and she closed her eyes as though she could forget the image of it entirely. "Leave me," she said curtly.

"Miss, doncha want —"

"Leave me!" Amber shouted at the top of her lungs. Her hands were balled into fists at her side. "This is my room and my house, and when I ask you to leave, you will do as I say!"

"Miss."

This time it was Suzanne's voice, and Amber opened her eyes to glare at the servant who would abandon her in a few days' time.

"If the servant's quarters are in line with what I have found here, you have reason to be as outraged as I. Leave me."

Mrs. Dariloo scurried through the doorway after lighting the candle in the lamp on the dresser.

Suzanne's expression was chastising, but Amber did not care.

"I shall help you undress," Suzanne said.

"There is nothing for you to attend to," Amber said. She pointed to the door. "Leave me alone."

Suzanne's expression did not soften, but

she nodded once, then bobbed a curtsy and backed out of the door, pulling it closed behind her.

Amber stood in the middle of the unpolished wooden floor and looked around at the disgraceful furnishings of the horrible room. *My parents sent me to this place,* she said to herself again. She had already acknowledged their lack of compassion toward her but had not imagined that their disregard could extend to this. Her father had said she would be comfortable here. Did he feel that losing her hair equated to losing all respectability?

She ripped off her bonnet and cap, throwing them against the pitched wall and then ran a hand over her gruesome head, not needing to see it to know how disgusting it was. She grasped two of the remaining tufts of hair and pulled at them, not expecting them to come away from her head so easily. She began to cry and grabbed another portion and pulled . . . and pulled . . . and pulled some more, her body racked with sobs as she threw the last of her hair onto the floor around her. She sank to her knees on the braided rug, covered her face with her hands and cried as she had never cried in her life.

It was clear to her now that she had not

been sent simply to Yorkshire; she'd been cast into hell. Was she truly so terrible to deserve such punishment?

# CHAPTER 17

Amber had been lying in bed and staring at the single window of her new bedchamber — though she found the term overstated — for well over an hour the next morning when there was a tapping at the door. She didn't respond and instead pulled the quilt higher to her chin, knowing Suzanne would come in without an invitation.

Suzanne let herself into the room, and Amber turned to face the wall. The bed was large enough to be comfortable, but the pitched roof above her felt confining, especially when compared against the four-poster bed in the London house and the equally grand bed at Hampton Grove; her room there was the size of the entire upper floor of Step Cottage.

Amber listened as Suzanne picked up the discarded clothing from the floor, shaking out each piece. Amber refused to watch Suzanne's movements as she went about the room, folding clothing and pulling out drawers in order to put everything away. The last thing Suzanne did was fetch the chamber pot from beneath Amber's bed, then she left the room as silently as she'd entered, pulling the door closed behind her.

Imagining Suzanne taking the chamber pot to the privy — wherever that might be — reminded Amber of the discussion they'd had before departing for London regarding Suzanne performing tasks meant for housemaids. And she would be leaving.

The thought of Suzanne's departure terrified Amber. Not only would she be responsible for herself, she would be alone in this house — this prison. Though she'd told both Suzanne and Lady Marchent that she could be without a personal maid, now that she had a fuller grasp of the situation and realized there were no other servants here, it was impossible. Perhaps she could find a new maid, but how? She had never hired anyone. How would a new maid react to her situation? Her father had said he was sending correspondence to people in town — who? Would he outfit the house with servants? Even if he did, where would they stay? With only one room for a servant, the cottage could not accommodate the attendants Amber needed. Her father had to know that.

The questions finally drove her out of bed. She picked up the dressing gown from the chair where Suzanne had left it, adjusted the cap on her head without surveying the damage she'd done last night, and tied the gown about her waist. She exited her room and took a fresh look at the house in the daylight.

The plaster looked no better in the day than it had the night before; the swirls of the trowel used to shape it were reflected in the texture, and the dark wooden beams that ran through the ceiling and walls were rustic and stark.

She peeked into the second bedroom, the same size as her own, and found it furnished equal to her own but cluttered with discarded household items and dusty trunks and crates. As it was the only other bedchamber, Lady Marchent would stay there upon her visit in July, but Amber could not imagine her mother tolerating such accommodations. If not for her father's assurance of familiarity with Step Cottage, Amber would think he had never seen it.

The third door, directly across from the top of the stairs, led to a closet, dark and narrow, which ran the width of the top floor with shelves stuffed with all manner of linens and crockery. It smelled of musty dirt. She pulled the door closed without further inspection.

Amber descended the narrow staircase that creaked beneath her feet and found herself in the foyer she had entered the night before. From where she stood she could see into the small parlor, and she ventured further down the hall to an equally confining library. The leather settee and chair that flanked the empty fireplace were dark and heavy, but improved somewhat by the daylight coming through a window set above a small desk. The day was quite bright for what Amber had imagined the North Country would be.

Amber followed the hall to the kitchen where she could smell something baking. She inhaled deeply, her stomach tight with hunger. She stopped just over the threshold and looked around the room. So primitive. So small. There was no water pump for the basin set within the counter that ran along one full side of the room. Beneath the counter were shelves filled with simple dishes and pans, but nothing of the quality at Hampton Grove. Nothing fit for someone of her station. A bricked hearth, blackened from use, sat against the interior wall it shared with the servant's quarters. The impoverished room was barely fit for servants, let alone women of genteel birth.

She must be expected to take her meals beside the fire but could scarce believe it. She wondered if she should insist on returning to London, but Amber would choose this exile above having to withstand her mother should she go back begging for consideration.

An outer door opened, and Amber startled until she saw it was Suzanne returning from outside, chamber pot in her hand. The maid met Amber's eyes quickly but said nothing as she headed toward the corridor that led to the rest of the house. Amber heard Suzanne's steps creak upon the stairs, cross the ceiling, and then come back again.

When Suzanne reentered the kitchen, she went to a washbasin set up on a table against the wall nearest the door and washed her hands. She dried her hands on a dishcloth and moved to the cooking fire where she used a crooked metal hook to pull the heavy iron pan from the coals. With the same hook, she lifted the lid, intensifying the smell of fresh-baked bread, which further tightened Amber's stomach. She was not used to feeling hungry and could not remember ever having wanted food so badly.

"I'm afraid it might be a bit burnt on the

bottom," Suzanne said without looking at Amber still standing in the corner. "I suspect the coals were too hot when I set the pot upon them. I don't often apply myself to baking." She placed the lid on the hearth and then removed two wooden plates from one of the shelves beneath the counter. "Mrs. Dariloo was kind enough to stock some things in the larder." She nodded toward a cupboard set within the back of the house. "There's a smokehouse out back too, and a cellar space that will be good for vegetables once there's a harvest."

Amber didn't want to hear such low details of household management and sat at the table, staring at the steaming bread on the other side of the room. It didn't look burnt to her, and she would scarcely care if it were.

"Don't you agree it was kind of Mrs. Dariloo to be so attentive?" Suzanne asked.

Amber met Suzanne's reprimanding expression and looked away quickly. She did not give a fig for Mrs. Dariloo. Not when so many things of greater consequence were so devastating.

"Your father's man of business did not make contact with them until Monday evening — late in the day," Suzanne continued. "They spent Tuesday pulling off the

Holland covers, sweeping and cleaning everything in sight, and clearing the chimney. Three days' work they managed to do in but one. Come yesterday they filled the larder, removed the shutters, and readied the stables for the horse and gig. Very kind of them, don't you think?"

"My father is their employer," Amber said, feeling defiant as she stared at the wood grain in the table that wasn't even varnished. "They will be well compensated for their service."

The spoon banging against the iron pot made Amber jump, and she looked up at her maid whose mouth was in a tight line. "Is that why you think people do what they do for you? Only because they are paid?"

"Of course," Amber said. "What other reason is there?"

Suzanne narrowed her eyes, then shook her head and went back to slicing the bread still in the pan. "You know nothing about regular people, Miss, and it is perhaps your greatest failing, though certainly not your only one."

"I beg your pardon!" Amber recoiled. "How dare you speak to me like —"

The spoon hit against the pan again, and Amber went quiet for a second time, shocked that Suzanne would act so out of place.

"Miss Sterlington," Suzanne said, facing her, the spoon in one hand and her other hand on her hip. "May I speak plainly?"

"Have you not been plain enough?"

"I spent a great deal of time speaking with Mrs. Dariloo last night. Step Cottage is four miles from the town of Romanby and Northallerton is a mile north of that. The nearest neighbor is no less than three miles from here. You are not going to live the life you lived in London or on your family estate. You will not be surrounded by servants who will cater to your interests and move about silently doing their work as if they have no mind or will of their own. Your father's solicitor asked the Dariloos to find a housekeeper who can come in once a week and —"

Amber gasped and clenched her hands into fists on the tabletop. "Once a *week*?"

"Yes, *once* a week," Suzanne repeated. "Mrs. Dariloo will try to find someone willing to come more often, but you are so far out of town that she feels it is unlikely."

"I shall have a housekeeper who *lives* here," Amber demanded. She pointed to the servant's room. "They shall live in the quarters afforded them and meet my needs on a daily basis."

"I do not believe you will find such an arrangement," Suzanne said. "Romanby is a small village, and Mrs. Dariloo seemed to think that living in the cottage could not compensate for live-in help even should you find someone. People here have families they return to at the end of the day or end of the week. They do not live at the place of their employ when there is but one person and a small lodging to care for."

"My father will pay whatever is required," Amber said. "He will want me to be comfortable."

Suzanne said nothing, which was perhaps the strongest answer she could give. Lord and Lady Marchent had sent their daughter as far from them as possible to live in miserable conditions. Why should Amber think they would listen to her request? She was not only a pariah to society, she was also an embarrassment to her parents. A blemish. An imperfection.

"I shall die here alone," Amber said, unable to breathe for the shock of reality falling about her. "I shall be alone for all but one day of the week?" She shook her head, panicking at the idea as a lump rose in her throat. Was that why her parents had sent her here? Did they expect she would disappear completely; perhaps die as an outcast? Would they prefer such an end?

Suzanne came to sit on the bench across the table from Amber. "Miss," she said in a well-controlled tone. "You are going to live as most people in England do — caring for your own needs and having *purpose* in your days."

Amber raised her eyes. *Purpose?* Why had Suzanne emphasized that word? Until now Amber's purpose had been to maintain her family's reputation, one day serve as an admired wife of an admired man, and seek pleasure and amusement in any way she liked. But that did not seem to be Suzanne's meaning.

Suzanne clasped her hands together upon the table. "There is great satisfaction in accomplishment, Miss."

"I am accomplished," Amber argued.

"Not only in music and embroidery and poetry, but also in creating useful things, in cooking and laundering and —"

Amber grabbed Suzanne's clasped hands. "I cannot launder my own clothing. Surely you are not suggesting such a thing!"

The slight smile on Suzanne's face confused her even more. Had she not truly awoken this morning? Was she still abed, caught within a nightmare?

"Miss," Suzanne said, "nothing will be as it was. That's what I realized as I spoke with Mrs. Dariloo. We've no idea the changes we will have to make to exist in this new place, but there are kind people, this is a good house, and the country is quite beautiful. You shall rest and heal and learn that there is more to life than parties and fashion. I daresay that at the end of it, you shall be better for this trial — a kinder, wiser woman with a better understanding of the world most people of your station never know. We shall make the best of this and find contentment if we can."

The tears rose like a tidal wave and Amber did not wipe them away. "We?" she whispered out loud.

Suzanne looked at the tabletop. "After speaking with Mrs. Dariloo and further considering the circumstance, I have decided to stay until your mother comes. I do not know how you could care for yourself and, in all honesty, I'm not sure there's another maid in the county who could handle your moods, should you manage to find one. I shall need you to appeal to your parents for an amount at least equal to what I was making in London so I may send it to my family. They are dependent upon me, you see, and I cannot choose to stay here without assurance that they will be cared for."

"Oh, Suzanne," Amber said, squeezing her hand. "I shall make sure of it, even if it means I pay you from my own quarterly stipend. Thank you."

"But I can't be expected to run this household myself," Suzanne said. "You will need to take on a new level of self-sufficiency, Miss, and you will need to be kind, not just to me but to everyone."

"I shan't be meeting anyone," Amber said, mindful of the damage beneath her cap. "I wish no one to even know I am here. I want no one to call on me, no one to wonder why I have been sent to this godforsaken place."

"I don't know if that will be possible," Suzanne said.

"It must be," Amber insisted, her thoughts working furiously. "I shall go by a different name; surely everyone my father corresponded with would afford me such protection. Should I have the chance to enter society again, I can't take the risk of anyone knowing what has become of me at this moment."

"Perhaps," Suzanne said, sounding doubtful and perhaps a touch frustrated. "The more important aspect of this conversation is that I need you to agree to be *kind.* I know you can behave with gentleness; you were kind during our travel. If I am to stay I shall need your word that you will treat me, and anyone else we might meet, with respect."

Amber did not feel she had any choice but to agree, even though she wasn't sure she understood the importance. She had treated servants as servants all her life. She had treated merchants and tradesmen as was their due. Still, it was not difficult to reflect on the tantrum she had thrown last night, or the way she had ignored Suzanne this morning to realize what Suzanne meant. Suzanne would stay, but not to coddle Amber or let Amber act within the sphere of their social positions, as had been the case previously. She was uncomfortable with this change but knew that without her agreement Suzanne would not stay. She nodded.

"I need your word," Suzanne prodded, lifting her eyebrows.

"You have it," Amber said, though she would need to determine the exact nature of Suzanne's expectations. It would not do to lose her bearing completely, but she had never felt so dependent on anyone in her entire life and truly feared that without Suzanne's assistance she would not last the month in this wild place.

"Then I shall stay," Suzanne said with a nod.

"Oh, thank you," Amber said, realizing that perhaps how she felt toward her maid right now was what Suzanne meant about being kind and respectful. Suzanne was choosing Amber and Yorkshire over the life she had trained for and the family she had in London — family who wanted *her* there with them while Amber's family wanted nothing to do with her at all. "I understand your sacrifice," she said to further reassure Suzanne.

Suzanne's expression drooped. "I'm not sure that you do, but I am committed. I hope that by the time Lady Marchent joins us we shall have a better sense of your condition and prospects. She can then make arrangements for your continued comfort until you return to London in time for next season."

"It is my greatest wish to return," Amber said breathlessly. Though when they left London she had felt as though she could never return for her embarrassment of the ball, this house being the alternative to a society life had her reconsidering her pessimism. If her hair would repair itself, she could arrange it in curls, perhaps combed forward in the Titus style some women wore with bands and ribbons. So long as a marriage afforded her the comforts she missed already and secured her future, she could accept a far lesser arrangement than she had expected. There were any number of men she had not given a second look to who may consider her once she had recovered.

"Then we are agreed," Suzanne said with a sharp nod. "Jeffery and Cornelius stayed in the grooms' room attached to the stable, though they said it was vastly uncomfortable when I spoke to them this morning. They are even now in town delivering the correspondence your father sent and procuring us a carriage and some animals."

"Animals?"

"Your father requested a horse for the gig, a milking cow, and some chickens. As I said, we are too far from town to rely on the resources available there. There is a path behind the house that leads to the stable, which is not far, and a structure in disrepair that could serve for the chickens. I asked Jeffery to seek out Mr. Dariloo in town and ask him to come see about repairs. It is not too late to start on a garden, I think."

"I can scarce take this in, Suzanne," Amber said, a quiver to her voice as she imagined picking eggs up from nests. Suppose they wanted chicken soup — would they have to kill their own dinner? The thought was repulsive. "How shall we do this ourselves? You are from the city, and I have never imagined doing such things."

Suzanne let out a breath and did not smile. "I do not know how we will make it work," she said with perhaps more honesty than Amber was prepared to hear. "I have little experience with animals, but understanding our need for them outweighs my fear somewhat. We shall simply have to learn what to do through our mistakes, I'm sure, but also our successes. I do believe that we shall come out all right." She looked over her shoulder at the pan of bread beside the cooking grate. "I believe the bread is sufficiently cooled. Why don't you serve each of us a portion while I write a letter to my sisters for Jeffery to deliver upon his return to London?"

Amber stared at the pan, then looked at Suzanne. "You want *me* to serve the bread?"

Suzanne nodded.

"I have never served food from a pot in my life." Amber said. The extent of her "serving" was to take teacakes from one plate and put them on another when entertaining. "I shall do it wrong."

"I am hungry enough to eat it no matter the form it is served in, but if we are to work together, serving bread from a pot is but the simplest of tasks for you to begin with."

Amber looked at the pot, swallowed, and stood up from the table. *London may as well be a thousand miles away,* she thought. She found a fork she hoped would work to lift the slices of bread from the pan. Was it not even a week ago that she'd sat at Mrs. Middleton's table and laughed about hair rinses over strawberry tarts? She had worn a dress that day that was finer than any she would dare wear in this part of the country, especially if she were to be involved in household tasks.

*Today I serve bread for the first time. What can I possibly expect tomorrow to bring?*

# Book Two

*Romanby, North Riding, County of York*

# CHAPTER 18

*July*

Dear Amber,

I regret that I am unable to deliver this letter in person but by the end of my words I hope you will better understand the necessity of the change in plans.

After your removal from London and the eventual settling of the gossip resulting from the events at Carlton House, Lord Sunther continued his attentions to your dear sister, and it is with great joy that I announce to you that they are engaged!

Due to the passing of Lord Sunther's father in the spring, the wedding will not take place until after the proper mourning period has been observed. However, Lord Sunther has invited Darra and myself to join him at his estate near Ipswich so as to become acquainted with his mother, the Dowager Lady Sunther, and the county of his residence.

We are most eager to make these connections and plan to sojourn to Suffolk after a brief return to Hampton Grove where we shall replenish Darra's summer wardrobe. Because of such pressures, we are unable to make the journey north as we had planned. However, we will visit after our time in Suffolk comes to an end — September, I expect.

I see from your letters that you are struggling to find the settlement of mind regarding your circumstance. While I am sympathetic of the difficulties you face, I would counsel you that you shall find greater happiness if you spend less time in regrets and more time gaining acceptance of the situation. Perhaps you shall make better progress in time for our visit in September. Your father tells me that Yorkshire is quite beautiful in autumn.

I shall let you know when I have a more exact date of our arrival. I wish you all that is good during this time of respite.

Your loving mother,
Lady Marchent

Amber read the letter twice before setting it on the desk in the library and looking out the six-paned window. The low-quality glass left the view warped and wavy, but she was not focused on the distorted scene of leaves and flowers in the bloom of summer.

"She is not coming," she said out loud. A part of her wondered at her shock; in the seven weeks she had been at Step Cottage, this was only the second letter she'd received from her mother. Suzanne checked the post once a week when she went to Romanby using the gig the groomsmen had procured before departing for London. Mr. Dariloo had taught Suzanne how to manage the gig, and she was now quite comfortable with it.

When Suzanne had returned with Lady Marchent's letter that afternoon, her eyes had been bright with anticipation. Finally, Amber's mother would be telling them when she would arrive to remedy this circumstance.

Amber had snatched the letter from Suzanne's hand and run into the library so she could read it by the light of the window. But her mother was not coming. Not for two more months. The only reason Amber had survived these last weeks was her increasing belief that once her mother saw the conditions of this place, she would ensure that Amber be removed from it immediately. Tears rose in her eyes as she realized she was not to be rescued after all.

"Miss?" Suzanne asked from the doorway. "When is Lady Marchent to arrive?"

Amber paused before speaking to be sure she didn't take out her frustrations on Suzanne, who had little patience with Amber's sharp tongue. She took a breath, let it out slowly, and then spoke in an even tone. "She is not coming."

She refolded the letter and tucked it into the vertical slot in the desk where the first letter from her mother resided. The other slot was overflowing with the correspondence Suzanne had received since their arrival. While this was only the second letter Amber had received, Suzanne received letters every week from her family, who was increasingly eager for her to return.

Amber turned to look at Suzanne's shocked expression.

"Darra is to marry Lord Sunther. She and my mother were invited to his estate in Suffolk for the summer. She will come in September."

Suzanne blinked as her face paled, triggering Amber's anger that her maid should feel so affected. It was not *Suzanne's* sister marrying ahead of her, and to a man of such high rank. It was not *Suzanne's* mother who had abandoned her a second time.

And yet, though Amber's immediate thoughts were still those of the Rage of the Season she had once been, she did not react with selfishness as easily as she once had. Suzanne had already extended her stay in North Riding far past their original agreement; no wonder she was eager to return to her family.

Amber made the decision she knew to be right, even though she wanted very much to do otherwise. "I shall write to Mr. Peters and request the funds necessary for you to return to London by mail coach. It won't be as comfortable a ride as my father's carriage, but it may be a faster trip as they do not stop for the night." She wanted to say something that might convince Suzanne to stay, through guilt or profit, or any other means necessary, but her intent was not pure, and she could not hide from her own awareness of that truth.

"How will you get on without me?" Suzanne asked after the shock had subsided. She sat on the leather settee facing the cold fireplace. They only kept the kitchen fire day to day, but Amber would likely need to utilize the other hearths when the weather cooled. She would need Suzanne to show her how to properly lay the paper and coal; she had avoided the task as the coal was so dirty.

"I shall manage," Amber said with a shrug as though Suzanne weren't doing the majority of the household tasks. Amber tried to assist in the management of the cottage, but more often than not stormed to her room in frustration and slammed the door to indulge in tears and regrets. Never in her life had she imagined she would need to live like this. *The tantrums will have to stop now,* she told herself. No amount of pouting or fits would get her out of undesirable tasks once she was the only one left to do them. The idea filled her with terror, but she refused to show it on her face. Not that Suzanne would offer sympathy. She did not coddle Amber in the least. "Mrs. Haribow will still come in, so I shall have my cakes." She smiled at her attempted joke — Mrs. Haribow came from Romanby one day a week and baked and cooked while attending to household organization.

Amber and Suzanne would stretch the bounty of Mrs. Haribow's cooking as long into the week as they could, but it never lasted more than a few days as cakes and breads dried out and stew was no longer palatable after it had simmered too long.

They were then resigned to whatever meals their meager skills could create.

From the beginning, Amber had enjoyed more than her share of the small cakes Mrs. Haribow made; they were the closest thing Amber had to the tarts and pastries she was used to in London. When Suzanne pointed out the unfairness of Amber taking more than her share, Amber had spouted a tirade about how her experience with fine food should give her greater right to the cakes.

Suzanne had cut her off and reminded her — again — of her promise to be fair. Amber had stormed out of the room, and the women had not spoken for two days until Amber explained her reasoning to Suzanne in a more teaching manner. She had expected praise at such a selfless discovery, perhaps even agreement, but instead Suzanne had said they would divide cakes equally upon Mrs. Haribow's leaving to insure that each of them had an equal share. Suzanne had kept her cakes in her room since then.

Would another maid be so patient with Amber's outbursts when she encountered some new task she could not accomplish, such as churning cream into butter? The side of the churn had splintered when Amber had kicked it across the yard, necessitating its repair the next time Suzanne went to town. Would another maid be mindful of teaching Amber to do something over and over again, such as how to properly slice potatoes so that they cooked evenly in the pot set over the fire? It was tedious to be so attentive, but crunchy potatoes were unpalatable.

Amber took a breath, determined not to let her fear show in her expression. "I shall be well," she said with false confidence. "Should you want to take a trip to Northallerton tomorrow to take the missive to Mr. Peters or wait until next week?"

Twice Suzanne had gone to town on a Sunday to attend church services. Amber, of course, never went to town. The Dariloos and Mr. Peters had agreed to present her name as Mrs. Chandler, a widow with a poor constitution, and her mother had addressed both her letters to Mrs. Chandler as well. Suzanne presented herself in town and at church as Mrs. Miller, the housekeeper, though Amber still called her Suzanne so as not to let her completely forget her place in this household. It was spread about town that Mrs. Chandler was not inclined for visits, and the few people who had called — the vicar and his wife one time, and two visits from the three-mile-away neighbor obviously hungry for some gossip to share — had been turned away. The ruse had worked thus far, and Amber was confident it would continue.

That she was very much in need to continue the ruse was something she was still attempting to accept. Her eyebrows were gone and her eyelashes were falling out every day. She held onto the hope afforded by a patch of hair that was growing at her crown, a fuzzy spot of red on her otherwise bald head which she always kept covered with a cap. Amber checked the spot of hair every day, but it was the only new growth, which meant that even if it were the beginning of all her hair's return, she was months away from being presentable again.

Suzanne's eyes focused on Amber, and she blinked quickly. "I shall go to town now," she said. "Sally has had some time to refresh, and I . . . I need some fresh air."

Amber did not point out that since Suzanne had already been to town once today, she had enjoyed more than enough fresh air. "You may not reach Northallerton in time to find Mr. Peters still at his office. Wait for tomorrow at least."

Suzanne stood. "I shall stay over with the vicar and his wife. They have offered me accommodation before." She did not meet

Amber's eyes, which had gone wide with fear. She would be at the cottage alone? *All night?* It was bad enough that she was alone for hours on the days Suzanne went to town. But at night?

Suzanne continued, "There is a dance held for the working class, you know, at the Northallerton assembly hall on the third Wednesday of each month, which is tonight. I think I should like to go."

"A dance," Amber repeated. It took all her skills at acting a part not to demand that Suzanne stay. The fact that Suzanne would be leaving for good within the next few days was not far from her thoughts, however. Even if Amber insisted she stay tonight, it would not change their course. Suzanne's opinion had become oddly important to Amber these last weeks, and she did not want the maid's last memory of her mistress to be unpleasant.

"That sounds lovely," Amber said with false sincerity while holding her emotions close. "Certainly, you should go." She turned to the desk and extracted a fresh sheet of paper, her hand shaking slightly. "Let me write the letter to Mr. Peters while you change into something fit for such a party. You can then deliver the note to Mr. Peters in the morning."

She fought the growing panic with every word she wrote, then stood on the porch and watched as Suzanne drove away for the second time that day. She wrapped her arms tightly around herself, though she wasn't cold, and went back into the cottage, locking the door behind her. She checked every window and put the board in the braces across the kitchen door.

Mrs. Haribow had been there two days ago — Amber always kept to her room on those days — and Amber's remaining portion of seed cakes were still wrapped in a cloth. She ate every one of them while she cried about her mother not coming, about Suzanne leaving, and about being alone for the first time in her life. How would she care for herself? How could her mother be so ignorant of how much Amber needed her?

When the world outside the windows grew dark, Amber sat in front of the mirror in her room and touched her newly growing hair, wishing for it to spread. It was her only hope of rescue from a horrific fate of living this way indefinitely. Surely if she could tell her mother she was healing, Mama would accept her back into their world. Surely she could then enjoy a future of comfort and pleasure again. Her time in Yorkshire would be nothing but a horrid memory.

Though she was not inclined to piety, that night Amber knelt beside her bed and prayed that her hair would grow. It was the only solution she could conceive, the only way she could gain entrance back into the life she once had.

Without Suzanne, it fell upon Amber to execute the morning chores. Gathering eggs and emptying the chamber pot had been previously avoided at all costs, but she could not ignore them now. Did the eggs always come from the coop so soiled? Suzanne must wash them before bringing them inside. As for the chamber pot, Amber nearly retched over the task of it, then sat against the side of the smokehouse and screamed at the heavens until she could not breathe and the fingernails of her clenched fists dug half-moons into her palms.

This was her *life.* This was her reality. After indulging in her misery until she felt quite ridiculous, she stood and told herself that if Suzanne could do such things, Amber could as well. She wanted Suzanne to be proud of her, and she *had* to take care of herself now. Fits and anger and avoidance would no longer be her friends.

It was not quite noon when Amber heard

the sound of the gig on the drive in front of the cottage. She was out of the kitchen, where she was attempting to make soda bread by herself for the first time, and down the wide stone steps before Suzanne had pulled to a stop on the lane.

Suzanne turned to look at her from the seat of the gig and then removed a letter from the folds of her skirt. She held it out to Amber who took it, turned it over, and frowned at the name "Mr. Peters" scrawled across the front in her own script. She turned it again to find the wafer unbroken, then looked up at Suzanne in confusion. "You did not take this to Mr. Peters?"

Suzanne shook her head, but looked past Amber when she spoke. "I shall stay until your mother comes in September. I have written to my sisters, explaining the circumstance."

Amber covered her mouth with her hand. Suzanne would stay? She would choose Amber over her family? The knowledge humbled Amber as nothing ever had before. "I am so sorry, Suzanne," she said when the shock had passed. *And so grateful.*

"As am I, Miss," she said, clucking at the horse and flicking the reins to continue to the stable. Amber hurried up the steps, through the kitchen to the back door and down the path leading to the stable so she would be there in time to help Suzanne unhitch the horse, another task she had always avoided. *Were there any tasks I haven't avoided?* she wondered. She felt wretched for being so happy Suzanne was staying, and more committed to do her share of the work about the cottage. Not only to relieve some of the burden, but also in hopes it would show how thankful she was for Suzanne's kindness.

She was staying.

Thanks be to the heavens.

# Chapter 19

*September*

Dearest Amber,

We have had such a lovely time in Suffolk. Lord Sunther is the most gracious of hosts, and we have fairly crossed the county ten times over enjoying the sights and history of the place while meeting friends and relations. The family is very well connected, which has only increased our excitement for this most advantageous match.

Because of our extended visit, I regret to inform you that we will not be able to come to Yorkshire. Your father has told me of the terrible winters there, and I fear that should I come so late in the season — for I could not be in readiness until late October, I am sure — I may very well be forced to stay longer than expected. I cannot take such a risk, not with Darra's wedding plans. The ceremony shall be at Glenhouse — Lord Sunther's estate — in April, when the year of mourning for his father is passed.

You have not spoken of your hair so I shall hope that it is continuing to grow back; I will be glad to see what takes place over the course of the winter. Your father assures me that when he met with Mr. Peters and the caretaker a few weeks ago everything was in order and you are doing well. It did my mother's heart good to hear such a happy report. Mr. Peters is to arrange someone to sew you and your maid some winter clothes. He shall contact you when the arrangements are in place, and your father shall burden the expense.

Mind you remain attentive to your health and do not over-exert yourself. I fear you may lose your fine manners without opportunity to exercise them but am glad the tone of your letters has improved.

I shall let you know when to expect me in the spring. Take care over this winter season and know that I am thinking fondly of you despite our distance from one another.

Your loving mother,
Lady Marchent

This time, Amber hurled the letter into the kitchen fireplace and then railed against her mother in a most unladylike display of fury and emotion for several minutes before turning to look at Suzanne, whose face was flushed, surely as much as Amber's own.

Seeing her maid's distress moved Amber past thoughts regarding her own situation and reminded her that Suzanne, who was quickly becoming the dearest friend Amber had ever had, was also affected by this change of course.

In the past months, Amber had pondered often on her family and their lack of thought and compassion toward her. According to her mother's letter, Amber's father had even come to Northallerton and not even stopped at the cottage to see how she fared. It was humiliating and hurtful to realize how truly abandoned she was by her family.

Suzanne's situation, however, was entirely the opposite. Her family missed her, wanted her back, and asked in every letter they sent when they could expect her return. Her mother's condition had been failing all summer. Consideration of Suzanne's position calmed Amber's rage much sooner than it would have even a month earlier. She had to do right by Suzanne; her own situation could be faced afterward.

"I shall write to Mr. Peters this instant and have him make arrangements for your travel to London." Amber took a breath she hoped would calm her increasing panic. "If you leave for Northallerton in the morning and deliver my letter to Mr. Peters early, we could have the funds secured in time for Monday's mail coach. I do believe travel is lighter this time of year, so perhaps it will not be too overcrowded."

Suzanne did not respond directly, but stood from the table and looked out the window set near the kitchen door. The sky was dreary, but though there had been rain most of the week, today had only presented them with angry skies which had allowed Suzanne to go to town that morning and return without difficulty.

Amber watched Suzanne with a heavy heart. How would she get on without her? After Suzanne's agreement to stay in July, Amber had successfully negotiated additional funds through letters exchanged with the solicitor so that Suzanne could send the same amount to her family that she had before and still have finances here in Yorkshire. Could Amber increase Suzanne's wage even more as an inducement for her to stay? But that only reminded Amber of the comment she had made regarding servants only wanting money. She was embarrassed to have ever believed such a thing. A larger wage had not been Suzanne's motivation, only a way for Amber to attempt to show her gratitude and keep Suzanne's family from suffering.

"I shall go to town," Suzanne said suddenly. Her face was flushed and her jaw was tight, but her eyes reflected sorrow she did not seem inclined to share.

It was not the third Wednesday of the month so there was no dance to use as her excuse, but sometimes Suzanne just needed to be apart. She would take long walks or even ride Sally as an excuse to leave the cottage. Mr. Dariloo had taught Suzanne to ride and being outside — or perhaps just out of Amber's company — seemed to renew her spirits.

"Shall you stay at the vicarage, then?" Amber asked. Suzanne had done so four times since that first overnight in July, either after the Wednesday dance, or when members of the congregation had invited her to dinner. The two women did not talk about Suzanne's friendships with people in town but Amber knew Suzanne had become a part of the community, at least as much as she could living so far out of town and protecting so many secrets about her employer. The irony that Amber's maid could participate in her own class of society, while Amber remained hidden from hers, did not escape her. Suzanne had so much more in her life than Amber did.

"The Clawsons have extended an open invitation to stay with them at any time," Suzanne said. "I shall return tomorrow afternoon."

"Let me write a letter to Mr. Peters before you go, then."

Amber was grateful she had applied herself better to the tasks about the cottage. She could bake soda bread on her own now, and make all manner of roasted vegetables and soups. She could care for the chickens and horse. She still avoided the milk cow as it was filthy, and Suzanne did not mind caring for that animal as much. They hired out the laundry to a washerwoman in Romanby, but Amber could make beds, place fires, sweep floors, clean pots, and fetch water. She was more assured than before of her ability to care for herself, but her heart was heavy at the prospect, and heavier still at the thought of how eager Suzanne must be to leave.

Amber wrote the letter to Mr. Peters and then helped hitch Sally to the gig. She did not remain to watch Suzanne disappear down the lane and instead returned inside and exchanged the lacey mobcap she wore at all times for the knitted cap Suzanne had made her the week before. Thus far Amber had only worn the knitted cap at night as it was not the least bit attractive, but now she was alone and there was no reason not to enjoy her own comfort. The cap fit tightly against Amber's head and helped keep her warm, something that was becoming increasingly difficult as she was almost without any hair at all and the season was sharply cooling.

The new growth of hair that had given her so much hope in July had fallen away in August. There were some fuzzy wisps on the left side of her head and her right eyebrow was nearly grown back, but she was not inclined to give either development much credibility. Rather than hoping for deliverance from her affliction, she found herself feeling the need to find a way to accept it. She had hoped that after her mother's visit she could return to Hampton Grove and find a place within her family again. It was difficult to accept that would not be the case. Would it ever be?

Amber spent the evening beside the kitchen fire reading *A Midsummer's Night Dream* — the library was well stocked with several familiar collections — and she was slowly making her way through literature she had once only attended as a topic of conversation. Now she read them from a different perspective of wanting to better understand their contents, context, and acclaim.

She tried not to think of the howling winds outside the window or how she would cope when winter would set in and the weather became more severe. She would have to find a way to get supplies from town. Suzanne interacted with Mr. Dariloo when he made his visits — Amber had not seen him since her arrival — and she did not know if he would be willing to fetch foodstuffs and supplies. Perhaps she would have to hire a servant, but how could she expect anyone to replace Suzanne?

When she finally took a candle to her room and curled up beneath the layers of quilts on her bed, she allowed herself to feel the day's despair. Why had her father not stopped at the cottage when he'd come to Northallerton? He would have passed the road leading to Step Cottage on both his arrival and departure, but he had not stopped in at all? What had she done to deserve such spurning from her family? How would she cope without Suzanne?

Suzanne returned to the cottage late the next afternoon just as Amber was placing the pot of water, chicken bones tied in cheesecloth, and potatoes in the coals for soup. Amber looked up from the hearth to see Suzanne set the unopened letter addressed to Mr. Peters on the table.

"Suzanne?" Amber said with regret even as warmth filled her chest. She stood and wiped her hands on her apron. She'd sewn it herself a few weeks earlier so as to protect her dresses, adding a flounce to the bottom. Though it was completely impracticable to have done so, the weight of the flounce helped the fabric lay better and gave it a feminine touch. "You should return to London. You have already stayed too long."

"I have made my decision," Suzanne said, moving to the fire to stare into the flames and hold her hands to the heat.

Amber watched her for several moments, her heart heavy for so many reasons, some of which made her feel horribly selfish and unkind. "But your mother . . ."

"Mama passed on three weeks ago, Miss." Suzanne said it so quietly that Amber nearly did not hear it over the crackling of the fire.

"What?" she asked, certain she had misheard.

Suzanne glanced at her quickly, then stepped closer to the fire. "She was very ill when I left," she said, unable to hide the regret in her tone. "And, as you know, my sisters had informed me of her increasing frailness throughout the summer. It was not as much of a surprise as it might have been. She passed away peacefully with my sisters and their families around her, for that I'm grateful. By the time I received word, she was already interred."

"Three weeks ago?" *And you did not tell me?* Amber added in her mind. While she awaited Suzanne's confirmation, she was reminded of an evening when Suzanne had returned from town complaining of a headache. She had taken the rest of the evening in her room and remained out of sorts for a few days following. Amber had feared she was ill, but Suzanne stated she was simply not sleeping well and in time returned to her usual self, which was naturally subdued. Though they worked side-by-side and Amber dared feel they shared genuine care for one another, they had not lost all distinction of rank. Suzanne did not confide in her mistress.

"I did not tell you for fear you would expect me to stay now that Mama's care was not a reason to return." She began removing the pins securing her bonnet. In the process she met Amber's eyes. "Or perhaps some part of me knew that Lady Marchent would not come and I feared for you to be alone."

"I am not to be your priority any longer," Amber said with a lump in her throat as Suzanne moved to hang the bonnet on one of the pegs near the door. "I am so sorry you were not there to say good-bye to your mother. If not for me you would have been."

"I am not holding blame toward you for it," Suzanne said, smoothing her hair away from her face. "And I have not regretted staying, Miss."

Amber was surprised to hear it. How could Suzanne *not* regret it? They both had to work so contrary to their inclinations just to have the smallest degree of comfort, and a great deal of their time was centered on the most base and repulsive necessities of self-sufficiency. However, Suzanne's peace of mind stirred Amber's awareness of the increasing peace she felt as well. She rarely raged, out loud or in her mind, over the unfairness of her situation or the primitive conditions of the cottage. She no longer pined so strongly for society and fine things. But she had never considered that Suzanne's feelings may have changed, and she did not entirely trust the possibility as it was exactly what Amber would want to hear.

"I shall never be able to adequately thank you for all you've done," Amber said. "But I renew my sentiment that you should return to your family. You have done more for me than anyone else in my life ever would." She wiped at her eyes and turned to the fireplace so Suzanne would not see her tears. She turned the pot using the metal hook, embarrassed to have shared such feeling, though a part of her was relieved to be so honest.

"Miss," Suzanne said softly, causing Amber to turn toward her again. "I have considered all aspects of my circumstance. I have heard tell of the harsh winter we are to expect in this place and had already determined that should Lady Marchent not keep her word regarding her visit, that perhaps God would be telling me I was better suited in the county of Yorkshire than in London." She gave a small smile. "I shall stay until your future is settled."

After several seconds of silence, which Amber used to contain her emotions, she cleared her throat. "Thank you," she whispered.

Suzanne nodded and folded back the sleeves of her dress, preparing to work anew upon the life they had made for themselves.

Amber went about finishing the preparations for dinner. She had saved the eggs from yesterday so as to attempt a Yorkshire pudding. She had tried twice before and failed but hoped tonight would result in success.

After a few minutes had passed, she spoke again. "I wonder if we could have Mr. Dariloo bring someone to move the trunks and things from the other upstairs bedroom and put them in the servant's quarters. If you shall be staying the winter, you need better accommodation and the upper floors stay quite warm."

"You would allow me to take the second bedchamber?" Suzanne said, her eyes wide at the prospect.

"I would insist upon it," Amber said, glad the idea met with Suzanne's favor and did not make her uncomfortable. "I believe we shall both be in need of every comfort possible these next months. I would be honored if you would take the other room."

"If that is the case," Suzanne said, smiling herself, "I would be honored to do so."

"Thank you for staying with me," Amber said again, without looking up. The sincerity of her words made her feel both vulnerable and comfortable, as though she'd discovered something new that felt oddly familiar.

Suzanne looked at her for quite some time before Amber looked away, embarrassed though she could not determine exactly why. Suzanne was quiet for a moment before she answered in an equally reverent tone, "You're very welcome . . . Amber."

# Chapter 20

Thomas had been overseeing the workers in the apple orchards on the east end of what he hoped would soon be his own lands when the rain drove them from the field. Despite feeling frustrated with losing half a day of work, he was pleased with the overall harvest thus far and had talked himself out of a poor mood by the time he reached the back entrance of Peakview Manor, the family estate located nearly equidistant between Northallerton and Romanby where he resided with his brother, Albert, and Albert's growing family. Since Thomas's return from London in July he had immersed himself in the management of his land and had never found more contentment in all his days.

Thomas hung his oilskin coat on the hook inside the doorway and then removed his working boots, placing them on the woven mat left beside the door. Lady Fielding had pointed out the mud and wet he brought in from the fields on more than one occasion, and he was determined not to give her more cause to complain against him.

He'd left his top boots by the door that morning and began to pull on the right boot before his foot encountered something inside the leather. He extracted his foot quickly, then turned the boot upside down, smiling when a far smaller shoe fell to the stone floor. He picked up the small black lace-up shoe, which most certainly belonged to his niece, then turned his attention to the other boot, which contained a similar treasure.

Thomas had always found Lizabeth endearing but had increased the time he spent with her in hopes of quieting some of her more *spirited* moods that had begun when her little brother — the next Lord Fielding — had been born.

The Dowager Lady Fielding, Thomas's mother, had assured the other adults that it was a normal phase when a new baby usurped the position of the reigning youngest child in a household, but suggested privately to Thomas that perhaps a bit more attention toward Lizabeth would help remind her she had not been replaced. It was not a difficult task to fulfill, and Thomas enjoyed seeking out his young niece on the evenings he came in before she'd been put to bed. He would indulge her with whatever game or story or adventure she requested of him, and he felt his own cares soften in response. Apparently, today, she had escaped her nursemaid long enough to start their games early. Lizabeth was already showing a disposition more similar to her father than her mother, something which concerned Lady Fielding quite a lot.

After pulling on his shoe-free boots, Thomas took the dainty shoes and made the rounds to the drawing rooms and breakfast room on the main floor. Lady Fielding had fresh flowers placed in the rooms twice a week, and if Thomas was careful, he could remove a bloom or two from each arrangement unnoticed.

Once he had adequately gathered his ammunition, he went into the study long enough to write a note, which he then took with him to the third level, where the nursery was located. Lizabeth had reading time following luncheon each day, and although he feared he would get into trouble for interrupting, he arranged the shoes, now filled with chrysanthemums and rosebuds, in front of the door, then placed the note in front of the display. He knocked quickly, then ran several feet down the hall to a recessed window where he pulled himself tight against the wall so as not to be seen.

The door opened, and he bit his lip to keep from laughing at Lizabeth's exclamation of delight. "What does it say?" she asked, surely addressing her nanny regarding the note.

"It says that if you are a good girl, your uncle shall join you for tea this afternoon."

More squeals and hand clapping and then a reminder from the nursemaid that she would have to finish her lessons. Pray, what type of lessons was a three-year-old child to learn? The door closed, and Thomas removed himself from his hiding place, quite pleased with his quick answer to her game and wondering how she had gotten away from her attendant long enough to hide her shoes in the first place. A scamp indeed. Only time would tell if her baby brother inherited his father's free-spirited disposition. Whatever would Lady Fielding do if he had?

As Thomas made his way to the family rooms on the second level, his mind moved from shoe bouquets to how he would spend his afternoon. Coming in from the fields early allowed him more time to work on organizing the estate records.

After Thomas's return from London, he had taken upon himself the task of gathering the documents necessary for the transfer of land from the Fielding estate holdings to Thomas himself. Albert, busy with matters of his own, hadn't attended to it over the summer, so Thomas had undertaken the task of setting in order nearly two hundred years' worth of ledgers and documents which had been stored in numerous places throughout the manor.

When Thomas entered the library, Albert was at the desk looking over some papers with a quizzing glass held to his eye. As the second son, Albert had not been raised to take over for their father and never been studious toward the requirements of *being* Lord Fielding. Only when their older brother, Charles, died following a debilitating bout of pneumonia did anyone consider whether or not Albert was capable of the position. Only two years later their father had passed too, giving Albert the title and the responsibility at the age of twenty-four — the age Thomas was now.

Albert had been sent immediately to London for a wife — it was their mother's belief that only marriage would settle his mind to his responsibility. Despite the mourning period, Albert married Miss Diane Broadbank in a private ceremony and set to work getting an heir of his own, which had been accomplished this summer. He'd done what was expected of him, but had been a bit of a bear those first years. Thomas had been at Oxford during that time but heard of his brother's struggles through correspondence from their mother, who worried greatly. However, in the end her wisdom had been proven. Albert had risen to his position and performed his responsibilities admirably.

Albert looked up from the ledgers and quickly hid the quizzing glass. Thomas did not comment on it, as he knew Albert did not want to draw attention to the fact he could not properly see the figures without his instrument.

"Did our fine weather drive you indoors?" Albert asked with a smile, seemingly pleased at the interruption.

"Much to my displeasure," Thomas said, looking out the large window behind his brother's head at the expansive grounds where the trees were just beginning to change color. "If I could have three fine days together I could finish the harvest."

"Three fine days together?" Albert repeated. "Does such a thing happen in England this time of year?"

Thomas smiled. "One can certainly hope, can he not?" He looked toward the crates of files, loose papers, and ledgers stacked in one corner. They had gathered records from all over the house and stored them here for Thomas to attend to as he could. They could easily have set the task to Albert's secretary, but both men were of a mind to have a better understanding of the estate and this proved to be a good way to become educated. "At least there is plenty to occupy me indoors."

"You say that with such — dare I say it? — affection."

Thomas smiled. "Despite how it troubles you to hear it, I find establishing order quite satisfying. Each of the Barons had a different system — or no system at all — and putting the records together will create a far more manageable system for future use. I find it an exciting prospect."

"You are a queer man," Albert said with an exaggerated expression of concern.

"Better a queer man than a blind one."

Albert laughed, and they returned insults and disparagements while Thomas chose which crate of papers to start with.

"Enough of that," Thomas said after Albert called him a bird-witted nincompoop. "Now you're just repeating yourself. Have you not reports to go over?" He waved toward the papers in front of Albert, then turned his back and ignored his brother's mumbling. It was all in good fun, as it had always been between them.

Thomas pulled a crate in front of one of the leather chairs near the fire and picked up the stack of papers resting on top. It took nearly an hour to sort the papers into time periods, then he took one portion at a time to a set of shelves in the back of the library that they had cleared for the purpose of organizing the records. He tried not to be discouraged by the fact that despite the hours of sorting he had already completed, he had yet to find two of the documents necessary for the transfer of title he'd hoped would have been finalized by now. He and Albert were running their lands separately, even if the legalities were not yet in place. Still, Thomas wanted a deed of his own. He wanted to feel like his own man.

Thomas finished the first crate and moved onto the next.

"Did you hear me, brother?"

Thomas broke away from his focus on the papers and looked at his brother. "Forgive my distraction," he said. "Do repeat yourself."

"I asked if you ought not make your way

to the Dower House about now."

"I'm sure I have no reason to call today," Thomas said, returning his attention to the paperwork. He visited with his mother a few times every week, and she joined them at Peakview for dinner more nights than not. "I had planned to be in the fields until sunset, though now I have a date to take tea with The Honourable Lizabeth Richards. I shan't live it down if I were to stand her up."

"I told you not an hour ago that Mama wanted you to visit *her* for tea this afternoon, and you nodded your agreement," Albert said with a laugh.

"I did?" Thomas had a tendency to become so absorbed in his tasks that he was all but unreachable, so it was not beyond belief that Albert was right. Thomas enjoyed his mother's company but hated interrupting his work. It could be weeks before he would have the free time again, and they were running out of season to finish the harvest, till the ground, and plant the new trees in the central portion to replace those older trees that had not produced well this year.

"Yes," Albert said with a laugh. "You are to present yourself at three o'clock. I shall have Lizabeth readied to accompany you."

He stood and moved to the bellpull that would call a footman.

Thomas lifted the timepiece pinned inside his vest, then jumped to his feet. "It is nearly a quarter to three now."

Albert smiled. "Then you should get to it."

Thomas turned immediately, ever the attentive son, then stilled as he remembered the pattern of invitations his mother had created since his return from London. She had been quite disappointed that he had come home without an engagement and instantly set herself about the task of remedying the circumstance. She had instructed him to find a woman of his equal in London, and that he had not done so seemed to have convinced his mother he should have no requirements at all in a wife.

The fact that he worked fourteen hours a day had certainly complicated her efforts to find him a match, but she had not been dissuaded. There could be no doubt that he would not be the only person joining her for tea today.

# CHAPTER 21

Thomas turned back to Albert. "Who might be attending this tea in addition to myself and Lizabeth?"

"However should I know?" Albert said, leaning back in his chair with his hands behind his head and grinning. Then he nodded toward the window that overlooked the lane leading to the Dower House.

Thomas moved to the window in time to see a familiar barouche traveling through the pounding rain toward his mother's lodging. A footman came into the library and received Albert's instruction regarding the young Miss Richards while Thomas continued to observe the scene beyond the window with resigned disappointment. "So I am to be seated between the adolescent daughters of Mr. and Mrs. Kemmer, then?"

"Are you not *delighted* to be in such fine company?" Albert said with mock surprise.

"The eldest is not yet sixteen years of age.

I would feel as though I were robbing the schoolroom."

"Many men before you have done so without complaint."

Thomas narrowed his eyes toward his brother. "Not every man wants a silly girl as a wife, Albert."

Albert shrugged, good-naturedly. Lady Fielding had only been seventeen when they said their vows. "I daresay good breeding and a willingness to please her husband and position should be of far more account. As they age, women become more independent, you know, and that is a fearsome trait."

"Such an argument does in no way dissuade me from my own interests in the type of woman I desire." Despite himself he heard the sound of Miss Sterlington's voice in his head and shook it away. A woman of Miss Sterlington's airs and disposition was certainly *not* the type of connection he wanted. Very far from the mark, in fact. Since returning to Yorkshire, he was more convinced than ever that he needed a woman of practicality and even temperament who would not mind being a gentleman farmer's wife. He was willing to wait as long as it took to find such a woman and therefore did not share his mother's concern for his continuing state of bachelorhood.

"Ah, yes, you are looking for an intellectual," Albert said.

"A woman I can converse with, yes, but who does not mind that I shall be my own man or bring mud in on my boots." A woman, he sometimes feared, who did not exist. He had become reacquainted with a number of women in Yorkshire in recent months but found not a single one of them interesting enough to pursue. Perhaps what he called patience was actually an unwillingness to admit defeat.

"Good grief," Albert said, lifting his eyebrows as though alarmed. "I shan't expect you to find any woman of breeding who will tolerate muddy boots. And did not both of the Kemmer daughters attend school in Bath? I believe the only young women Mother has attempted to catch you with are women of education. She understands your interests."

Thomas did not answer. How could he adequately explain that while equanimity of mind was certainly a priority, he *also* wanted admiration and, he admitted, desire. What a selfish man he was to want for so much, and yet he could not seem to help himself.

He had watched the married couples of his community when he was about town or in church. It was easy to see the difference between those partnered through arrangement, and those who had a true affinity for one another. Now and then he would catch a shared look of such depth and contentment that his own heart would tighten in longing for it. Was it only a matter of chance for such feelings to develop between a husband and wife? Or had they married for love and then thrived within it? He felt sure it was the latter, and therefore did not want to give up the hope of finding a woman who would meet his very particular interests. What he did not want was to disregard his hopes and find himself saddled to a woman he could not tolerate. Life was far too long for such an unhappy arrangement if a man expected to keep his vows, which Thomas did.

"It surely does not do to point out that those requirements of yours are without fulfillment," Albert said, breaking into Thomas's thoughts. "Which then brings us to consideration as to whether or not your expectations are as valid as you have made them out to be."

The two men stood with hands clasped behind their backs as they watched the carriage stop outside their mother's house. The groom jumped down from the seat and opened an umbrella, which he held over the carriage door, allowing the two Misses Kemmers to step out. One was head to toe in pink while the other was equally arrayed in purple. Both colors looked too bright set against the gray landscape surrounding them and seemed to flaunt the girls' age and immaturity. In addition, their choice in dress did not flatter their eyes or figure anywhere near the way Miss Sterlington's clothing had always flattered her person.

Albert's tone continued with a serious air. "There is great peace that comes from establishing a proper marriage, Thomas. I do not mean to make light of your preferences; you have always been a studious and attentive fellow who puts much thought into your direction, which is a credit to your character. But as your land will require your attention, if you are to secure the future you often talk about, I would advise with all seriousness that having a wife in place to support your efforts and create for you a legacy more precious than land will be of greater comfort and relief than you can imagine."

Thomas looked at his brother in surprise. It was quite out of character for Albert to wax so sentimental. "I daresay you are more satisfied with matrimony than I have ever supposed before," he said without attempting to cover his doubt. "Did you not feel it a heavy obligation at the time you and Diane made your vows?"

Albert inclined his head. "I did not take much care to conceal such feelings, did I?" He paused before he continued in the same sentimental tone. "When Father passed so unexpectedly and I found myself burdened with the responsibility of his title, I viewed marriage as a decidedly limiting aspect of my future. I had expected several more years before I had to rise to the level of duty Charles had left me, and I resented the quick end to my youth. No one could accuse me of being a happy groom upon the day of my nuptials." His paused for a breath before continuing. "Rather than it being such a limiting burden, I have, instead, found marriage to be a great comfort, brother. I am the first to admit there is an air of flippancy about Lady Fielding at times, and she does care for gossip far more than my patience can stand, but you do not hear the way she encourages me, or her confidence in my ability to be the man circumstance has determined me to be. I have come to believe with every part of my heart and mind that a good wife can truly make for a better man, to say nothing of holding a child in your arms that only she could give."

He stared out the window a few more moments, then seemed to remember himself and smiled in his familiar, jovial way. He slapped Thomas on the back and then nodded toward their mother's cottage. "Well, get on with it, man. They shan't grow in age or intellect quickly enough that delaying their acquaintance will be of any benefit — especially as our mother is surely counting the minutes you are late so as to flog you with your lack of manners. I shall have Lizabeth wait for you in the foyer as soon as she is readied. I am sure she will consider a trip to her grandmother's house a grand adventure."

Thomas parted company with Albert and hurried to his bedchamber where he traded out his working coat for a finer cut in charcoal gray. For an instant he thought of the coat he had given to Miss Sterlington nearly four months ago and wondered what had become of it. Thinking of the coat naturally led his thoughts to Miss Sterlington herself. Was she healed? Would she return to London next season and renew her flirtations with the bucks so entranced by her? He shook his head to rid himself of thoughts that did him no good, and instead focused on improving the shape of his cravat. To his great relief, thoughts of Miss Sterlington were becoming easier to push away. In time he hoped to forget about her completely.

He hurried toward the foyer where he bowed elaborately to Lizabeth, who wore a small blue cloak tied beneath her chin while her brown eyes sparkled with excitement. Lady Fielding stood beside her, an expression that seemed a mixture of amusement and concern.

As Thomas straightened from his bow, he put out his hand to Lizabeth, palm up. "It is my pleasure to serve as your escort to the Dower House this afternoon, Miss Richards. Shall you want to walk or ride?"

"Ride!" Lizabeth shouted, jumping up and down which caused her honey curls to bounce.

"She shall walk, Thomas," Lady Fielding amended.

Thomas gave his sister-in-law a surprised look. "In the mud?" he questioned. He was never quite sure how to best get on with his sister-in-law, but after hearing Albert's compliments, he felt a bit softened toward her. "I shall of course do exactly as you say, but I fear for the state of the poor girl's shoes."

Lady Fielding looked toward the window, frowned, and seemed to realize the wisdom of Thomas's words. "Very well, but please help her be well behaved."

"Of course," Thomas said with a wide smile that elicited a decidedly distrustful narrowing of Lady Fielding's eyes.

He turned to his niece, put his hands on his knees and squatted, which was all the invitation she needed to scamper onto his back.

Lady Fielding made a disapproving comment, but Thomas could not hear it for the squealing in his ear as he secured Lizabeth's hands around his neck and hooked his elbows behind her knees as he stood.

"To the castle!" he exclaimed before galloping toward the door, which an amused footman opened for them at precisely the right moment. "And to the Kemmer girls who are far more suited in age for your company, Lizabeth, than mine."

# Chapter 22

*December*

Dear Darra,

I woke this morning and realized it was your birthday. I can hardly believe it has been a year since the cook made you those lovely spiced flat cakes for breakfast. Then we went to town where you bought that hat with the blue bow — do you remember?

I have taken much inventory of myself these last months as I have been so far away from everyone I love, and I have come to regret deeply my treatment of you. You accused me of giving no consideration of your feelings once we arrived in London, and I realize now how true that was. I was of one mind when we embarked upon our season: that of enjoying myself regardless of the cost it might have to anyone else. I did not have the character necessary to realize what that must have felt like for you. I am especially sorry for my behavior regarding Lord Sunther after I reentered society. I think of that evening at Carlton House and feel humiliation that has nothing to do with anyone's behavior but my own. I knew he had high regard for you, but I let my competitive spirit cast aside sisterly affection.

Because of the understanding I have discovered, I want you to know that I hold no ill will regarding removing my hairpiece. I am resigned to the result of that evening on my part, and have come to bear this form of banishment — I cannot find a better term — as due for my behavior, but I have been increasingly uneasy with the strain that continues to exist between us as sisters.

It is my dearest wish that you will feel of my love, which has not diminished toward you, and that you will be able to forgive me for my poor behavior, which caused you so much pain.

I would also like to attend your wedding if you will have me. I will do all I can to appear as would be expected. I am truly happy for your future and want very much to be a witness of your vows.

I have already requested it of Mama, but she has not responded. If it is better that I not attend, I will understand. I in no way want to take away from your wedding day, only to share in it as we always dreamed we would.

I wish you every happiness, dear sister, and pray you will extend my love to the rest of our family. May you all have a Happy Christmas.

With all love and felicity,
Amber Marie Sterlington

"I best be going," Suzanne said from the doorway of the library as Amber pressed her stamp into the quickly cooling wax used to seal the letter. "Pray that the roads will allow me to get back tomorrow."

"I'm finished," Amber said, standing from the desk. She fanned the letter as she crossed the room to ensure the wax was properly set, then handed it to Suzanne already dressed in her coat, shawls, and cape.

It had become agonizingly cold and travel to town had become precarious, which had Suzanne attempting it less and less often and Mrs. Haribow coming hardly at all. But there were several matters they could no longer put off, and so Suzanne had watched the skies carefully and deemed today the time to go to town to procure some essentials, such as tea and salt and sugar, and some luxuries, like cinnamon. They also needed a new broom — Amber had left the prior one on the hearth where the bristles had burned. As winter had become reality, the women better understood the need to have enough stores to take them through the weeks, and possibly months, when the roads might be impassable.

"Come back only when the way is safe. If it is a few days' time, I will manage well enough," Amber said, though she hated the idea of being alone for an extended period of time. Still, it had been two full weeks since Suzanne had last gone to town, and the trip could not be put off much longer.

Suzanne nodded. "I shall try my best to return quickly."

"I know you will," Amber said, then shooed her toward the door. She did not want Suzanne's concern for her to keep her any longer in case the weather turned, as it could do quite quickly. They walked to the stable together, and Amber helped Suzanne into the gig, a difficult task when she was so encumbered with petticoats and layers of clothing meant to keep off the chill. They had had a few bouts of snow already —

something rarely seen in Somerset where Amber grew up. It had melted quickly each time, but left enough cold and mud behind to keep things unpleasant.

Suzanne set Sally to move with a flick of the reins, and Amber hurried back to the cottage. She thought of the letter on its way to the post and wondered how Darra would receive it. Amber had not heard from her sister in all the months she'd been at the cottage and feared her letter would invite a reply full of anger and resentment that would burn into Amber's heart. Even if that were the result, however, Amber did not feel comfortable allowing their relationship to remain as it was now that she better realized her part in the circumstances.

Perhaps if Darra wrote back with kindness Amber would share the details of some of the activities that now filled her time. Her sister would scarce believe such tales, but rather than feeling ashamed at the prospect, Amber smiled to think of Darra's reaction. How she hoped to one day be restored to the comfort they had once shared. She vowed not to see such a connection as a small thing again.

# CHAPTER 23

The day was cold but the skies were a brilliant Yorkshire blue when Thomas turned Farthing up the lane that led to Step Cottage — as it had been referenced by his brother's solicitor, Mr. Llewelyn. The pursuit of the records, specifically a bill of sale for a sixty-acre piece along the riverfront, had led him to what was once the caretaker's house of the parcel.

It had been some years since the cottage had functioned as such, Mr. Llewelyn had said, but as Thomas had looked everywhere else for the document, it was his last hope. If the document were not produced as proof of the Fielding estate's ownership, they would have to take secondary documentation to the magistrate and attempt to have it rectified that way. Which could take months. It was nearing the end of the year, and Thomas was still not the legal owner of the lands he worked. If they could find the document, the end of this transfer would be in sight.

In preparation for this journey, he had asked after the cottage's occupant, Mrs. Chandler, hoping to learn what to expect when he arrived. Based on the general feelings around town toward her — that she was isolated, eccentric, and not even accepting of clergy — he feared he was being too optimistic to hope she would allow him access to her library. Or perhaps desperate was a better description of what he was feeling.

Lady Fielding felt he should send a letter asking for audience, but with the weather so unpredictable he feared he could be delayed a week or more awaiting her response. Mrs. Chandler's housekeeper, Mrs. Miller, came to town only once a week, or so the vicar had told him. He hoped Mrs. Chandler would be less inclined to turn him away if he were upon her doorstep, even if he were uncomfortable with the demanding nature of the visit.

He brought Farthing — his horse named by Lizabeth — to a stop at the bottom of the steps and jumped down before tying her to a post. He knocked three times on the heavy wood door before stepping back and waiting for it to be answered. It wasn't an impressive cottage from any perspective, but he could see it was solid and there was smoke rising from the chimney. In addition to hoping Mrs. Chandler would let him in, he hoped it was warm. He was quite chilled from his ride despite today being the best day to travel these last two weeks.

He waited some time before stepping forward and knocking a second time. When more time passed and no one answered his knock, he found himself in quite a quandary.

Because of the distance from town and the unreliable nature of traveling so far this time of year, never mind the urgency he felt about the business that had brought him there in the first place, he was not much inclined to simply come back another day.

Thomas stepped around the side of the cottage. Perhaps Mrs. Miller was out back, though the temperature was such that he did not imagine she would be lounging about. He stepped through some of the sodden patches of brown grass around the edge of the house, but eventually found himself behind the cottage. There was a privy, a smokehouse, a coalshed, and what looked like a cellar entrance all close to the kitchen door.

He knocked again. Perhaps this woman whispered about in town was deaf and had not heard his knocks from the front of the house. Rumor had it that she was a cripple too, but certainly her housekeeper wasn't.

The back door was not answered either. What poor luck on his part if both occupants had gone to town. If they were gone, however, could he let himself inside to look around on his own? As soon as he thought it, he rejected the idea. His morality would not allow such a trespass despite how much his lack of patience encouraged it.

He spied a path leading away from the cottage and decided to follow it. Perhaps there was another outbuilding where the residents of the cottage were occupied. The further he moved from the house, however, the more discouraged he felt. Why could not one part of this transfer be easy? Just one?

# Chapter 24

The footsteps retreated but Amber did not relax one whit until they had disappeared completely. She did not think she had ever been so terrified as when this unwelcome guest had pounded on the door just two hours after Suzanne had left for town.

She had been in the library sketching out a pattern for a new shift she wanted to attempt to make from fabric Suzanne would be purchasing in town when the knock came. A man, based on the heaviness of his knock. Amber had immediately run for the kitchen and sat in the corner near the washstand where she could pull her knees to her chest and know she would be unseen through any window or door.

In all the months of living in Step Cottage no one had come when Suzanne was gone, and Amber could barely breathe until after she heard him leave — toward the stables, she thought. Did that mean he would come back to the house?

Once Amber was sure he was gone, for the moment at least, she crawled to the kitchen door and lifted the wooden plank into the braces on either side to secure it, then hurried to the front door and turned the lock before going about the house and pulling all the curtains closed.

Despite her overwhelming fear, there was an edge of excitement to the situation as well.

"Don't be a goose," she chided herself as returned to the kitchen. Suzanne would be laughing if she could see Amber's actions and read her silly thoughts.

She pulled back the curtain over the washbasin just a bit to survey the yard, then squealed when the long legs of a man came into view. She dropped the curtain and resumed her position in the corner with her hands over her mouth, torn between laughing at herself and crying in fear. What if he were a highwayman come to murder her? And yet why would anyone come to Step Cottage for such a thing; there were plenty of people to murder not so far from the road.

Perhaps he was a bandit, hiding from the law! She nearly screamed again when there was another knock at the door beside her, sending her heart racing faster than she thought possible.

"Madam?" a man's voice called. "I have seen that your carriage and horse are not in the stable, which means your housekeeper must have gone to town today. Please forgive me for such an inopportune visit, but it truly is of great importance that I speak with you. I am in need of your assistance with a matter of business."

Amber didn't move, but clearly this man was not a highwayman or a bandit; he had all the high tones of genteel breeding. The realization only gave her a modest degree of comfort. He was still a stranger — a *male* stranger no less — and she was still alone.

Yet if his assertions were correct, he needed her help and that made her curious at the very least. It had been a long time since she had conversed with anyone but Suzanne, let alone a *man.* In London, Amber had simpered and flattered her way through so many conversations with so many men; could she not talk with this one man now when he was in need of her assistance? The idea made her heart flutter. She was quick to remember that she was not Amber Sterlington, Rage of the Season. She was exiled and different in every way. But then, she did not need to flatter this man. She simply needed to *talk* to him. Could she do it?

"Madam," he said again, his tone sounding less hopeful. "I saw the curtain move. I have come all the way from Romanby to look into your book room and can promise that if I could obtain access for just a short while I shan't bother you again."

*Book room?* There was a book room at Hampton Grove where her father's bailiff worked on the ledgers and kept documents associated with the estate. Here at the cottage, she assumed Mr. Dariloo kept those records at his own house, though she had seen past documents in the library from a time when the records were kept in residence. This had once been a caretaker's house according to Mr. Dariloo, and the records had remained even when the cottage and connecting lands had been sold to Amber's father.

Her neck was hot and her heart still racing when she made the momentous decision to respond to the gentleman outside. There was a door between them, and a braced one at that, so there was no fear he would see her. With such protections in place, she simply could not resist the temptation.

She lowered her hands from her mouth

and moved on her hands and knees to the doorway. "What need have you for the items of the book room, sir?"

He was quiet for several seconds before he responded. "I understand that this house was once part of an estate that was divided out over time and sold. My father purchased one of those parcels, and I am seeking to get the legalities properly settled. I'm looking for a sale agreement and have looked everywhere in the county that might possibly have a copy except this place."

Amber slowly stood, then pressed her back against the door and straightened the knit cap on her head. She had three of them now and rarely bothered with the lacy caps anymore. "The records here are not current, sir."

He paused for a moment. "I'm afraid I did not understand you through the door, Madam."

She cleared her throat and spoke louder this time. "Mr. Dariloo manages the land and keeps the current records."

Another pause. "I am not looking for current records, but for records from twenty years ago."

"Well, the latest records in my library are from ninety-four, I think." She had had ample time to peruse the shelves of the library, though she certainly hadn't read the estate records. "And I believe the earliest of them was sixty-nine."

Again he paused before he replied, and she wondered at how often he did so. "I-I would be most obliged if you would allow me the opportunity to look at the documents to see if I may find the transaction in question. I believe the record was made in ninety, when the parcel in question was sold to my father."

Amber was surprised at how much she wished she could help him. His interest seemed sincere and his presence was wonderfully diverting. Regardless, she could not bring herself to let him in. "I am afraid your timing is quite poor, sir," she said. "My, uh, housekeeper is in town, and it would be most improper for you to come inside with no one to attend me."

"Might I be so forward as to ask your name and station that I might address you properly as Madam or . . . perhaps as Miss? My name is Thomas Richards. My brother is Baron Fielding. He holds title to a parcel of land that connects to the eastern border of your property."

*My name?* Amber's mind spun, trying to remember the name she had decided upon for her stay. She was to be a widow, she remembered that much, and disliking of company. If she sounded too agreeable would it conflict with the reputation Suzanne had shared in town? Amber had delayed an awkward amount of time before she recalled the information and answered his question.

"You may call me Mrs. Chandler. I am a widow." She rolled her eyes at how stupid that sounded. Six months out of society and she couldn't maintain the simplest of conversations. Besides, why was he asking her name so directly? It was highly improper for him to be so forward. But she had answered him all the same, and she couldn't deny she had been equally curious as to his identity. Perhaps him talking through a door to a widow in the country was as unusual to him as it was for her to be talking through the same door to a man of gentle birth. Surely conventions could be set aside for such unique circumstances as this.

"Uh, my condolences," he said, though it took her a moment to realize that he was referring to her deceased husband. How very considerate of him.

"And you think the record you seek is here?" Amber asked.

"Yes, and it is of great importance that I find it. Would it be at all possible for me to come in and look through the records?"

She had already told him that she was home alone and could most certainly not let him in. Beyond that, she felt no reason to refuse his request. It was simple enough to fulfill, only not today.

"My housekeeper shall be here the day after next. If you would be so kind as to return then, I shall see that you have full use of the library for as long as you desire." Only when she finished did she realize that as a widow she would not need a chaperone. She frowned, but could not reverse her insistence.

"That is very kind of you," he said, but the disappointment in his tone made her frown deepen. "I shall return on Friday then. What time would you like me to arrive?"

Amber calculated how long it would take to bake a cake, dust the library, and ensure Mr. Richards enough time to travel from Romanby and back without risk of being caught in the dark. "Eleven?" she asked. "I can have some tea and cake for you."

"I shan't need such consideration," he said. "I shall return as you said, at eleven on Friday, assuming the weather holds."

Imagining that he was turning to leave, Amber found herself eager to keep him talking. She faced the door and placed a hand upon it, though it seemed an overly dramatic gesture. "I am sorry you have had to journey so far, sir," she said, hoping he could hear her sincerity.

He was quiet again, perhaps so angry at her refusal to let him in that he needed time to better control his words. "Thank you," he said. "It was nice to meet you . . . Mrs. Chandler."

"And I am most pleased to meet you . . . or, well, talk with you, Mr. Richards. I will look forward to seeing you on Friday . . . or, well, I shan't be seeing you but Suza— my housekeeper will show you the library and all will be in readiness. I shall pray for clear skies on your behalf."

"Very good," he said. "Until Friday."

"Until Friday," she confirmed, then listened to his footsteps retreat toward the west side of the house.

She waited a few seconds and then ran on her tiptoes to the window of the parlor. She moved the curtain aside in time to see him pass by the window so closely that she squeaked again and dropped below the sill while clapping her hand over her mouth.

After another moment, she hurried to the front window beside the door to watch his back as he retreated down the steps, soon disappearing all together. She turned and ran up the stairs, knelt below the window of her bedroom that overlooked the lane, and peeked over the sill to watch him untether his dark brown quarter horse from the post, turn it around, and then smoothly mount with only the stirrup for assistance.

She could not see him well, what with his high collar, heavy coat, and beaver hat, but he had chocolate-colored hair that showed beneath the brim and a very nice seat on his horse. His greatcoat split so that it fell on both sides of the animal. He looked back at the house one time, and she dropped to the floor before looking up again in time to see him disappear around the bend.

Amber kept her eyes on the road for some time before turning so her back was against the wall below the window and pulling her knees to her chest. She could not reasonably account for the fluttering invigoration she felt in the wake of Mr. Richards coming to the house and dared diagnose it as giddiness until she reached a hand to her head, where two knit caps protected her from the cold. Her happy mood faded along with her smile.

What good would giddiness or excitement do her in reaction to any man, much less a gentleman? Did she fancy herself able to make any kind of impression upon him with her condition? He would not see her. He would not ever know her. And she'd required him to make a second trip all the way from Romanby rather than allow him the access he'd requested. He could very well be married, though if he were, it would be expected for him to bring his wife with him for such a visit. Regardless, he was certainly used to better treatment than she had given him.

She was embarrassed to have been affected by such a minimal exchange and lowered her hands to her lap, somber as she reflected on the meeting. He would likely return to his friends and family and laugh at the ridiculous nature of his visit. She could not blame him if he did. She surely would have a year ago had she been on his side of the conversation.

"It is a relief to be honest with oneself," she told herself as she stood and smoothed out her now grease-stained apron that covered her simple blue woolen dress. If he had seen her true person, he would never want to come back. Not even to find the record he sought. She took a breath and let it out, lifting her chin and choosing not to wallow. "However, I am still a gentleman's daughter, and I shall most certainly have tea and cake to serve on Friday."

# Chapter 25

Thomas removed his hat before letting himself into the magistrate's office only minutes before it was set to close for the day. The clerk, a rather jovial man with a shiny pate and thin shoulders, smiled up at him. "Mr. Richards," he said. "What can I do you for today?"

"I should like some help determining the owner of a specific parcel of land." It was all Thomas could do to keep his anxiety out of his voice. He had argued with himself the whole way back to town.

It was impossible.

He should be consigned to Bedlam for even thinking it.

But that voice . . .

Mr. Kimball moved to the area map posted on the office wall. It showed roads, rivers, and the individual parcels of land — hundreds of them at least. "I'm happy to help you if I can, Mr. Richards. Which plot are you asking for?"

Thomas scanned the map until he found the Romanby road, then followed the line with his finger until he found the lane that led to the cottage. His finger stopped at what he thought was the appropriate distance given the scale of the map. "This parcel here, I think." It was larger than he expected, perhaps two hundred acres. "There's a house called Step Cottage set on the incline of the hill there."

"Right, right," Mr. Kimball said, nodding his shiny head. "I know just what piece you mean. It used to be attached to that field of yours that runs along Willow Beck, right?"

"I believe so, yes," Thomas said.

"Let me double-check our records," Mr. Kimball said before disappearing behind a partition.

Thomas tapped his fingers lightly on the countertop in an attempt to contain his anxiety. "It can't be," he muttered under his breath. "You have lost any sense you may have ever had."

"What was that, Mr. Richards?"

Thomas looked up to see Mr. Kimball coming toward him and put a smile in place. "Oh, just talking to myself, I'm afraid."

"Ain't no harm in that," Mr. Kimball said.

"I sometimes go all day long without another body to talk with. I've had some of my best conversations with my own self." He put a folder on the counter, opened the cover, and ran his finger down the lines of neat print. "Ah, yes. I didn't want to say as much in case I was wrong, but that there piece is owned by a Viscount — not a local, mind you. This one's seated a cry south, I believe. Viscount of Marchent."

"Lord Marchent," Thomas said as he felt the blood drain from his face, his wild thoughts confirmed. "And is not the family name Sterlington?"

"The very same," Mr. Kimball said with a smile.

Thomas took a deep breath in hopes it would restore his countenance, then let it out slowly. "I assume there must be a manager I could talk to. I, uh, I would like more information about the parcel."

Mr. Kimball looked back at the paper. "Right. The name I have on record here as overseeing Lord Marchent's interests is Mr. Arnold Peters. He's a solicitor with an office on High Street. I imagine there's a caretaker or bailiff managing the land itself, but I don't have that name on record so Mr. Peters would be the man to talk to."

Thomas didn't bother unhitching Farthing

from the post but instead cut through alleyways and side streets in hopes of catching the solicitor before he returned home for the evening. He reached the right office on High Street within minutes, found Mr. Peters at his desk, and began peppering him with questions about the cottage until Mr. Peters raised a hand to interrupt him.

"I'm sure I can't understand why you are so interested in the cottage or the occupant," Mr. Peters said, fidgeting uncomfortably with his quill. " 'Tis nothing remarkable about either one."

"The operating fields are in good order," Thomas said, developing a feigned motive as quickly as he could in hopes it would afford him more information. "And they meet up with some acreage I'm already farming. I am wondering if Lord Marchent might be inclined to sell —"

"He is not interested in selling," Mr. Peters interrupted.

"You're certain?"

"I am absolutely certain," Mr. Peters said. "He was here not three months ago, reconciling his accounts and advising the caretaker on how to manage the coming season. There was no discussion regarding any interest in selling."

"It isn't a large enough parcel to be very

profitable for the Viscount, especially if he lives so far south."

"It makes a small amount," Mr. Peters said.

"Certainly not more than it takes to keep the cottage operational," Thomas argued. "A good portion of the fields are fallow and the cottage itself would not be fit even as a hunting lodge for a Viscount. Surely Lord Marchent would entertain an offer." If necessary, Thomas could talk Albert into making a request himself. Mr. Peters might respond better to Lord Fielding.

"Lord Marchent retains the house for sentimental reasons." The man's nervousness was increasing.

"Sentimental reasons," Thomas repeated. "And so who is it that lives there? A family member perhaps?"

"Yes. She is a widow in need of some convalescence. Elderly and crippled." He seemed to add the last part as though to dissuade Thomas from making any designs on the woman as a way to acquire the land. Thomas ignored it.

"And she has been there for how long?"

"Since the summer," Mr. Peters answered.

Thomas had last seen Miss Sterlington in May. He had assumed she'd returned to her family estate when she left London. Why would her family send her so far north as this? And to such a confining house? Was she *alone* except for her housekeeper? "And how long will she be staying?" Thomas asked.

"Certainly I do not know nor would I be at liberty to say if I did." The man's nervousness was changing to irritation. "I have told you far more than you are entitled to, Mr. Richards. I'm afraid I can't tell you anymore."

Thomas stood, fairly towering over the man even though Thomas was not of large stature. "You have helped me quite enough," he said, putting his hat back on before turning and striding from the office, his head miles away in a cottage off the Romanby road, thinking about a woman who would only talk with him through the door but promised him tea when he returned on Friday.

# Chapter 26

"I fear it has too much cinnamon. Does it have too much cinnamon?" Amber asked, wringing her hands as Suzanne cut another bite from the piece of spice cake Amber had made. Mr. Thomas Richards was a gentleman with all manner of experience with fine foods made by better cooks than she. If it were too poor she would not serve it and settle for biscuits from a tin. At least the weather had held so as to allow him the visit.

Suzanne swallowed the bite of cake and looked at Amber. "It is the perfect amount of cinnamon. Truly, it is perhaps the most delicious cake you have ever made."

"You are certain? You are not flattering me?"

Suzanne laughed. "I am not flattering you," she said and took another bite.

"I shall still drizzle it with some sugar glaze."

"That will complement it nicely."

Amber frowned. "You said it was delicious before I mentioned the glaze. Does that mean it is not as delicious without it?"

Suzanne laughed and stood from the table. "I must say I have not seen this side of you in all these months, Amber."

"A gentleman is coming to the house," Amber said by way of explanation. "It is the first time I have been a hostess."

"And yet you will stay in your room?"

"Well, of course," Amber said. She had not for a moment considered otherwise.

"Perhaps you should simply don your cap and meet him. All of town talks of you as though you are deformed or some such thing."

"As long as they do not know how truly deformed I am, I shall be at peace with their gossip."

"You are not deformed. Or crippled or ill. You have simply lost your hair."

"I have simply lost everything," Amber clarified, hating how quickly her excitement over Mr. Richards's visit was fading now that they were talking of her condition.

"I would suggest again that we invite Dr. Marsh from Northallerton to attend you. Perhaps he —"

Amber cut off Suzanne's words. "I will not talk of that when we are preparing for a visitor. I want any guest in my home to be comfortable and welcome."

Suzanne seemed to consider her words for a moment, before speaking. "I have no doubt Mr. Richards will feel welcomed. It is kind of you to attend to his comfort."

Amber was relieved to have Suzanne drop the argument. She turned her attention to the tea set and moved the pot to the left side of the tray, then back. It was porcelain and old, which didn't bother her or Suzanne but seemed awful now that she anticipated a gentleman seeing it. She placed the nicest cup on the nicest saucer, then moved the sugar bowl far enough from the creamer so that the dishes wouldn't hit together when Suzanne carried the tray into the library. Last of all, Amber drizzled three slices of cake with sugar glaze and set the platter, as well as an empty plate, on the tray.

She could not explain why she wanted Mr. Richards's experience to be comfortable, but it was all she had thought about since talking with him through the door, and while it might simply be a symptom of her loneliness, it was a welcome change to feel so energized about anything at all. When she had told Suzanne of Mr. Richards's visit, Suzanne had informed her that he was unmarried and most certainly of her station. Amber told both Suzanne and herself that those aspects made no difference, but she feared they did. Having an eligible man in her home was exciting even if she would not see him.

Amber rearranged the tea tray three more times before there was a strong knock at the front door.

"He is here," Amber said, wiping her hands on her apron as she looked toward the door. She hurried into the foyer and stopped, staring at the door that separated her from her visitor. Suzanne came up behind her.

"Are you certain you will not join him for tea?"

Amber did not bother answering — they had argued over the topic quite enough — and instead lifted her skirts and quickly went up the stairs. She had planned to go to her room and close the door, as she did whenever Mrs. Haribow or Mr. Dariloo came to the cottage, but instead she moved to the side of the stairway as Suzanne opened the front door and welcomed Mr. Richards, who thanked her. Amber liked that she was already familiar with his voice, which was low in timbre and strong. If it were any reflection, his bearing was equally good, and she wished she dared peek around the corner to catch a glimpse of him.

Instead, Amber listened to their exchange as Suzanne led him to the library, making it harder for her to hear what was being said. After a minute, she heard Suzanne's footsteps cross in front of the stairs for the kitchen.

Certain Mr. Richards would be staying in the library — she could trust a gentleman to stay in the room to which he'd been invited — Amber carefully moved down four steps in hopes to hear his reaction to the cake she had made especially for him. Each stair creaked slightly but she hoped he was so intent on the records he would not notice.

Suzanne obviously did not expect to see Amber when she crossed the stairway with the tea tray and startled slightly, causing some of the dishes to hit together. Amber covered her mouth with her hand, worried Suzanne would drop the tray completely. But Suzanne recovered without incident, sent Amber a narrow look, and then repaired her expression before continuing into the library.

"I informed your mistress not to trouble with tea," Mr. Richards said. "I am in her debt for the opportunity to search the library as it is."

Amber smiled at the pleased tone in his voice. He truly was a gentleman and she relished his kind words.

" 'Tis no trouble, sir," Suzanne said. "She wants you to feel welcome."

Amber came down a few more steps, so as to better hear their exchange. She made sure to stay hidden from view of the library.

"I had hoped I would get the chance to meet your mistress during this visit."

"She is not one for visiting, but I shall pass along your kindness, sir. Please let me know if you need anything. The papers and ledgers you are wanting to see are located on the back bookshelf. I shall look in on you in a little while."

He thanked her, and Suzanne left the room — sending another irritated glance Amber's way as she passed the stairwell on her way to the kitchen.

Amber sat on the stairs and listened to Mr. Richards move around the room; she was ready to run if she heard his footsteps leave the hooked rug.

He seemed quite attentive to the library however, and her tension faded as the time passed. He would walk to the back of the room, presumably extract some documents from the shelf, then return to the desk and turn pages for an impossibly long time. It was perhaps the most uneventful afternoon Amber had ever spent, and yet she enjoyed visualizing him in the room she herself was so familiar with. She wondered what he thought of the book collections — they were impressive for such a house as this — and she suddenly wished she could discuss some of those books with him. She leaned her head against the wall and let out a breath. She missed the company of other people.

When Amber's backside began to get sore, she realized that he may finish his investigation soon. It would be better if she left her hiding place before he discovered her. She stood and tiptoed up the stairs.

She returned to her bedroom and lay on the bed unable to say why his presence gave her such satisfaction except that to be a hostess and ensure the comfort of her guests was part of what she had been raised to do. To use such skills and attentions connected her to that part of herself she sometimes feared was gone forever. She felt she had attended to his comfort well and that pleased her. How long it had been since she had attended to anyone's comfort but hers and Suzanne's? And that attention was required, not chosen.

Amber looked to the window on the far wall and tucked her hands beneath her cheek. She closed her eyes and indulged herself in memories of the life she had once lived. She recalled waltzing at Almack's. Attending the opera at Covent Gardens. Riding through Hyde Park during the fashionable hours. The opera. Card parties. Lemonade.

If only the memories were not so tainted by knowing how every dance was measured against whether or not the man was of acceptable rank, or if he had asked for a dance before she had an excuse to refuse him. Had she enjoyed any of those nights? *Truly* enjoyed them?

It had felt like pleasure then but now she wondered if she knew what pleasure was. Had she simply adjusted to this life so well that she could not remember the true enjoyment she had felt amid the *ton,* or had the fripperies of London been so gilded in expectation and falseness that they had not been pleasure at all but simply appeared to be?

If she woke up tomorrow with a full head of hair, but with the knowledge of what she had learned these last months, would she be a different woman than she had been in London? Could she dance for the enjoyment of it? Could she talk with men because she was sincerely interested in what they had to say? Or would she become the girl she'd been before? Would she manipulate and position herself because she was once again acceptable to society?

Would she give up the perspective she had now for the beauty and consequence she had then?

# CHAPTER 27

Thomas laid a well-preserved paper on Albert's desk upon his return to Peakview Manor. It had rained during Thomas's return trip from the cottage, but he barely felt the cold for the thoughts he'd stoked throughout the ride. Albert glanced at his brother before exchanging the letter he was currently writing for the document Thomas had presented. He scanned the contents while Thomas sat in one of the leather chairs opposite the large desk.

"I promise not to spread the tale if you use your glass," Thomas said, resting one ankle over the other knee. His trousers were wet from the rain. He should trade them for a dry pair, but he felt too tightly wound to attend to mere comfort.

"If documents were not written in such impossibly small print, the glass would not be a consideration." Despite Albert's argument, the quizzing glass appeared, and Albert scanned the sale agreement with greater attention.

"Praise the heavens," Albert breathed when he reached the end of the page. He looked up at Thomas, his face bright with excitement. "The record was at the cottage, then?"

"All this time," Thomas said, unable to hide a satisfied smile. "The caretaker who kept the squire's records from eighty-seven to ninety-four was quite diligent."

As Albert reread the document, Thomas was miles away in his memory, sitting in a small library while Amber Sterlington sat on the stairs. He had known she was there; he could swear he could feel her breathe while he had waited for her to present herself. Even after he found the record, he had extended his stay. She did not appear, however. Instead, after nearly an hour, he heard the stairs creak as she returned to the upper level of the house. The Miss Sterlington he knew would not have hidden herself away.

Curious as to whether she would return — perhaps after making herself presentable — he had stayed at least half an hour longer, until the three slices of cake were gone, and he could find no reason to extend the visit he had already drawn out far past the deadline of polite society.

With his curiosity unsatisfied regarding Miss Sterlington, he had spent the ride back to Peakview pondering her being in his county at all.

At Carlton House, he had seen the condition of her hair from the rinse gone poorly — could that account for her being here all this time and not showing herself? It did not explain why she had given a false identity, however, and he could not help but wonder if there was perhaps another reason she was in hiding. A much more damning reason.

Thomas had defended her virtue to Fenton, but a *delicate* condition would necessitate a complete removal from a society intolerant of indiscretions of its young women. Miss Sterlington had been in London seven months ago, which, if she were in fact increasing, could explain why she would hide from him. Could that be the true reason for the fear and vulnerability he'd seen on her face that night? Was she afraid of far darker secrets coming to light?

It was not difficult to cast his memory to the night at Almack's when she'd snubbed him and shattered his security amid the society of London. Or to recall her manipulations at Fenton's card party. Was it so hard to consider that her character was more failing than he had thought?

"Thomas?"

He looked up at his brother who was regarding him with a questioning expression. "Are you well?"

"Quite," Thomas said, attempting a smile he knew must look as stiff as it felt. "Would you like me to take the document to Mr. Llewelyn?"

"It can wait until tomorrow," Albert said. He pushed away from his desk and moved to the door. "I should like to tell Lady Fielding of the success of your visit, however. If you'll excuse me."

Thomas waited until Albert had left the room, then stood and walked to the fireplace. The chill from his journey was beginning to settle about him, and he shivered as he leaned his forearms on the mantel and dropped his head onto his arms. His stomach was tight with continued thoughts of Amber Sterlington and her reasons for being so far from her rightful place. He had thought of her less and less in recent weeks and had counted that a success. Yet now she was back, closer than ever. Why could he not be rid of her completely? Why was she thrust into his path again and again when she brought such difficulty with her every time?

"Please," he said out loud, begging for relief of his pull toward her even while picturing Amber Sterlington sitting on those stairs. She had been unable or unwilling to show herself to him and yet for reasons he could not make sense of, he felt that she wanted to be near him.

Why?

Did she know who he was? Did she know it was he who had given her his coat?

More importantly, what would he do now? She was here, near his home and his comforts. Would he seek her out again? What would be his motivation? Did some part of him still hold on to the hope she might notice him?

He growled at the idea of it, embarrassed to admit wanting such a thing. That it followed his suspicions of her lack of virtue and goodness made him even more repulsed with the seemingly uncontrollable desire to find a reason to return to the cottage. What was his expectation?

"Nothing," he said to the room as he pushed away from the mantel. "She is nothing to me, and I shall do nothing at all to satisfy my curiosity."

With those words surrounding him, he

headed for his bedchamber, a suit of dry clothes, and perhaps a glass of port. He was a man of discipline and focus. He could keep his thoughts in check. He could rid his mind of her if he chose, and he would.

Each time thoughts of her entered his mind, he would think of something entirely different — like cows, or ditches, or Albert's silly quizzing glass. Anything to keep his thoughts off her — a woman undeserving of his attentions.

It would work.

He would make certain.

# CHAPTER 28

*January*

Thomas secured Farthing to the post and hurried through the open doorway of the blacksmith shop located on the west end of Northallerton. The shop was sweltering in the summertime but today it was a welcome heat that greeted him. He removed his hat and brushed the snow from it, then looked over his shoulder with a frown. The storm had moved in far faster than he'd expected when he'd set out on his errands in town. He would be glad to complete his business quickly and return to Peakview Manor for the duration of the tempest.

Yorkshire had received only a few bouts of snow so far this winter, though temperatures had been as cold as ever. He feared this storm would make up for what had been spared thus far. With St. Nicholas past and a New Year just begun, perhaps it was only fair that they welcome the season with open arms. It would be good for the new trees he'd planted in the fall to have so much moisture seep deep into the soil.

"Good day, Mr. Richards," Mr. Larsen, the smithy, said from where he stood beside the forge. Using a large set of tongs, he pulled a pot from the flame and set it on his anvil, immediately working the side of it with a small hammer. "The harnesses are just there if you'd like to inspect them." He nodded toward the workbench that ran the length of the north side of the shop. Though the shop had doors on every wall to accommodate ventilation, the temperature inside was quite comfortable.

"I've no need to approve the quality, I'm sure."

Mr. Larsen finished his hammering and used the tongs to dip the pan into water that hissed and bubbled in reaction to the heated metal. Mr. Larsen left the pot in the bath and removed his heavy gloves in order to join Thomas at the workbench and review the details of the work he'd done. As expected, the work was sound enough that it was difficult to tell where the repairs had even been made. Thomas said as much, and Mr. Larsen thanked him for the compliment.

As part of his attempts to keep his

thoughts focused on purposeful tasks, Thomas had created a list of tasks that could be done during foul weather. One such task was to organize the tack shed and though the stable master did not appreciate Thomas's supervision, he had relented when Thomas made it clear he had no other choice. Repairing all the broken bridles and harnesses was the first step. Then they would be hung by order of type and size along an interior wall of the stable which had been prepared with a series of hooks. It was not difficult, only time-consuming — which was exactly what Thomas wanted. His business complete, Thomas paid for the work before turning up the collar of his coat.

"Take care on your return to the manor. Looks like a blustery storm, it does," Mr. Larsen said, nodding to the weather to which Thomas was to return.

Thomas thanked him and had turned back to the open doorway when a bundled figure hurried into the sanctuary of the shop, forcing him to step aside to avoid being knocked down.

"Beg your pardon," a woman's voice said from beneath a heavy scarf wrapped around her head and neck. She didn't await his reply but instead continued toward Mr. Larsen, who looked at the new arrival with greater interest than he'd looked upon Thomas. "Is my pot finished, Mr. Larsen?" the woman asked.

"Just now, Mrs. Miller," Mr. Larsen replied, waving toward the bath. "But you can't expect to return home today. Not in a gig. Not alone."

"I'm afraid I must," the woman said, her concern evident as she pulled the scarf from her face. "I can't leave my mistress alone, not in weather like this. Mr. Clawson feels this storm will only get worse."

At the mention of her mistress, Thomas realized who the woman was and remembered her as he'd first met her, in the doorway of Step Cottage more than a month ago. A rush of heat and irritation moved through him, prickling his skin beneath the layers of clothing. Hearing any news related to Miss Sterlington would surely undo his determination to extract her from his thoughts. He told his feet to move, but they did not comply, and he remained where he was, listening to the conversation that did not include him.

"I fear the vicar is right, Mrs. Miller," Mr. Larsen said, stepping to the tub of water. He lifted out the cooled pot with his bare hands and shook the water from it. "You best return to the vicarage and wait it out."

Mrs. Miller began to wring her gloved hands and looked outside again, her face pinched with concern. She met Thomas's eye, and he saw recognition on her part.

"Mrs. Miller," Thomas said, accepting his obligation to greet her. He had no desire to snub the woman; he simply knew he should be hurrying home. "Is everything all right?"

"Yes, Mr. Richards," Mrs. Miller said, nodding quickly then pausing and shaking her head. "I mean, no, but it is no concern of yours." She looked past him to the falling snow, and her eyebrows pulled together once again before turning back to Mr. Larsen. "How long will this last, do you think? Could I expect to journey home tomorrow?"

"I wouldn't expect decent travel for a few days, Mrs. Miller," Mr. Larsen said with regret. "Even if it stopped within the hour, your rig can't make the trip in such mud as will be left behind from a squall like this. If there were *more* snow I would offer my sled, but it would take a week's worth of heavy snow to accommodate that."

The blacksmith's generous offer prompted Thomas to find a solution of his own, though even as he prepared it he wondered at his motivation. He had promised himself to keep a distance from that cottage and yet the words left his mouth without restraint. "My brother has a traveling coach and four that could make the trip if we left soon, Mrs. Miller," Thomas said. "I could have it readied in an hour's time if you are desperate to return today."

The woman turned eager eyes to Thomas, but then her glance slid to Mr. Larsen before turning to the ground. Thomas understood the response; she realized his offer was above that expected of her position. "I could not ask for such an accommodation, sir, though I appreciate your kindness. I shall confer with the vicar and see what solution he might propose."

Thomas smiled in an attempt to put her at ease. "If you truly appreciate my kindness, then allow me to help." He turned to Mr. Larsen. "The pot is finished?"

"Yes, sir," Mr. Larsen said, a pleased smile on his face.

Thomas's stomach, on the other hand, was sinking. What was he doing, going back to the cottage? How would he ever get past his obsession with Miss Sterlington if he did not keep himself out of her path? Doing the right thing bypassed his regrets, however. He could not *not* help a woman in need; he'd been raised to such things all of his life. He told himself he was doing it for

Mrs. Miller, though. Not for Miss Sterlington.

"Could you arrange to have Mrs. Miller delivered to the manor in one hour's time? Perhaps the vicar could assist you." He turned to the woman. "Your horse and gig can be cared for in our stables, and I shall have them returned to Step Cottage when the weather lifts."

Mrs. Miller blinked at him in surprise. "I should refuse your offer, sir, but I am most eager to return to my mistress as she has already been alone for two days' time. I am most grateful for your generosity. Thank you."

Thomas inclined his head before meeting Mr. Larsen's gaze. "See that Mrs. Miller gets to the manor, and I shall see that she gets home."

When Thomas explained the situation to Lord and Lady Fielding, Albert agreed to lend use of the coach and Diane offered to act as Mrs. Miller's chaperone. Thomas accepted her offer with a reluctance he hoped she did not note. He had already come up with a list of questions he wanted to ask Mrs. Miller. But with Lady Fielding in attendance, he could not be so bold. Thomas couldn't refuse his sister-in-law, however, and convinced himself it would be better if she came. It would ensure propriety and, he reminded himself, he didn't want to know more about Miss Sterlington. Lady Fielding's presence would secure his ignorance.

Mrs. Clawson, the vicar's wife, arrived with Mrs. Miller and intended to go with her, so it was a full carriage that made its way to Step Cottage, which was nearly four and a half miles from the manor. A very long and slow four miles.

Diane and Mrs. Clawson enjoyed some light conversation in the carriage about the weather and the parish and the health of one another's husbands and children. Mrs. Miller did not participate, she was a servant after all, and Thomas was content to stare at the words on the page of the book he'd brought with him — a book on architecture he hoped would help him with the design of the house he planned to begin this spring. He kept reading the same words over and over, however, unable to think of anything other than the fact that every turn of the wheel was taking him closer to the woman who haunted him.

When they arrived at Step Cottage it was late afternoon, and Mrs. Miller promised them tea if they would wait in the carriage just a few minutes for her to ready the cottage. Her nervousness made far more sense to Thomas than she could ever have guessed, and his whole body was taut with expectation as he looked up the steps that led to *her.* Miss Sterlington did not know they were coming which meant he might be able to catch her unawares.

"We do not need tea," Mrs. Clawson said, a bit presumptuously, Thomas thought. "Please give your mistress our regards, however. The groom will help you with your supplies, and then we should return to town as quickly as possible while the roads are still passable."

"I shall assist with the supplies," Thomas said quickly, finding a secondary reason to enter the cottage.

Mrs. Miller had come to town to refresh the stores, and thus was returning with two crates of supplies as well as the pot Mr. Larsen had repaired. Thomas exited the carriage first and then assisted Mrs. Miller.

As soon as both feet were on the ground, Mrs. Miller lifted her skirts and hurried up the snow-covered steps — not even giving instruction to the groom.

The groom removed the supply crates from beneath the carriage far too slowly for Thomas's mind, but as soon as Thomas had the first parcel in his arms, he took the steps as quickly as he dared. The front door had been left open in Mrs. Miller's haste, and Thomas smiled to himself, feeling anticipation of coming face to face with Miss Sterlington. What would she do? Would she know him from exchanges in London?

He ducked through the door in time to hear hurried footsteps moving on the stairs. Thomas looked up in time to catch a flash of blue skirt and snowy white petticoat as they disappeared around the corner.

# Chapter 29

Thomas clenched his jaw in frustration at having missed his chance, but turned his attention to Mrs. Miller who approached from the kitchen, an anxious but relieved smile on her face.

"Thank you so very much for your kind assistance," she said before glancing up the stairwell. Seeing it empty seemed to bring her greater relief.

"Of course," Thomas said. Miss Sterlington had set quite a pace for her escape — and *up* the stairs, no less. Could she have moved so quickly if she were nearing the end of her confinement? He hated thinking in that direction but found some of the weight in his chest lifted by what seemed to be proof against the condition he feared. What other reason would she be confined to this cottage?

"Would you mind bringing the supplies into the kitchen, please?" Mrs. Miller asked.

Thomas nodded and followed the footman — who had just now caught up — into the small but warm cooking area. As he set down his crate of supplies, he tried to imagine Amber Sterlington in such a room. It was primitive and confined, nothing like the kitchens of the great homes she was accustomed to. Then he realized that the fire in the grate would have to have been maintained by Miss Sterlington herself, since her housekeeper had been in town these two days. He scanned the room with greater attention and saw a potato quartered on the counter. He noticed the scent of recent baking and was stunned by the realization that Miss Sterlington . . . cooked?

"Are there any other servants here?" Thomas asked, turning quickly to Mrs. Miller. He felt sure she was the only help as he had not encountered any others on his previous visits, but it had become very important of a sudden that he know for sure.

"Only me, sir, which is why it was so kind of you to deliver me home. I am indebted to you. As is my mistress. It is a fearful thing to be alone too long in weather like this."

"Yes," Thomas said, nodding slowly while trying to puzzle through the situation. "Was . . . Mrs. Chandler well in your absence?"

Mrs. Miller turned her eyes to the counter and the fire, just as Thomas had, and he knew she understood why he was asking. Mrs. Chandler had been rumored about town to be a widow of genteel birth, yet she had cared for herself in her servant's absence. Mrs. Miller looked at the floor and seemed to be struggling with how to answer, which made Thomas feel badly for having put her in an awkward situation. He knew the true identity of her mistress; there was no reason to make the housekeeper uncomfortable.

"I am glad to have been of assistance," he said, saving the woman from a reply. "Is there anything else we can do before we return? Shall we fill your coal box from the shed?"

Mrs. Miller busied herself with something at the counter and gave them a nervous smile. "You have done so very much already. I do have some oat biscuits you can take for your return trip. I know it is not equal to your efforts on our behalf, but I have no other way to express our thanks."

"We are glad to have been able to help," Thomas said while ushering the groom outside to fill the coal bucket. The maid passed him a basket lined with linen, and he pulled back the cloth to verify that the biscuits were still warm — biscuits Miss Sterlington had baked herself. He replaced the linen covering with a degree of reverence. "Please thank your mistress for the refreshment."

She smiled, then turned to instruct the returning groom on where to put the coal. As she led them to the door, Thomas looked up the stairwell but could see no indication of Miss Sterlington. Yet he knew she was there. Standing just out of view, listening to them talk. Unwilling to thank him herself. He did not know how he knew it, but he did.

When the door shut, Thomas felt sure Mrs. Miller was glad to have him gone.

The groom began to move down the stairs, but Thomas stepped back to the door and listened to the sound of muffled voices and the creak of stairs as Miss Sterlington surely returned to the main level. He could not hear what was being said and closed his eyes against the desire to throw open the door and confront her. But to what end?

Oh, the aggravation!

He looked at the confused groom, shifting his weight on the porch, and then nodded him forward, reluctantly following the man away from the cottage.

Once inside the carriage, the three occupants dismissed manners and ceremony in order to enjoy the biscuits. "If I'd known how long this journey would take, I'd have brought us a full picnic," Lady Fielding said, eating her biscuit one pinch at a time. "Specifically a crock of milk to go with these cakes. They are good, if perhaps a bit dry."

Thomas did not find them dry. He found them delicious even as he told himself to dislike them on principle. "The mistress of the house baked them," he said, causing both women to raise their eyebrows. He turned his gaze to Mrs. Clawson. "Have you met her?"

"Mrs. Chandler?" Mrs. Clawson said as though Thomas could mean anyone else. "Not myself, no. A queer woman from what I've been able to gather, though I know very little."

"You surely know more than anyone else," Lady Fielding said, wiping her fingers on her handkerchief and unknowingly saving Thomas from having to ask the question himself. "No one in town seems to know much about her. Thomas even came to search the library for a document, but Mrs. Chandler did not even make an introduction."

Mrs. Clawson smiled at him. "Yes, Mrs. Miller said you had come for the use of the library. I sense she'd hoped her mistress would have been more welcoming."

"She was quite welcoming," Thomas said, rising to Miss Sterlington's defense far easier than he would have liked. He thought back to that afternoon and wondered if the cake she'd served him could have been made by her own hands. The idea was exciting to him, yet the excitement annoyed him. "But, no, she stayed above stairs and did not introduce herself." Well, *on* the stairs, actually, but he was not going to explain that part.

"She has met with no one in town, not even her man of business," Mrs. Clawson said as though trying to soothe his feelings. "And Mrs. Miller does not often talk of her. She is oddly protective of her mistress."

"She seemed quite eager to return despite Mrs. Chandler's apparent self-sufficiency," Lady Fielding said.

"I'm sure you know that a bond often develops between the staff and their betters. Mrs. Miller is rather fond of the widow, I think. Never disparaging or cross about her, which says a great deal about both of them."

"How odd that she would develop such a kindness in her staff, but be so inaccessible to the town, especially clergy," Lady Fielding said, her eyes bright with the anticipation of gossip. Thomas clenched his jaw and wished again that his sister-in-law had not come.

"I have the impression she had some great difficulty before coming here," Mrs. Clawson continued. "Lost her husband, of course, and no family to speak of. I believe she is a cripple."

"She is not a cripple," Thomas said quickly, thinking again of the footsteps he heard and the flash of skirt on the stairs. Only when he noticed both women looking at him did he realize he would need to explain, which he did.

"Odd," Mrs. Clawson said, her eyebrows knit together. "I feel certain Mrs. Miller said she had some trouble with her legs, but I suppose Mrs. Chandler has had to learn some measure of independence for Mrs. Miller to leave her for town." She shrugged as though it was an inconsequential detail.

"Perhaps her husband was a scoundrel and she has run from his reputation to live in peace," Lady Fielding said, seeming to like the idea. "Or maybe *she* was a scoundrel and all the doors of her acquaintances were closed to her." Thomas's breath caught at the remarkably astute assessment and he tried to cover it with a cough. Fortunately, Lady Fielding kept her attention on Mrs.

Clawson. "Did she not turn away you and the vicar not once but twice? Only someone out of favor with the church would do such a thing."

"Or perhaps she is simply an eccentric woman who prefers her own company. I've no reason to doubt that nor speculate on her situation if she is unwilling to share it." Mrs. Clawson's smile was befitting the wife of a clergyman, but her reprimand did not go unnoticed. "There was another woman who lived there years ago, you know. It seems that Mrs. Chandler has much in common with the former occupant."

"Oh?" Lady Fielding said, raising her eyebrows. Thomas was equally interested. The cottage had been owned by Lord Marchent for more than two decades. Who had lived there before his daughter?

"She was very much the same as this one, I believe. It was before Mr. Clawson and I came to North Riding, so I don't know much myself. With Mrs. Chandler's arrival we have heard talk, however. *That* woman was not a widow, however, but rather a spinster. Stayed in Step Cottage as Mrs. Chandler does, but was far more forceful regarding people leaving her be. Her servants avoided anyone in town and were not even allowed to go to church."

"How long ago was this?" Lady Fielding asked.

"I believe the former occupant passed away about six years ago. There was a rather difficult year of influenza and she did not survive it. Her servants quit to London once she was buried. The house has been empty ever since."

"Until Mrs. Chandler," Lady Fielding said, a thoughtful smile on her face. "Curious. I wonder if the wife of a local baron might receive different reception if *she* called upon Mrs. Chandler. Perhaps her position would earn her an audience."

Thomas looked out the window, irritated with himself for envying Lady Fielding's courage to present herself. He did not think Miss Sterlington would receive her, however. Surely if she were to meet anyone, it would be Mr. and Mrs. Clawson. Yet she had lied to them as much as she'd lied to everyone else. She had worked hard to keep herself hidden.

"Perhaps," Mrs. Clawson said reluctantly.

When the silence stretched on too long, Thomas glanced toward the women to find Mrs. Clawson looking at him, a smile on her face that seemed determined to change the topic of conversation. "Now, Mr. Richards, I have been meaning to ask you about the progress you have made toward the transfer of land you and Lord Fielding are orchestrating. I must say it has caused quite a stir for a man of your station to want to wear a working man's coat."

# Chapter 30

Amber bent over the paper, her quill hovering over the page as she stared at the words she'd written so far: "Dear Mr. Richards." She put the quill back in the stock and pushed away from the desk. Suzanne was in the kitchen, washing the dishes from breakfast when Amber entered.

"Should I be addressing the letter to Mr. Richards or Lady Fielding?" Amber asked Suzanne. "She was the highest-ranking member of the party who escorted you home."

"But Mr. Richards was the one who offered the help and served as escort." Suzanne smiled slightly though Amber had no idea why. This was important. She must do it properly.

Amber thought of something else. "The carriage belonged to *Lord* Fielding. Perhaps I should address the letter to him as he outranks everyone."

Suzanne fixed her gaze on her mistress, eyebrows raised. "Perhaps you should stop trying to talk yourself out of writing a letter to Mr. Richards."

"I only want to do it correctly," Amber defended, but that was not entirely true. She was anxious about this letter — this reaching out. She was unsure if it was putting her situation at risk.

"Then perhaps you should write to all three of them. A letter to Lord and Lady Fielding for the carriage, and another one to Mr. Richards for orchestrating the travel."

"Yes, that is an option." But it still made her nervous. Even though he did not know it, she had spent far too much time thinking of Mr. Richards since his visit to the library a month ago. It was surely due to her removal from the society he represented, but the attention her mind gave to him was not helpful. She feared that writing to him would be some kind of . . . invitation. Openness. Interest. She could not risk any of those things.

"Write the letters, Amber," Suzanne said. "You are making this far too important in your mind."

Amber nodded, knowing Suzanne was right and that she ought to just get it over with. She returned to the desk in the library and took a breath. Writing two letters was a good idea, so she pushed aside the one already addressed to Mr. Richards and started a fresh one that, thankfully, was much easier to write. She thanked Lord and Lady Fielding for the generosity of the carriage and the chaperone, emphasizing that she was writing two days after Suzanne's return and the storm *had* left the roads impassable. Had Suzanne not returned when she had, Amber would be alone still.

It wasn't until after she had signed her name "Miss Amber Sterlington" that she remembered she was Mrs. Chandler now. Grunting with frustration, she balled up the letter and threw it in the fire, where it crackled before being swallowed up in flames. She wrote a second letter, as equally eloquent as the first but signed Mrs. Chandler.

While she waited for the ink to dry, she read the words over and worried they were *too* kind. It didn't seem right to be *less* than kind, but it would not do to sound as though she would welcome a continued acquaintance. Goodness, what if Lady Fielding called at the cottage? Turning away someone of her station would be nothing short of an insult, but a visit would be impossible.

Amber groaned again and crumpled the letter, as she did with her third and fourth attempt until, finally, she felt she struck the right balance of gratitude and distance. Never mind that it was also the most pathetic letter she had ever dared write.

Dear Lord and Lady Fielding,
I am writing this letter to thank you for the use of your carriage and for Lady Fielding's attendance in returning my housekeeper to me on January the sixth. I am quite dependent on her as I am disinclined for anyone's society but hers and am glad to have had her delivered safely.

Sincerely,
Mrs. Chandler

She was still shaking her head when she sealed it, hating the coldness of her words but knowing no better course. Moments later she was staring at the letter to Mr. Richards again, no better prepared to write it now than she had been an hour ago. She didn't want to be so cold and distant with him as he was the one who had come to Suzanne's rescue. As he was of greater importance in her thoughts, she wanted greater honesty in her letter to him. Surely he would not call on her himself if her wording was *too* kind; single men did not make calls on crippled widows. With that in mind, she took a breath to calm her nerves, cocked her head, and simply said what she wanted him to know.

Dear Mr. Richards,

I cannot adequately thank you for the kindness you showed to both Mrs. Miller and myself on January sixth when you returned her to Step Cottage. As I write this letter, the roads are quite impassable, which means she would still be in Romanby if not for your generosity. It was surely a great sacrifice of your time and your household, and I want to be sure that you know what a blessing it was to me. Though I know few people in this area, you and your family seem to be the very best of them and I thank you again for your kindness and attention.

Sincerely,
Mrs. Chandler

How she wished she could put her own name on the letter and feel a sense of ownership for the words. It was not possible, however. She waited for the ink to dry before sealing it up and putting Mr. Richards's name on the front. She stacked both letters on the edge of the desk where they would wait until Suzanne was next able to go to town.

She looked out the window in front of the desk and frowned. It was snowing again, and she wondered how long they could expect to be trapped here. They had enough necessities, but it was uncomfortable to know they were cut off from town completely. Even when the weather cleared, however, they were without Sally and the gig, which were being kept at Peakview Manor. She wondered if Mr. Richards would return the items himself. The idea made her smile.

She glanced once more at the letters on the desk and allowed herself the contentment at having written them. Thanking those who had returned Suzanne had been the right thing to do, and she felt as though she had lived up to her station in having done it.

The task complete, she returned to the kitchen where Suzanne was bent over a book. Amber paused in the doorway and smiled. She'd been helping Suzanne improve her reading on these cold winter nights and was glad to see she was taking the time to practice. She must have sensed Amber in the doorway since she looked up and then closed the book and pushed it away as though embarrassed to be found with it.

"I didn't mean to interrupt you," Amber said, crossing the room to take the stool on the other side of the table. "What are you reading?"

Suzanne turned the book over so Amber could see the title.

"*Romeo and Juliet*?" Amber's knit cap moved up a bit instead of her eyebrows. "I would not have guessed you to be such a romantic."

Suzanne shrugged. "When I looked over the bookshelves for something to practice my reading, it was the only title I recognized."

Suzanne's talk about Mr. Larsen, the blacksmith in town, had increased these last weeks, and Amber wondered if the choice of literature might have something to do with the attention the man seemed to be paying Suzanne.

"And do you like the story?" Amber asked.

Suzanne frowned. "I don't know that I read well enough understand it. The Capulets and the Montagues dislike one another, but I don't understand why."

"That is part of the brilliance of the story," Amber said, leaning forward and tapping the book. "Whatever it was that caused the discord was so long ago it has been forgotten. Their hatred has simply become a . . . tradition, I suppose. They hate each other simply because their families always have."

"Seems a poor reason."

"As prejudice usually is," Amber said, thinking of how she had always looked down on people below her class simply because it was how she'd seen it done. Tradition. "How much have you read?"

"Not much at all," Suzanne said, still frowning. "I have to read some portions three or four times to try to understand it."

Amber nodded, she could understand that. She had done much the same thing when she'd first revisited some of the Bard's works this winter. He wrote with such eloquence and power that without strict attention the details of the story could be lost. "Perhaps you could read it to me and together we can sort out the meaning; I'm sure I could benefit from such study." Specifically she needed a distraction that would keep her from reading the letter she'd written to Mr. Richards over and over again.

Why did the honest gratitude she'd shared on paper make her feel so vulnerable?

# Chapter 31

It took another five days before the skies and the roads were clear enough for the gig and horse to be returned to Step Cottage. Thomas helped ready the heavy farm wagon that was to make the trip — the lighter carriages would have a harder time on the slick roads — but declined to go with the party of four groomsmen who facilitated the delivery.

He watched them leave the stables in a procession of wagon and gig and told himself he'd chosen correctly. Keeping distance between himself and Miss Sterlington was still his primary goal. As it was, these past five days had been filled to overflowing with thoughts of her, many of them confusing.

He had seen a change in her, or perhaps a different side of her, that night at Carlton House. Perhaps anyone — no matter how horrid — would have looked as vulnerable, so in need of protection in such a dreadful situation. He then added that sincerity of expression with the self-sufficiency of her present circumstance, her accommodations to him regarding the use of her library, and the genuine care her servant had for her. Mrs. Miller seemed to regard her mistress as a friend, a companion. Together, all these details were enough to build new theories that churned in Thomas's head and chest.

He sought to occupy his thoughts elsewhere, but even digging postholes in the frozen ground and mucking out horse stalls, while ignoring the concerned looks of the staff, did not distract him completely. That morning, as preparations were made to return the horse and gig, he had almost convinced himself to attempt one more visit to see her. Yet in the end, he did not go. Instead, he busied himself in the stables until the most minor of tasks was accomplished and then he saddled Farthing for a very cold and uncomfortable ride in the opposite direction from Step Cottage. Perhaps the cold would numb his brain completely. Such a thing would be most welcome.

Thomas returned to the stables in time to see the wagon roll through the gates without the gig following behind, proof that the journey had been successful. He'd been longing for a hot cup of tea and a chance to thaw his frozen face and fingers in front of the fireplace but could not resist knowing what had happened at Step Cottage. He was waiting for the men in the stables when they entered.

Under the guise of helping care for the horses, which he knew made the stable hands uncomfortable, he helped remove the harnesses and store the supplies, all the while asking about the roads — muddy, but passable — the wagon's maneuvering — good, sturdy rig — the gig's ability to navigate in the trail made by the wagon — slow, but certain — and, finally, the occupants of the cottage.

"The woman was a bit surprised to see us, I think," said Mr. Sharp, the stable master. "Came to the door all flustered, then said she'd meet us at the stable. Couldn't thank us enough once the horse was in the stall. Right nice woman."

"Did you see anyone else at the cottage?" Thomas asked as he removed the bit from one of the horse's mouths, then patted her neck while she moved her teeth back and forth, whinnying in contentment.

"No, sir," Mr. Sharp said, shaking his head. "The housekeeper — Mrs. Miller — brought us some tea and soda bread." He grinned. "Apologized for not having anything better, if you can believe it. Right nice woman. I see why the blacksmith is sweet on her."

Thomas considered this as he returned the bridle to the tack wall. He'd thought Mr. Larsen was rather attentive to the woman, and knew the man had lost his wife some years ago. Would he know more about the occupant of the cottage? Would Mrs. Miller have confided in him?

"Oh, and Mrs. Miller wanted me to bring these back to the manor."

Thomas looked over his shoulder at Mr. Sharp, who held out two letters. Thomas hurried to take them and felt his heart skip a beat when he saw his own name printed on the front of the first letter. The fluid feminine hand had to belong to Miss Sterlington, and he traced his fingers over the loops and curls of her penmanship. The second letter was addressed to Lord and Lady Fielding.

Not wanting to seem too eager, he put the letters in the inside pocket of his coat and continued helping Mr. Sharp care for the horses. Only when the horses had been led to their stalls, where grooms waited to brush them down, did he excuse himself. He made it through the back entrance of the house before he removed the letters, found his, and turned it over. The stamp was a simple fleur-de-lis, not a monogram.

He broke the wafer and unfolded the letter while his boots dripped onto the mat inside the door. It took concentration to keep from skimming the words too quickly so he slowed his mind and his eyes and read every word one at a time. When he finished, he took a breath and read the words again. As he did so, he felt some of the continued defenses he'd built around himself weaken, like the mud-and-stick dams he and his brothers used to build in the irrigation ditches when they were boys. Their dams could never withstand the rushing water for long and in time were washed away completely.

"Thomas?"

He looked up from his reading and dripping and thinking to see Lady Fielding standing a short distance away.

"Diane," he said, trying to fold his letter inconspicuously with the one hand he'd dropped to his side.

She looked at it, then raised her eyebrows and looked back to his face, awaiting an explanation.

Rather than give it, Thomas reached into his coat for the other letter and handed it over. "This came from Step Cottage. We had the gig returned to Mrs. Chandler this morning."

Lady Fielding took the letter, but looked at the one Thomas was trying to hide behind his back. "Two letters?"

"The other was addressed to me."

She raised her eyebrows again. "I see you did not wait to open yours."

Thomas would usually peruse correspondence in private, not in the servants' area of the house. In his defense, he had been alone when he'd opened it.

Thomas had no explanation that Lady Fielding would find satisfactory, however, and so he simply shrugged, quickly folded up his letter, tucked it into his coat, and began removing his working boots. As he did so he heard her break the wafer of her letter.

Thomas was tugging on his second boot when Lady Fielding spoke again. "She might be gentle bred, but she is quite lacking in manners, if you ask me."

"Pardon?" Thomas said as he straightened. His letter had been nothing but kindness and sincerity.

Lady Fielding held out her letter to him, and Thomas read the direct and specific language. It did not seem possible that the letters could have been written by the same person, the tone was so different. But the writing was the same. He could feel Lady Fielding watching him, awaiting his reply.

He looked up and returned the letter to her. "She *is* an eccentric," he said by way of explanation. "Perhaps we should be glad she was well-mannered enough for her to have written at all."

Lady Fielding nodded, but her scrutiny of Thomas was more intent than he liked. "Your letter was similarly abrupt?"

Thomas paused to construct as honest a reply as he dared to give. "It was perhaps a bit more gracious, but I suppose that is to be expected since it was I who put forth the idea to return Mrs. Miller." The arrogance of his words made him cringe inwardly, and he knew Lady Fielding wouldn't hesitate to remind him that the plan to return Mrs. Miller could never have been executed without the baron's carriage and blessing. Thomas did not give her time to speak, however.

"I'm afraid I must attend to some business. If you'll excuse me, Diane."

She nodded, but he felt her eyes on his back as he stepped away. He was still wet and cold so once he reached his room, he changed into dry clothes and then spent far too much time at the fireside, reading and rereading the letter Miss Sterlington had sent him. That she had crafted this letter to him was more intriguing than ever in light of the letter she'd written to Albert and Diane. What did it mean? Did he dare to speculate?

# Chapter 32

Amber,

I'm afraid the demands of the holiday kept me from responding to your letter sooner than this but perhaps it was a blessing as I had time to think over your apology and prepare my response.

While I hope your words are sincere, I am unsure you can fully understand how it felt to be treated as I was at your hand during our time in London. I cannot express the hurt and betrayal I felt, and yet I harbor my own guilt for what happened at Carlton House. Perhaps one day I shall be able to tell you the whole of it, but for now I can only admit to having been infected by the same selfishness and jealousy I believe inspired your own actions that night.

After your letter, I admitted the whole of it to Lord Sunther, and though I feared his disgust at my behavior, he has given me good counsel on the importance of forgiveness toward you.

I can say with confidence that I have no wish to be cruel to you, Amber, or press further infliction upon your circumstance. I am accepting of your apology, and I am trying very much to think only of the goodness we once had. I hope my honesty is understood and not taken poorly.

I am glad to hear you have become comfortable in Yorkshire. I have spoken with Mama about your request to attend the wedding, and she is concerned that your appearance at what shall be the event of the county would serve as a reminder of what happened at Carlton House. I have told her of the number of acquaintances who ask after you as well as suggesting that having you attend might resolve any concerns that have developed regarding your well-being. I also feel it would give credit to our family, as well as to Lord Sunther, to include you at such a happy event. Mama would like some time to consider my words.

Perhaps you could write her and promise to follow her direction in all matters of the wedding. Perhaps you could use it as a reason to return to Hampton Grove. Mama and Father shall be leaving for London in April; there would be time enough for you to procure the necessary arrangements to attend with them.

She mentioned you had not given her an update on the state of your hair, so perhaps include that as well for her peace of mind. I shall continue to encourage your attendance, though you know as well as I that if Mama is set against it, my opinion will not change her mind.

I wish you well, Amber, in body and spirit.

Sincerely,
Darra Elsinore Sterlington

Amber folded the letter carefully and put it in the slot reserved for her correspondence — five letters in all the months she had been at the cottage. Six, if she counted the one she'd thrown into the fire last September. Amber was relieved by Darra's desire to forgive her, but unsettled about her mother's reluctance to include Amber in their family again.

Darra had given her hope, however, and she would make sure to follow Darra's advice and write another letter to Lady

Marchent as soon as possible; Suzanne could post it the next time she went to town. Weather prevented frequent travel, but yesterday had arrived with blue skies and dry roads so Suzanne had made her trip, returning today with Darra's letter.

Amber entered the kitchen where Suzanne was finishing a bowl of stew, shivering from the cold air outside.

"How were things in town?" Amber asked, gathering the ingredients for bread. Suzanne had brought back yeast with her and Amber was determined to use it properly this time.

"Very well," Suzanne said, a lilt in her voice that caused Amber to look at her.

"*Very* well?" Amber repeated with suspicion.

Suzanne's cheeks were still pink from the cold, but Amber felt sure they went a shade darker.

"I saw Mr. Larsen at the mercantile, and he assisted me to the gig with my purchases and asked after my next trip to town."

Amber abandoned her ingredients and sat across the table from Suzanne. "Did he now?" she said with a smile. "You must tell me the whole of it, then."

Suzanne did not hesitate and told Amber of every expression and movement Mr. Larsen had made during their time together.

Amber was careful to be excited and positive even though the continuing attention of Mr. Larsen filled her with fearful anticipation. He was a widower with three small children. Amber was sure he was attempting to court Suzanne but had not yet said as much out loud.

When Suzanne finished her account, she updated Amber on the other matters she'd attended to in town, including delivering apple cakes to both Mr. Peters and Mr. Dariloo.

"Mr. Peters seemed rather surprised by it, but grateful. The Dariloos, however, were quite taken with the kindness and asked that I relay their most sincere thanks. He will be coming next week to see about any repairs we might need. I promised we would make a list for him."

Amber smiled. "I am glad they were pleased, though a cake now and again does not account for much."

"What did your sister say in her letter?" Suzanne asked, changing the topic while scraping out the final bite of stew from the wooden bowl. "Shall you attend your sister's wedding?"

Amber looked past Suzanne to the window while offering a soft smile and a shrug. "My mother is still deciding, but Darra did encourage my attendance so there is cause to hope. She suggested that perhaps I should return to Hampton Grove permanently at that time." Amber did not mention Darra's suggestion that Amber could then go on to London. She did not think she would ever go to that city again.

"Is it your wish to return to your family's estate?" Suzanne asked.

Amber shrugged again. "I do not know. When I think of the comfort of the place, being part of my family again, and planning for my future once more I feel eager for it. But I cannot believe it will ever be as it once was, or at least how I thought it was. I found happiness with my family because they loved me, and although I am hopeful that Darra still does, she will be making a life for herself as Lady Sunther in Suffolk and . . ." She paused for a breath. "I have not told them the truth regarding my hair. Should they know of it, I fear they would reject me again. By saying nothing I have led them to believe I am healing."

Suzanne glanced at Amber's head, covered in three knit caps. Amber no longer bothered with the lace caps, but needed the knit ones to stay as warm as possible. She had lost all of her hair, including that fine layer that covered her body. She did not even have eyelashes any more.

The few times she dared look at her reflection she noted how deformed she looked without the familiar facial landmarks of lashes, brows, and hairline. Her forehead was enormous, and her eyes looked wide and stark against her face. She supposed there was some artistic merit to the curves of her face and the shape of her head, but not enough to lift her in anyone's opinion she was sure.

"When last they saw me, I could hide my condition with a cap, but I can do that no longer. Without brows and lashes, I am unable to even pretend to look as a woman should, which makes me wonder if I ought to attend the wedding at all."

"Could you not use paints for your eyebrows?" Suzanne asked.

"The only women I know of who paint their faces are of dubious character."

"But you are not."

"If I paint my face, I shall be assumed to be."

Suzanne paused before she spoke. "I am not sure you need to make such attempts. This is your family. Perhaps they deserve another chance to accept you as you are."

Amber shook her head at the suggestion of presenting herself as she was. The idea filled her with fear and dread and doubt. "They shall accept me only in as much as I can play the part assigned to me. I know you cannot understand it, but it is the truth. My only chance to attend the wedding is to look as normal as I can — perhaps with another wig, perhaps with paints as you suggested, if I could make them look right. To go as I truly am is not an option."

"But, Miss —"

"I shall make the bread later," Amber cut in. "I feel in need of a rest, as I am sure you do after your journey."

She did not look back as she hurried from the kitchen, up the stairs, and to her room. She lit the fire she had laid that morning and curled up in the willow chair beside the hearth with a quilt. She attempted to compose in her head a letter for her mother that would entreat her consideration without revealing the fullness of Amber's condition. She did not like that she might have to trick her mother in order to get her support, but was she willing to tell the truth and risk spending the rest of her life in this stone house?

The cottage was comfortable and she felt secure within its walls, but if Suzanne made a match with Mr. Larsen, Amber would be alone. At least at Hampton Grove she would have . . . what *would* she have? She did not expect acceptance from her parents, nor did she expect to renew childhood acquaintances or pursue a marriage. Amber was a pariah, an embarrassment, a complication, and should she return to her family they would be forced to endure it. She wanted to be loved, not endured.

For the first time since arriving at Step Cottage, Amber wondered if perhaps she would find more comfort and happiness here than anywhere else. Perhaps it was best for everyone if she did not return. Could she live the rest of her life in isolation? Without Suzanne for company, she felt sure she would go quite mad.

There was a light knock on the door. "Come in."

"There was something else I wanted to speak to you about," Suzanne said as she came into the room.

"Of course," Amber said, forcing a smile to hide her discouragement.

"While I was in town, I purchased some fabric and wondered if you might sew me a gown for the Winter Ball in two weeks' time."

Amber blinked. "Sew you a gown?"

"You are an excellent seamstress, Miss, and —"

"I embroider well, is what you mean," Amber said.

"And make aprons and shifts and caps, to say nothing of the dress you picked out and redid with side panels," Suzanne said. "I should very much like a nice gown for the dance. Would you please help me?"

Amber leaned back in the chair. "I have never sewn clothing except for a few shirts for my brothers. I cannot imagine you would be happy with the result. Could we not contact the woman in town who outfitted us for winter?"

"I have seen the care you take with other things you've created, and I feel sure you will do right by this," Suzanne assured her. "I cannot think to pay someone else when I am sure you will do well."

"I could ask Mr. Peters if he might extend the funds to —"

"I do not want you to ask Mr. Peters," Suzanne said with directness. "I am asking you to sew me a gown. You have an eye for fashion and drape that I feel will do my figure as much credit as I can expect at my age. Please say yes."

Amber felt backed into a corner by the request; she could not refuse Suzanne anything. "If you are certain," she said, oddly humbled by the request while also invigorated by the challenge. "I should be most happy to give it my very best effort."

# CHAPTER 33

"Are you ready?" Suzanne asked from the doorway of the library.

"I don't know that I shall ever be ready," Amber said, her hands over her eyes. "But there is no point in delaying it."

She heard Suzanne's footsteps and could scarcely breathe as she waited.

"All right, then," Suzanne said.

Rather than move her hands, Amber spread her fingers so she could look between them. Seeing that the dress was not atrocious, she lowered her hands. If she'd had eyebrows they would have risen as she looked upon Suzanne, who put out her arms and turned around slowly enough for Amber to inspect the rose-colored dress she had spent the last two weeks creating. After Suzanne completed her turn, Amber smiled. "You look beautiful," she said in a breathy voice.

"The *dress* looks beautiful," Suzanne corrected, looking at the skirt as she swished the fabric back and forth.

"You look beautiful in the beautiful dress," Amber further amended. She stood up from the settee and came closer. "I had so feared the bodice would be puckered there in front where I did not get the gather quite right."

"It is exactly as I had known it would turn out," Suzanne said, fairly beaming. "And look —" She twirled, causing the skirt to bell out with perfect symmetry. "It is just the right length for dancing but will not drag upon the floor when I walk." She demonstrated by taking a few steps toward the door — while a train was fashionable in London, it was impractical in the country.

"The color is perfect for your features," Amber noted. In London it had never occurred to her to consider whether or not Suzanne was a handsome woman, but she had taken note of Suzanne's solid beauty here in Yorkshire. She had dark hair, always gathered into a braided knot at the back of her head, and wide brown eyes that danced when she was in a good humor. Her teeth were well set, and her complexion was quite smooth for a woman of thirty-two years. The rose color enhanced every good thing about her.

Amber inspected the dress again, amazed

at how lovely it looked. She had used one of her own dresses as a pattern, adjusting it for Suzanne's larger frame and the formality of the event by adding puff sleeves and a sweetheart neckline. Certainly she knew it was not nearly as fine as one an actual dressmaker could create, but she felt proud of the result. She had feared it would be hideous.

Every cut of the shears and stitch of the needle had filled Amber with dread, but having been fitted for dresses all her life, and learning the "accomplishment" of embroidery considered suitable for women of the *ton* had created more ability than she had expected.

Suzanne had tried on the different pieces a dozen times as Amber attempted to fit them to her just right, but tonight was the first time Suzanne had put on the completed dress.

"I have something else for you," Amber said, then hurried behind one of the heavy bookshelves and returned with a reticule and a hat, both sewn from scraps of the fabric. She'd taken the Swedish lace from one of her morning dresses unsuitable for cottage life and made an edge on the hat that set it off to even further distinction. Amber had embroidered an elaborate design on the bag, working late at night in her room so as to hide it from Suzanne's notice.

Suzanne's eyes went wide as she took the items and turned them in her hand. "They are beautiful." She smiled like a schoolgirl and ran upstairs to look at her reflection in the looking glass. "I shall be the belle of the ball in this," Suzanne called from the top of the stairs, quite improperly.

It felt good to make something useful, but even better, Amber felt as though she had in some way begun to repay a debt to her friend. She wondered how Mr. Larsen would react to Suzanne in that dress and smiled at the expectation that he would be well pleased with it. For an instant she imagined that she were wearing such a dress and attending a ball. Perhaps Mr. Richards would ask her to dance. She entertained the idea for only a moment before brushing it away. Dances and balls were a lifetime ago. Mr. Richards was simply a kind man — one of the few she'd met since relocating to Step Cottage — and his kindness had given him the status of the hero in all her girlish fantasies.

"I shall serve supper while you change," Amber called. It was only four o'clock, but as they tended to rise with the sun and sleep by the moon, it was sensible to prepare dinner when it was still full light outside. Today was storming, however, and they had been forced to burn candles during the day.

Suzanne returned a few minutes later, dressed in a gray working dress that further emphasized the advantage the rose-colored dress gave to her. "I folded the dress and packed it along with the reticule, stays, and hat in the small trunk. You're sure you don't mind my taking it with me?"

"What use have I for it?" Amber said without feeling the level of regret she once had. The finer things in her possession were quite useless in her present circumstance, and she was glad they would benefit Suzanne. She glanced to the window, streaked with rain. "I do hope the storm lifts before tomorrow, though. Even the hood of the gig won't protect you from such elements as this."

"I shall go rain or shine," Suzanne said and smiled again, which, as always, made Amber smile too. For two women so opposed to their situation in the beginning, they had come to find a level of joy that surprised them both.

Amber served roasted potatoes with a bit of mustard powder and dried thyme, some ham from the smokehouse, and yesterday's leftover soda bread. In the beginning,

Amber had been unable to entertain the idea of a meal without meat, and they had gone through their winter stores faster than they should have. She was now accustomed to vegetable stews and meatless pies, but as Suzanne was going to town, Amber wanted to serve a fancier meal than usual. Mrs. Haribow had only come three times since November due to the condition of the roads. They missed her cooking, but it had challenged Amber to better hone her own skills.

All things considered, life had become quite comfortable at Step Cottage. Amber was less inclined to pine for the life she had had; in fact it seemed like a story in a book when she thought back to it. Had she truly stayed out until three or four o'clock in the morning simply to gossip and flirt? In Yorkshire she never went outside after dark and, according to the clock in the library, no longer stayed up past ten o'clock.

Had she worn very fine dresses only once before refusing to be seen in them again? At Step Cottage she had three dresses for winter — all of them plain, comfortable, and practical — that she interchanged from day to day. No one saw her in them but Suzanne.

Had she sat at her dressing table for hours

in order to have her long, thick hair perfectly arranged? That was perhaps the memory that felt most like fantasy. Her head was so smooth she could scarcely remember what it looked like before. She'd moved the looking glass from her room to Suzanne's and in its absence she become all but unaware of her appearance. Quite a change from the girl she had been before.

"Shall we play loo before bed?" Suzanne asked after they scraped their bowls clean and wrapped up the remaining soda bread.

Amber had begun teaching Suzanne how to play cards when they'd run out of other evening entertainments and Suzanne was not in the mood to read. Teaching her loo had reminded Amber of an evening in London when she had pretended not to know the game so as to beg help from the gentlemen at the table. It was embarrassing to recall the ways in which she manipulated the people around her.

What a fool she'd been to ignore the chance to truly get to know someone. What she wouldn't give for the chance to try again. This time, she would try to learn about the inner workings of a man rather than weighing and measuring him against her expectations. Perhaps if she had done so the first time, she *could* have found a kind man willing to overlook her condition. Until the end, however, kindness had not been a consideration. And now, when she wished for another chance, it was not to be.

She thought of the coat hanging in her wardrobe at the London house. Surely the man who had helped her that night would have been worthwhile to know, and yet Amber did not think she had bothered to even meet him. How shallow she had been to have ignored someone of quality. She wondered what had become of him. And Lord Norwin too — had he married the girl of his fancy?

"Amber? Shall we play loo?"

Amber shook herself out of her thoughts and smiled. "If you don't mind, I think I should like to read for a bit. I have almost finished another volume of the Roman history. They were far more advanced than I ever realized before. When I finish, I believe I shall go to Shakespeare's histories. I've always avoided them, you know, but now that we have read some of his other works I wonder what I might have missed."

Suzanne tsked her tongue and shook her head while giving Amber a playful look. "You have turned into quite a bluestocking. I hope you shall not spout off about the barbaric nature of Ancient Rome again. I can assure you it is lost on me."

"As it was on me when I was first taught it as a girl," Amber said, shaking her head. There was so much she had relearned now that she cared enough to be attentive to the information. "To think they threw men together in a ring and had them fight to the death, often tearing one another limb by limb to the delight of the crowd. Deplorable." She looked sideways at her friend. "I daresay our current society is not so different in some respects of class and distinction."

How often had she been one of the observers, watching someone's reputation be stripped through an oversight of etiquette or dismissing someone due to poor connections. She had never once considered that she would one day find herself in the arena.

# Chapter 34

Suzanne left for town the next morning, the rain falling steadily but the road not too muddy yet. Amber had wanted to talk her out of taking the trip in such weather, but knew how excited Suzanne was for the Winter Ball and so she held her tongue and offered a dozen prayers that her friend would make it to town and return tomorrow, safely. As always, she hated to be alone at the cottage and began counting the hours before she could expect Suzanne's return.

It was a quiet evening which allowed Amber time to finish the Roman history and begin reading *Richard II.* She was in bed early and awake with the winter sun. That the sky was clear enough to show the sun improved her mood, and she quickly moved through the morning chores before putting on a stew to cook for supper. She kept an ear for the road and the wheels of the gig, but the afternoon dragged on and Suzanne still had not come home.

Bored and feeling anxious, Amber tried to read, but put the book aside when she could not focus on it. *Richard II* was rather tedious, but she was determined to give it her best effort.

She went out to the front porch, frowning at the sun that would set in two hours' time. Where was Suzanne? The weather would not have prevented her return. Had Mr. Larsen declared his intentions? Could Suzanne even now be trying to craft an explanation to Amber about her changing future? The thought seized Amber's chest in a cold grip. If Suzanne left and her parents did not allow her to return to Hampton Grove, what would become of her?

More eager than ever for a distraction, Amber began walking through the cottage, sweeping out this corner, oiling that windowsill until it gleamed. She arranged the foyer area with the hat tree on the left, then on the right, then back on the left again before centering it in front of the small window on the east wall. She rearranged some of the books in the library, moving Shakespeare higher so as to accommodate the entire collection in the center portion of the bookshelf where it was more of a focal point. It was when she turned away from that task that her eyes landed on the limp curtains hanging on either side of the window above the desk.

The brown fabric was threadbare and coarse enough to appear like burlap — until she pulled the fabric out to straighten the creases and realized it had been burgundy in color. Amber rubbed the fabric between her fingers. She had sewn shifts and aprons and, now, a dress. Could she not create curtains that would cheer this room? There were so many dark and heavy items in the cottage that a splash of green, or even yellow, would certainly lift the overall mood.

She spent half an hour going through the excess linens stored upstairs — none of which matched the idea she had for the curtains — and then looked through her own dresses that she had brought from London. There were three gowns she had not worn even once at the cottage, not wanting to soil them, and although she doubted her need to keep them — when would she ever need such fine clothes again? — she did not want to destroy them.

The four gowns she had worn until having the winter dresses made were stained and quite ruined, unless you were a cook and a cleaner. Which she was. Because they were still serviceable and spring would be arriving some time — she hoped — she did not want to destroy them either. But that left her without fabric for the project that had captured her attention and distracted her from her growing worry about Suzanne's return.

It was then she remembered the trunks that had at one time been in Suzanne's bedchamber. At the time Mr. Dariloo had come and moved them to the servant's quarters, Amber and Suzanne had talked of going through them at some later date. Yet, they hadn't. Instead Suzanne had learned to read quite well and play loo. Perhaps it was time to examine the contents of the trunks. Perhaps there would be some garment that would prove acceptable as curtains and thus spare Amber's own dresses.

With that goal in mind, Amber was skipping down the stairs when the front door opened. She froze, put her hand on her cap-covered head, and turned to run back up the stairs, her heart in her throat and her lungs refusing to fill with air.

"Amber?"

At the sound of Suzanne's voice, Amber relaxed, but she still peered around the edge of the frame to make sure Suzanne was alone. Suzanne had always come in through the kitchen on prior trips to town. Why had she come through the front? Was she alone?

When the door shut behind Suzanne, Amber dared come around the corner. "You scared me near to death." Amber took in the maid's disheveled appearance and tired expression and hurried to the bottom of the stairs. "Suzanne, are you all right?"

Suzanne looked at the floor and tried to hide the mud on her boots and the hem of her dress. "The gig slid off the road two miles from town. I had to walk back and ask Mr. Larsen for his help. He freed the gig, but it took some time and . . . the left wheel was broken." She looked up. "I'm so sorry, Miss. I don't know how it happened."

"It is of no trouble," Amber said. "But are you hurt? How did you return?"

"I rode Sally back after Mr. Larsen loaned me a saddle and said he would look after the gig. I feel like such a dunce."

Amber shook her head at Suzanne's self-recrimination. "We knew we were taking a risk having you drive to town before the roads firmed up. It will all turn out, but let's get you into the kitchen and warm you up. I'll see about heating some water for a bath. You must be half frozen."

"Thank you," Suzanne said, showing the level of her fatigue as she let out a breath. "I had to leave my purchases in town, as well as your traveling trunk — I'm sorry."

"It's no mind at all," Amber said, ushering Suzanne into the kitchen. Dried mud fell from her hem to the floor; Amber would have to sweep up later. "Stop apologizing."

She pulled one of the stools from the table closer to the fire and set Suzanne upon it. Suzanne leaned forward, soaking up the warmth and seeming to relax. Amber put a pot of water on to boil for tea, then a larger one to heat for a bath, added more coal to get a better blaze, and then led Sally the rest of the way to the stable, where she combed her out and treated her to a full bucket of grain.

By the time Amber returned to the kitchen, Suzanne had poured her own tea and the larger pot was heated. She poured the hot water into the tub, filled the pot again before putting it on to boil, and set the screen around the tub.

"I'll not having you attending to me," Suzanne said when Amber attempted to help her out of her dress. "It isn't right."

"Don't be a goose," Amber said, pushing Suzanne's hands away. "You're only making it harder."

It was nearly an hour before Suzanne was warm and clean and had fully given up her fight. Amber found the reversing role rather humorous, mostly because it so discomfited her maid, and she therefore took extra measures for Suzanne's comfort. When Suzanne was dressed in fresh clothing, Amber attempted to take the tub out of the kitchen but found it far too heavy. Suzanne had been the one to attend to bathing previously, and Amber had not once considered how it was done and was lost as to how to complete the task.

"You have to empty it in portions, just as you filled it," Suzanne said as she jumped to her feet. "I shall do it."

"You shall not," Amber said, fixing her with a hard look. "After all the effort it took to get you dry, I shan't risk starting all over because you soak yourself with bathwater." She took the pot and removed a portion of water, dumping it out the back door. Once she'd removed enough water for the tub to be moved, she took the tub to the yard and finished emptying it.

"Now, what do we do with your clothing?" Amber said, eyeing the pile of sodden and muddy fabric. "Perhaps I shall hang it to dry until it can go to the washerwoman in town."

"I shall hang it," Suzanne said, rising to her feet again.

"You will not!" Amber retorted, quickly

gathering the soiled fabric and hurrying into the yard. If it did not rain, the articles could dry outside, which seemed a far better course than hanging them on the line that stretched across the kitchen. The sun had been down for some time, and she shivered in the cold. Maybe a little rain would help clean the wretched things.

She was in the process of shaking out Suzanne's coat when she heard the crinkle of paper from one of the pockets. Of course — Suzanne had retrieved the post while in town, but as she had said she'd left her parcels behind in the gig, Amber hadn't thought to ask after any letters.

With eager hands Amber retrieved a letter addressed to Mrs. Chandler, the name written in an unfamiliar hand. She set it aside, then checked the rest of Suzanne's pockets before returning inside.

"Was this in the post?" Amber asked, closing the door behind her and trying not to sigh in relief at the kitchen's warmth.

Suzanne looked over her shoulder. "It's from Mr. Richards. I meant to tell you of it as soon as I came in."

Suddenly eager, Amber broke the seal and unfolded the letter.

Dear Mrs. Chandler,

Thank you for your kind letter. I simply did what any other gentleman would do, but I am glad it added to your comfort for Mrs. Miller to be returned. I hope it is not too forward of me, but in your letter you said that if there was some way to repay the kindness you would be obliging. In the process of searching your library for the record I found last November, I noticed that you had a volume of John Donne's early poetry. I am a great lover of his work and wondered if I might borrow the book and copy from it a few of his more poignant verses. I promise to take great care of it and return it quickly.

If this is acceptable, I should like to come Tuesday next, assuming the roads are clear, and promise not to bother you for long. There is no need to prepare anything on my behalf, I shall only retrieve the book and be on my way.

Sincerely,
Thomas Richards

Amber read the words through twice, quite forgetting that Suzanne was awaiting a report until she turned back to the fire and saw the woman standing there. "My apologies," Amber said. "He would like to come on Tuesday and borrow a book."

"Would he now?" Suzanne said with a grin.

"Apparently there is a rare book of poetry in the library." Her stomach fluttered. "Do you object to his visit?"

After a slight pause, Suzanne shook her head. "Not at all. Mr. Larsen is coming for Sally and myself on Sunday in the vicar's carriage so I may attend church. I can return with the gig on Monday. Tuesday is acceptable."

Amber smiled, relieved, and gave into her building excitement. "Is it not rather invigorating to have someone in the cottage?" she said. "It is as though it brings new air into the very rooms, does it not?"

Suzanne simply inclined her head. She must not feel the same invigoration Amber did, but then, Suzanne interacted with townspeople on a regular basis. For Amber a possible visit from Mr. Richards was new and exciting, even though she knew she should be uncomfortable and anxious. Her jumbled feelings only underscored how strange her life had become. She had not *interacted* with Mr. Richards at all, but still, she had enjoyed his previous visit and had spent a great deal of time thinking of him and wondering about him. She liked very much that he felt welcome here. In fact, she realized, she was eager to have him come.

The idea of his visit gave Amber a fresh burst of energy as she went about the evening, seeing to Suzanne's needs and finishing supper. Eventually she remembered the idea for her curtains — she would so very much like to have the new ones in place before Mr. Richards's visit.

"We said we would sort through those trunks one day," Amber said to Suzanne, "but we never have. Perhaps we could bring in one trunk at a time and sort it in the parlor. With both of us exerting ourselves on either end it shouldn't be too difficult. It shall be like buried treasure!" She headed toward the sideboard to put away the dishes, then turned back to put a hand on Suzanne's arm. "And you must help me come up with another cake! We cannot possibly serve him the same variety on Tuesday as we did the last time he came."

# Chapter 35

As with many things, the *proposition* of removing the four trunks, a wooden crate, and a lidded basket from the servant's room to the parlor the next morning was far easier than the action it required. It did, in fact, take nearly an hour for the two women to complete the task. The furniture in the parlor was pushed to the walls, and they lit some coal in the grate they had not used all winter. They spent the majority of their time in the kitchen or library, which was why the parlor was the best choice for the project that was becoming more and more exciting to Amber. In the parlor, the trappings of the trunks would not get in the way of their daily activity.

After they had lunched on cold beef sandwiches and apple cake, Suzanne expressed her concerns about completing the other chores around the cottage since she had been gone two days and would be leaving again tomorrow when Mr. Larsen came for her.

"I can delay the sorting," Amber said, hiding her disappointment. She wanted to see what those trunks held, but she also wanted Suzanne's company. "I shall have time enough after you go to town."

"You are more invested in the contents of those trunks than I shall ever be," Suzanne proclaimed. "I am quite content to do our shared tasks before we go."

She wrapped a shawl about her shoulders, crossing the ends over her chest and then tucking them into her apron band so as to free her hands as she went about her work. She tied on a rather worn bonnet against the chill wind that had picked up overnight and then pulled on a set of Amber's leather gloves. They were too fine for stable work but as Amber had no other use for them, they served well enough.

Amber made Suzanne promise to fetch her if she needed help, then removed to the parlor where she was indeed eager to explore the trunks. She hoped to find fabric suitable for curtains, but she also wondered if perhaps the trunks belonged to a former occupant of the cottage. Who had lived in Step Cottage prior to Amber and Suzanne's arrival?

Surely Mr. Dariloo could answer such questions should Amber have asked, but it had not occurred to her to do so until her mind had been turned to the trunks yesterday. She could hardly contain the intrigue of such a mystery.

Amber settled her attention on the largest trunk first and flipped the clasps, pressing the locks until she was able to pull the lid back with a great creaking. The packing paper had yellowed enough to testify that it had been some time since the trunks had been opened.

She moved the paper aside carefully, and then removed perhaps the most ridiculous hat she had ever seen. It was a large frothy looking thing so heavily adorned with ribbons and feathers — all of which were badly damaged from the storage — that Amber laughed out loud imagining someone attempting to balance such a creation upon one's head. It was outdated and crisp with age. She set it aside and removed two other equally horrific pieces before moving aside another layer of paper to reveal what she thought was a costume of some sort.

Amber stood and pulled from the trunk a heavy brocade dress of dark red, with buttons of paste diamonds and eight inches of lace at the cuffs. The waist was low to the hip, the cut severe and the skirt billowing enough to accommodate hoops, no doubt. Her mother had worn similar gowns during her season more than twenty years ago, which at least gave Amber an idea of the age for the woman who may have owned this dress.

There was surely enough fabric in the large skirt to accommodate library curtains and the color would complement the room very well. She would feel bad cutting up such a remarkable — though completely unwearable — garment, however.

She laid the heavy dress across a chair before continuing on her pursuits, which resulted in three more equally elaborate and, in the case of two of them, quite hideous gowns. A green velvet thing with flounces and ruffles and a section that moths had gone to work on replaced the brocade for curtain consideration; the green would better suit the surroundings, Amber thought, and she would not be destroying a dress that was not already damaged.

Below the dresses was more paper and then eight pairs of shoes, including a very nice pair of classic white satin slippers she would insist Suzanne try on. They would serve her well at the next Wednesday night ball. A pair of half boots were also of value due to their solid construction, so long as the wearer could bear boots the color of daffodils.

At the very bottom of the trunk Amber found what looked like an invitation, but turned out to be a dance card for an event titled EverSpring Soiree. She opened it to find that every line was filled, though only a few bore legible names. Amber wondered why a woman of such attention would have removed to Step Cottage at all. Had this woman lived here alone?

The thought stilled her for a moment and her eyes darted to the elaborate dresses now draped around the room. Had Amber not dressed in the finest of fashions and danced every dance at any number of events in London not even a year ago? Though her ball gowns had not been sent with her from London, would it have been such a surprise if they had ended up in storage just as this?

It was with quicker movement and less attentiveness to style and quality that Amber opened the next trunk and sorted its contents: clothing more appropriate for everyday use, the styles of some more modern than others but still outdated. There were shawls and a great variety of mobcaps, the sheer number of which quickened Amber's eagerness even more.

At the bottom of the trunk, amid a few pairs of practical shoes, Amber found something that quite caught her breath. With a trembling hand, she removed a knitted cap of yellowed yarn not so discolored as to have been in the trunk for long.

Prior to her time in the cottage, Amber had only ever seen such caps for very small infants, but she was now quite familiar with the pattern. She pulled the knitted cap she wore day and night from her own head, then held it side by side with the one she'd found in the trunk. The design was too exact to be coincidental.

Whomever had lived in this cottage previously had found herself needing something to keep her head warm during the long winters.

# Chapter 36

Suzanne put on her bonnet in the kitchen Sunday morning, though she left the ribbons undone. She gave Amber a concerned look. "Perhaps I should not go. I am not feeling resolved to it."

"I am *quite* resolved," Amber said as she whipped together the two eggs they had found in the coop that morning. The bounty would allow her to make a cake today. She was of a mind to use some of the apples and carrots from the cellar as she felt sure the flavors would complement one another. "And your blacksmith is coming all the way from town to fetch you so you must go."

"Amber, you need not cover your feelings at what you have discovered."

Amber stopped beating the eggs, her stoic façade replaced by an expression of fatigue. She stared into the mottled yellow mixture and let out a long breath. "I do not mean to concern you by hiding my feelings," she said. "And I will not deny that I would like nothing more than for you to stay — but then I always feel that way."

Suzanne removed her bonnet and patted the wayward strands that had pulled away from her braided knot. "I shall stay. Mr. Larsen will understand, and I shall simply fetch the gig later in the week."

Amber shook her head. "You did not let me complete my thoughts. I am *also* quite eager to receive whatever reports you may find about Constance Sterlington as well as to see that my letter to my parents is posted tomorrow morning." The woman's surname — discovered in yet another trunk — was proof that she was a relation to Amber herself: another Miss Sterlington sentenced to Yorkshire to hide a condition that was not to be tolerated. But Amber did not know what exact relation they shared as she had never heard her name in her life. It made her extremely uneasy to think of this woman's existence being hidden from her by purposeful action.

Suzanne frowned, then almost immediately brightened. "Come with me," she said, crossing to Amber and putting a hand on her arm. "Whoever she is, we know she was not about the town or I certainly would have heard about her before now. Use this discovery as reason to hide no longer. Not everyone will be so dismissive as those who sent you here."

The idea of leaving the cottage filled Amber with absolute terror and she shook her head. "As much as I thank you for such encouragement I cannot do it."

"You can if you shall make the decision for it," Suzanne said. "Mr. and Mrs. Clawson would welcome you fully and —"

"I will not go and insist you stop asking it of me!" Amber snapped, shocking them both with the strength of her words. They shared a look for a few moments, then Amber turned back to the eggs. "I'm sorry, Suzanne, forgive me," she said by way of apology, but she did not look up.

"I should not have insisted so strongly, Miss," Suzanne replied, her tone formal and submissive. They both worked in silence until there was a knock at the door. Suzanne bade Amber good-bye without meeting her eye, and Amber stayed hidden in the kitchen while Suzanne greeted Mr. Larsen and followed him out of the cottage.

Amber went to her room and watched from the window as the carriage, with Sally tethered to the back, disappeared down the drive. It was rare for Amber to revert to her waspish ways, and she felt deep regret for having succumbed to it, yet glad it had stilled Suzanne's arguments. Suzanne could not possibly understand how much Amber both longed and feared for connection with people. The fear, of course, won out as she could not imagine that anyone could look past her defects. What good would it do to make acquaintances who would then avoid her? Fear her? Judge her?

When Amber returned to the kitchen, she finished mixing the cake and adjusted the coals before putting the pot amid them. Only when the dishes were rinsed and drying did she permit herself to return to the parlor. The contents of the trunks were still strewn about the room. She stirred the fire, added some coal, and turned her attention to the fourth trunk — the smallest one she had opened very last.

While the others were filled with different varieties of clothing, this one had been filled with sketchpads and correspondence and all manner of documents. There was even a small crockery that held a kind of paint in a shade of light brown — face paints. Suzanne had suggested it was to remedy Constance Sterlington's missing eyebrows. Amber agreed that it was likely, but felt sick knowing someone else had suffered as she had.

Amber had glanced through the papers

quickly last night but the emotion of the discovery had eventually sent her to bed with a headache that had lingered through the morning. She had not told Suzanne she was still so afflicted, of course, as she knew it would serve as another reason for Suzanne to stay at the cottage. Despite her dislike of being alone, Amber was glad to have the time to focus on the papers she hoped would put flesh on the bones of understanding Miss Constance Sterlington.

So engaged was she in her research of the prior occupant of Step Cottage that she burned the cake. And the soda bread she attempted for a light supper. Finally, she let the kitchen fire die out and brought a quilt from her bed so as to remain beside the fire in the parlor while she continued to read through the letters and journals that detailed the feelings of young Constance.

The girl had been presented to court at the age of sixteen and enjoyed the attention of many suitors for her first season but refused any number of proposals only to return for a second season the following year. According to her journals, she was simply too amused to trade the entertainment for matrimony. Amber's chest burned at the similarity to her own feelings.

Constance spoke of balloon ascensions,

balls, and visits to Ascot, theaters, and parks that first season. It seemed her company was in high demand and her suitors were of high station befitting a Viscount's daughter. Constance was her father's sister, Amber's own aunt, and yet Amber had heard nothing of her before.

The journal entries became less effusive and less frequent during Constance's second season, until one emotional entry reported that she was being removed to Hampton Grove due to some illness affecting her hair. She was miserable to leave her friends and suitors but shared a greater fear that something was very wrong, something that would not be easily remedied. There was only one entry after that: three sentences explaining that her family had left for London — Amber calculated from the date that it would have been her third season — and Constance was to stay behind.

> What shall become of me? How shall I get on?
> Why must I be so afflicted?

There was nothing written after that, no mention of when she had come to Step Cottage or how her thoughts and expectations of her future had changed after her illness. If not for her trunks being in storage here, there would be no reason to suspect from the journals and letters that Constance had been here at all — no correspondence between her family, no record of her thoughts of life in Yorkshire.

As the coals cooled and the wind howled, Amber pulled the quilt up to her chin, sure that she could feel Constance's restless presence. Had Constance ever been reconciled to the life she'd once had? Had she returned to her family? It seemed that if she had left this place she would have taken her things with her. That they remained and no one had ever claimed them caused Amber great unease.

She was therefore eager for any account of Constance Suzanne might be able to gather from town. Amber hoped that Constance *had* left this place and continued her life elsewhere without the items she'd brought to the cottage. It did not explain why Amber had never heard her name spoken within her family, but perhaps there had been some additional reason that accounted for her situation. The caps found in the trunk made it impossible to hope that her loss of hair wasn't part of her reason for being here, but it did not mean that it was the only reason.

If Constance Sterlington had in fact recovered, however, regardless of other causes for her removal to Step Cottage, Amber could have hope that she would too. That she could be beautiful again. Confident again. A darling of the Polite World again. And yet even as she attempted to revive her hope, she feared that having gained such perspective on a way of life so different than the one she was raised to expect had changed her so that she would never find joy in the place she had once thought to be the only source of it. She could not imagine trusting people of her station when she knew how fickle their acceptance was, how superficial, how small. She could not imagine spending such time and attention on frivolous things and meaningless conversation.

She gathered the quilt around herself and blew out the candle; she did not need the light to see her way to her room. Once in her bedchamber, she lit the coal she'd put in the grate that afternoon and snuggled under layers of quilts as the flames licked and popped. As she closed her eyes, she said a silent prayer that Suzanne would return tomorrow with hope. She felt more in need of it than ever.

# CHAPTER 37

Suzanne returned late Monday afternoon, shivering and wet from rain that had picked up the last mile. Fortunately the weather didn't prevent her return as the storm had three weeks earlier or end in disaster as it had on Friday when the gig had slid off the road. Amber had her friend sit in front of the kitchen hearth with a cup of tea while she warmed their dinner and Suzanne began her account of Constance Sterlington.

"She passed away before Mr. Clawson had taken over the parsonage. Two women of the congregation I spoke to knew *of* her, but had never met her. She did not go to town but instead employed an attendant and a manservant to transact her dealings. Both servants came with her when she arrived at the cottage and returned to London after her passing. They did not travel to town much either, but kept to the cottage."

"Did you speak to Mr. Dariloo? Mr. Peters?"

"Mr. Peters claims to know only the barest facts about her even though I feel sure he managed the estate while she was here. Perhaps he would be more open to your inquiry than mine."

Amber had not considered that Mr. Peters would be less forthcoming with a maid and was embarrassed to have put Suzanne in an uncomfortable situation by having her ask. "And Mr. Dariloo?"

Suzanne gave her a hesitant look over the rim of her cup. "Mr. Dariloo lived in this cottage before Miss Constance came. He was removed to his current residence to accommodate her."

"So he knew her."

Suzanne nodded. "He interacted with her several times, but not pleasantly. He referred to her as bitter and cross — very disparaging of lower classes and critical of his efforts with the land. She would send him letters through her servants, often calling him to task for not accommodating her in one way or another, or demanding to look at ledgers for the land and then reprimanding him for bothering her with such information."

"And her hair? Did he know of her condition?"

"He did not say that anything ailed her, rather he believed she'd chosen to live away from society for her own particular reasons, but then seemed very disagreeable to life here. He felt she was a bit . . . touched."

Miss Constance was not touched. She, like Amber, had been exiled. She had lost her future and prospective happiness and had not had someone such as Suzanne to direct her toward purpose and contentment. It was not difficult for Amber to imagine her first night at the cottage being followed with hundreds just like it if not for Suzanne. How would such anger and resentment *not* fester and canker a person?

"How long did she live here?" Amber asked.

"Eight years," Suzanne said. "She came in aught one and died of influenza in aught nine though she was not quite thirty years of age at the time. She is buried in Northallerton. Mr. Dariloo said he could direct us to the grave."

"Her grave is *here*?" The Sterlington family had a burial plot outside of Hampton Grove that had been established when the grand house was built. Six generations of Sterlingtons had been buried there, including her father's brother who was killed in France. They had seen to it that his remains were returned and properly interred with the family — but not Constance's? Was losing her hair enough to cut Constance off from her family even in death?

The thought ushered in another one that left Amber feeling unsteady on her feet and in her mind. Constance had *died* here, which meant she had never recovered. She had never returned to society or her family. Amber sat on the kitchen stool beside Suzanne and stared at the stone floor.

"I'm sorry to have been the bearer of such things," Suzanne said, regret laced through her words.

"It is alright," Amber said as her own future spread out before her with a brittle detail she wished she could deny. If she did not get well, she would not return to her family. They had not brought Constance back into their fold; they had not even spoken her name. Like Constance, Amber was to be forgotten until some further ailment took her life and sent her to the cemetery in Northallerton too.

"Amber."

She looked at Suzanne and tried to blink back the tears she had not realized were forming. Without lashes to contain them, there was no barrier preventing the tears from streaming down Amber's cheeks. Her stomach felt hollow.

"You are not Constance," Suzanne said. "You do not have to take her same course."

"I am already on her same course. Constance had a season in London — two of them. She was sent here as I have been and was not accepted back to the family, even for burial. How can I expect anything different except to live and die as she did?"

"Perhaps knowing of her fate can help you avoid it."

"How?" Amber said, wiping at her eyes. "Nothing has stemmed the loss of my hair and none of it is growing back. If it were simply a wish and a will that would repair me, I would not be here even now."

"It is not your lack of hair keeping you to the cottage."

Amber blinked, confused as she regarded Suzanne's determined expression. "I don't understand your meaning. Of course it is my lack of hair."

Suzanne shook her head. "It is your lack of *confidence.* It is your fear of being turned away that keeps you here — not your ailment."

Amber felt anger rising in response to Suzanne's reprimand and looked past her. The memory of the faces at Carlton House when she'd sat at the bottom of the stairs without her head covering filled her chest with a heat burning of pure fear. It was something Suzanne could not understand any more than Amber could adequately explain it.

"I think I shall retire for the night," Amber said, unable to abide the discussion any longer. "I mixed the gravy from Saturday night with some potatoes. It's warming in the pot on the coals. There are a few biscuits left in the tin as well."

"Stay and eat with me," Suzanne said.

"I'm afraid I have already eaten my share of biscuits in my anxiousness for your report. I am not hungry."

Suzanne stood from the table, but did not move. "I am sorry to have upset you, Amber."

Amber looked at her cautiously, pulled between staying with her friend and running for the solitude of her room. "I know you mean well, but you cannot know my position," she said, though her honesty made her nervous as she did not want it to sound like a set down. "I cannot risk rejection, Suzanne. I know that may be difficult to understand but . . ." She paused a moment to gather her thoughts. "Already I have lost my family and my society — if not for you I should be entirely alone. To ask for consideration of the people here in Yorkshire would risk further rejection. I cannot endure such a thing again."

Suzanne regarded her for several moments. "I understand, Amber, and would have you remember one additional thing. I know all of what you have become and have not rejected you."

Amber looked up at her, struck by what she'd said even as doubt and fear lingered in her mind.

Suzanne continued. "No one can expect approval from every other person in the world — even the young woman you were in London did not expect such a thing — but I believe all of us can expect those few who matter to us to see past our limitations.

"My sister has had a twist in her back all her life which leaves her walking with an awkwardness that appears painful, though she assures us it is not. She married a good man who saw past her physicality, and they have three children, one of whom is of simple mind and yet loved as wholly as his brother and sister. I would have hoped your family would be the first to accept you regardless of this circumstance, but even if they should not, I do not believe everyone would be so dismissive. In fact, I am certain they would not. Mr. Richards, for example, has been courteous and kind from the start. I believe he has an interest in knowing you better and that his request to borrow a book is an excuse to be close to you."

"He is curious," Amber said dismissively.

"And what if it is more than that? What if he is the very kind of man who has seen your goodness already and would therefore accept the whole of you?"

"How could I possibly know that he would accept me?" Amber asked, a plea in her voice. "And how could I survive it if he did not? If so a kind man as Mr. Richards cannot accept me, what hope would I have for others to do what he could not?"

Suzanne frowned but Amber continued before Suzanne could pose another argument. "While I am humbled by your family's difficulties and even envious of such acceptance, I could not expect to be included in *your* class and have never seen such acceptance reflected in the people of my station — simple-minded children are given to others to raise. I dare not think how a girl child born with a twisted back would be received. How can I *know* who within my society might accept me and who would not? Without knowing I would be safe, I could never take such a risk."

Suzanne frowned and turned away. "For that I have no answer," she said softly, regretfully. "I only believe that there are people in every society who would prefer the heart you have grown, to the beauty you left behind to find it."

# Chapter 38

It was fortunate for Thomas's peace of mind that the weather had warmed enough to keep him working in the fields every spare hour until Tuesday morning and his planned visit to Step Cottage. He rode out to his property only long enough to plan the day with his bailiff before returning to Peakview and updating his ledger. Though he had attempted to distract himself from thoughts of the mistress of Step Cottage, he had been unable to cast them from his mind completely, no matter how many fence posts he set and ditches he cleared.

The day was cold so once he was in the saddle he turned up his collar and pulled his hat down low. He kicked Farthing into a run, which fairly froze his face but would make the trip to the cottage faster. When he slowed down to turn onto the road that led to the cottage directly, he adjusted his scarf and had the thought enter his mind that he was being drawn here for a reason. He shivered for a reason other than temperature.

He believed in God's hand directing the lives of people, and Thomas had felt such promptings and positioning in his life before. He could not discount the possibility of it happening again. True, Miss Sterlington had flaws, but he found himself doubting that those flaws were as prominent as they once were. The traits that seemed more important to him now were her graciousness regarding his helping Mrs. Miller return to the cottage, her humility in caring for herself, and her willingness to let him peruse the library and organize the records. To say nothing of the invigoration he felt that was exactly as it had been in London. She was different now. She was changed, and those changes increased his interest more than ever. It was frightening, and yet he was here all the same. Curious. Eager. Drawn.

Mrs. Miller let him in, and he removed his coat and hat while surveying the area in hopes of catching a glimpse of Miss Sterlington. In a cottage this size, she could certainly not be far but it seemed as though she was once again in hiding.

In the parlor there was quite an array of trunks, but Mrs. Miller led him to the library where a set of candles had been lit, presumably to offset the gray skies outside the single window. The fire warmed the room quite comfortably. "I shall bring in a tea tray straight away."

"I told your mistress in my letter that I am not in need of such attention," Thomas said, just as he had the time before.

"It is the wish of my mistress that you should be most comfortable, and the tray is already prepared." The woman bowed out of the room and disappeared. She had been gone only moments before Thomas heard the creak of the floorboards and knew that Miss Sterlington had returned to her place on stairs, just as she had for his prior visit to the library.

How easy it would be to move quickly to the bottom of those stairs and see her there before she could escape. It was a deliciously tempting thought that brought a grin to his face, and yet he did not do it. Instead he turned his attention to the library and perused the bookshelves while awaiting the maid to return with tea. He had come for the book of Donne's poetry, but realized that some of the books had been moved, re-arranged. Had Miss Sterlington organized the books?

He had not been exaggerating when he'd said in his letter that the library at the cottage held an impressive collection of literature in English, French, and Latin. The book of poetry he was looking for was not where he'd found it before, and so he took his time perusing the shelves and becoming familiar with the entire collection. It did not take long to find the slim volume he recognized between two other books. He had only just removed it when the maid returned and placed the tea service on the small table beside the settee.

"Thank you, Mrs. Miller," he said as she added cream and one spoonful of sugar to his tea. She'd obviously remembered how he liked his tea from his last visit. There was only one cup on the tray but he pretended not to notice. "Will your mistress be joining me?" he asked.

"No, sir," Mrs. Miller said as she set the pot back on the tray. "She is not one for company."

"And yet she goes to such pains to be welcoming," he pointed out.

"Yes, sir," she said with a slight incline of her head. She met his eyes with an expression he did not fully understand, though he had the strangest sense that she wished she could tell him more. He kept his own expression open and inviting, but Mrs. Miller turned to move out of the room and left him to his own company. His eyes moved in the direction of the place where he believed Miss Sterlington sat upon the stairs and he wondered if she felt the least bit tempted to accept his invitation.

He sat in the leather chair that creaked slightly beneath his weight and when he moved to set down Donne's book of poetry, he noticed a book on the end table. He knew Shakespeare's *Richard II* well from his days at Oxford where he had first pursued the study of playwrights and literature before turning his full attention to agriculture.

He opened the pages to the bookmark, a slip of rose-colored fabric embroidered with flowers. He set the book, page-side down, upon his leg then rubbed the fabric between his fingers, sipped his tea, and contemplated the woman on the stairs.

# CHAPTER 39

Amber leaned her head against the wall and listened to every foot-fall as Mr. Richards crossed to the bookshelves and back, every page he turned, and every chink of the cup and saucer as he enjoyed the tea and lemon cake she'd baked that morning. Suzanne had brought four lemons from town the day before, and Amber was quite pleased with the resulting confection. She hoped Mr. Richards would also be pleased, and was glad that there hadn't been time to cancel his visit, as she'd told Suzanne she would like to do. After learning of Constance and considering more deeply her own circumstance, Amber felt more lost than ever. Mr. Richards's visit seemed a silly thing to allow — what did she hope to gain from it? And yet when Suzanne had insisted they could not cancel, Amber had not argued much. She *did* want him to come, she simply feared she shouldn't. That he was here, however, was quite lovely. The house felt different with him in it, and she allowed herself to push away the heartache of the last few days. She closed her eyes and instead of wallowing in her self-pity, she imagined she *had* accepted his invitation to join him for tea.

She fantasized that she wore her blue-striped day dress and sat on the settee while he sat beside her in the chair with the table between them. He would cross one foot over his knee and hold his saucer in one hand while they talked of the weather and the coming spring. How she wished she knew his face so that she could add it to her daydream. She did not let that take her out of the fantasy, however. In light of these past days, she was content to be lost in this ideal, just for a moment.

Perhaps he would share a humorous story regarding his last hunting trip, and she would tell him of . . . of what? Of how to perfectly flavor a chicken stew? Or how long to let the coals cool before putting a pan of bread upon them?

She opened her eyes and allowed the daydream to slip away. Reality was a heavy thing. She listened to the creak of the very chair she had imagined him sitting in as part of her daydream and smiled sadly. He was so very close to her, and yet in ways that truly mattered, he could not be further away.

Eventually, Amber heard the turning of pages and suspected he was looking through the book he'd come to borrow. Then a rumbling sound came from the library. It took her a moment to realize it was his voice, quiet as though not wanting to be overheard. Amber held her breath to better hear what he was saying, then rose carefully and came down a few more steps until she could decipher his words. She realized quickly that he was not simply talking to himself, rather he was reading.

Before the discovery of the trunk contents had distracted her, she had finished the first act of *Richard II* and left the book out so as begin act two upon her return to the material. It seemed he was reading where she had left off. He had beautiful oration, and his words left her feeling both chilled and warmed in the same moment. She leaned her head against the wall that separated them and closed her eyes, allowing his voice to move through her.

"With eager feeding food doth choke the
feeder:
Light vanity, insatiate cormorant,
Consuming means, soon preys upon itself.

> This royal throne of kings, this scepter 'd
> isle,
> This earth of majesty, this seat of Mars,
> This other Eden, demi-paradise,
> This fortress built by Nature for herself
> Against infection and the hand of war,
> This happy breed of men, this little
> world . . ."

Amber wished she had left out something other than one of Shakespeare's histories, and yet it seemed beautiful in his low-toned timbre. She felt sure he would stop when he reached the end of Gaunt's monologue, but he did not. Instead, his voice changed in intonation enough to define a new voice — Edmund, she thought — and he continued with an impassioned speech. Amber soon found herself lost in the patterns and lyrics of his voice as the story of Richard II came to life within the cottage.

When he stopped reading some time later, she blinked her eyes open and straightened on the step. How long had she listened to him? And only two steps from the main floor! She heard the cover of the book close softly and came to her feet. He stood as well but then seemed to cross the room away from her direction, toward the window and the desk.

She should run up the stairs and secure her hiding place before he found her, and yet instead she tiptoed down the two remaining steps and peered around the stairwell, allowing herself only a few moments to take in the back of his charcoal coat pulled tight across broad shoulders. Her heart rate increased as she took note of the way his coat tapered at the waist and the dark brown sheen of his hair. In the candlelight from the mantel, it looked like chocolate not yet set.

She both saw and heard him open the desk drawer and remove a piece of parchment. He pulled back his coat and sat in the wooden chair before the desk — the very same position she would take when writing a letter. He reached for the quill from the stock, and she became fairly giddy with expectation of what he might be writing.

She realized, suddenly, that a quick look over his shoulder would reveal her. She picked up her skirts and made her way as quietly as possible to the second floor. Certainly he wouldn't hear the creaking steps, would he? She remained out of sight at the top of the stairs and therefore heard him stride from the room.

"Mrs. Miller?" he called.

Suzanne hurried to meet him in the foyer as he retrieved his outer coat, hat, and scarf.

"Did you find the book you wished to borrow, Mr. Richards?" Suzanne asked him.

How Amber wished she could watch him again without being seen. She wanted to memorize the shape of the mouth that had read so beautifully and see into the eyes that must reflect great feeling. She knew the basics of his carriage now and sensed his manner to be gentle. She ached to know more of him, ached to speak with him, and learn of him. Such foolish longings were ridiculous, of course. The fact remained that she could not gain closeness without him being equally close to her and that was not a possibility.

"I did and would like you to extend my thanks to your mistress for allowing me to borrow it."

"She would extend her welcome to you, of course," Suzanne said.

Amber heard the creak of the door open and footsteps as Mr. Richards took his leave. She moved toward her bedchamber so as to watch him ride away but then remembered the letter he had written and changed her direction.

As soon as the front door closed behind him, she ran down the stairs and fairly flew into the library. Her eyes located the cream paper on the desk without her feet ever having to stop. With the paper in her hands, she sat down on the chair still warm from his occupancy and unfolded the letter. Out of the corner of her eye she saw Suzanne come to stand in the doorway.

Mrs. Chandler,

I express my most sincere thanks for the loan of your book and would very much like to repay your kindness by inviting you to tea this coming Friday. I know you do not care to venture out, and I would therefore bring all the requirements if your housekeeper could but have hot water available. I can promise absolute discretion in regards to our appointment. Such a visit would also allow me to return the book I have borrowed.

It is my greatest wish that you will allow me this opportunity, and unless I am informed otherwise, I shall believe my invitation is as agreeable to you as it is to myself. I shall plan to arrive at one o'clock.

Most kindly yours,<br>Thomas Richards

Amber lowered the letter and the shock she felt must have shown on her expression.

"Amber?" Suzanne asked, coming into the room. "What is it?"

Amber blinked. "He wants to return and bring tea on Friday."

Suzanne pulled her eyebrows together. "*Bring* tea?"

Amber looked back at the letter. "He says that due to my not wanting to venture out, he would bring tea here for both of us to enjoy at the cottage. All he needs from us is hot water, which is reasonable. I suppose it would be impossible to transport hot water such a distance."

"Oh," Suzanne said, her eyebrows rising this time as a smile played across her lips. "He is to *call* on you."

Amber leaned back in the chair and lowered the letter to her lap as reality descended like a stone. "He cannot *call* on me," she said, turning to look toward the copy of *Richard II* now returned to the end table where she had left it, the scrap of fabric she had used as a bookmark draped from the new place within its pages. Her spirits, so lifted a moment ago, sank into the too familiar state of regret. "I shall have to send you with word that I am unable to accommodate his request."

Suzanne crossed the room and sat on the settee. "Would you read the letter for me?"

Amber read the letter aloud, then looked to Suzanne, whose expression was far too pleased. "He is most sincere in his attentions and seems mindful of your desire for privacy," Suzanne said.

"He cannot call," Amber said again, hating the truth but unable to ignore it. She had been too welcoming from the start and given rise to his curiosity. To welcome him to the library but not meet him in person, to have been presented to the town as reclusive and yet attentive to his every comfort during his visits — it was no wonder he was interested in better understanding her person. What a fool she was to have let this go so far. "I cannot receive him."

"Are you most certain of that?" Suzanne asked, reminding Amber of the discussion they had had on this very topic just last night.

"I am repulsive, Suzanne," she said, quietly and filled with regret. "I cannot hide it from him, and I cannot bear his reaction. I know it is hard for you to understand, but my society is not like yours. He *would* reject me. I know it."

"You are not repulsive," Suzanne said.

"And you found that paint in those trunks belonging to Constance Sterlington, did you not?"

"I have already told you my feelings about using face paints."

Suzanne crossed to the candelabra near the fireplace. She blew out the flames, taking the room into shadowy darkness thanks to the skies dulled with gray clouds. She crossed to the other candleholder near the door and blew out that flame as well, inviting even more darkness.

"He thinks you an eccentric widow. Let him come and enjoy tea in a darkened room. We could tell him that the light is painful to your eyes or some such thing. With the shadow and some carefully painted brows in place of your own, you shall appear unobjectionable and his curiosity will be appeased, as will yours."

"I couldn't possibly," Amber said, breathless at the very idea. Yet it was the true reason for her breathlessness that concerned her more than the suggestion. As Suzanne laid out the potential plan, Amber felt such a stir of excitement and possibility that she could not deny her desire to do exactly what Suzanne suggested. To sit across from him and sip tea and eat biscuits as she once had done with any number of gentlemen? To see those eyes and hear that voice directed toward her?

"What would we talk about?" Amber said, realizing as she did so that she was agreeing to Suzanne's plan. Why was she even considering such a thing?

Suzanne moved to the table beside the chair and picked up the leather bound volume of *Richard II.* "You shall talk of literature, of course. And perhaps, if we are lucky, he shall read aloud to you again. He has quite a fine voice, do you not agree?"

Amber looked at the book and remembered the effect his words had had on her. She thought back to Suzanne's assurance that the world was not made up only of people who would reject her, that there would be those — even amid her own society — who could see beyond her appearance. Maybe even Mr. Richards. The idea had seemed impossible last night, painful and frightening. And yet she felt a smile pull at her lips now. He would not be seeing the whole of her, and certainly this would be his final visit to the cottage once he had met her and returned the book. Could she not take this smallest risk, if only to appease her own curiosity regarding the man?

She could not give him the chance to reject or accept her; it was still far too much of a risk. But if she were to live an isolated life, bound by her illness to spinsterhood and loneliness, could she not take some joyful memories with her? Would not tea with Mr. Richards — perhaps the last gentleman she would ever entertain — be a delightful memory to have? As soon as she thought of it, she wanted it so very much that she felt a physical ache. With her future so uncertain and so heavy upon her shoulders, could she not make the choice to enjoy one afternoon in a gentleman's company?

"Perhaps he *will* read again," Amber said softly as her heart fluttered in anticipation. "Perhaps so."

# Chapter 40

Thomas came in through the back door of Peakview Manor Friday afternoon and removed his coat and boots. It had rained most of the night, leaving the grounds choked in mud that clung to his boots. Out of habit he turned his polished top boots upside down before attempting to put them on; no patent leather shoes fell onto the stone floor, however, and while he would miss playing a game with his niece, he was running later than he would have liked.

He proceeded to his rooms where he dressed himself presentably for the cottage. He had never been a man of fashion but quite liked the pieces of clothing he'd purchased on Fenton's recommendation in London. The tailoring was superior to anything he'd had before, and since his return, he'd used them as a guide for his tailor. Now all of his coats fit so perfectly they seemed to snap into place like a peg in a hole. He knew he cut a better figure, though such things had never concerned him much in the past. Today, however, he was going to meet Amber Sterlington and he wanted to look his very best. He wondered if she would recognize him and how he might react if she did. For good measure he added some of the spiced cologne he wore for society events; he had been in the fields most of the day, after all.

"Good day, Mrs. Berdsten," he called loudly to the cook after he entered the kitchen, causing her to startle from where she stood at the stove. She turned and gave him a narrow look.

"You ought not to be sneaking up on me like that, Mr. Tom. It's time you grew out of such childishness."

Thomas smiled and continued toward the woman who had served his family all of his life. He still felt as welcome in her kitchen as he did in his mother's parlor. "I shall never grow out of such things," he said as he looked around the kitchen. His eyes fell upon a basket covered in a yellow cloth, and he looked from it to the merry eyes of Mrs. Berdsten. "Is that my request?"

"There is no one else who asked me to organize tarts, crumpets, and jam for a mysterious visit. I included some chicken sandwiches in order for you to have a proper picnic."

" 'Tis not a picnic I'm of a mind to produce, but I thank you for the consideration. Now, all I am needing is a tea service." He worried that perhaps Miss Sterlington only had the one serviceable cup he'd been served with each time he'd visited.

Mrs. Berdsten pulled her heavy brows together and shook her head, covered in a cap that did not hide her steely curls. "I would caution you against making a visit to a woman who's not got a tea service of her own."

Thomas raised his eyebrows, only half in jest. "Who's to say I'm visiting a woman?"

Mrs. Berdsten let out a hearty laugh and turned back to the pot she was stirring on the stove. "Who's to say," she muttered. "As if anything else would draw such attentions."

Thomas could only hope the cook would not be too vocal in her suspicions as he moved further into the kitchen quarters in pursuit of the dish room he had only ever visited once or twice before. By law everything in the house belonged to Albert, but if Thomas were to divulge the motivation behind his actions, he felt sure Albert would allow him use of a tea service currently set in storage. However, he would prefer not to divulge anything until he better knew his own mind.

It took some time to find an appropriate set, small enough to be easy to transport but not so fine as to be at risk for the journey. When he settled on his decision — a white porcelain set decorated in yellow flowers — he wrapped each piece in a dish-towel, packed them into a crate, and then brought it into the kitchen where he set it beside the basket.

He kissed Mrs. Berdsten on the cheek then put the parcel under one arm and lifted the basket with his other hand. He made his way to the stable, mindful of avoiding the patches of mud he had stomped through when wearing his working boots.

He had already asked the stable hands to prepare the curricle, as Farthing would not be able to accommodate such a load. The rain was still falling, and Thomas could drive the vehicle himself rather than need the assistance of a driver — though it was more dashing than necessary for this particular visit.

He loaded the crate and the basket into the curricle and was stepping up when he heard his brother's voice.

"Where are you headed, Thomas?" Albert approached on horseback, likely coming in from surveying his own fields just as Thomas had done this morning. "I thought you would spend the day celebrating the victory."

Just yesterday Mr. Llewellyn had informed them of the approval to properly transfer the parcels to Thomas's ownership. Albert had come home with a full report. It was a great success after so many months of effort, and yet it had strangely paled in comparison to the eagerness Thomas felt toward having tea in a simple stone house this afternoon.

"I have been about the place since sunup," Thomas said. "You can be certain that my celebrations were great."

His brother's attention turned to the curricle. "What is this?" Albert dismounted his horse, which was quickly taken in hand by one of the groomsmen, and looked at his brother curiously.

"None of your concern," Thomas said, knowing that was not an adequate explanation but unwilling to offer more. "I had best be on my way though."

Albert leaned against the side of the curricle and regarded his brother with suspicion. "I am quite used to your mind being filled with tasks and figures, Thomas, but I cannot help but wonder what additional things are taking priority amid your thoughts these past weeks. I had thought it was the transfer, but now wonder that it's something else."

Thomas turned to the horses — a beautiful pair of chestnuts Albert had secured on a trip to Tattersalls two years earlier — and busied himself with double-checking the harness of the one nearest to him. "Nothing of much consequence, I assure you."

"I do not believe that," Albert said with a laugh. "Diane seems to think it's in regard to a woman, though I made her promise to withhold such suspicions from Mama."

"I thank you for that," Thomas said with sincerity. Should his mother begin to entertain such thoughts he would not hear the end of it until he admitted the whole. Should that occur he did not doubt she would be on her way to Step Cottage in a trice to see for herself the subject of his interest.

Albert's commentary, however, made him mindful that he was not being as clandestine as he had hoped. If both his brother and Lady Fielding had noticed his change in focus, his mother would not be far behind.

"And I thank you as well for not pressing me on this issue."

"Am I not pressing you?" Albert asked, raising his eyebrows. "For indeed I think that I am."

"Then I should thank you not to." Thomas knew his brother well enough to know that he would not be quick to cast aside such interest without a compromise. "I shall see that my man fills the ruts in the western road if you shall spare me some consideration in this, Albert."

Lord Fielding threw his head back and laughed. "You think grading a road is at all equal to my brother's interests in a woman? You have not hidden your visits until today, but as you rarely visit anyone I cannot help but be curious about this Mrs. Chandler. No one seems to know a thing about her, and yet this is your third visit, is it not?"

"It is not what you think," Thomas said, imagining how Albert would react if he knew Thomas had sat in a humble cottage reading Shakespeare to an empty room. How could he possibly explain any of this without giving Miss Sterlington away?

"What is she like?" Albert asked.

"I have not met her and am not inclined to add *on-dit* to the gossip mill should I have such an occasion to become acquainted with her today. She prefers her privacy, and I am of a mind to respect it." His voice had become sharp, and he cleared his throat as though that were the cause of it.

"Don't get so high on your horse," Albert said. "I am merely curious. He paused, regarding Thomas for a few moments longer. Thomas shifted beneath his brother's gaze "How old is this widow? I realize only now that I've had the impression of age, but perhaps I am mistaken."

Thomas was determined to learn more himself before he invited anyone into his confidence but knew he would have to negotiate Albert's support. "Please allow me my peace on this, Albert," he said with all sincerity. "It is a delicate situation I do not yet fully understand myself. I would like your assurance that you will not speak of this to anyone, even Lady Fielding." Especially Lady Fielding if she were trying to learn more about the woman in the cottage. "In return, I can promise you that when I am prepared to share my thoughts, you shall be the first to hear them."

"You will give me no promise as to when you will confide? After the Thorton dinner tonight, perhaps? Or maybe Sunday afternoon we could go riding."

"I will make you no promise other than

the assurance that you will be the first to know."

Albert frowned and shook his head. "You are so difficult at times." He let out a dramatic breath and stepped aside so Thomas could enter the curricle. "Very well, I shall keep Diane's curiosity at bay and press you no further, but I *shall* hold you to your word."

"Thank you," Thomas said gratefully.

Albert slapped the side of the vehicle and gave his brother a wink. "Carry on, then. Godspeed and good luck."

# CHAPTER 41

Amber paced back and forth in front of the fire in the library, mindful of Mr. Richards's arrival, which could happen at any moment. She kept looking to the slot of the desk where she kept letters from her family and the anxiety regarding the newest letter did nothing to settle her nerves.

The weather had stayed fair and so Suzanne had gone to town again on Wednesday to dine with her blacksmith and returned the next morning with a letter from Lady Marchent, which could not have been a greater surprise to Amber. After all these months away, Amber was being invited home, and she could scarce decide how she should feel about it. Grateful? Nervous? Excited? Her mother's letter had been written before Amber's request for information about Constance, so there was no mention of her.

Darra's wedding date was set for March

4, five weeks away. Amber was invited to return to Hampton Grove three weeks prior so as to be in attendance for a wedding ball held in Darra and Lord Sunther's honor. The actual wedding would take place at Lord Sunther's estate in Suffolk, and since Lady Marchent had not specified that Amber would attend that event, Amber assumed her behavior at the ball would determine whether or not she would receive greater inclusion.

It was not difficult to ascertain that Amber was being called back only to preserve the appearance that all was well with the Sterlington family. Lady Marchent also said that Amber and her parents would find time to discuss her future. Amber did not know whether or not that meant her parents were willing to accept her back with full favor but she could not forget that Constance had died in Yorkshire. Again, perhaps that answer hinged on how she presented herself at the wedding ball — her first social event in nearly nine months.

Two weeks ago Amber would have eagerly packed her bags in anticipation for the comfort of her childhood home. However, that was before she knew of Constance's rejection from these same people. It was before she had put on her blue-striped day dress for the first time since her arrival at the cottage and had exchanged out three different caps before deciding on the one with the tighter ruffled trim. It was before Suzanne had painted on the eyebrows that did not look quite right to Amber, although Suzanne assured her they would appear to greater advantage with the low light of the library.

"Are you quite sure my appearance is that of a decrepit old woman?" Amber asked, looking upon her reflection with a critical eye. Since she was known as a widow, she thought it best to appear as an elderly one. Amber was quite certain she was only creating a joyful moment, not a step toward any kind of future.

"Quite sure," Suzanne said. "The lighting will make the difference."

Amber wondered at the maid's confidence and almost dared suspect that Suzanne was hoping for Amber's discovery since to herself she looked like a debutante wearing an old woman's cap. But she was eager to meet Mr. Richards and trusted Suzanne, so she had stilled her arguments and been ready in the library a full half hour before he was to appear, giving her time to further obsess over her mother's letter.

*Would I refuse the request to return?* she

asked herself, then shook her head. Of course she would return to Hampton Grove. She was taking tea with a man who would think her elderly, not accepting a call from a potential suitor. And yet her concern at returning home was tied to him in ways her mind had not yet deciphered, and it made her uncomfortable. Perhaps if her mother's letter had been worded with eagerness and a strong desire to know of Amber's well-being she would feel differently. Perhaps Mr. Richards was nothing more than an excuse Amber was holding on to because she feared further rejection if she accepted her mother's unspoken terms.

The knock at the front door caused Amber's heart to race and she stopped near the edge of the carpet. *He is here!*

Suzanne's footsteps crossed from the kitchen to the front door while Amber moved to the side of the settee furthest from the chair, settled a rug across her legs to conceal her youthful figure, and adjusted her cap. The morning gown had a high neck and long sleeves, keeping her well covered.

Suzanne welcomed Mr. Richards and then led him to the kitchen where he could set down the items he'd brought for tea and which Suzanne would prepare. Amber caught sight of a candle on the mantel that had not been extinguished at the same time she heard his boots returning toward the library. She jumped up to extinguish the flame, returning to her position moments before Mr. Richards arrived in the doorway, blinking in the low light as he scanned the room. When his eyes settled on her, she *felt* it and had the strangest sensation of calm and tension woven together like a blanket.

Amber did not know if he could see her smile in the darkness, but she smiled all the same and straightened her carriage while taking in the look of him fully for the first time. He was neither fat nor thin, and his shoulders were broad and his legs long, which she already knew from her peeks at him on his prior visits. His smile was genuine and his eyes were intelligent. The sense of familiarity she felt must be from his earlier visits and their unusual interactions. She certainly didn't know him past that, did she?

It was when she realized that those intent blue eyes were as focused upon her as hers were upon him that she looked away from his inspection. She smoothed the rug on her lap and took another breath she hoped would calm her heart, which was beating most erratically. What a goose she was to be reacting so intensely.

"The low light is easier upon her eyes," Suzanne explained from behind him. "I hope it is not too uncomfortable for you, Mr. Richards."

"It is quite fine." Mr. Richards remained in the doorway, however, and after a few seconds, Amber remembered her role as hostess. He was awaiting her invitation.

"Do sit down, Mr. Richards," she said, waving toward the leather chair he had occupied on his other visits. She caught sight of her hand — her youthful and elegant hand — and quickly drew it back, hiding it under the edge of the rug.

"Thank you, Mrs. Chandler," he said, finally entering the room and crossing to the chair she had indicated. She dared a quick look at him now that he was closer, and when their eyes met, she was unable to look away. She found herself quite conflicted between wishing he could see her as she was, Amber Sterlington, and *needing* him to see her as the widowed Mrs. Chandler. She looked away and turned toward Suzanne, who was watching in the doorway. "Is everything in readiness, Suz— Mrs. Miller?"

"It shall be soon, Madam." She bowed out of the room, and Amber took a breath before looking back at her companion. This time, he was the one to look away, much to her relief, but she wondered at the pleased expression on his face as he held out the slim volume of Donne's poetry. She paused a moment before reaching for it.

"I thank you for the loan of the book. I am a great fan of Donne's work and was able to copy out two of my very favorites. Have you read it?"

"I'm afraid I have not," Amber said, quickly drawing the book back to her lap. She knew she would read it now that she had his recommendation. "I have, however, enjoyed many of the other volumes from this library through this winter. It seems to be a rather good collection for so small a library."

"Based on my experience, it most certainly is," Mr. Richards confirmed, his eyes locked upon her in a way that made her shift awkwardly. "Have you always been a great reader, Mrs. Chandler?" he asked, bringing his attention back to her.

"Not always," she answered truthfully, though it seemed odd for him to ask about her past reading rather than discuss her current choices. "I was taught from the classics, of course, and was familiar with all manner of literature from my youth, but it has only been since arriving at the cottage that I have turned my mind to reading for pleasure or edification." She met his eyes briefly and then lowered her head, hoping the brim of her cap would prevent him seeing her too closely. She was only six or seven feet away from him and mindful of his scrutiny. "Do *you* enjoy reading, Mr. Richards?"

"Very much," he said. "My mother is a great lover of literature — poetry especially — and encouraged me from childhood. There was a time when I thought I might pursue my education in literature but then my interests turned. Though I would not mind being a professor, I think I would mind very much living away from Yorkshire, which would be necessary if I wanted to make a future of teaching."

"You are born and raised in Yorkshire, then?"

"All my life save for my time at Oxford and a brief foray in London. Have you ever lived in London?"

Amber shifted in her chair and fidgeted with the braided edge of the rug in her lap. "For a short time only," she said, eager to direct attention from herself. "What of your mother's people? Are they Yorkshire-born as well?"

He graciously took the lion's share of the

conversation from that point forward, telling her of his mother — who *was* Yorkshire-born and bred the same as his father, though her family was Scottish only a few generations back. Amber was tempted to tell him of her own Scottish roots, but feared moving the focus to herself.

He had just asked after her family when the tea arrived on a matching service. Suzanne set the tray on the table and withdrew, leaving Amber to serve the tea which she had not expected. She hesitated a moment, but was unwilling to call Suzanne back.

"What a lovely service," Amber said, lifting one of the cups to inspect the yellow flowered pattern and hoping to direct his attention away from her. "I did not know you were bringing such accommodations."

"I feared that you might only have one cup," Mr. Richards said with a smile that warmed her neck and face.

Amber had to move closer to him to serve the sandwiches and strawberry tarts he had brought, not to mention the tea. For ease of movement, she pushed the rug aside and hoped he would not look too closely. She held tight to Suzanne's assurance that the lack of light in the room would hide her youth, though it seemed ridiculous to consider.

Amber complimented the tarts he proclaimed to be his favorite since his youth, and then asked him about the document he had found in the library two months earlier. He went on at length to explain his arrangement with his brother and she found herself quite fascinated. "And your brother was agreeable to your request?"

"I am most indebted to him for it."

Amber sat back against the settee and regarded him. "I hope I do not sound impertinent, but does it not feel more secure to have your interests managed by your brother for a guaranteed income? Being dependent on weather and yield seems worrisome."

"But land is a heritage of another kind," Mr. Richards explained, then went on to speak of his desire to have his own children as well as future generations possess something of rising value, which would give them security rather than having to rely on a good marriage with gentry of higher order than themselves.

It was quite a remarkable explanation and presented a perspective she had never before considered. She wondered what her situation would have been if she had not been raised simply to look for a husband who would secure her comfort. It was beyond consideration that she, as a woman, could own and manage land, but the more Mr. Richards spoke of the satisfaction of working with one's property and having investment into his own living, the more she wondered what options might be open to her should she seek independence her own way.

Amber did not mind asking Mr. Peters for financial consideration when a need arose, but she was always fearful he might deny her request. He had when she'd requested new furniture for the main floor last October; she could barely abide the heavy old-fashioned stuff, which was as uncomfortable as it was ugly. He had refused her, claiming that it was an expense beyond what he was entitled to release, and while she now saw the request as rather frivolous, what if she did not have to ask after such things? What if she managed her own ledgers and accounts and could decide for herself where the money went?

"And what of society?" Amber asked, hoping that her forwardness would not upset the ease between them. "Are you not choosing a station for your family below the one you have enjoyed? Is that not a worry?"

"There are those who may close their door to me. I daresay there are some who see my independence as impertinent. Luckily, another man's opinion — or the opinion of all of a singular society — does not define my course. I have had enjoyable interaction with men of many different levels and find them as good and intriguing as men of our class. It does not bother me to proclaim myself one of them, nor does it concern me for my children. I have always found greater security in a man's character than in his station."

Amber could do naught but regard him as she pondered on his feelings. They were quite singular, yet entrancing too. To regard character above position was a progressive idea indeed, and one that sparked an odd hope in her chest as she reflected on Suzanne's opinion that there were people who would prefer Amber's changed character to the beauty she once possessed.

She also reflected on Suzanne's character. From infancy Amber had been taught that she was superior to the classes below her, that she was of greater intelligence and morality than all other classes simply because of her station. Interacting with Suzanne had proven that quite false, as Suzanne possessed qualities of goodness and determination Amber had never seen in her life. That awareness presented the further possibility that people of character could reside in any class. In fact, perhaps there was greater chance of such attributes in people not raised to disparage others as Amber had been.

"I have quite bored you, Mrs. Chandler," Mr. Richards said when she did not answer him. "I apologize."

"Do not apologize," Amber said, widening her smile in hopes of easing his mind. Again she found it difficult to look away but forced herself to do so. His eyes were far too intense for her comfort, and she feared at any moment he would call her out on her charade and demand the truth. "I have found your explanations most interesting. I can now better understand the comfort of managing your own interests and having to account to no one."

One side of his mouth came up in a crooked grin that made her breath catch. "I am glad to hear you are not overly scandalized by my self-sufficiency."

She forced herself to look away again. "Not in the least, Mr. Richards." Her heart rate increased, and she found herself not minding it in the least.

# Chapter 42

"Might I ask after *your* history, Mrs. Chandler? I hope it is not too much for me to say, but you are not so old as I had supposed you to be."

Heat filled Amber's face and chest, and she pulled the rug back onto her lap as she fumbled for an answer. What could she tell him that would not reveal her deception? How could she explain herself without speaking further untruths — an idea that settled miserably in her chest? She felt her breathing becoming shallow as she failed to find an adequate lie she would not hate herself for saying.

"I have made you uncomfortable," Mr. Richards said, embarrassing her further by admitting notice of her discomfort, but also giving her relief. "You have been nothing but gracious to me, and I have overstepped my bounds. Please forgive me."

"There is nothing to forgive, sir," she said,

though she kept her eyes on the floor. "I understand your curiosity, but I have had . . . a difficult time of things and came to Yorkshire in need of relief from certain pressures. I fear I am unprepared to speak of it."

"I repeat my apology," Mr. Richards said. "I am certain your reasons are just."

"I assure you they are," Amber said with a nod, relieved that he did not press her.

"It is obvious to me that you are from a privileged class, which, if I may be so bold, are not often found in such circumstances as you are, though the house is quite pleasing. Is it a trial to have but one servant to attend you?"

Amber hesitated, not wanting to be rude and dismiss another request of information he'd made of her. Surely she could answer him without revealing too much. "Mrs. Miller is very capable and perhaps, given your unique perspectives, you might understand an odd kind of pride in my attendance to those things necessary for daily life. As you guessed, I was certainly not raised to it, but Mrs. Miller has been patient with me, and I have come to find great security in knowing how to meet our needs, though I could most certainly not do it without her."

"Fascinating," he said under his breath,

causing her to give him a quick glance. He smiled when she met his eye, and she looked away before his gaze captured her completely. Had she heard derision in that reply? Had she embarrassed them both by admitting to such things? The chair creaked as he straightened his posture. "I am sure I have stayed quite long enough," he said, though he sounded reluctant to go, which gave her hope he was not turned away by her confession. "I wonder if I might call on you again. I have found this afternoon quite enjoyable."

*Call on you again,* Amber repeated. Her thoughts began spinning in circles as she argued with herself over the wisdom of such a thing. Of course she *wanted* him to come again, but to what end? He had already realized she was not elderly — what else would he discover if he came again? It would be difficult to darken the room any more without it being quite ridiculous, but beyond that she could not bear to know him better as it would only make it more difficult when she did not see him again. She had created her enjoyable memory of sharing tea with him. That she wanted more, and he did too, was both exciting and frightening.

Suzanne's voice from the doorway drew

Amber's attention before she could answer. "I should be happy to have the service in readiness to return to you on your next visit, Mr. Richards."

Amber felt her eyes go wide at the maid's forwardness, which was far beyond her bounds. Suzanne was focused on their guest, however, and did not see her mistress's displeasure.

"If it is all right with you, Mrs. Chandler, I should like to give this service to you as a further sign of my gratitude. After hearing my tale, you certainly better understand the importance of the lease agreement I only found because of your generosity."

"I could not keep your service," Amber said, turning her attention to the set. It was quaint compared to the silver sets her mother insisted upon at Hampton Grove and the more delicate porcelains of the London house, and yet it fit this cottage and this man so perfectly she found herself wanting it very much.

"I insist that you keep it," Thomas said. "It seems perfect for this house."

She looked up at him again and realized that the tea set represented more than the cottage — it represented him and she would cherish the connection. "I had thought the same thing."

He smiled broadly. "Then we agree that it must stay and that we shall share in its use again when next I come to visit. Would tomorrow be acceptable? I do not mean to sound overly eager but I believe the weather may hold a few more days yet, and I would like to take advantage of the fairer skies for my travel."

Those eyes had her quite trapped, and she found herself nodding. He thanked her for the afternoon and then followed Suzanne to the door. When Suzanne returned to the library after showing him out, Amber was holding her teacup in both hands as though it were a baby bird.

"I should not have agreed to let him return, Suzanne." She looked up, panicking over what she'd done. "And I do not thank you for putting me in such a position."

"Did you not enjoy his company?"

"Very much," she said, a bit breathless at the truth of it. "But I cannot allow him to continue his attentions. He could see that I was not an old woman as he'd expected. What shall I do if he discovers my deception?"

Suzanne began gathering together the tea service to return to the kitchen. "Do not worry yourself so much," she said. "Take joy in things that are joyful, there is no harm in that."

"Allowing him to return — tomorrow no less — is far too inviting. What if he becomes . . . interested in furthering his acquaintance with me?"

"You still have a say no matter what *his* interests are," Suzanne said as she stood with the tray in hand. "And formalities are not the same here in the country. As he said, the weather may not hold long enough for him to schedule a return further out — we have had nearly two weeks without preventative weather as it is. Enjoy another afternoon with him and then tell him not to return if that's what you've a mind to do."

*Could I tell him not to return?* Amber wondered as Suzanne left the room. She stood and folded the heavy blanket from her legs before returning it to the basket beside the fireplace. It would have been easier for everyone if she had told him *today* not to return. And yet her selfish heart had not been able to do it when the opportunity presented itself. Would she be any more able next time to request he not return should he ask again?

She found Suzanne in the kitchen with a pleased smile on her face as she set about caring for the service.

"If I am to receive Mr. Richards again I

must exact from you a promise, Suzanne."

"Yes?" she asked with her eyebrows raised expectantly. One did not consider the impact of eyebrows in communication until one no longer had them.

"I must have your word that if I should need to refuse him another visit you will not stand in my way as you did today."

Suzanne pulled her eyebrows together. "I would not have thought my reply stood in your way. Did you *truly* mean to refuse his request after such a comfortable afternoon?"

"In truth I do not know if I shall be able to say it to his person, perhaps I will be a coward and send a letter, and if that is the case, I shall need your promise to assist me in that as well."

Suzanne's disapproval was evident but Amber spoke first. "I know you are conspiring to make a match between us, but I continue to assert that you and I are of a different mind toward that possibility. If I am to entertain him tomorrow I must have your word that if I am intent to sever my relationship with him afterward that you will support me in it."

"And if I won't promise such a thing?" Suzanne said, displaying an irritating measure of cheekiness.

"Then I shall refuse to see him when he

arrives. I will let him take that long journey in the cold and the wind and deny him entrance to the house so as to prevent your interference."

"That would be most ill-mannered of you," Suzanne said, but Amber could see she was conflicted. She was choosing between one more visit she very much wanted Amber to enjoy, or an extreme inconvenience to a man who did not deserve it. Amber felt certain she could never be so rude to Mr. Richards as to turn him away; she was counting on Suzanne's romantic sensibilities to prevent it from happening.

"I will not hesitate to be as ill-mannered as I must be. I am an eccentric widow living in the home of a woman who was known for her discontent," Amber said. "And you know I am perfectly capable of such rudeness if I'm of a mind to do it, though I find no joy in such things as perhaps I once did. I need your word that you will assist me in whatever way I request."

Suzanne regarded her a few moments longer and then finally nodded. "I promise to help you refuse him *if* you choose to do so."

# Chapter 43

For Thomas, the invigoration of an afternoon in Miss Sterlington's company lasted well into the next day. Upon finishing a meeting with the architect, Thomas hurried in to change his clothes and then retrieved a basket of refreshments from the kitchen, kissed Mrs. Berdsten on the cheek, and took Farthing at a faster pace than he ought. His boots were splattered with mud by the time of his arrival, and he was glad for his greatcoat that protected his riding coat from similar treatment.

He arrived at Step Cottage with a fresh determination to gain Miss Sterlington's trust enough that she would reveal herself. It would not do for them to continue with a deception between them, but he wanted it to be Miss Sterlington who broke her silence rather than he who called her out. From the ease between them the day before, he expected she would find great relief in confessing the whole of it. She could not be comfortable in her ruse, and yet he believed she *was* comfortable in his company. Comfortable enough to trust him, he hoped.

Mrs. Miller answered his knock, smiling a welcome as he entered the cottage and removed his coat, hanging it himself rather than expecting her to do it. "It is very good to see you again, Mr. Richards."

He grinned broadly and bowed to her. "And very good to see you again as well, Mrs. Miller." He handed over the basket, which she took, eagerly pulling back the cloth to inspect the contents before looking up at him with raised brows. "You are too good to us," she said.

"My cook insisted on filling the basket to the brim after the compliments I shared of her former selection."

"Ham and preserves — and is this a cherry cordial?" She lifted out a bottle.

"Indeed it is. Some of the very finest you'll find in the county I'd wager."

"We are much indebted," Suzanne said. "Miss . . . *Mrs.* Chandler awaits you in the library." She paused and held his eyes in a way he believed meant that she had deliberately given Miss Sterlington's correct form of address. She was leaving him bread crumbs without knowing he was in possession of nearly the full loaf.

In an equally bold response, he smiled and nodded slightly, causing her to widen her eyes in realization of his part. He wished he could pull her aside and learn more but that was out of the question, and he preferred Miss Sterlington to share the truth with him herself.

"I shall return shortly with a tray if you would like to show yourself into the library," Mrs. Miller said with a pleased smile.

Thomas thanked her, then turned his attention to the library, which was as dark as it had been on yesterday's visit. It made him smile that Miss Sterlington felt the darkness concealed her bright eyes and fine features. He stood in the doorway until his eyes adjusted to the low light and he was able to make out the figure sitting properly on the settee.

She was dressed in a light green gown today with not so high a neckline as the one yesterday, though it was modestly appointed with a trim of lace, and Thomas was reminded of his encounter with her in London and how the color matched her eyes and complimented her hair. *No,* he corrected himself, it would be better not to think of her hair as he knew it to be a casualty of the situation that had sent her here.

The cap she wore today, and had worn during his other visit, concealed the current state of it but if her hair was shorn last summer, it would not be much longer now than Thomas's own. Certainly this was a matter of great insecurity for her but it was not for Thomas. Even with a short coiffure, she was the most beautiful woman he had ever seen and hair would grow back. He had seen for himself that Miss Sterlington's overall health was unaffected — she was as beautiful as she had ever been, mobcap and all — and yet he could praise her ailment in regard to the part it had played in the woman she had become in response to her circumstance.

"Mr. Richards." As always the tone of her voice invigorated his senses. "Do come in."

He did as she asked and sat in his familiar chair. Once seated he wondered if he should have been more forward and seated himself beside her on the settee instead, but he did not want to cause her undue anxiety. He must contain his eagerness. She did not know as much as he did, and he would need to be patient.

"How are our Yorkshire skies this day?" Miss Sterlington asked. He enjoyed that she seemed to have taken ownership of those skies. He liked to think she was beginning to feel she belonged here in Yorkshire.

"Fearsome, I'm afraid," Thomas said, frowning slightly. "There was rain most of the morning and though it has given some respite, I daresay it will start up again soon. The temperatures are cooling, which makes me wonder if we are due for snow."

"I shall not expect you to stay so long as to get caught in the storm, then."

Thomas leaned toward her, causing her to pull back and lower her chin, which kept her face in shadow. How he wanted to pull the cap from her head so he could see her face and those eyes that had kept him up at night. "I shall welcome any force of nature the skies shall deem fit to bestow upon me in trade for a hour of your company."

"Oh, how you talk." The nervous twitter in her voice did not disguise the pleasure of her response. "You are doing it too far thick, Mr. Richards. It is not like you."

Thomas leaned back in his chair. "Perhaps it is quite like me. Perhaps I am a man who does nothing too thick but is neither insincere in his feelings."

Mrs. Miller brought in the tray and set it on the table before them. "Mr. Richards's cook sent treacle tarts as well as a cut of ham and bottle of cherry cordial."

"That is most generous," Miss Sterlington

said. "Please return our compliments to her, Mr. Richards."

"I certainly shall," he said with a nod.

Mrs. Miller quit the room and, after hesitating a moment, Miss Sterlington pulled forward on the settee in order to pour the tea. He watched her elegant hands move about the tray with all the etiquette of the *ton,* and when she handed him his cup, his fingers brushed against hers. He realized that he had never actually touched her before and was startled at the energy that shot through his arm and down his spine. He quickly looked at her face and felt a new rush from the surprise of her own reaction. She stared back at him with those big green eyes that rendered him speechless for the time it took her to remember herself and pull her hand away from his.

The swagger and confidence he'd had upon entering the cottage only minutes ago shifted and settled within him at the reaction to her touch, confirming every feeling he'd felt toward this woman in all the months of his having known her. He had been so irritated and even embarrassed by the draw he had felt toward her when she was spoiled and arrogant, yet seeing her transformed character led him to admit that his feelings were not merely biological or even emotional. He was in *love* with Miss Amber Sterlington. She had changed his heart and fate or God or some such force had brought them to this place.

Miss Sterlington looked away first, breaking the spell, though not completely, as she attended to her own cup of tea. He watched every movement of her fingers and expression as she lifted the cup, blew across the surface, and took a small sip before returning the cup and saucer to her lap, which she had not covered with a rug today.

There was silence for a few moments before Amber found a topic to provide rescue. "Suzanne tells me your family is very generous to those of us situated so far from town. She says you often deliver boxes of goods to outlying settlements when the snow is too deep."

Thomas ducked his chin in modest acceptance. "Living in a place such as this inspires the community to work together. Fortunately we have been spared the worst of the season this year. So far at least."

"It is certainly generous for you to be so charitable."

"Traditionally one of the purposes behind a title was that the bearer would care for those within his stewardship, and while those boundaries are not quite so set as once they were, my family has always taken its position as a place of responsibility." He hoped it did not sound pompous, as it was not how he meant it. However, he *was* proud of his family's tradition of genuine charity.

Miss Sterlington cocked her head to the side. "I suppose I had not thought of titles in such a way. I fear most men graced with them do not feel such responsibility."

"I beg your pardon but I am sure most of them do," Thomas said with a confirming nod. "They may have bailiffs that do the watching, but the men of my acquaintance bound by position seem to understand that they are in a place of benefit for those that work their lands. Though there are a fair amount who spend their time hunting or gaming or some such endeavor, I should hope they are in the minority."

"That is an optimistic position," Miss Sterlington said. "I'm afraid as a female I am kept apart from such considerations."

"And does this bother you, Madam? Do you wish not to be apart?"

Miss Sterlington lifted her shoulders, which drew attention to the line of her neck and collarbone. He was careful to keep his attentions on her face, however, to prevent too much distraction. "I have not lost much time in regret over my sex," she said. "I have known a great many powerful women in my life, and while their place within society might be different, I have always felt they are equally positioned to have influence if they choose." She looked up at him. "If we might tie this conversation into Shakespeare, for instance, do you not find that many of his female heroines possess a great many strengths of quality reflective of Queen Elizabeth's own turning of traditional roles for men and women?"

Thomas was mesmerized by the workings of her mind and could not hold back a smile. "Indeed. I do not feel the Bard was subtle in his positioning of his women characters. I had a professor in Oxford quite enamored of this topic. I can't help but wonder what turned your head toward it."

She gave him a smile he knew to be far more dazzling than she expected it to be, otherwise she would never have shared such a bold gesture. It fairly made his fingers tingle with the desire to touch her fine lips, preferably with his own. "I suspect that any woman left to read the entirety of Shakespeare's work over the course of a winter would be hard-pressed not to find such patterns within his stories."

"You would be wrong in such suspicions,"

Thomas said with assurance. "Forgive me for sounding critical, but I have discussed Shakespeare with any number of women and the best I can expect from them is a passing understanding of his more memorable characters. You would be hard-pressed to find a single one with the barest familiarity with any of his histories, for example. Rather they shall sigh over Romeo and perhaps laugh with Petruchio, but they will see Lady Macbeth as rigid and mad rather than regal and powerful until her guilt overtakes her. They only reference Kate when attempting to contrast their own good nature against what they see as her failings."

It was brave indeed to introduce Kate — a woman of such similar likeness to the woman sitting across from him — into the conversation. Kate was a veritable Shrew, as the title of her story proclaimed her, but she was intelligent and sought for equality amid men who were of no mind to give it to her. Perhaps Thomas was making too many comparisons in his mind, but he saw many of Kate's qualities reflected in Miss Sterlington.

"Do you not feel that Kate has great failings, sir?" she asked.

"I do not," Thomas said, causing her to lift her too-dark brows that looked odd, though perhaps it was only the lighting that made them so. "I find Kate to be one of Shakespeare's most fascinating heroines. She is proud and intelligent, but chooses to soften her character in order to find equanimity within a position she initially refuses. It is my belief that through the courting process — the taming, if you will — she comes to realize the strength of a solid marriage, that it helps her to share in the position of her husband as no other arrangement can give her. I do not see that she gives up her strengths, rather she hones them into a more useful position and finds herself triumphant."

"Perhaps such matters of her character are neither good nor bad, then," Miss Sterlington said in a thoughtful tone as though forming the ideas even as she spoke them. "Rather it is how they are utilized that determine their nature."

"Precisely," Thomas said, even more invigorated by the depth of the discussion. "She chooses to use her strengths alongside a husband who allows her to do so rather than to fight against him, which would be a battle she would surely lose. You will remember that at the end of *Taming of the Shrew,* Kate and Petruchio retire to their marital bed, while Hortensio and Lucentio are left to worry about their own marriages. It seems obvious to me which couple found greater joy within their union. Petruchio could have dominated any number of women into the role of his wife, but he chose a woman of strength who then complemented him far more than Bianca or the widow did their husbands."

"That is a very interesting observation," Miss Sterlington said after a few moments of contemplation.

"It is very much in line with your observation regarding women finding position in society if they have a mind to do so. My mother is part of a woman's society here in Yorkshire that studies matters of politics and history; they meet together to discuss a new topic each month. My sister-in-law, Lady Fielding, has headed an effort to send supplies to an orphanage in Ireland quite depleted in resources. Neither of them were afforded a critical education and both were dependent first upon their fathers and then their husbands — yet they have both flourished within their spheres, just as, I believe, Kate did."

Miss Sterlington leaned forward slightly as he spoke, as though unwilling to miss a single word. When he stopped, she remained silent for several seconds and he could only assume she was pondering his bold words. She seemed to realize herself and sat back against the settee, repairing her thoughtful expression with one of a bit more ease.

"I wonder if I could ask you to read me that final speech of Kate's. I have read it myself but have never seen beyond the seeming servitude of her thoughts. I have learned before now that your skills at oration can give new meaning to such things." She smiled and Thomas's heart flipped within his chest. He had not seen such a radiant smile from her since London, and yet there had been a falseness to the expression back then — a calculation. This smile, here in North Riding, was perhaps the truest he had ever seen upon her face.

"I would be most pleased to read that passage," Thomas said once he recovered himself, flattered and quite validated by the request. He had known she was listening when he read from *Richard II* and was as pleased to have her admit it as he was to see her comfortable in their company. "If you shall direct me where to find the volume?"

"I shall retrieve it, sir," she said, setting her saucer on the table before rising and crossing to the bookshelves that filled the interior wall of the library.

Thomas rose when she did and observed her movements as the fire within him, already kindled by her intellect and smile, began to grow. She bent to position a small stool beneath the shelf, and he did not hesitate to cross the room in order to be of assistance; he ached to be near her even if only to retrieve a book she could not comfortably reach.

"Allow me," he said, coming up behind her and reaching the topmost shelf for the book — a collection of several plays bound together in one volume. He was close enough to smell the scent of lavender and closed his eyes as he inhaled the warmth of her. He was only fractionally aware of her turning to face him until he opened his eyes — quite caught in his moment of sensory attention — and found her looking up at him with eyes that reflected the same awareness of their closeness that had him rooted in place.

He could scarcely breathe as he looked into those eyes that were far more the vulnerable girl at Carlton House than the haughty woman at Almack's. The way the air between them increased in temperature seemed proof that she was not opposed to his nearness.

Rather than remove the book, he braced

his hand against the bookshelf and waited to see if fear appeared in her eyes. Instead he saw reflected in her gaze a willingness and welcomeness that fairly caused his chest to burn through with rising heat.

Miss Sterlington lifted a hand to his chest but rather than push him away, she grasped the lapel of his coat. It was more invitation than he could refuse, and he lowered his mouth to hers, pulled by a force he could not define until his lips touched her soft and willing ones. The sensation that filled him was of a magnitude far greater than that when their hands touched over the tea tray. The hand gripping his coat pulled him closer and he did not resist as perhaps a better gentleman might have.

Instead he deepened the kiss and placed one hand alongside her jaw while placing his other hand over hers, flattening her palm against his chest so that she could feel the way his heart raced in response to her. She slid her hand up his chest to the back of his neck, pulling him even closer until he felt sure the very room would soon catch fire.

It was only when he felt sure he was about to lose control completely that he pulled back and allowed them both the chance to breathe. He searched her face, afraid he might see regret within her expression. Her eyes fluttered open and she smiled, putting his fears to rest. He smiled back and leaned in once more to kiss her cheek, allowing his lips to linger as he gained further control of himself. He moved his mouth toward her ear and whispered, "Upon thy cheek lay I this zealous kiss, as seal to this indenture of my love."

He felt her intake of breath and knew that despite how much he wanted to stay, it was time to take his leave. He had moved far faster today than he had anticipated, and things had not occurred in the proper order — she still had not revealed her true self to him.

Likewise he needed time to plan his response when next they saw one another. He had made his attraction quite clear and needed to align himself in order to declare his full intentions. He took a step back and bowed over her hand, kissing the back of it with a lingering press of his lips to her skin.

"I think it best that I take my leave, Madam, but might I request an audience come Tuesday?"

"O-of course, sir," she said breathlessly enough to bring another smile to his face and another flip of his heart. To know she was as affected as he was left him steeped in warmth and invigoration.

He released her hand and tapped his finger on the tip of her perfect nose. " 'Til Tuesday, then," he said quietly.

She blinked and nodded while raising a hand to adjust her cap, though it had not shifted. " 'Til Tuesday."

# Chapter 44

"I am sorry, Amber, but I will not do it."

Amber looked at Suzanne in surprise. She was to leave for town within the hour for church and her usual Sunday evening activities. Tomorrow she would be posting the letter Amber had written in response to her mother's invitation to attend the wedding ball.

"Suzanne, I need your help with this." Amber held out the note she had written to Mr. Richards and shook her hand to emphasize that Suzanne should take it from her.

Suzanne clasped her hands behind her back. "And I will not do it. Mr. Richards has been nothing but kind to you, and if you are not to see him again, he deserves to hear it from your own mouth."

"You promised me you would help me," Amber said, disliking the whining tone of desperation in her voice.

"Which should impress upon you how

seriously I feel that Mr. Richards deserves more than words on paper. I would never break my word unless I felt this strongly."

Amber let out a breath and glanced around the kitchen as though there might be something that would support her argument. She could not *tell* Mr. Richards to cease his attentions — she could barely write the words much less say them aloud — but she was certain that sending a letter was a better course. Feeling she had no choice, Amber stood up straight, put the hand not holding the letter on her hip and drew all the *ton* left within her veins to the surface. "As your mistress, Suzanne, I *demand* you take him this letter."

Rather than be cowed, Suzanne smiled slightly. "If that be the case, then I shall quit your service entirely." With both hands she lifted her skirts and curtsied quite elaborately. Once she had straightened, she smiled even wider. "And you are left without a maid to deliver your message or fetch your foodstuffs or transport your laundry. Now what shall you do?"

Amber frowned and allowed her shoulders to slump. "Please take him this note," she asked in a completely different tone. "It shall hurt him worse to hear the words than to read them."

"You believe it shall hurt *you* less, and yet if you should think on that a bit more you know it is not true." She moved toward Amber and looked at her hard, no longer smiling. "You know as well as I that your heart will break in a hundred pieces if he does not call on you again. The man is full in love with you."

Instant tears filled Amber's eyes and spilled down her cheeks. "He knows nothing about me. It is for the best that he forget me, Suzanne, even if it means he is disappointed for a short time. Surely you can see that."

"I can see no such thing. You are in love with him too."

"He does not even know who I am."

"He knows your heart, at least as much as he has been allowed to see. Tell him the truth; let him show you the kind of man he is. I am sure you will not be disappointed."

Amber shook her head. "I cannot bear his rejection. He has been such a brightness for me, and I want to treasure those memories, not be haunted by the look on his face when he realizes my deception and my truth."

The intensity of Suzanne's dark eyes bore through Amber's senses. "Do you truly believe he comes all this way out of chivalry? Do you not see that his heart is as affected as your own? Did he not kiss you as a man in love kisses a woman of his desire?"

The kiss had filled her with such light and hope and goodness that for the space of an hour she had quite forgotten who she was and what ailed her. It was perhaps the most pleasurable moment of her life and she would forever cherish it. Should she have to see his censure when she rejected him, or, worse, be forced to tell him the truth — which would result in his rejection of her instead — she might lose that moment even within her memory. She dared not risk it and therefore must ensure that the last memory she held of Mr. Richards was one of such joyful pleasure that it would sustain her for the rest of her life.

"But he does not know me," Amber said for the third time. "And when he learns the truth of my dishonesty and deformity he will not wish to associate with me any longer."

"I feel you are denying both of you great happiness," Suzanne said, sounding frustrated. "If you could for one moment see the changes that have taken place these months, you would see the very thing Mr. Richards has fallen in love with. You are unwilling to accept that you are worthy of a man such as he is."

Amber wished she could believe it, but nothing in her life or education gave the idea any credibility. To emphasize her point she reached up and pulled off her knit cap. It had been months since Suzanne had seen Amber's head, and Suzanne backed up a step in shock.

"This is what I am," Amber said loudly, her arms spread wide. She walked to the table and slapped the note upon it. "If he knew, he would not feel anything but revulsion for me no matter what improvements have taken place with my character. I am not a woman who could be accepted by his family or friends, and I will not ask him to choose me over his future, his connections, and his obligations to both. I would never make him happy and have deceived him from the start. Between that deception and revelation of the truth, he should want nothing to do with me. You have to understand the wisdom of my choice to give him leave before either of us is hurt more by this game I have played with him."

Suzanne said nothing. Amber turned away from the maid's wide-eyed stare and replaced the cap as she returned to the sideboard, embarrassed by the depth of Suzanne's reaction, which confirmed her fears. She could not bear to see such a reaction in

Mr. Richards's face; the anticipation of it alone was enough to bring tears to her eyes.

"I appreciate your hopes for my happiness," she said in a softer voice. "Truly I do, but I will appreciate even more your taking the note to Mr. Richards. It will be better for him to read the words in privacy and accept what is inevitable." She took a breath before revealing the remainder of her decisions, hoping that perhaps Suzanne would understand this next choice better than she had the first.

"The letter I asked you to send to my mother is an acceptance of the invitation to Darra's wedding ball. It is important for my family to have me seen by their society, and I have chosen to leave Yorkshire. I have made a request from my parents in regards to retaining my inheritance and setting up a home similar to this one, but in a different place so as not to be so close to Mr. Richards and cause him further harm. I believe I am able to care for myself so I shall not allow you to make such sacrifice as to attend me again. I am hopeful that without my situation to confine you, you will feel free to pursue your man in town and provide for yourself the happiness you deserve."

She had to stop as emotion threatened to overcome her at the idea of losing Suzanne, but she took a breath and straightened her posture. She kept her back turned, however, unable to look Suzanne in the eye as she delivered her final words. "My mind is quite set on the matter, and I would remind you that I am still your mistress and you are still my servant. I expect you to fulfill my commands, which are for you to deliver my letters and abide my wishes."

"Miss," Suzanne said in a choking tone that cause Amber to close her eyes as she struggled to contain herself. She could not absorb Suzanne's sorrow when her own was already so overwhelming.

"Please go," Amber said, a waver to her own voice. "I have made peace with this decision, and if you care for me at all I ask that you leave me to my choice and set about the tasks I have asked you to perform in my behalf."

Suzanne did not speak, and Amber did not turn to face her. After a moment, Amber heard her maid finish her preparations to leave, move to the door, pull it open, and then close it again. Amber braced her hands on the edge of the sideboard and dropped her head, waiting for the emotion to wash over her. She had hurt Suzanne. She would soon hurt Mr. Richards. Had she hurt every person who had ever cared for her? Was that the true reason for her exile?

Mr. Richards would surely be angry, but he would then leave her alone, assured that her heart was not bound to him in any way. She had not been gentle in her letter, and he would have no doubt that she had no interest in seeing him again. Sometime in the next fortnight her father's traveling carriage would collect her, she would endure discomfort at the family estate for a time and then move forward with a life of her own choosing — protected from a fantasy that had only resulted in pain. Perhaps in time she could interact with whatever community surrounded her, perhaps working through the local clergy as Suzanne had encouraged her to do.

Regardless, she would never allow such a connection to take root in her heart again, not as it had with Suzanne, Mr. Richards, or her own family. She would protect this heart Suzanne so admired, take comfort in purpose, and . . . she did not know what else. She did not want to live as Constance had, but it was safer, not only for her but for those who would be hurt by her.

"It is best," she said out loud. Mr. Richards deserved a wife he could respect, admire, and desire. Amber could never be those things, and even Suzanne, the one person who had attempted to convince Amber she could be accepted, had seen the wisdom in the end.

Amber would never see Mr. Richards again, and she would soon leave this place, which had become a sanctuary, forever. How it broke her heart to know it.

# Chapter 45

"Thank you, Nelson," Amber said to her mother's maid as Nelson put the last of three ostrich feathers into the folds of the expertly draped turban Lady Marchent had procured. It was the same soft green fabric as the dress Mama had chosen for Amber's presentation tonight. The dress was meant not to draw attention — it was Darra's ball — but it still complimented Amber's eyes and figure.

The wig Amber had worn in London was considered but eventually dismissed by her mother who wanted no memory of that night's display to accompany this evening. Amber was to attend the wedding ball, make polite if not shallow conversation with their connections, be part of a toast to Lord and Lady Sunther's happiness, and then fade away secure in the knowledge that friends and family would no longer worry about her well-being. Perhaps she would be invited back to Hampton Grove for family events now and again, but never to draw attention back to her own self. Never that.

Amber fingered the pendant resting just below the hollow of her throat. The jewel had once felt like a trademark, and though it was as well-crafted and lovely as it had ever been, it felt strange and foreign now. Heavy. Cold. Everything felt that way.

"I need but paint on the brows and ye shall be ready," Nelson said, sounding nervous.

"I can paint on the brows," Amber assured her. The paint her mother had purchased was a finer quality than what Amber had from Constance's trunk, and it more closely matched the true shade of Amber's eyebrows — if she'd had them. "I have painted them on many times now and know just how it is done."

After the brows, she painted a very thin line along the edge of her eyelids in order to give the shadow of lashes; it was the best she could do. If the attendees at the ball looked long enough they would see something awry, but Lady Marchent had asked her to give as few opportunities for scrutiny as possible and Amber agreed that would be best.

"Thank you, Nelson. You may go. The

dancing has already begun, has it not?"

"It 'as, Miss. I 'eard the strains of music when I was comin' up to 'elp ya."

Lady Marchent had requested Amber show herself after the formal introductions of the other guests. While Amber could not say she was not wounded at being asked to come late, she did not mind so much. These last days at Hampton Grove had revealed to her that the company of her family was no longer something she craved.

The older boys were still away at school, and while William, the youngest, was still in the schoolroom at Hampton Grove, she suspected her mother was purposely keeping him apart from his eldest sister. It would be easier for him to forget about her entirely if they did not renew whatever affection might lie between them.

Darra had come to Amber's room the first night of her return. They talked for hours of Darra's wedding, and Amber had hoped for more time exactly like that, but it was not to be. Beginning the next day, Lady Marchent seemed determined to keep the girls apart and, but for family meals and a few promises of finding time to talk again, Amber had seen little of her sister.

At least they had resolved the difficulties between them. She would forever be grateful for the chance to be reconciled to her sister again and hoped that once they were removed to their separate futures that connection would continue.

Amber had seen her father only long enough to repeat the request she'd sent in the letter and receive his assurance that a man was looking for a location she could remove to. She had asked after Constance, and, without meeting her eyes, Lord Marchent had given a brief description of what she already knew — his younger sister became ill toward the end of her second season and was removed from London in hopes of a recovery that sadly never came about. After two years of convalescence, she removed to Yorkshire where she lived her life in isolation. She was not buried in the family plot because of the influenza, not her "other condition."

Amber did not accept his explanation, but did not argue with it either. What was the purpose? He was determined to justify his family's treatment of Constance just as surely as he justified his treatment of his own daughter. He was resolved that he had done the right thing and Amber would be unable to change his mind about it.

"It was her choice to go to Yorkshire, Amber. No one forced it upon her. She simply realized, as it seems you have, that causing discomfort to the people around her was a great source of her own discomfort. I believe she was quite happy in the cottage, so much that she chose not to come to the funerals of her own parents when they passed. It's a shame you are not willing to stay there. It would be far simpler for you to return to Yorkshire than to arrange a new location."

"I should like a more mild climate," Amber said, inserting the reason she'd invented to explain herself.

Since there was no affection between her and her father, she hoped it meant she would not be too disappointed by the loss once she left the family estate again. He was working to secure her independence as a yearly income she could control and hoped to have all things in arrangement by the end of the month. She had chosen simply to be grateful for his assistance rather than hurt at his eagerness to dispose of her.

With her family so uncomfortable with her presence, and Darra frequently unavailable to talk, Amber had spent the majority of her time walking the grounds of Hampton Grove alone and enjoying the nostalgia of childhood memories. At times, she removed her bonnet and cap when she was assured she was alone. The weather was fine and the sound of birds and wind in the trees was a comfort. It had been many months since she had been outdoors, except for trips to the cottage stable, and she wondered why she had resisted it while she had been at the cottage.

*The cottage.*

Her head was as full of thoughts regarding Yorkshire as it was with thoughts of her current surroundings; she could not be free of them no matter what she did to distract herself. It seemed everything brought her thoughts back to the quaint house and Suzanne, whom she missed terribly.

Suzanne had not spoken of the letter she'd delivered to Mr. Richards and had not treated Amber any different upon her return from town that day. They had worked and lived side by side until Lady Marchent had arrived to take Amber back to Somerset.

The night before their parting, Suzanne admitted that Mr. Larsen had declared himself to her the week before. She had not said that without her mistress she had no reason to refuse him any longer, but Amber understood it all the same. Amber wished her dear friend happiness and the next day bid her a tearful good-bye on the cottage steps. Suzanne, who rarely showed emotion, had been crying into her apron when the coach pulled away.

It was only her mother's frigid disapproval that dried Amber's own tears. The woman was only a servant, Lady Marchent had said. Why waste tears on one such as that?

Knowing that Suzanne would be happy with her blacksmith made it easier for Amber to mitigate her regret at disappointing her. It was not so easy to think of Mr. Richards, however, whose memory brought so much conflict to her heart and mind.

Amber had tried to read *Hamlet* upon her arrival at Hampton Grove, but Shakespeare's words now sounded with his voice in her head. The sound of hoofbeats made her think of him arriving at the cottage, her morning chocolate was the same color as his hair, and her own solitude reminded her of what it felt like to be in his company. She had only known the enjoyment of his presence a handful of hours, and yet every hour without him she felt as though she was missing something. Something she could never have. Something she could never forget.

Each time the sadness seeped inside her, she tried to think only of that kiss, the feel of his heartbeat beneath her hand, the scruff of his face against her own, the way he smelled of wood smoke and leather and tasted of tea. It was a bittersweet remembrance to be sure, but she hoped that in time the ache in her chest, the question of "what might have been," would fade and leave only the sweetness behind. She hoped it with her whole battered, bruised, and broken heart.

"Enough of this," she said before taking a deep breath and looking at her reflection in the mirror. She must be mindful of the moment at hand — Darra's wedding ball. The gown and turban drew upon the color of her eyes and complimented her skin, browned from the time she had spent in the Somerset sun. She would look wild to the rest of society but to her mind she had not looked this beautiful for many months. The brows she'd painted on looked very much like her true eyebrows once had, her figure was as well defined — though not so prominently displayed — and she was grateful for the chance to feel as much an equal with the other women here as she could ever hope to.

Yet her optimism could not protect her entirely from the discomfort she knew awaited her. There would be whispers regarding her appearance after so long an absence, a few braver guests would ask after her health, and everyone would comment when she was out of range how changed she was, how she was a shadow of the woman she'd been in London. What a pity. What a shame. Amber knew precisely how they would look at her and talk of her because she had been one of them only a year ago, eager to put herself above someone else, quick to find another's flaws.

But perhaps a few generous young men would ask her to dance — how she longed for a dance. Never mind that she would wish it were Mr. Richards's hands she held through the steps, wish it were Mr. Richards's arms around her, and wish it were Mr. Richards's compliments she folded into her heart to pull out and read over on future nights.

An unexpected memory of her last ball came to mind, but instead of shrinking from it she remembered the man who had given her his coat. She could only assume the coat was still in London, where she had left it in the wardrobe. Remembering him reminded her that there *was* kindness amid the *ton* — not everyone was cruel. She would take Suzanne's counsel and look for those of her society who would not dismiss her for being imperfect. No, she would never be one of *ton* again and they would never know the extent of her deformity, but perhaps for one night — this night — she could expect better of people. The man with the coat was to be a reminder of the possibility.

"You shall find joy in this night," she said to her reflection, lifting her chin in her most regal expression. "Your sister is marrying her prince, and you are allowed to celebrate with her. Every happy memory is that much more light you will take with you. Be glad for it."

It was one thing to give herself such direction, but quite another to enter the ballroom and feel the glances turn toward her and hear the whispers rise out of the surprised guests. In that moment she wanted nothing more than to slip back to her room and beg off the evening, but she knew her role and lifted her chin as she made her way to her parents. They welcomed her with a kiss on the cheek and a press of her hands. Only she could see the wariness in their eyes, but it served to raise her determination to be exactly who they wanted her to be tonight. She would give them no reason to regret allowing her to attend. If she played her part well she hoped to be allowed as a guest for the wedding to be held in a few weeks' time in Suffolk.

"Amber?"

She turned with a polite smile toward her

Aunt Janice, her mother's youngest sister. Janice had married a vicar and though no one spoke of it being a disappointment — he was clergy, after all — it was understood she had not made her parents proud. Amber had once thought her softheaded and plain, but perhaps for the first time, Amber noted her kindness and sincerity rather than her lack of fashion and position.

"Aunt," she said, leaning forward to press cheeks with the woman so unlike Lady Marchent. "How are you?"

"I am very well," she said. "How are you? I hear you have been recovering from an unfortunate reaction to, what was it, a hair rinse?"

"It was nothing some country air could not remedy," Amber said, more sincere than either of her listening parents would believe. The country had healed her, in a sense. However, there was more healing that would need to take place now. Realizing that she had a safe companion for a time, Amber looped her arm through that of her aunt's and turned in the direction of the refreshments on the other side of the room. "Would you accompany me for a drink and tell me of my cousins?"

Being with Aunt Janice helped increase Amber's confidence as they encountered family and friends. Amber was careful not to engage any one guest too long; she could feel them looking at her and realizing that something was not right in her face. She would turn away when their confusion appeared, wave at someone on the other side of the room, or begin a topic of conversation.

In time her aunt became engaged with some other distant relation, however, and Amber felt herself panic as she stood alone on the edge of the dance floor. While a few gentlemen had approached her in greeting, they had kept a polite distance and, in truth, she had not tried over much to engage them. She was increasingly nervous about having so much attention from any one of them. She was not the Amber Sterlington she'd been before, and under a gentlemen's gaze she felt more aware of what she was not. Perhaps she would not dance after all tonight. Perhaps, just as leaving Yorkshire, that was for the best.

"Upon my word," said a lyrical voice behind her. "Is it truly Miss Amber Sterlington my eyes are seeing?"

# Chapter 46

Amber turned and smiled at the man dressed in gold pantaloons and a salmon-colored coat with gold trim upon the lapels. "Lord Fenton," she said, allowing him to bow over her hand, which he exaggerated, of course, though he was careful not to spill the glass of white wine he held in one hand. "I did not know you were attending this evening."

While Amber was acquainted with Lord Fenton from her time in London, his family was not so connected to hers that she would have expected him to attend Darra's ball. Perhaps it was an association to Lord Sunther's family that warranted him an invitation.

"I hope you are not disappointed to see me, then."

"Not at all," Amber said, smiling. Fenton was a flirt but his insincerity was comforting; his affections were a game for him rather than true intention. "It has been an age, has it not? How have you filled these months since last we saw one another?"

He waved his free hand through the air with aplomb. "Oh, I stay quite busy with all manner of dissipation, I assure you." He shrugged and leaned toward her, which prompted her to fix her gaze to the floor as though listening intently so as to keep him from looking directly into her face. "Should I tell you the half of it you would be quite scandalized."

"Well then, you must tell me the whole of it," Amber said, glancing up enough to catch his eye and give a sincere smile. "For then I shall only believe half, which will likely still be far above the truth. You only *wish* to appear the rake, Lord Fenton, but your true nature is not so well concealed."

Lord Fenton threw back his head and laughed loudly, causing Amber embarrassment as several guests turned to look their direction. When he met her gaze again she noticed a rather sincere look in his eye. "Would you join me for the next set, Miss Sterlington? I believe it is a cotillion."

"Certainly, Lord Fenton, but I hope you will not abandon me before it begins. Tell me of your family. What travels have you had this winter?"

Fenton raised his eyebrows in surprise. "My family?" he repeated. "For what should you have interest in so boring a topic? Would you not prefer an accounting of London, perhaps some *on-dit* concerning a few of the more *nefarious* characters of our society?"

"Those things hold little interest for me," Amber said, then watched his eyebrows rise a second time. She faced the dance floor, avoiding his scrutiny.

"A girl spends a few months recuperating in Yorkshire and suddenly cares nothing for the society of her peers?"

Amber snapped her head back to look at him. "You know I was in Yorkshire?"

He took a seemingly contemplative sip of his wine before answering her question. "I do believe it has changed you, Miss Sterlington," he said when he lowered his glass, all the while looking at her closely. Too closely.

"How did you know I was in Yorkshire?" she asked again while looking away from his piercing gaze. It was only after she she'd spoken that she realized if she'd been more coy in her questioning, she would not have confirmed the truth. Her family had assured her no one knew the humble nature of her retreat. They wanted the impression that she was in a grand place, waited upon and coddled for her recovery, not hidden away.

"Did you like it there, Miss Sterlington?"

Amber turned her head to find him looking even more strongly into her face. His voice had lost its flippant quality, and she was quite speechless with surprise. She took a step away but he moved with her, causing her heart rate to increase.

"Did you, Miss Sterlington?" He sounded very intent, which unnerved her. "Was Yorkshire to your liking?"

"What are you about, Lord Fenton?" Amber said, casting her eyes about as though someone might rescue her. Of course no one would. They were all keeping their distance.

"I am asking you a simple question, Miss Sterlington," he said. "I would like to know how you feel about your time spent in Yorkshire. I can explain my intention once I know your mind, but I fear I *must* know what you thought of it. I have heard it to be quite savage."

"It is not savage," she said, unsure what her course should be even while she looked about the room for some means of escape. His attention was most discomfiting. "Wild, perhaps, in land and weather, but it was peaceful and . . . generous and comfortable, too."

"And the people?"

"Were good and kind," she said easily, thinking of the Dariloos — and Mr. Richards. They were the only people she had actually met from Yorkshire. "Among the best I have ever known."

"One might wonder, then, why you left a place toward which you feel such warmth."

Amber looked away from him as a volley of memories washed over her, the final one being the expression on Mr. Richards face when he'd promised her a visit the following week — a day now long past.

"One might wonder that, yes," she said in almost a whisper, then looked at Lord Fenton again. Why did he speak as though she were not returning to Yorkshire? How would he know she had been there at all? "I'm surely unable to explain adequately my reasons for leaving, Lord Fenton, but it was for the best, and I would ask that you not press me further."

"And where shall you go now? Shall you remain at Hampton Grove? Will you return to London in time for the season?"

"I shall set about my own household," she said, content to make her intentions known. Lord Fenton would certainly share her plans with everyone of their acquaintance, preventing her from having to do so herself. "My father has agreed to settle my inheritance upon me, and I shall live a quiet life, which I have come to prefer. I am to be an independent woman."

"In Yorkshire?"

"Not in Yorkshire," Amber said, wishing she did not feel a stab of disappointment at the admission. "Why are you asking such —"

"Why not in Yorkshire? If you were so very happy there and found the people and way of life so pleasing, why would you not return to it for your life of independence?"

Amber did not answer him and wondered if he had been sent for information — perhaps from her parents, though she did not know why they would be interested or why they would not ask her directly if they were. There was obviously a purpose behind his questions, however. She backed up another step and dropped into a curtsy.

"Upon greater thought I am feeling rather . . . drawn at the moment and shall not be able to stand up with you for the next dance. Please excuse me, my lord."

"Do not go," Fenton said, sounding alarmed. He reached for her arm, but she moved out of his grasp and then met his eye and lifted her chin in defiance. What was he about? "I am sorry to have been impertinent."

"I do not feel well and insist you let me leave," Amber said strongly, prepared to make a scene if necessary.

He seemed to sense her determination, and she thought she might have seen regret regarding his behavior already. "I would not prevent you from leaving, of course. Will you return when you have recovered?" Lord Fenton asked. "Perhaps you would give me the chance to explain myself."

"Certainly," she said, but only so he would allow her to leave. She had no intention of returning.

He did not detain her any longer as she slipped from the ballroom and then to the drawing room next door. It was not lit for the evening, and she closed the door, more comfortable in the darkness and the solitude. She shivered slightly — the fire from earlier in the day had died out — and moved to the French doors that led to the same veranda connected to the ballroom.

The veranda was lit with torches, and a number of guests stood about the stone balustrade conversing and sipping wine despite the cold, or perhaps preferring it to the heat of the ballroom. She crossed her arms over her chest and rubbed the exposed skin between her long glove and puffed sleeve. Had she appeared long enough to fulfill the curiosity of the gossips and satisfy her parents' need for the appearance that all was well with their family?

She was considering how she might best make her excuses when a flash of a salmon-colored coat on the veranda drew her attention to the view from the window. There were not many men who would wear such a coat, and upon closer inspection, she verified that it was indeed Lord Fenton heading toward the garden stairs, though his steps were longer and his movement more masculine than she had ever seen before. He still held a glass of wine in his hand, but hurried as though unencumbered.

The garden was not lit for the assembly tonight — it was too cold to be inviting to the guests — but Lord Fenton was intent upon it nonetheless. Amber watched him hurry down the steps, then continue toward an arrangement of benches beneath a trellis that would be heavy with wisteria in a month's time. A movement from beneath the trellis caught her eye, and she leaned closer to the glass as a man stepped out of the shadows.

Lord Fenton's step slowed as he reached

the unknown man, and if not for having seen him leave the ballroom, she would not have been able to identify Lord Fenton now for how dark the gardens were. He had fled the ballroom just as she had. Had he been intent on a conference with this man hiding in the gardens?

Amber thought back to Fenton's strange questions and the even stranger intensity behind them and felt her breath catch in her throat. Her nose hit against the glass as she tried for as clear a view as possible. The man Lord Fenton conversed with had broad shoulders. Long legs. Conservative dress. Dark hair.

"It cannot be," she whispered to herself, then fumbled for the doorknob. She could not stop herself from exiting through the French doors once she pushed them open. She lifted her skirts as she fairly flew down the steps, along the garden path, and then came to a stop as the two men turned to face her.

Her eyes, however, were on only one of them.

"Mr. Richards?"

# CHAPTER 47

For a moment Mr. Richards's expression showed only shock — likely the very same she had on her own face — but then he smiled, and her heart fairly melted until her mind caught up with the understanding that he was *here,* at her family estate in Somerset. That meant he knew who she was — who she *truly* was. He knew she'd deceived him.

And then she remembered the fabric wound about her head to hide the further truth she was determined he never see. She took a step backward.

His smile fell. "Amber," he said as he moved toward her.

The sound of her name on his lips should have been honey to her ears, but instead it burned within her a sharp point of shame, pain, and regret. She had sent that letter to avoid this — all of this.

"You should not have come," she said, taking another step away from him. Would he follow her when she ran away? Why did some traitorous part of her hope that he would when she knew it would make everything worse?

"I *had* to come," he said.

Tears filled her eyes, overflowing immediately as she shook her head. She turned to the ironic refuge of the ballroom and lifted her skirts. She *needed* the last memory of him to be that kiss — that beautiful and encompassing kiss full of enough passion and goodness to last her a lifetime.

Mr. Richards grabbed her arm, but she wrenched it from his grasp and took another step only to have him grab both of her arms to further restrain her.

"Wait," he said, his mouth close enough to her ear to make her shiver despite her panic. "Let me explain."

She could not spare the hope sparked by finding him here. She could not risk a different parting memory even as she realized she would never forget *this.* Already her memories of him would include *this.* She lunged forward, twisting in an attempt to pull out of his grasp. She was not a blushing debutante playing a game of refusing advances she wanted him to accelerate. She could not stand for him to know —

She choked on a scream when she felt a pull upon her turban. She tried to lift her hands to her head, but Mr. Richards's grip on her arms prevented her, which meant someone else had hold of the turban. *Not again.*

"Fenton!" she heard Mr. Richards yell.

"You wanted her to stay," Lord Fenton said as the fabric slid off her smooth head.

Mr. Richards released her as her chest caught fire and her knees gave out. She crumpled to the gravel path, and the rocks cut through the thin fabric of her gown as she crossed her arms over her head and clenched her eyes closed.

"Go away!" she pleaded, curling into herself as a firestorm of fear and emotion erupted within her. They had seen her; they *knew.* The horror of the moment swirled together with her memories of Mama and Darra seeing her for the first time and the looks upon the faces staring down at her when she dared lift her head at Carlton House. Those reactions had haunted her all these months, and she pulled even further within herself, desperate to hide.

She should never have let Mr. Richards use the library at the cottage. She should never written him that thank you letter or joined him for tea. She should never have believed that a little bit of happiness was worth this risk. Great sobs broke from her chest. If they would leave her now, if they would just go, she could at least be spared *seeing* their reaction.

Mr. Richards's voice — so close to her huddled body — broke through her sobbing. "Amber, this isn't how the evening was supposed to go. Please don't cry. Let me explain."

She only pulled herself into a tighter ball. "Go," she sobbed with her head nearly between her knees. How repulsive and indecent she must look. Why would they not go? "Leave me. You owe me nothing. Please go."

"This is not as I planned."

She could hear the pleading in his voice, but she recoiled from it. A hand reached beyond the fortress of her arms to touch her face, and she pulled away, wishing she dared throw the skirts of her dress over her bare head, wishing she could disappear completely.

Suddenly, strong arms gripped her waist and she was lifted from the ground. She did not fight, only tried to protect her head as she was carried to a bench where she was deposited. She bent over at the waist, her arms protecting her head in a position that surely looked as though she were fearful of being struck.

"Look at me, Amber," Thomas said gently as he knelt before her. "Let me explain."

Her arms were now preventing her seeing him rather than him seeing her. She heard the crunch of gravel as he moved closer, took both her wrists and pulled her arms away from her head — just as her mother and Darra had done on the night they learned of her state. She clenched her eyes even tighter.

"Amber," he said in a soft tone that washed over her. Softness. Kindness. Would he speak to her so if he were here to exact revenge upon her? Would he go to such efforts?

She felt the smallest glimmer of hope in the measure of his tone, and she lifted her head. When she met his eyes, he smiled.

*Smiled?*

She stared at him, shocked and confused that he could see her for exactly what she was and not react with revulsion. He turned his head to the side. "Fenton, your wine."

Amber's eyes left Mr. Richards's face only long enough to see Lord Fenton step forward. She looked away from his expression, which was decidedly shocked. And yet Mr. Richards's had not been.

Thomas took Lord Fenton's wine glass and removed his handkerchief from his pocket. After dipping the edge of the cloth into the wine, he turned to face her, and she looked him over, certain she would see proof of his mask, his disguise of the disgust he must be hiding. He did not show even the shadow of being repulsed, however. He did not even seem angry or embarrassed, and she did not know what to think as he lifted the wet handkerchief to her face.

She held his eyes as he cleaned first her cheeks, which she feared were stained by the lining she had put around her eyes, then wiped at her painted-on eyebrows. She closed her eyes under a wave of fresh humiliation and attempted to gain control of herself, caught between fear and the effect his gentle touch had upon her. He continued dipping the handkerchief into the wine and clearing the paint from her face until he sat back upon his heels and waited for her to open her eyes. When she met his gaze, he was smiling still. She could not speak. Why was he not running away? How could he abide to look at her?

He leaned forward and placed his hands on either side of her face. The effect of his touch was instant, and her body shivered in reaction to the warmth she felt. "You are the most beautiful woman I have ever known," he whispered. He leaned in and kissed her lightly on the lips, then the right cheek, then the left. And then he pulled her head forward and kissed her upon the top of her hideous, horrible, terrible head.

She began to cry again as relief and hope she would never have imagined replaced the fear that so recently had strangled her. He straightened her head and stared into her face.

"My intent was to find you in the ballroom and lead you to the floor for a waltz," he said. "Fenton was to assure your sentiment for me and for Yorkshire before I did so to make sure you would not be opposed to my attention, but I fear he pressed you too much."

Lord Fenton spoke from the side. "I was only attempting to —"

"Fenton," Mr. Richards said, turning his head. "You will allow me this after having so poorly played your part thus far. Could you remove some distance and afford us some privacy?"

Lord Fenton snorted as Mr. Richards turned back to face Amber, and his expression softened again. "I wanted you to know that I knew who you were, that I knew of your condition, and that my heart was not restricted in the least. I wanted your family to see it; I wanted them to know that you were not to be hidden away for the rest of your life. I wanted them to see that you lacked nothing of any consequence in regard to all you have become."

Amber shook her head. "I don't understand, Mr. Richards. How did you know?"

"Please, call me Thomas."

She repeated herself. "How did you know, T-Thomas." The intimacy of calling him by his Christian name further impressed upon her the remarkable nature of this moment.

"You do not remember me from London, do you?"

*London?* It felt years ago that she had been in London. He had been there?

He began with her dismissal at Almack's, which she did not remember, and she ducked her head in embarrassment until he touched her chin and lifted her eyes to meet his. He told her of his avoidance of her despite his continued desire to be in her company, and, finally, he told her of offering her his coat at the ball at Carlton House.

"That was you?" Amber breathed. She had thought back on that kindness a hundred times, but the emotion of the experience had always obscured the memory of the man who had assisted her. Looking at him now, however, she could supplant his face in her memory and felt a rush of competing reactions wash through her veins. "After I had treated you so poorly?"

Mr. Richards — *Thomas* — explained how he had then recognized her voice from behind the heavy wooden door the day he had come to the cottage to look for the sales record. He admitted his hope that learning of her scandalous character would finally drive thoughts of her from his mind.

"Imagine my surprise when the woman I came to know instead was kind, and good, and humble, and more dear to me than she could ever have been before."

She tried to look away but once again he would not allow it and drew her face back to him. "When Mrs. Miller brought me that note . . . I am afraid I would not let her leave without her confirmation of everything, though she was not hard to convince."

"S-Suzanne?" she stammered, lifting a hand to wipe at her eyes. "She told you?" Should she feel betrayed or grateful?

"I already knew much of it, and she suspected other interests behind my visits. All that she confirmed to me was that your condition seems to be permanent and that your leaving Yorkshire was not because of your indifference to me, but rather because you feared I would reject you as everyone else in your life had already done."

She looked down and he awaited her reply. "Not everyone," she finally said. "I gained a dear friend in Suzanne I shall forever cherish. But how could you ever . . ."

"Love you?" he said when she could not finish.

She blushed in embarrassment and did not reply. Could not reply. Could not believe this was happening.

"I have a question I would like to ask you, Amber — may I call you Amber?"

She smiled at this sudden nod to propriety after all that had happened between them. "You may call me whatever you wish."

"I wish to call you Amber, then," he said with a wink. "Actually, I have two questions to ask you if I may."

Amber simply nodded, then tensed in anticipation.

"The time we spent together in the cottage showed you to be very different than you had been in London. Would you agree that your character was improved upon your time at the cottage?"

Amber bowed her head. "The girl I was . . . it pains me to think of her."

Thomas nodded as though to tell her the answer was acceptable to him. "If you could, would you take back your hair and never have come to Yorkshire?”

# CHAPTER 48

Amber took several seconds before she answered; she wanted to be sure she didn't give an answer simply because she knew what answer he wanted. She would not be anything less than honest with him or herself from now onward. "I would not change it," she said, her voice soft, surprised, and yet sure as well. "I would not trade the things I have gained from having endured these difficulties. I only wish I could have learned them another way."

He leaned in and kissed her, allowing his lips to linger. She closed her eyes and placed a hand alongside his face, wishing the kiss could quiet the rising awareness that was building like a sob in her chest. After several moments, Amber pulled away and looked into his eyes. "Thomas, you come from a respectable family. You have responsibilities to them, and I fear you have not thought this through."

"I have thought of nothing but being with you for weeks, Amber. You must know my intention is to ask for your hand in marriage, to share my life with you in every way."

She felt her cheeks heat up but she did not answer, which caused him to move closer, bringing him only inches away from her face. The air between them warmed with his proximity and the scent of him was familiar.

"Do you mean to refuse me?" he asked in a soft voice, as vulnerable as her heart felt. He could not realize the reality. Had his feelings — which were still so shocking to her — clouded his understanding of what it meant to join his life to her?

"Thomas, a wife such as me will limit you. People will not accept me as you have. Our society does not tolerate imperfection."

"Our society is riddled with imperfection," Thomas said with a chuckle that Amber could not share.

"*My* imperfection will change everything for you, especially as you are already establishing a unique position. I could ruin every hope you have of retaining social standing."

"I embrace it," Thomas said, squeezing her hand.

"Your family will be affected as well. Your

brother is titled; he has responsibilities to uphold."

Thomas shook his head. "I assure you that the people who matter to me will accept you and love you."

How could that be possible when her own family had not done so? "You cannot expect so much from people, Thomas."

He regarded her for a thoughtful moment. "You believe that the people I want in my life will not accept you because you are without hair?"

She nodded.

Thomas sat beside her on the bench and took both of her hands in his, invigorating her with his touch. "I have never taken the course chosen for me by societal expectations, and I can promise you, without a moment's hesitation, that I am full in love with you and those feelings have nothing to do with your hair or lack of it or how people might choose to react to it. I do not believe they will be as discounting as you fear, but if they are, it is of no consequence to me. You know that I am not relying on my station to provide for my future. Part of that independence is because I refuse to allow society to dictate my future and my happiness. I cannot give you the lifestyle your father did, but —"

"I care not about that," she said quickly.

"And if I believed you did I would not be here," Thomas continued. "But I can give you my love, my respect, and my promise that my feelings for you will not be compromised by the opinions of others. Not ever."

She stared at him, stunned by the sincerity of his words and unsure how to answer him.

Thomas looked past her to Fenton, who had not removed himself as Thomas had asked him to and now leaned against the beam of a trellis, watching the exchange. "Could you see that a waltz is played next?" Thomas asked his friend.

Heat rushed up Amber's face to know Lord Fenton had been a silent audience of their declarations. She felt her heart race as she glanced toward the veranda, partially blocked from view by the trellis. Thomas did not mean to dance with her in front of all these people, did he? She looked to her turban, crumpled amid the stones, the feathers scattered beside it.

Fenton nodded as though it were a small thing to change up an orchestra's repertoire and strode past them to the steps, leaving Thomas and Amber alone.

Thomas turned back to Amber, whose hands he still held. "I expect to live a full life with a good woman — with you — and I would hope that you would take confidence in your character as I do. If people of our class reject you — us — it is to their own detriment. If they accept us, it is to their own credit. Give them the chance to accept us, rather than live your life with an expectation of rejection. Do you recall when Cassius says to Brutus 'Men at some time are masters of their fates: the fault, dear Brutus, is not in our stars —' "

" 'But in ourselves,' " she finished for him as she applied his words to the last several months of her life. It had been her choice to hide and live in fear of people's reactions. It had been her choice to deceive him of her true identity. *She* had been the one most unwilling to accept her imperfections. Could she not also be the first — or perhaps the second, or third when she thought of Suzanne who had said these exact things — to accept herself? Could she not be assured of her internal improvement despite a physical flaw she could not control? She found herself unable to discount Thomas's earnestness and certainty.

"We are only underlings to fate if we choose to let the wills of others shape our lives," Thomas said softly.

Amber looked into his eyes, stunned by

the capacity of this man she had once rejected because he had not seemed to be *enough.* Now she stood on the threshold of proving to him that she would do all she could for his comfort, including taking the confidence of his love and support to do such a hard thing. "You truly believe I am as whole as anyone," she said.

Thomas's eyes sparkled in the moonlight. "I believe you are *more* than anyone I have ever known. I want you to believe it as well and feel, as I do, that becoming my wife will make me a greater man than anything else in this world ever could."

The orchestra completed the strains of the cotillion and the guests applauded the conclusion of the dance. The waltz would be next, assuming Lord Fenton had been successful. Thomas stood before reaching for her hand. She resisted, looking at the raised veranda in fear again. She could not face a roomful of people and the judgments they would hold.

"I cannot replace my turban without help of my mother's lady's maid," she said, raising a hand to her head and looking at the discarded fabric that had served as her shield.

"I mean to dance with you tonight, Amber," he said. "It is your choice whether we dance here in the garden, or in the ballroom. You have no need for a covering regardless of which venue you choose, but I leave the choice to you."

Amber let out a breath of relief. "I do not feel prepared to present myself to so many people and would not want to be the cause of disruption at Darra's ball."

He smiled, nodded, and reached his hand closer to her. "Then shall you dance with me here in the garden?"

She took his hand and rose to her feet before following him to the base of the steps where tightly fitted stones provided an improvised dance floor. They were close enough to hear the opening strains of the waltz but far enough to preserve their privacy.

He bowed. "Miss Sterlington, might I have this dance?"

"Most certainly, sir," she said as he straightened and took her hand. He pulled her close, deliciously so, and she adjusted her arm as he took her hand. They danced in perfect time with the music flowing through the ballroom doors, over the veranda, and down the stone stairs to meet them.

She had waltzed with any number of gentlemen — men she had deemed worthy because of their fortune and title — and yet now she was in the arms of the man she'd once spurned who had been willing to know her as the new woman she had become. She could not understand how this had happened, how he could forgive her and still pursue her. That he saw so much good in her, however, made her want to see it too.

His hand on her back was warm, his hand holding hers was strong, and the depth of his eyes and what she saw reflected there was overwhelming enough that she did not hear footsteps on the stone stairs until she saw a flash of pink out of the corner of her eye. She stumbled to a halt.

Darra and Lord Sunther descended the steps while a dozen people gathered on the veranda behind them. Amber pulled away and stepped behind Thomas, covering her head with her hands as panic shot through her. Thomas turned to face her, still blocking her from the guests, and took hold of her shoulders. "It's all right," he said. "Take a moment."

"You told them?" she said, quick to suspect the worst.

"Of course not," Thomas said, his eyebrows rising. "I would not betray you, Amber. Never."

She glanced past him and watched as

Lord Sunther and Darra began to waltz in the same space Amber and Thomas had been using. Darra turned and locked eyes with Amber, smiling slightly at her sister and beckoning with her head for Amber to join them.

Lord Fenton suddenly appeared at the base of the steps with a wide-eyed girl Amber did not recognize. He helped her adjust to the right position and then counted under his breath before they too began waltzing.

Amber watched the two couples swirling around her and Thomas standing in the center of the stones. Thomas moved closer, and when she met his look of confidence, she remembered all he had explained to her these last few minutes. He believed her to be as whole as any other woman and had been willing to dance with her in the ballroom to prove it. With a staggered breath to release her fear, she lowered her arms from her head.

She looked toward the people on the terrace and caught the angry glare of her mother from amid the growing crowd. Though her mother's reaction filled her with regret and insecurity — as it had all of her life — she knew she did not deserve the censure. She had not done anything wrong

— even to the point of dancing here in the garden rather than attempting to detract from her sister's ball. But Darra had joined her, had shown her support by extending her ball to include her imperfect sister.

"Should we continue?" Thomas whispered in her ear.

He would leave with her if she chose to go, and yet instead, she turned to him and put her hand on his shoulder once again. He did not hesitate to take position for the dance, and they moved together as though they had danced a hundred times before.

Her chest still felt tight but she had tried to hide and it had nearly cost her this future. She would be brave now. She would be honest and, as Thomas had said, she would let people make their own decision about her. If they chose to allow her outward appearance to make up the whole of her measure, she could not change it. But if they, like Suzanne, Thomas, and even Darra and Lord Sunther, could see past it, she would offer more by way of character and compassion than she ever had been capable of before.

Thomas adjusted his arm on her waist, pulling her close enough that she caught her breath and quite forgot her lingering insecurity. The waltz was a scandalous dance indeed.

"Is this truly happening?" she whispered. "Have you really come from Yorkshire after knowing the whole of my deception and condition and asked me to become your wife?"

Thomas grinned. "Indeed it feels like a dream, does it not?"

"A dream I fear I shall awaken from at any moment."

"Perhaps on the morning you awaken beside me you will finally know it is not a dream." He leaned in closer. "It is my hope that such a morning is not far distant."

She knew she should blush at his words, but she did not. Instead she felt a thrill of anticipation and said a silent prayer of thanks for every bit of what had happened that had brought her here. *This* was what it felt like to be loved. This is what she had once felt a paltry reason for marriage.

"Is there something more I can do to convince you that this is not a dream, that the moments we find ourselves within are very much real?" Thomas glanced at her lips, and she gasped sharply at the implication. If Thomas were to kiss her here, in front of all these people, it would be nothing short of a proposal, a public display of his intentions that would leave no room for interpretation or retreat. He looked back into her eyes, and she knew that his thoughts were the same as her own.

There were half a dozen couples dancing with them now, creating a rather haphazard and crowded dance floor. The remaining guests were gathered on the stairs and veranda, the sound of their whispers all but covering the strains of music from above. Did any of their judgments matter when a man such as Thomas Richards had claimed her heart and promised it safekeeping?

She slowed her steps and he followed suit. She lifted her face toward his and he smiled at her silent invitation. Without a word, Thomas cupped her face and lowered his mouth to meet hers in a kiss of promise, a kiss of hope, a kiss to invite a thousand more.

# EPILOGUE

*August*

Thomas jumped from the carriage pulled by two butter-colored horses — a wedding gift from Lord and Lady Fielding — before reaching up to help Amber from the seat. She gathered her skirts in preparation to step down, but Thomas's hands grasped her waist and lifted her to the ground instead.

He rarely let an opportunity to touch her pass him by, and she had become quite accustomed to the brush of his hand across her shoulders when he passed behind her or his hand resting on hers when they sat beside one another in the library, to say nothing of his arms around her at night and the kisses he planted on her smooth head whenever she was without a covering.

After meeting with the local physician — whom Suzanne had told her to consult months ago — Amber had accepted that she would likely never have a full return of her hair, though she currently had her left eyebrow and some regrowth near the back of her head. Dr. Marsh, unlike the doctor in London, had seen similar conditions, which he said were related to the body's ability to grow hair. She was at peace with it, though at night she sometimes dreamed of what she'd once taken for granted.

Thomas brushed her cheek and she smiled. She had no complaint for the reminders of his affection, but since typical British society was not so demonstrative, his affection in public concerned her. In this way, however, as in many others, Thomas had little concern for convention. Even after placing her firmly on the street he did not release her and instead tipped his head so it fit beneath the brim of her bonnet and kissed her soundly.

"You are a scoundrel, Mr. Richards," she said when he pulled away.

"Only with you, Mrs. Richards."

She laughed as Thomas paid a boy to care for the carriage and horses for the duration of their appointment with Mr. Peters.

Once in the solicitor's office, they were shown to a room where they sat side by side at the large table. When Mr. Peters entered a minute later, Amber ignored the slightly narrowed look he gave her; women did not usually accompany their husbands on errands of business. Thomas, however, had felt that since it was her matter of business as well it was only fair that she attend.

She had been right that there were those of their society who did not welcome them, but Thomas had also been correct in the fact that his family, and a handful of others, had embraced them far more than Amber had expected. Lady Fielding had even thrown a ball at Peakview Manor in their honor, which had been well attended and filled with congratulations and well wishes.

Mr. Peters sat opposite them and began explaining the different papers he had brought with him. He gave them to Thomas to sign, who gave them to Amber to look over though only Thomas's signature was required for the legalities. It took nearly half an hour before Thomas and Amber had signed the final page. Mr. Peters gathered the papers and tapped them together on the tabletop.

"I shall have this recorded straightaway," he said. "The new title shall be delivered to you within a month's time."

"Excellent," Thomas said, standing along with Amber. "Please share our thanks with Lord Marchent for the ease of this transaction and assure him that his daughter is doing well."

"And is quite happy," Amber added, keeping her smile in place though Mr. Peters did not return it.

She did not believe her father cared all that much for her happiness, but perhaps some part buried beneath his presentation and social position would like to know of her contentment all the same. She had not seen her parents since Darra's wedding ball, though Darra and Lord Sunther had attended Amber's wedding at the Northallerton church in May.

Today, her marriage settlement — Step Cottage and the lands connected to it — had been properly joined to Thomas's land, increasing their combined holdings by nearly forty percent and further ensuring their future. Currently, she and Thomas were living at Step Cottage until their house was built. That they lived so far from town without a daily servant was but one more thing to shock the county. What would they think when Thomas drew up his will dividing his land equally between their future sons and *daughters*?

They exited the office to the welcoming blue of the Yorkshire summer sky. Thomas assisted Amber back into the carriage and then took his position behind the reins. "To the Larsens?" he asked.

"Yes," Amber said, checking the watch pinned to her bodice. She was glad for having allowed additional time between appointments so as not to be late for supper, which would be served promptly at five o'clock. "How do you think Suzanne will react to our happy news?"

"The happy news of the land transaction?" Thomas asked with his eyebrows lifted in mock sincerity.

"Of course," Amber said with equal playfulness. "She shall be *ever* so excited about the land transaction. Why would I think her excitement would be for any other purpose?"

Thomas's broad hand on her belly caused a lump in her throat as she reflected on how truly happy she was. She placed her own hand over his and her heart filled with gratitude for a man such as this, who she knew would love their child regardless of what afflictions he or she might face, who would value a daughter as highly as a son, and who would do all he could to allow them to find their own happiness in life. A father with such a progressive mind and open heart were the greatest things she could ever give to her children.

Thomas leaned toward her and smiled

widely. "Suzanne shall know, perhaps better than any but the two of us, just how wonderful this truly is. Ten to one the woman gives in to tears."

Amber smiled. "You do not know her as well as I do. She was the only one not crying at the wedding."

Thomas frowned. "Must you bring that up again? I told you I had something in my eye."

Amber placed her hand on the side of his face. "Oh, how I love you, Mr. Richards."

"Then come on, and kiss me, Kate."

She did as he'd requested and hoped that the kiss communicated all the things she felt. It might take a lifetime to assure this man of all he had given her, but she was determined to see that he never questioned his choice. She was sure that she would not.

# AUTHOR'S NOTE

The condition Amber suffers from is now called Alopecia Areata, an autoimmune disorder where the hair follicles essentially die and therefore no longer grow hair. There are varying degrees of Alopecia Areata, but the one represented here is Alopecia Universalis, which presents itself as a complete — universal — loss of body hair and accounts for approximately 10 percent of Alopecia diagnoses.

Though modern research has found treatments that have been helpful for some, for many patients the hair loss is irreversible and cyclical, continuing throughout their life. The condition is often hereditary but there is not yet a cure.

In the early nineteenth century, there was no name for this disorder, but I believe that the fear and insecurity was likely not much different than it is now. Identity, appearance, and social expectation is something each of us face, and so I hope that the difficulties and eventual acceptance Amber faced is something we can each relate to in our own way.

You can find more information, and read the stories of real people living with this disease, on the website for the National Alopecia Areata Foundation: www.naaf.org.

# ACKNOWLEDGMENTS

The very first book I ever dared write — way back when — was a Regency romance novel. I had read hundreds of them and had wanted to show off all I had learned about the time period. That book will likely never see the light of day — I might have known the time period but I did not know how to write — but revisiting the genre that first made me think I had a story of my own to tell was fabulous.

I owe big thanks to my writing group, Nancy Allen, Becki Clayson, Jody Durfee, Ronda Hinrichsen, and Jenifer Moore for encouraging me and helping me find my voice. Jen and Nancy, specifically, provided me with research materials and fact checking that helped immensely.

Once I finished the story, Jennifer Moore and my sisters, Jenifer Johnson and Crystal White, read the book and helped me know where to improve. I am indebted to those people in my life who trust me with their honest feedback in order to make me better.

Big thanks to everyone at Shadow Mountain for believing in this project and making it happen. Specifically, Heidi Taylor, Lisa Mangum, Suzanne Brady, Heather Ward, Malina Grigg, Karen Zelnick, Michelle Moore, and Ilise Levine. I so appreciate my relationship with the team of people at Shadow Mountain, and I have loved working with them on something new.

Hugs and thanks to my family, especially my husband Lee, who is the basis for every romance I write. I am greatly blessed.

# ABOUT THE AUTHOR

**Josi S. Kilpack** published her first novel in 2000. Her seventh novel, *Sheep's Clothing,* won the 2007 Whitney Award for Mystery/ Suspense — several others have been finalists in subsequent years. She was also the Best of State winner for fiction in Utah 2012. She has written twenty-two novels, including the twelve-volume Sadie Hoffmiller Culinary Mystery Series.

Josi currently lives in Willard, Utah. For more information about Josi, you can visit her website at www.josiskilpack.com.

The employees of Thorndike Press hope you have enjoyed this Large Print book. All our Thorndike, Wheeler, and Kennebec Large Print titles are designed for easy reading, and all our books are made to last. Other Thorndike Press Large Print books are available at your library, through selected bookstores, or directly from us.

For information about titles, please call:
(800) 223-1244

or visit our website at:
gale.com/thorndike

To share your comments, please write:
Publisher
Thorndike Press
10 Water St., Suite 310
Waterville, ME 04901